PRAISE FOR

THE MAHDI

"This gripping tale sheds the needed light on today's white hot Middle East strife. A withering take on ancestral anger, a captivating cast, and a gripping story with vivid dialogue carries us to a memorable conclusion."

—**JACK BRAY,** author of *Alone against Hitler: Kurt von Schuschnigg's Fight to Save Austria from the Nazis* and *The Tudor Wolfpack and the Roots of Irish America*; retired Senior Partner, King & Spalding, LLP

"Cook employs the lens of a Bedouin American protagonist in his tale of the West Bank and Gaza before it all went bad. Great story, wonderful dialogue, fascinating view of things."

—**TANIA AMOCHAEV,** author of *Mother Tongue: A Saga of Three Generations of Balkan Women*, native Russian/Serbian speaker, Stanford MBA, software executive, educational philanthropist

"An exciting look into the future of technology in warfare, driven by a powerful Bedouin American hero with a chip on his shoulder. Serious geopolitical possibilities with lots of violence, dialogue, and simmering personal relationships."

—**DAVID CAMPBELL,** philanthropist, Founder of All Hands and Hearts, former President of Raytheon BBN

"A lot of people won't like the outcomes in Cook's thriller *The Mahdi*, but his thesis makes one consider alternatives and their likelihood. The portrayal of the impact of quantum computing on encryption is accurate, but we are not near that point in technology. Handheld quantum cell phone? Oh, no, no, and that's been going on for three books! Once again, Cook writes a good thriller!"

—**RICK CRANDALL**, Founder of Enterprise Software CEO Roundtable, Chair of the Cyber Committee of the National Cybersecurity Center

"An action-filled thriller set in Gaza and Israel. It makes one really think about how this region can solve its problems. It's a thinking person's thriller."

—**BRUCE T. COLEMAN**, Baker Scholar, Harvard Business School, software entrepreneur

"As a geopolitical thriller, it is fantastic. Great characters, brilliant women, great dialogue, lots of action. *The Mahdi* gives the reader an exciting look at Israel and the Middle East through the lens of a Sunni Arab."

—**JUDITH HAMILTON**, corporate director, wildlife philanthropist, software entrepreneur

"A compelling read that mirrors the current world situation. A thought-provoking book, it made me seriously consider if Kufdani's vision for a better Middle East could someday become a reality."

—**STANLEY B. JOOSSE**, Colonel, USA (Ret)

MAHDI

Other books by Robert Cook

COOCH | *PATRIOT & ASSASSIN* | *PULSE*

THE
MAHDI

THE FOURTH IN THE COOCH SERIES OF
NATIONAL SECURITY THRILLERS

ROBERT COOK

RIVER GROVE
BOOKS

Published by River Grove Books
Austin, TX
www.rivergrovebooks.com

Distributed by River Grove Books

Design and composition by Greenleaf Book Group and Brian Phillips
Cover design by Greenleaf Book Group and Brian Phillips
Cover images: © Tatkhagata, Wakajawaka, sergio34, Vandathai, and Kambiz Pourghanad. Used under license from Shutterstock.com

Publisher's Cataloging-in-Publication data is available.

Print ISBN: 978-1-63299-790-6

eBook ISBN: 978-1-63299-791-3

First Edition

For PJ, my rock

ACKNOWLEDGMENTS

FOR THIS, THE FOURTH OF THE COOCH SERIES, THERE ARE MANY TO thank. First, thanks to my readers with their enthusiastic reviews and word-of-mouth support, which are key to my efforts. Judy Hamilton and Sally Krueger, MD, again provided early support. For military matters and issues of national security, special thanks go to Admiral James Loy (Ret) and Admiral Thomas Fargo (Ret). Writer support and comments came from Art Allen, Jack Bray, David and Gay Campbell, Bruce Coleman, Bob Corman, Stan Joosse, and Rich Moore among many others.

AUTHOR'S NOTE

I CALL THEM NATIONAL security thrillers, for lack of a better term. They have the violence, sex, and intrigue common to good thrillers. There is always a national security aspect to them, since Cooch became a legal adult while training at the CIA's Farm. It was fun to give him the hook into the Muslim world with a Bedouin mother.

Pulse, the thriller before this one, was a story about a US preemptive attack on Iran over a planned deployment of a nuclear weapon against Israel.

Patriot & Assassin was about Yemen and a nerve gas attack at an NFL championship game in Dallas.

Cooch, the original thriller that won an IPPY Gold Medal for thrillers, is about how Cooch evolved and his teen summers in the desert of Morocco.

I do my research for the Cooch books. Descriptions of modern weapons and their capabilities are accurate. Of course, no one has built a quantum computer into a cell phone or even used cloud computing, but it's fun to invent what is needed for the story. Besides, if one existed, it could do what is described and more. Think of ChatGPT without the starter wheels. Think about our society with Emilie, our heuristic AI chatbot, in charge.

The education backstory is personal. I've been involved with K–6 education for forty years starting with producing a video for a troubled elementary school in Baltimore (*The Battle of City Springs*) and with educating the intellectually gifted, financially challenged child for thirty years (Cook Honors College at Indiana University of Pennsylvania). I care and I keep track of what seems to work. Little I do has gained traction in the broader world.

The foundation idea for *The Mahdi* arose while I was reading the *Economist* magazine several years ago and read of the conflict in Israel over Bedouin ownership rights in Israel. Since I had been writing about Cooch as half-Bedouin for quite a while, I decided to pursue research to see if there was a book in there for me. There was, it was a great fit, and remains that way today. Netanyahu is still pursuing the right-wing agenda, confiscating Arab land and destroying the rule of law in Israel. The Israeli intelligentsia is going crazy, protesting in the streets, pretty much as I predicted. I heard one Israeli citizen say, "I don't want to live in a repressive, failing, Middle Eastern Jewish theocracy. I like Israel the way it is." Now we have the Hamas conflict with no good solution in sight, except, of course, perhaps the one I present with this fiction.

The Mahdi is the first novel where Cooch so broadly expresses himself as a Muslim. I describe the novel as one seen through the lens of the modern Muslim liberal. I don't know of other fiction that so overtly does this.

If there is to be a solution between Israel and Palestine, it is likely to evolve from religious leadership, not politics.

—ROBERT COOK

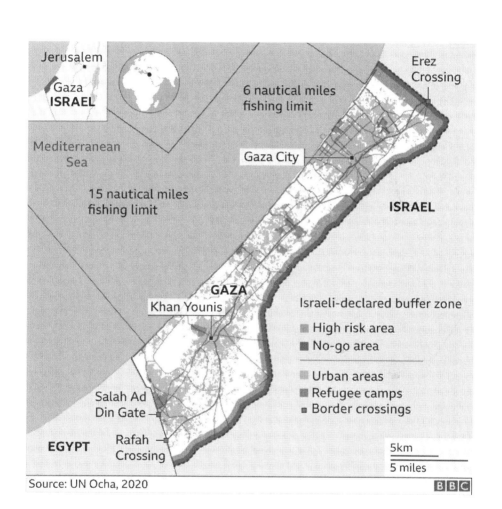

Source: UN Ocha, 2020

SOUTH OF TANGIER

THE MOROCCAN DESERT SOUTH OF TANGIER WAS HOT AND DRY, AS WAS usual at this time of year, with a wind stirring fine sand from the Sahara to the east and south. Shadows cast by the northern hills inched across a rock-encrusted sandscape toward a tented encampment, where a large group of men were seated in a circle between two large, ornate tents. Camels were tethered just beyond the circle, and an assortment of trucks were parked nearby. On the far side of the tents, women worked around several cooking fires, watching the men.

The man named Kufdani sat cross-legged in the circle's center, atop a mound of dirt and sand. His eyes were closed.

A calloused open hand drove a slap toward Kufdani's left cheek. His head jerked back enough to cause a miss, except for one ragged fingernail that caught his forehead near the hairline, bringing a thin line of blood to the surface. It matched several other bleeding scratches that mingled among a cluster of small, half-moon scars, similar but long healed. The slap from the opposite side followed immediately, but Kufdani dropped his head and lifted his right forearm to bump the slapping hand away from its target. The right-hand slap came again, part of an unceasing pattern, and again ended with a miss.

The breeze picked up another waft of sand, and another and another as the day grew into late afternoon. The watchful Bedouin crowd grew more still with each attempted slap, mesmerized, as blow after blow from a series of assailants failed to make direct contact.

"Time!" a male voice shouted at last, in Arabic.

A spontaneous shout erupted from the sitting crowd. "Kufdani, Kufdani!" They leapt to their feet and ran to help him from his perch, attempting to congratulate him by collectively pounding on his back. Several men hoisted him on their shoulders.

The Bedouin ritual was over. Kufdani had prevailed once more: no one had been able to slap him from the center spot, even though his eyes were closed. Nineteen Bedouin men from various tribes across the Middle East had entered the contest along with him. Even though their eyes remained open, each had been dislodged from his perch within the allotted three minutes of blows suffered per contestant.

Kufdani jumped from the shoulders of the men, who staggered under his shifting weight and slapped his back yet again. The others surrounded him still, waving their hands, reaching for him.

As he fought through the crowd, Kufdani decided it was time to figure out what all the excitement was about. An eager tension filled the desert encampment, and the chieftains clearly wanted something from him. The Bedouin rumor mill—active as ever—said it was about the West Bank.

It was always about the West Bank.

Pushing through the swarming crowd to the trough past the big tent, Kufdani dipped his head in the water, letting it run over his blood-spattered, sweat-soaked shirt as another tribesman pumped the handle on the aging well. Then he peeled the shirt over his head and rinsed again, until the water flowed from his thick black hair and down across his naked chest. He was tall—not quite six feet, four inches—with the muscularity of a gymnast, but thicker in the chest and stomach. A random series of ragged lines and puckered, half-inch circles appeared randomly across his torso and arms, healed masses of white flesh against his dark skin tone. Among the special ops community, where he had spent eight years, these scars were called "zippers" and "assholes," depending on the shape and the cause: shrapnel and knife wounds versus bullet holes. A single, long scar ran down the side of his face too, beginning in the wrinkles beside his left eye.

Someone handed Kufdani a towel, and he wiped his face before accepting a dry shirt from one of his former assailants, who was grinning at him and squinting through a swelling, newly blackened eye from his own time on the contestant perch. Pulling the shirt over his head, Kufdani moved through the crowd, grinning and slapping the impatient hands that swayed in the air, toward the largest tent in the complex. A flap was pulled back, and he eased through the crowd, stepped inside the tent, and looked for a seat.

"Here, Kufdani!" a grizzled man in traditional garb shouted in heavily Bedouin-accented Arabic. "You are next to me. We have business."

After slipping through the last of the admirers, Kufdani stood beside a colorful cushion woven from goat's hair where the man sat. When he shook the man's hand, applause broke out among the throng assembled in the tent. These were tribal leaders from the large Bedouin tribes—desert people who live traditionally by tending cattle or camels inland across the Middle East. They represented more than a million Bedouin Arabs who recognize no central government or authority. Kufdani waved to them and sat down.

The tent flap was dropped, and air circulated from the skirt as it was raised waist-level around the tent's base. In a ring just outside the flap, other men gathered in the dust, legs crossed, to listen to the elders. Body odor was prevalent both inside and outside the tent.

Mint tea was served. The aging man in the traditional honor seat was named Badawi, and he had recently been elected the leader of all Bedouin tribes—by a substantial voting margin. A successful trader in livestock, he owned a prize-winning herd of camels and kept Arabian horses in several locations, all tended by his fellow Bedouins.

Badawi wore a scarf looped around his neck and a loose cotton shirt that fell around his waist. His face was a map formed by his life's history in the bright desert, his skin a deep mahogany, built layer by layer from decades of exposure to the Saharan sun. Wrinkles pulled at his face and puddled near his chin and under his eyes, and hair grew densely from his ears and nose. His hands were dry and mottled with prominent purple bruises.

"Congratulations, Kufdani," the old man continued. His speech was modulated by breath whistling past a missing incisor. "You are again victorious in our traditional game of slaps. Welcome back to the contest and to our gathering of Bedouin peers."

"It is my honor to be here," Kufdani replied, bowing his head slightly. "Thank you for allowing me to sit beside you during this meeting."

"Yet something is more critical now than your honor alone," Badawi said loudly, his voice quivering with emotion. "I have been elected spokesman for the tribes' leadership. We need your winning skills, your leadership, in preserving the honor of the Bedouin nation."

As he looked around the room, expectant faces peered back. "Honor is a vital component of our people's being," Kufdani replied in a strong voice audible to all seated in the tent. "How may I help preserve it?"

"It is the Israelis. They treat us as animals. They have stolen our land. We get no respect."

Badawi's voice rose.

"The Israeli government has bent our Israeli Bedouins over! The Orthodox Jews, the Haredim, are raping our Bedouin tribesmen. Their government moves our Bedouin people—Israeli citizens—from lands on the West Bank of the Jordan that we have occupied for two hundred years and then settles us by their garbage dumps. They build homes on our land for Russian Jews who don't work, don't serve in the military, and weren't born in Israel. They attack our children on their way to school. A large percentage of them may not even be Jewish by DNA, though they are certainly Russian—Cossacks, mostly. Strange, no?"

"I know the story," Kufdani said, his eyes narrowing. Knowing it didn't make it any easier to stomach.

The Bedouin were a million strong—Sunni by religion, but Semitic by blood and historic language. Their ties to this contested land, and to their neighbors who also lived there, were strong. And yet these cousins were afforded none of the rights or respect due as a result of their history and lineage.

"We have long lived by our code of honor, hospitality and courage, and now we ask that you help us restore Bedouin honor," Badawi repeated. "Tribes have banded together across the Bedouin nations to discuss the Israeli outrage. After endless discussion, we finally agree: we have little chance of defeating a nation like Israel. But we are Bedouin. Our honor is at stake. We *must* fight back."

Kufdani contemplated the old man. "And what do you say is to be done? What would you have me do?"

Badawi waved his arms to the heavens. "We choose you to lead the way! You are an imam and a business leader. You have brought prosperity to Tangier's Yahia Bedouin." He paused. "Our honor has been violated, and without it we are nothing. With the new Israeli leader, things will get worse. But we have the courage to fix everything—if we have the right leader."

"I understand," Kufdani said, nodding. The Yahia tribe in Morocco had actively fought Israel's policies on the West Bank, even filing suit in the International Criminal Court and arranging for the Moroccan foreign minister to successfully file a United Nations motion condemning Israel's actions as a violation of the Geneva Convention. "The United States warned the new Israeli government not to annex the Bedouin land in the West Bank. Pressure is being applied."

"Bah!" the old Bedouin scoffed. "You talk like a woman. Pressure, indeed. Why not just kiss their tiny, bald members and ask them to treat us nicely?"

Kufdani sighed. "Again, Badawi, what would you have me do? What would the tribes have me do?"

"Do what your grandfather Kufdani would have done!" Badawi cried. "*You* are now Kufdani. Use your resources to fight to regain Bedouin honor! If we can't regain our lands by peaceful negotiations, we must make Israel's actions terribly expensive for them. We will shed Bedouin blood if necessary so our children can live with honor, the Bedouin way."

Kufdani held Badawi's gaze. "You speak of shedding Bedouin blood," he said. "If it is to be shed, it must be shed under the total control of the Bedouin nation. All the tribes. There should be no holdouts, no exceptions. Sacrifices must be made, both in time and in blood. We Bedouins must be in this together."

Discipline, he knew, was everything. The old man was talking about the loosely organized Bedouin nation making war on a strong, violent sovereign nation—a military that was, person for person, the best in the world. It couldn't be done in any traditional way. Yet Kufdani was an American, Bedouin through his mother's side only, and his influence had always been limited.

"Each tribe has committed to doing what is necessary to recover our nation's honor," Badawi insisted. "We will depend on you to guide us."

Kufdani looked around the room at the silent, attentive men. "There is a time for dissent and discussion. If I am to do this, that time is over. To be your leader, I must have both obedience and dedication to my command."

He sat back on his cushions for a few moments, silent as he considered what was to be done—and whether he was willing to be the one to attempt it. Then he spoke.

"Collectively, you will recruit all tribes—even those not represented here—to our cause, and you will demand that they follow my rules as part of the Bedouin culture, as though our lives depend on it. Because they will.

"This is going to be hard. I require each tribe, depending on size, to devote one or two of its best men to our effort. Not slackers! You will provide leaders—under forty years of age would be best. I may call for assistance, and I expect to get it."

Kufdani thought for a brief moment and then announced he would send a list of requirements to the tribes, each of which would then supply names and qualifications in response. When these chosen leaders returned home from their efforts, the remainder of their tribe would be influenced by their guidance.

"This is not the time for independent action," he continued. "The full measure of the Bedouin nation effort is impossible without the involvement and enthusiastic participation of our women too."

He explained that each tribe would also pick a female leader for its women—one without constraint on her education. She would be chosen for her wisdom and treated with respect as a Bedouin leader, following the guidance of other Bedouin women affiliated with Kufdani Industries, in southern Spain.

Furthermore, education would be provided to all Bedouin children without exception, both girls and boys, with the help of teaching materials provided by Kufdani Industries—the same educational approach that gave rise to the commercial success of the Yahia tribe in Morocco. Together they must create a new model of the Bedouin worker, Kufdani insisted, by educating their people better than others did. Their tribes would need to develop strength going forward if they were to stop the Israelis from violating their honor again and again.

"All tribes must participate!" he said, raising his voice for all to hear. "Those that don't will answer to Badawi and to the rest of the Bedouin nation." He turned to the tribes' spokesman. "I will investigate what can be done, Badawi. You will take a new reading of the tribal leaders, their followers, and their ability to obey instructions, and we will talk again in a few days."

"No," Badawi said. "These discussions have taken place at length already."

Kufdani stood before the crowd of hopeful faces, thinking what an unfamiliar sight it was. "Then gather everyone's information," he commanded, looking down at Badawi but addressing all of his people too. "Choose your leaders, and tell me about them in writing. Prepare to send them to me. I will contact you with guidance in a few days and then expect your response within a week."

The spokesman nodded enthusiastically. "The Bedouin nation is committed to you as our leader in this matter of honor. We await your command, Kufdani."

Kufdani nodded in return. "I expect obedience if I am to undertake this matter. If I, as your leader, commit fully to this endeavor, I expect each of you to respond in kind."

Dinner was within sight, and Kufdani longed for a good night's sleep before his return to Tangier in the morning—the sleep he could find only in the dark emptiness of the desert.

"Now," he announced as he sat down, "let's get back to our tea."

TANGIER

ALEJANDRO MUHAMMAD CUCHULAIN STROLLED DOWN A HALLWAY SUR-rounded by stone and then turned north, toward a large office space with massive windows overlooking the Mediterranean Sea and the old city of Tangier. What had started many decades ago as a cavern for holding inventory of various trading goods, cut into the hills above the city, had evolved into Kufdani Industries, a huge office and manufacturing facility that extended deep into the mountainside. Five independent executive facilities, including offices and residences, filled the north wall of that complex—behind which were four hundred thousand square feet dedicated to offices, a warehouse, a medical center, a cafeteria, and a computer processing center—all perched six hundred feet above the Mediterranean.

"Here he is!" Brooks Elliot said, standing with a grin for the tall man built like a gymnast who had entered the meeting room. "Is it Kufdani or Alex today?"

"I think I've had enough Kufdani for a while, so I'll answer to the latter," Alex said, smiling as he clasped Elliot's hand. Each man clapped the other's shoulder. "I didn't plan for the Bedouins to call on me for much, but—well, this is as good a time as any to discuss what's going on."

Alex studied the group of four middle-aged adults lounging around an enormous ceramic table inlaid with colorful tiles: two men sitting cross-legged on a padded circular bench, and two women stretched out on enormous cushions covered in a complex weave of orange and brown with yellow flecks, sipping mint tea from heavy ceramic mugs. On the floor in front of the women sat a small, ornate wooden table with a battered ceramic teapot warming over a burning candle.

Each of the five owned a stake in Kufdani Industries, an investment group that included a venture capital firm in New York; majority ownership of Axial Systems, a software and physics company; and a private venture finance firm. At its center was Kufdani Trading Company, a decades-old trading company with more than thirty thousand employees and offices across Europe and the Middle East.

Alex had been looking forward to the whole gang getting together again.

He had been an American for most of his adult life, first as a US Marine and then for eight years as an operator in the CIA special operations unit, but had spent each summer with his Bedouin grandfather as a child, learning about Islam and life as a Bedouin. Several years earlier, Alex had inherited the Kufdani Trading Company from his grandfather and began to build the company it had become, first adding Kufdani Ventures and then purchasing most of Axial after being an investor since its IPO and seeing it through a few financial challenges. Once Kufdani Industries had taken Axial private, the US National Security Agency had discovered its power. Revenues had skyrocketed while costs stayed subdued because, once conceived and written, software is cheap to reproduce, copy after copy.

Now here he was, with some of the people he cared most about.

The Kufdani Industries executive strategy team waited for Alex to suggest where the discussion should go. One of the women was blonde, stunningly attractive, distractingly busty in a polo shirt, and relaxed. Her hair was wet from a recent swim and carelessly arranged, and she wore loose, casual blue cotton shorts and flip-flops. She was Caitlin O'Connor, the smartest person in the world—or so she claimed. Few argued. She was also Alex's live-in lover.

The other woman was LuAnn Clemens, a tall, broad-shouldered Texan with sun-streaked brown hair cut short. She wore a white shirt that had experienced many washings, tailored in cowboy fashion across the yoke, and baggy cotton shorts similar to her friend's. Her feet were bare. LuAnn had once edited the *Michigan Law Review* and soon after became a managing partner in the seventh-largest law firm in America. Now, she was the wife—and better half, really—of Brooks F. T. Elliot IV: Princetonian, former US Navy SEAL, Rhodes scholar, and advisor to the president. His father was an aging US senator; hers owned an oily portion of Texas.

Brooks sat down next to Alex and across from the women: relaxed, smiling, waiting. He was slim and ordinarily handsome despite standing well under six feet tall, with regular features. His brown hair was conservatively cut, and he wore an ironed, blue cotton button-down shirt and khaki shorts. He waited patiently, a skill nurtured through countless business and political meetings.

On the other side of Alex sat Jerome Masterson, his longtime friend and CIA special ops field partner. Jerome was dark-skinned, with a full beard and long, thick arms sticking out from a gray polo shirt adorned with the US Marine Corps symbol on its chest pocket. Whenever there was trouble, Jerome was nearby and often useful: skilled at logistics and training, he was also a legendary sniper.

Alex reached into the refrigerator, pulled out a beer bottle, and popped the lid. He stuck it to his lips. "I'm tired of mint tea," he said, letting half the bottle's contents run down his throat. Then he leaned back. "So, my fellow Bedouins say I'm the last hope for restoring the honor of the Bedouin nation. They want to reverse Israel's confiscation of Bedouin land in the West Bank. If I succeed, they'll back me with citizen commitment and, of course, pay me with tribal accolades."

"What do the rest of us get?" Caitlin asked, frowning and smiling at the same time.

"You get everything I get, less the tribal accolades," Alex said, smiling around the neck of his beer bottle. "Plus, we're going to start educating the rest of the Bedouin nation—nearly a million people. That is a commitment I got and am going to enforce."

"Works for me. Another million kids is a big deal," Caitlin said. The Bedouin leadership had resisted the Axial Systems education program despite the low cost and continued to under-educate women and children. From their experience teaching in Morocco, however, Caitlin and Alex had seen that people get hooked on learning. "For me, that's the Holy Grail."

"It's a big risk." Brooks shifted on the padded bench. "Shall we cut to the chase here? Do you feel this is a personal matter, a matter of family honor?"

Alex nodded. "It is." Both his parents would expect him to defend his honor, however he defined it. "But a big potential education bonus will also help us meet our goals there. I'll have to do this."

Brooks shifted again on his seat. "And if we don't agree to support you, you'll go off into the sunset alone to fight this beast."

Jerome Masterson chuckled. "Cooch ain't going no place alone, especially if there's violence involved. He's with me, like always. I know how he thinks and acts when he's stressed: I like it." An African-American man by birth, now living in Tangier as a dark-skinned Arab with several wives, Jerome had some money saved and lived pretty well. For him, this could be interesting—maybe even fun. "I smell an op," he said. "And if there's an op, I'm in if Cooch is in."

"Yeah, I'm in too," Caitlin agreed. "I don't like that racist, theocratic bullshit they're pulling in the West Bank." The last time she was invited to observe at Israel's super-secret nuclear location, the Israelis had ignored her advice about how to mathematically describe a particular speculative phenomenon. "They treated me like the help. They came back later, but still."

Alex smiled to himself. Caitlin viewed the world as her intellectual property. She could make every conversation about herself.

"Anyway, what are they going to do, give me another Fields Medal? Take the old one back?" she continued.

"I get it," Brooks broke in. "If everyone is committed to this ill-defined, boundless, and most assuredly dangerous venture, so am I. We agreed on the education part long ago, and we knew it would be slow and incremental. I guess this is just as good a way as any to get there."

"What am I, chopped liver?" LuAnn asked. "Do I get a vote?"

Alex grinned. "For sure you get a vote, and for sure we need you. You make money for us, don't you? Plus, you're with Himself."

"You sure are a smooth talker," LuAnn snorted. "I vote to spend as much as we need to, and involve all of us to support Alex in his mission."

"I really appreciate this vote of confidence or complicity or whatever it is. I'll go to Israel to try to sort this out with their leadership," Alex said, walking to the wet bar and grabbing another beer. If nothing else, the five of them would have a good time planning it all. He wouldn't be looking to engage the Israeli people in this venture—only their government. "I can't imagine I'll get much of a hearing, though. What we do after that is what should get their attention."

He popped the cap and stood, gazing at Tangier harbor. Yesterday he had been getting his face slapped. Today he was looking over one of the best views in the world, thinking about his new mission and the many, many moving parts he would have to put in play all at once.

"You'll need to get your ducks lined up in DC if you're going to engage with the Israelis," Brooks called out from behind him. "I assume you'll be making that trip before long, so I'll head there in the morning and get to work doing the prep. Good thing the president likes you . . . for now."

"Yeah," Alex chuckled. "I have to stop and see my sister in New Jersey anyhow. My mother is over there right now."

"Oh, visiting with Elena's family should be fun," Brooks said. "Has your brother-in-law warmed up to you yet?"

"Not in the fourteen years since he married my sister, so I suspect it's a lost cause."

"If the Israelis get intransigent, I have a few ideas that could be enjoyable for us while inconveniencing them quite a bit." The focus was back on Caitlin, who had worked full-time for over a decade on developing "Emilie," the name she chose for her software product that tied big-data analysis with predictive analytics. Emilie collected vast amounts of data in the cloud, then produced stunningly accurate predictions—what the requestor should do next, and where—using the power of artificial intelligence combined with the speed of a top-secret quantum computer: the Kphone, cleverly disguised in its cheap plastic case.

Alex turned to look at Brooks, who had a faint smile on his face. "As a representative of the president of the United States, with the rank of ambassador," Brooks retorted, "I do not want to hear about ideas like that from a woman like you."

"Yeah, well, fuck you too." Caitlin grinned.

"Caitlin and I will talk it through. Get some rest, everyone," Alex advised.

He thought for a moment. The Israelis owed him big-time, so perhaps Mossad could arrange a meeting with the new prime minister.

Now it was his turn to grin. "I'll call Guns Epstein tonight and catch up."

MOSSAD HEADQUARTERS, TEL AVIV

THE FOLLOWING AFTERNOON, AT MOSSAD HEADQUARTERS, NORMAN "Guns" Epstein put his heels on the edge of his steel credenza and turned slightly to the older woman sitting across the desk. Sheila Pelzer had tight gray hair and an aging, formerly attractive face atop a body pointing to age seventy. She was alert as ever, though—by necessity.

Epstein had asked her for a short-notice meeting, which was unusual behavior for him. Still, he was on the shortlist to succeed her as head of Israel's foreign intelligence body, Mossad, so the meeting was easily arranged. She studied him over the rim of her teacup. His enormous biceps stretched the sleeves of his shirt—thus the nickname "Guns." He had long run Mossad's intelligence efforts in the United States under the cover of an electronics engineer teaching at the graduate school at New York University, returning from New York with upper arms the size of tree trunks. Now he was firmly in place in Tel Aviv as her number two.

"I got a call yesterday from a friend in the dark world—a Bedouin sheik, half American," Epstein began. "He's upset about the recent West Bank business and the stolen land argument. The Bedouin tribes have collectively appointed him to discuss the issue with the new prime minister."

Pelzer understood his concern. "What makes him think he can see the prime minister?"

Epstein shrugged. "He wants us to arrange it for him."

"And we should do that for him . . . why? Because we're known as the softie Mossad?"

"No," Epstein replied. "Because he was the guy who put together the Iran attack."

Now Pelzer got it. "Ah, it all comes together now," she said. "Cuchulain, the CIA guy."

Some kind of a tactical-explosives maven, this operative had told the Israelis exactly when the attacking Arabs would be coming and, at no small personal risk, bootlegged several thousand of those terrific Coochmore mines that the Israeli forces had used so effectively. Pelzer remembered the exact number of dedicated Muslim antagonists who wouldn't be fighting the next round because of Cuchulain's warnings and equipment: 8,721.

"That battle coverage was very well done, and slaughtering the cream of the local Islamists was a big win for Israel," she admitted. "I'll bring it up with the prime minister. A meeting is not much to ask, I suppose."

Epstein sat back on his chair and gazed blankly at the computer screen. Pelzer knew he was working out how to explain the risks and rewards of a situation like this to someone at least as smart as he was.

"We both know the arrogance Alex Cuchulain will face from our prime minister. How Cooch will deal with that arrogance is a national security risk," Epstein said. "Worrying about how to prevent national security crises is what we do. In this case, we worry about Cooch. He could be a problem."

"Mmm. This particular 'problem' is connected to the White House through Mac Macmillan and Brooks Elliot, no?" Pelzer asked. Although Epstein was familiar with this group from his younger days, when he was running Mossad's US division, Pelzer herself knew Colonel Macmillan well—a formidable opponent and a vicious, ruthless, experienced man. Alarm bells were beginning to tingle in her head. "Give me your assessment of the whole cabal, individually and as a group."

Epstein nodded, then leaned forward. "A cabal is indeed what Cooch heads. There are four key players in addition to Cuchulain. As you know,

Elliot is a special ambassador to the US president. And Macmillan is Cooch's former boss at the CIA—he's somewhere in the National Security Advisor's shop now, and well respected.

"Cooch is the leader," Epstein continued. "He's a cold-blooded killer wrapped up in a façade of civility. There's no one as cool in battle as he is. He was a US Marine assigned to CIA special ops for eight years—reflexively violent when confronted and enormously competent at committing violence, both personal and unit.

"Cuchulain then went to Pittsburgh for a computer science and electrical engineering degree at Carnegie Mellon," Guns explained, "before heading off to Oxford for a master's degree in Islamic studies.

"Now he runs a gazillion-dollar trading company out of Tangier, plus a big private equity fund in New York," Epstein said. "He's filthy rich and well connected. And his girlfriend claims to be the smartest person in the world. I'll get to her in a moment."

Epstein stood up to refill his cup from a coffee pot on a plain wooden table. The cup was clearly a favorite: the purple NYU logo was fading, and the porcelain was stained a little by age and countless refills.

"We can deal with Cooch and Brooks Elliot if we have to. They're just a pair of smart, well-connected wolverines. Cooch's number two guy in anything related to violence, Jerome Masterson, is a retired US Marine Master Gunnery Sergeant living in Tangier—a legendary Marine sniper and trainer," he went on. "Cooch and Masterson were battle partners. They are very close. We can handle him too, but he has reach."

Masterson was head of security at Kufdani Industries HQ in Tangier, Epstein told her—the largest trading company in the Middle East, with offices in twenty-eight countries, nearly thirty thousand employees, and a fleet of fat cargo ships and airplanes that carried premium cargo around the world. In addition to his offices and residence, Masterson had a 15,000-square-meter training facility. He was paid to run a very elite warrior training program for the Moroccan minister of defense—the king's cousin, who was a good friend of both Cooch and Elliot. Rumor had it that Masterson's program had trained some eight hundred warriors, mostly Bedouin, primarily using South African 40mm belt-fed weapons.

"Now," said Epstein, "about the girlfriend."

HOW CAN I POSSIBLY EXPLAIN *Caitlin O'Connor and the risks she represents?* Guns thought, uncertain of how to fully distill the dangers inherent in someone who won a MacArthur Fellowship at age twenty-five and a Fields Medal at twenty-eight.

Guns had an interesting character of his own. His reputation in the field, back when he was running the US for Mossad, was that of a strong, direct, and ruthless operative. Among Mossad's more politically sensitive and astute, he was seen as a bit of a cowboy, slow to get on board with consensus. That was probably why he was popular with the Americans—both local operatives and Jewish civilians. Sheila Pelzer liked him too.

"The one we might not be able to handle is the smartest member of this little cabal—a particle physicist named Caitlin O'Connor," he said. "She rents her brain to the NSA, which in turn pays her company, Axial Systems, several hundred million dollars a year—plus another twenty million to cover her residence and its security. What exactly they are buying is unclear."

"My word, that's a lot of money!" Pelzer exclaimed. "And she's a problem for us . . . how?"

"She's just so friggin' smart." Guns shook his head. "It's disturbing. Sometimes she talks casually about things no one is supposed to know—things we didn't know *anyone* knew. It's as if she's reading our mail, even when it's in a language she doesn't speak. She is intimate with electronics at the quantum level. Our brightest physicists marvel at her skills."

A decade or so earlier, he explained, O'Connor had invented predictive big-data analysis and never told anyone, claiming it was intellectually obvious and not immediately important despite great promise. She was done worrying about what the rest of the world had only started worrying about.

"Today we call it 'artificial intelligence,'" Guns said. "We're touting ChatGPT and OpenAI as miracles. Well, Caitlin O'Connor did all that stuff years ago. No one should give her a twelve-year head start on anything intellectual. I can't imagine the ways she could hurt us if she chose. We just need to steer clear of her."

Pelzer gazed at him. "Can I get her with a love hawk?"

Guns snorted. "Last time we tried that, we lost the hawk after she screwed him half to death and told him he was stupid. He quit Mossad and got a nice, quiet job teaching physics somewhere. And she's just as much a pain in the ass as ever." Guns had argued against that plan the first time and would argue all the more strongly this time around.

Pelzer raised her hands in front of her face. "What about your pal Cooch? Maybe he can be convinced to stray toward another woman . . . or maybe be goes both ways?"

"Not that I'm aware of," Guns replied. "And Cooch already is unfaithful to Caitlin, but only because she wants it that way." He'd heard that O'Connor liked to "interview" top post-grad physicists with a lip-lock or something even more intimate, and that Cuchulain had long since accepted that part of the relationship.

"That's odd. So, what is he like as a person?" Pelzer said. "Without O'Connor, and separate from business. As it affects *us*. How do you sum him up as a threat?"

There's the question, Guns thought. *Cuchulain is a massive threat, but how did he get that way?* Cooch's post-CIA relationship with Macmillan was already in place when Guns had started in New York over a decade earlier, and his youth was beyond Mossad's reach except in the most academic way. But Guns knew how to spin hearsay into a story.

"As an individual, Cooch thinks through things more than most I've met in this business," he continued, "and he's maybe the most lethal human being on the planet.

"Cuchulain's father, Mick, had earned the Congressional Medal of Honor in Vietnam and spent many years in a wheelchair from the wounds accompanying that award. When Cooch got into high-school trouble, his father used Macmillan to get the boy into the Marine Corps. Then Macmillan yanked Cooch out of Parris Island to CIA special ops."

"As I recall, Macmillan ran that group for years," Pelzer said. "I assume this Cooch person blossomed into whatever he's become?"

Guns took a big swallow of his coffee and thought about how Cooch had spent much of those years in special ops—studying with a master of violent movement—and how he'd ended up today.

Six-foot-three or -four, about 240 pounds, maybe 2 percent fat, he thought. *Senses movement as it occurs, without seeing it. Goes against dozens of people and comes out the other side. It affects how he thinks, drives his anticipation.*

Guns had seen it over and over, and it was scary. He wasn't sure how to explain that to Pelzer, but it would be important for the longer term when dealing with Cuchulain.

"Yes," he said, "it's safe to say he blossomed."

Pelzer got up, stretched her lower back, and turned to the teapot behind her. "So he could be a real pain as an individual, even aside from the group. But how smart is he?"

"Very bright and a good electrical engineer, mostly when it comes to explosive design. He'll know what he wants and be clear about it," Guns said. "And he'll do whatever he promises to do, if he can. He's a notable planner. And Elliot is a Rhodes Scholar, you know. Those two are best friends—I've heard them discuss Thucydides and Machiavelli, as if the two thinkers go together somehow . . . ?"

"Mmm, they do," Pelzer said. "The latter studied the former. As did I."

Guns nodded, though ancient philosophy wasn't exactly his specialty. "Anyway, it almost doesn't matter how smart Cooch is. O'Connor will be involved, and Elliot. They all will."

This was a cabal of true experts. Guns couldn't possibly stress that point enough.

"There's another woman too: Elliot's wife, LuAnn Clemens," he continued. "She runs the money-making side of Caitlin's business and Kufdani

Industries alike. She's a noted lawyer and quite competent—probably tangential to the West Bank thing. She's buddies with the American First Lady, so we should try not to piss her off."

"Mmm, I suppose." Pelzer gazed at the ceiling for a long moment. "So, it looks like this guy could do us some damage if he chose. Eliminating him would likely cause a giant problem with the Americans, so I'd recommend against that. Yet we don't know quite how to predict what he will do. So, it seems safer to set up the meeting and see what we can learn. Fair?"

"Fair," Guns agreed. "Let me know if there's a glitch, but I'm sure Cooch will make room in his schedule for the prime minister." He paused. "Oh, and in our world, he calls himself by his Bedouin name."

"Which is . . . ?"

"Kufdani."

TANGIER

A QUARTER MOON HUNG OVER TANGIER HARBOR. "ROUND MIDNIGHT" BY Oscar Peterson was playing on the extraordinary speaker system. Caitlin's large, luxurious living room—adorned with overstuffed, red leather furniture, facing a bay window that looked down on Tangier harbor from the second bench of land above the sea—was beyond comfortable. At that moment, in the small, superbly equipped corner kitchen (nearly unused), the gracious hostess was opening a bottle of 1990 Le Pin, a legendary Bordeaux merlot that LuAnn had never tasted.

Looks like I have a new best friend, LuAnn chuckled inwardly.

Her husband had returned to Washington that morning. Alex was off doing planning things, and Jerome had gone home to his several wives. This evening, it was just LuAnn and Caitlin against the world.

The previous afternoon over in Alex's offices, when LuAnn had raised her eyebrows at Jerome's casual disclosure, he'd merely laughed and said things were different in Tangier and the Muslim world. As Jerome told it, his first wife complained that she needed help keeping up their place. When he had said, "Hire someone," she suggested instead that he marry a friend of hers, who would help with things and perhaps bear more children. Jerome worked a lot, went the logic, and the first wife was bored.

Long story short: the second wife came with a sister who was slightly mentally challenged, and they demanded he marry her too. Now the three women, who bore him several children among them, had no problem getting the housework done, and passed the time (according to Jerome) by ganging up on him.

"So, I guess we have everything we need right now except a guy to share it with. Right, Caitlin?" LuAnn said, one foot on the floor and another on the bench of the rag sofa where she sat.

"I'm used to that, and I'm good with it, apart from the lack of sex," Caitlin said, handing LuAnn a glass of Bordeaux, one-third filled. "I like my own company. And of course, I like your company."

LuAnn smiled and considered how little she really knew Caitlin. Maybe she wasn't as earth-shatteringly bright as everyone thought. How could anyone truly know, anyway? *I've worked with many lawyers who thought they could move the earth with their intellect,* thought LuAnn. *They couldn't.*

"I am curious," she said, the wine making her bold. "How does one become the smartest person in the world? I mean, how do you know you're *that* smart?"

Cailin sat back and raised her glass to LuAnn. "There's a long story and a short one. Which do you want to hear?"

"Which one did you tell the president?"

"The short one, of course," Caitlin replied. "He's the president."

LuAnn rolled her eyes. "I'll take the long one."

"Okay," Caitlin said. "Much of it is on my parents, as they say." Her father was an astronomer and well thought of in that bunch, she explained, while her mother was a Leibniz scholar and called herself a statistician. Both were full professors at Princeton. So to begin with, in the world's IQ score bucket, Caitlin was the product of two people probably in the upper one-tenth of 1 percent. "They weren't exactly into parenting. I was a distraction that resulted from them being in love. But I was smart and thus perhaps could be a source of amusement to them."

Caitlin explained she spoke in full sentences at age two, read English at age three, and was consequently a voracious reader of any book she found in her parents' library, as long as she could reach the shelf.

"What did your parents think of all that?" asked LuAnn, amused by the image it conjured.

"They were amused, as planned," Caitlin said.

By age ten, she said, she was fluent in Latin and had read much of Sir Isaac Newton's work in the original language. After Latin, naturally French, Spanish, and Italian came easy. Then she'd discovered calculus. But her parents decided she should save thinking about that until she had finished the foundational work in Newton's *Principia*, so they put the calculus books on the library's top shelf.

LuAnn could hardly believe her ears. "What did your schoolteachers have to say about your learning style?"

Caitlin chuckled. "It was hard for me when I went to public school. Other kids picked on me for being a smarty-pants, and I thought the teachers were stupid and told them so. I got in lots of fights and learned to swear." Calling other kids "pus-nuts scumbag motherfuckers" was not a big hit, so she got sent home a few times. Her mother had to come for her.

LuAnn sipped her wine. This was an amusing conversation. "And how did your mother handle that?"

"She took me to the study and made me an offer I couldn't refuse."

"To wit . . . ?"

"She said I was interfering with her lifestyle, which was beyond what our relationship could bear, and she would put me in Catholic day school if it happened again. If that didn't work, they would find a Catholic boarding school for me. Good discipline there, you know? If you don't behave, they just hit you."

"Harsh, but to the point," LuAnn conceded. "Did you run to your dad?"

"Run to him? He was sitting across the room, reading a book. He looked up and said, 'You are an embarrassment. Get yourself under control. Think, then act.'"

"Whoa," LuAnn said, "a unified front."

Caitlin's mother had convinced the school administrators to let her daughter sit in the back of the classroom and read her own books, as long as she took their standardized tests and added to the school's academic glory. So Caitlin did her homework and didn't make much more trouble. At the playground, meanwhile, she played as rough as possible, so what friends she had were mostly boys.

"By sixth grade, I was into Newton's calculus at last and stayed busy with my books," Caitlin continued. "Mom and I would argue Leibniz versus Newton after dinner. Dad and I talked about stars and the galaxy broadly. He liked to talk about Jupiter. That was great fun."

LuAnn stood and went to the bar to fill her glass. "I'm getting it. You were a bit of a problem child. Did something come together after a while?"

"Yeah," Caitlin said. "What came together drives what I do and my business today." She'd figured out that calculus *enables* the natural sciences and that being good at calculus had enormous personal value. "Without calculus, you ain't good at advanced biology, physics, chemistry, any of it. And *with* calculus, you compete with me."

In studying physics and chemistry, Caitlin had noticed that much of the advanced work was in describing what was going on so others could then study it. In other words, any work in the sciences required calculus as the descriptor language—a nearly infinite one, and constant in its written nomenclature across every spoken dialect. One of her early mentors, theoretical physicist Richard Feynman, once said calculus was the language of God: it allows one to describe God's work.

"This explains why I get contracts around the world to consult on new ideas," Caitlin pointed out. "If I can understand a new scientific concept, I can describe it mathematically better than anyone I have met."

It was a lot to take in, even for a highly intelligent lawyer. LuAnn's hostess knew more about calculus and how to use it than pretty much anyone alive, and she had been working on it for thirty years or so. And she was quick, obviously. *But where's the beef?* LuAnn thought.

"I sort of get it," she admitted. "But why is that valuable? Why do they pay you so well?"

"Aha!" Caitlin said. "The benefit is that I make things smaller and faster. Small things run cooler; heat is important. An organization's current effort might take a lot of computer space and time, which makes it impractical. So they hire me to describe their product in a faster, more efficient way."

"I'm a lawyer," LuAnn said. "I don't see any math in my business, but I do see a lot of finance arithmetic wrapped up in opinions. Things are defined in varying shades of gray."

"Yeah, that's why I avoid fields with too many dependent variables, like the law and politics. Especially finance. There is insufficient precision in any of those fields to get a reliable, correct answer to a problem."

"Okay, so you were the smartest kid on the block, maybe the planet," LuAnn said. "You were born with a head start, and your parents put your already capable brain on metaphorical steroids."

"Yeah, that's pretty much it. But I wouldn't be here without Alex. He bought and bailed out my business ten years ago. After putting years into Emilie, I would have lost it all."

"So, he gets you." LuAnn nodded, smiling. "He gets it."

"He has always gotten it, and I adore him for his persistence," said Caitlin as a dreamy look came over her face. "And now I have a quantum computer in a cell phone case."

"So this Kphone is a big deal," LuAnn said. "Net it out for me."

It's not just the Kphone, Caitlin thought. *It's Emilie.*

The heuristic AI chatbot that powered the Kphone was what ChatGPT and other sophomoric AI implementations could only hope to be. Caitlin had named the software for her declared idol, Émilie du Châtelet, one of the few women to grace the pantheon of eighteenth-century Enlightenment natural philosophers. AI functions on data—lots of it—and Caitlin had been teaching Emilie to collect and index the world's data for ten years now, in the form of videos, meeting transcripts, emails, phone conversations, you name it. By now, Emilie was getting quite good at it.

Caitlin walked to the bar and refilled their glasses once more, taking a sip. "Nice wine," she confirmed. Then she shrugged. "It's a big deal," she admitted, despite being unsure whether getting into it with a lawyer was wise. "A Kphone is thousands of times faster than the world's largest, fastest air-cooled computer. One can do a lot with that speed, especially if no one else has it."

Quantum speed vastly enabled computers, just as calculus vastly enabled the study of the natural sciences. It provided Caitlin instant access and reference to all the data managed by Emilie, and from there—with unlimited cloud storage and unlimited quantum speed—anything was possible. Caitlin had designed the phone several years before, and a former colleague from Caltech used his Taiwan chip-fab to build a quantum chipset for it. Caitlin had bought thousands of the chips for just $100 each. Buying the phone software and the cheap plastic case was easier yet.

She ticked off her next points one by one on her fingers. "I have access to all the information ever recorded in modern history up until this morning—that's big data." *One.* "I have the ability to sift through it in minutes while questioning the content—that's artificial intelligence, and without speed limits because the Kphone is a quantum device." *Two.* "And then I draw conclusions from it—that's predictive analytics." *Three.*

Caitlin looked expectantly at her guest.

"Go on," said LuAnn slowly. "I think I'm tracking you. Except for the part about the NSA paying you and your firm $225 million a year . . . without receiving title to anything at all."

Caitlin strolled to the large plate-glass window and peered out at the lights around Tangier harbor. *What do I say now?* she wondered. *This is some seriously secret shit—so secret, even the NSA hasn't quite figured it out.* She turned back to LuAnn before she had even decided what to say—but suddenly figured if the tall Texan woman was good enough for Brooks Elliot, she was good enough for Caitlin.

"Okay, here it is," Caitlin confessed. "I can find out anything you want to know that has a recorded history and a communications connection, along with a set of observations—conclusions even—about the topic. The software, known as Emilie, does all the translations and research."

So, she explained, if you asked Emilie, *What were the results of the meeting between President Putin and his foreign minister last night?*, within twelve hours you'd get a transcript of the conversation in any language you chose, plus any observations made by other meeting attendees who had commented electronically or typed their response into a connected computer, plus conclusions with reasoning based on any recorded history behind the same topic. Putting it all together depended on compute-speed capability—enter the quantum speed of the Kphone.

"In other words," Caitlin said quietly, "no message is secret, no design is protected, and no act is ignored or forgotten."

LuAnn whistled. "Wow. I had no idea. That's . . . enormous."

Cailin smiled wryly. "And that's why they pay us the big money. The NSA finds that information valuable, for good reason. Until someone catches up, we own the game."

"Given Alex's latest project, let's hope the Israelis don't catch up anytime soon." Sensing an end to the evening, LuAnn drained her glass and put it on the bar.

"They won't," Caitlin assured her. "I'm watching closely. They have some very smart people, but this took me twenty years to develop. It's no picnic." She turned to stare out the living room window again, an empty glass in her hand. "We have what no one else has. And we use it."

TANGIER

"THE ISRAELIS ARE TOUGH," SAID ALEX EARLY THAT AFTERNOON. "IT will be hard to manipulate them to our point of view."

Alex and Caitlin sat in Caitlin's office, on a padded bench at a small wooden table, where teacups and teapots awaited clearing. It was a clear midday, with the bulk of Gibraltar visible from the office windows. Computer screens covered the walls. In one corner was a closet, where tiny blinking lights confirmed the presence of several servers connected to the main computer facility at Kufdani Industries, embedded deep in the mountain.

Alex, his bare feet in Caitlin's lap, stared blankly across the choppy water at the Gibraltar's gigantic promontory jutting hazily from the blue-green sea, just a few miles away. "For this Bedouin thing to work, I need to plan some kind of force multiplier. And Emilie just might be the key."

Caitlin applied thumb pressure to the ball of his foot and rolled it around. "How do you think that might start?" she said.

Ideas for how to restore the stolen land to the Bedouins as is, with the Israelis' developments in place but their Haredim Orthodox tenants back on the kibbutz, had been rolling around in the back of Alex's mind all day. "What if I could create some kind of central attraction to the cause of restoring Bedouin honor—and therefore Islamic honor—by making the Israelis give back the West Bank?"

"But what about the IDF?" Caitlin said. If Alex's plan got any traction, surely the Israel Defense Forces would immediately get involved. He would have to neutralize them somehow. "They're a bunch of bright, mean fuckers. And that's the first place the Israeli government will turn if it gets uncomfortable and they need to . . . fix things."

"Yeah, they're good," Alex said. "The IDF has technology that really makes things hum. Everyone talks to everyone. Their combined forces communicate and act in concert—securely, effectively. They have smart weapons."

Caitlin looked offended, as he'd known she would. "Securely? Well, hell, we can already read their messaging, and I've had Emilie hard at work figuring some shit out," she insisted. "What if I could mess with their communications, maybe even interfere selectively with their infrastructure?"

Alex nodded and wiggled his foot to demand more pressure. "If we can do that, it's an idea with potential. If I know what the IDF is planning, I have a decent chance of figuring the rest out."

"I already figured it out," Cailin said, digging deeper into the ball of his foot. "And if you make nice love to me, I'll tell you everything you want to know."

Alex put his hands behind his head. "And what if I *don't* make nice love to you?"

Caitlin laughed. "I'll tell you anyway. I just had a few thoughts that I'd like to ride for a while, and you do know how to make a thought ride pleasant."

"Ride them later," Alex demanded. "Tell me now."

"Okay now, stay with me," Caitlin replied, sitting up straight. "These are the CliffsNotes, and you ain't the sharpest knife in the drawer." She explained her interest in the mathematical and physical characteristics of an electromagnetic pulse, which she'd been studying for a while thanks to the NSA money.

"I know what you mean," Alex agreed. "EMP was a big component of my venture in the attack on Iran. It got my attention."

"That's when I started thinking more about it too. It changed the game on the ground," Caitlin said.

Alex wiggled his foot again. "Frying electrical circuits without killing people made it useful in Iran. We interrupted communications in a large part of Tehran and on targeted field units of the Republican Guard. It worked fine. So . . . ?"

"So, what if we could control the EMP impulse?" she said. "Make it big, make it small, maybe even make it shootable? We have some boss 3D printing capability now. That could be useful."

"That's huge." Alex nodded. "It's a good start."

"Want me to tell you all the dirty pieces?"

"Not right now. I want to ride that thought for a while. Care to join me?"

"Charmed, I'm sure," Caitlin murmured. "Who has the honors?"

"Happy to be of service," he replied, swinging his feet from her lap to the floor and sliding off the padded bench to his knees. Bob James—high on their go-to list, up there with Oscar Peterson—was busy on the piano, notes flowing from the speakers hidden in the ceiling. He felt Caitlin's hand ruffling his hair with one hand, her eyes closed, as she reached for the remote with her other hand and notched the volume up a little.

As he turned toward her, she continued running her fingers through his thick, graying hair. He knew she would be emptying her mind of thoughts and current events, succumbing to his skill. Alex was a master at the oral artistry of accompanying a complex, repetitive jazz beat.

LATE AFTERNOON SUNRAYS SLANTED THROUGH the windows of Caitlin's office. Through one window on the west wall, a two-lane, twenty-five-meter lap pool was visible. It was hers, extending beside a corridor leading to workspaces, custom made for her and installed years ago with a watertight door. She seldom let others use it.

Alex, freshly showered and dressed, picked up two Bordeaux glasses from a rack on the counter, then plucked out a bottle of water and one of red wine: a Napa Cabernet from recent wine venture Accendo Vintners. Caitlin watched him sleepily until he returned to the couch.

He opened the red wine, poured a third of a glass for Caitlin and another for himself, and then drained the water bottle. "I talked to Guns, asked him to set up a meeting with the Israeli prime minister as recognition for our help in Iran," he began. "We talked philosophy for a bit. I'm assuming the Israelis will try to placate me at first without agreeing to anything much."

"Now, there's a safe assumption," Caitlin replied, rolling her eyes. "If they even notice you at first."

"I need a plan to spin public opinion early," Alex said. He would need to figure out whom to convince, when, and how, and get the US political people on board—all before meeting with the prime minister.

"Okay. That's probably the key, really," Caitlin said. "Get the world on our side."

Alex nodded. "Brooks knows a lot of folks back there, so he's likely to be useful."

"The whole idea just has too many dependent variables, with no real predictability that I can identify," Caitlin pointed out. "But with my Kphone, I can definitely fuck up anything, anywhere, as long as it's connected to the internet." On the couch, she moved an inch closer to him. "But if it all goes bad, I'm willing to hire you as my personal sexual linguist. You have very special skills in that rarified field."

Alex grinned at her, then felt his Kphone buzz in his pocket. He took it out, glanced at it, and stood up quickly. "It's Mom. I'm going to grab this in my office."

Maria Kufdani Cuchulain lived just across the Strait of Gibraltar, in Algeciras on the south coast of Spain. Years ago, after growing up in Tangier, she had been teaching high school math in Algeciras—and seriously dating the mayor—when Alex's father showed up. He'd been stationed at Rota, the US Navy station strategically located nearby. When a group of four or five determined Spanish men demanded he look elsewhere for a girlfriend, Mick had revealed himself to be demonstrably (and violently) unintimidated.

The two were married, and when Mick was transferred to Vietnam, he moved his young family to Audley, South Carolina, near the Marine Corps base at Parris Island. When Mick came home from his second tour in Vietnam, he had a wheelchair and the Congressional Medal of Honor to show for it; the medal came with fifty bucks a month added to his medical retirement. Life for the Cuchulains changed.

Maria taught math at the junior college, while Alex and his older sister, Elena, adapted and grew up in the small South Carolinian town. Mick read a lot.

Alex planned to be a high school wrestler, and he was good at it—until he injured two of the town's high school jocks fairly badly after they assaulted Elena. A friend of Alex's father, Mac Macmillan, violently intervened in town politics to keep Alex from going to prison. Soon after, life sent him off at age sixteen to Parris Island to become a US Marine.

Elena survived the incident with the football heroes and went on to teach math at a small liberal arts college in New Jersey. She was married now and had a teenaged son, Michael. When Mick died, with no one left in South Carolina, Maria had moved back to Algeciras, where she had a sister, friends, and connections with Tangier, just fifteen or so nautical miles across the Mediterranean.

"Hi, Mom. All good in Spain?" Alex asked. He sometimes worried that his mother wanted to return to Tangier, where she could be a major society player if she chose. She missed Morocco, of course. But she could have anything money could buy, and with her house and her sister in Algeciras, she had all she needed. Plus she had the recent surprise of twin grandchildren living nearby—unacknowledged, but still flesh and blood.

"I'm sorry to bother you, Alejandro, but I am troubled," Maria replied.

Everything else on Alex's mind vanished in a rush of concern. "Are you okay?" he asked. "Is there anything you need?"

"I'm fine. I like Spain, and I am busy," she said. "But I am just back from visiting Elena. I think there is some trouble there."

Alex relaxed into his chair. Marital troubles *seemed* stressful but usually went away easily. "Oh yeah? I talk to Elena occasionally, but she hasn't been very forthcoming. I was planning to stop by and see her when I go to the States again. What's going on?"

"When I arrived at the Newark airport, Elena met me at baggage claim as always," Maria replied, "but this time her face was swollen and her jaw was cut."

Alex sat up.

"I asked her about it, and she had some facile answer, which I accepted. She is entitled to her privacy."

"Hmm?" Alex said patiently. He knew his mother well. Whatever this was, Maria had been thinking about how to say it for a while now.

"But then we got to their home—which is very nice indeed for a school-teacher—and when I walked in the door, Kevin's face was also swollen and . . . his nose was splinted."

Alex chuckled quietly. "She's a Cuchulain. She doesn't do the quitting thing. Kevin lost the fight, but he's alive. May there never be another."

"Don't be coarse, Alex," his mother scolded. "It does not become you."

"Sorry, Mom. So if not domestic violence . . . then what?"

"Michael had a black eye. My grandson had a black eye," she continued, her voice hardening. "He got it from a boy at his school."

"Mom, he has to learn to fight back. We all have to do it sometimes," Alex insisted. "Bullies are everywhere. We had a playground bully for a president who had never been hit hard in the face, and look what he's like! I mean, perhaps I can help Michael out when I visit in a few weeks—"

"Alejandro, you are beginning to irritate me. I was married to the legendary Mick Cuchulain. I am the daughter of Kufdani. I am the mother of Cooch, the warrior. I know about these things."

"So, what happened?"

Maria explained that it had taken several hours and a few tears to get the story from her grandson. "Michael is being bullied, just like you guessed. Some other boys stay close to the bully and help him out, and they get in a few punches and kicks too. The problem is, no one is allowed to fight back lest the bully's father get involved."

She's on a roll now, Alex thought. *It will all come out.*

Apparently the bully would direct the other boys to hold whomever he was beating on, then tell the teachers to stay out of the fight. The teachers were afraid of him ever since one called the police and promptly got a beating from the bully's father. The police, meanwhile, did nothing.

Kevin had gone to pick up his son at school one day, and there was Michael at the bottom of a pile, with the bully sitting on his chest, punching him in the face, and two boys laughing and kicking him. Kevin ran to break it up, only to be punched by the bully as well—and then beaten fairly badly by the bully's father, who had been watching his son's antics from a nearby car. The man broke Kevin's nose and loosened a few teeth too.

When the doctor called the police to the hospital after setting Kevin's nose, Kevin told them who had assaulted him. The sergeant told Kevin that his best bet was to stay away from the man, who was a big deal in a rough crowd.

"Mobsters of some sort, I suppose," said Maria.

"And Elena?" Alex said. By now he was pacing across his office, back and forth.

"Elena is her father's daughter," Maria said quietly.

The next day, Elena went to pick up Michael. The bully made a rude comment to her, and Michael yelled at him—and when the bully pushed Elena, she kicked him in the testicles, then elbowed him in the face with one arm and then the other. As he was falling, she kicked him in the kidney.

"The bully's father came running and pushed Elena to the ground," Maria continued. "When she came to her feet, he slapped her and called her a . . . a disgusting name. She spat in his face, so he knocked her to the ground with a punch to the jaw and kicked her a couple of times in the ribs. Then he picked up his son and carried him to the car."

"Not good," Alex said. "Did anyone find out the name of this 'rough crowd'?"

"The family is named Cabrillo. The police told Kevin that the father's a leader in the Bollito gang."

Alex smoothed his hair with spread fingers. "What do you want me to do, Mother?"

"Fix it," she replied. "You are a man of legendary violence, and they are people of only ordinary violence. It's that simple. I don't ask for much."

Well, she's right about that, Alex thought. *Mafia, huh?*

"Your sister has adjusted to the situation, just as you and your father would expect." A note of bitterness entered her voice. "She has grown cold and hardened. It's ugly. I cried and said hello to my new Elena."

"We're still nice people, Mom. You married one."

"I know, and I would do it again. But I didn't expect it for my only daughter. What are you people? Not just warriors. Wolverines. Something. And now Elena has joined you."

Alex sighed. "I'll figure it out, Mom. But you know Kevin thinks I'm a cretin." He wasn't worried about Elena—she was a Cuchulain and a Kufdani. But he would have to get some measure of Kevin and Michael. "I've seen my nephew maybe three times in thirteen years. I'll have to spend a few days with them to figure things out, sleeping in their house. Floor is fine."

"I'll talk to Elena, see where her head is, and then let you know. I'll make it happen," Maria insisted. "But no son of mine sleeps on the floor."

TANGIER

TANGIER HARBOR WAS BUSY AT MIDDAY. FISHERMEN SCURRIED ACROSS the waters in boats that looked tiny from halfway up the hill into which the Kufdani Industries' headquarters was built. Tankers and freighters made their way west to the anchorage and unloading piers at the city's new dock facilities.

Sitting at his desk many feet above the harbor, drinking mint tea while watching the scene through a window built into a sheer stone wall, Alex thought about what he and Caitlin had discussed the previous day: how to isolate the Orthodox Jews from their broad political support base in Israel. If he could win the goodwill of liberal Israelis while making life miserable for the Orthodox Jews in the occupied West Bank, his end goal would be in sight.

Their primary enemy was the Orthodox Haredi, a separate community of ultra-conservative Jews who had decreed that being Jewish was necessary in order to own property or have constitutional rights in Israel. They had arranged, based on that theory, to have Bedouin land confiscated by the government. A newly elected prime minister had endorsed that theory in exchange for the Haredi votes that had gotten him elected—which in turn had allowed him to avoid prosecution for a smattering of public fraud charges. The prime minister was expected to suck up to the Haredim, and he did.

Hardcore religious fundamentalists, the Haredim encouraged men to avoid traditional work and instead study religious texts at yeshiva seminaries. More than half the Haredi high schoolers attended institutions that did not even teach the Israeli national core curriculum of science, math, and English. Haredi women, on the other hand, were expected to maintain the house and have babies. With a reproductive rate of more than seven to one compared with below two for more liberal, left-leaning Israelis, the Haredim expected to dominate the voting population of Israel before the turn of the next century.

Traditionally, except for one brigade of hotheads called the 97th Netzah Yehuda Battalion, Orthodox Jews did not serve in the military, so Haredim lives were not in direct danger in any conflict. Regardless, the Israel Defense Forces would likely be directed to protect them from harm. After all, they voted in large numbers and as a bloc.

The IDF was competent and well led, so Alex would need to get them out of the way. Shin Bet, which served as the federal police or some such, akin to the FBI, would be a problem too. To neutralize this threat, he would need to change the nature of the conflict between the Israeli forces and the masses of largely unarmed Palestinians in the West Bank.

I'll have to move first with the liberal Jews, both at home and abroad, he thought. He would need to gain tacit approval, or at least avoid vocal disapproval, from the more modern Jewish community within Israel and the powerful diaspora of liberal Jews in the United States—six million each, broadly defined. *I'll need a way to reach them quickly and effectively.*

The trick would be making life uncomfortable for the upper-class Israelis without scaring them. He wanted discomfort without fear.

The Israelis had universal conscription, so soldiers at the fighting level came from upper-class families just like the others. In the likely event that the Israelis responded to his actions by attacking the Bedouin and Palestinian forces that Alex planned to create, he wanted to avoid killing Israeli soldiers and instead wound as many as possible. A thousand Israeli troops with stitches were much better than two or three flag-wrapped caskets shown all over the newspapers.

A good public relations plan was essential. Brooks could probably give him a hint of where to start and who to hire. But if the Israelis decided to punish the Palestinians for supporting his Bedouin position, there could be slaughter. No amount of PR would whitewash that type of mess.

At twenty-five miles long but only six miles wide, the Gaza Strip was narrow enough that any real fight became a very personal knife fight. The Palestinians controlled it, but they were basically leaderless and had no trained military force. They wouldn't get a chance to fight with slingshots, much less knives, and would lose the fight even if they did.

I need to figure out a weapon that untrained Palestinian troops can use, Alex thought.

He decided the M79 40mm grenade launcher, first used in Vietnam, was an excellent place to start. He had always liked the M79, even fifty years after it was introduced. It acted like a short-barreled, single-shot shotgun that fired a 40mm grenade.

Jerome had procured a bunch of modern, belt-fed South African 40mm weapons for the Kingdom of Morocco, so Alex would be able to count on his knowledge of the current use of area weapons in the hands of line troops, rather than using precision shot rifles. Jerome had thought through 40mm weapons tactics many times over, and the two men had some joint experience in how those tactics played out.

Rheinmetall, the German arms manufacturer, had built an international business in making and supplying 40mm arms and ammunition, including some new anti-drone and anti-armor stuff. Alex had worked with Rheinmetall on fusing its new 40mm fragmentation weapons; governments worldwide now had 40mm munitions for fragmentation, armor piercing, and smoke production. More recently, the manufacturer had announced a magazine-fed 40mm, shoulder-fired launcher with some electronic features that Alex found intriguing.

The Americans had long ago developed a new model to replace the single-shot M79: the Mk19, a belt-fed, shoulder-fired 40mm weapon, with all the hardware required for mounting on a truck, thus supplying a solid base from which to aim and shoot. The newer-design Mk19 performed better, and the Americans had tons of them, but these were now obsolete thanks to an even newer 40mm weapon developed with modern electronics and additional range. That left them eager to dispose of the Mk19s, and make available all the videos and training that Emilie would need to splice together a short, robust training video of how to shoot at dismounted ground troops within one hundred meters. The ammo would have to fit the weapon, but Alex didn't need all the electronic bells and whistles that could expand the window of lethal usefulness as on the Tangier Bedouins' more modern 40mm weapons. He wanted to cut, not kill.

The South African weapons had a longer range and employed a plethora of special-purpose ammunition—somewhat fatter than the chamber of the Mk19, often supplied by Rheinmetall. The vast majority of Mk19 ammunition Alex might procure from Rheinmetall would be used against dismounted infantry. By design, only the cutting rounds were small enough to fit into the chamber of the Mk19; the lethality of the larger rounds would be reserved for the better trained troops.

That should be just right for our purposes, he thought.

Alex thought about delivering 40mm projectiles that were fusible, both for range and power, to given targets—thus exploding only under specified conditions. Now *that* would be a cool capability to have! If the Israelis attacked his Bedouin and Palestinian forces, the one-hundred-meter range of the 40mm could wreak havoc on ground troops. Airplanes and armor would be a more challenging problem to handle, but Alex remembered that Rheinmetall had done some development work on 40mm anti-aircraft weapons, and the Bedouins coming from Morocco would be using the more capable South African weapons, not the Mk19. The Israelis' armor, or at least the lightly armored personnel carriers targeted by his Bedouins, would be toast. If tanks became a problem, the Swedes had developed some great shoulder-fired antitank weapons. And Jerome said he could get a few of the new American Javelins from the Moroccan army, thanks to Alex's buddy Admiral Sino ibn Nahir, the minister of defense.

Presiding over the whole communications operation would be Caitlin, hanging out in Tangier with a bird's-eye view and control of the entire Israeli military communications complex, thanks to Emilie. This extraordinary software had constructed a chart of each communications node in the complex and a click-path to destroy it, neutralize it, or keep it on hold. Caitlin's little EMP trick, if she could manage it, would have a huge impact on the Iron Dome—Israel's air defense system, which depended on its electronics to function—if the conflict moved to Israeli soil; their Iron Dome close-in air defense system was also dependent on its electronics to function. The Iran war had introduced electromagnetic pulse weapons to Alex's mind as big, area weapons riding Tomahawk missiles to knock out electronics in a base or a whole city. He and Caitlin would have to discuss this option further, but shootable EMP had promise.

Zap! Big area. Zap! Small area, he thought. *Very cool, if Caitlin could pull it off.*

The wreaking of havoc—cutting, not killing—was essential to Alex's thinking. It would take two Israeli men to carry each injured soldier off the battlefield and a raft of doctors to sew up their wounds. The phones would be going wild. Maybe Caitlin could shut down one of the Israeli support centers; that would delay the news to mothers and other loved ones. Delays in welcoming their wounded kiddies back to civilian life would cause discomfort and stress.

And that would be good for his primary goal: mobilizing disapproval among moderate Israelis. The way Alex was planning it, in the back of everyone's mind would be the reluctant vision of high-fragmentation weapons driving lethal shrapnel fired from the very same guns—and their kiddies coming home to them in flag-wrapped caskets the next time.

One loose strand did bother him, though: the likelihood of losing control of the Palestinian fighters, who would want to kill Israelis anytime they could. The Palestinian shooters might be appeased by knowing that by shooting 40mm rounds from hiding, they wouldn't have to get too close to wound as many troops as they pleased. And they would have only the ammunition Kufdani provided to them: the razor rounds, which wouldn't kill shit and weren't useful at close range. So it seemed like just a problem of controlling ammunition inventory, rewarding those who attempted to wound only and punishing those who used excessive force. Alex would worry later about how to get field support from the Palestinian leadership—whoever that might be—and how it would play with Hamas, the real power in Palestinian politics, at least in Gaza.

Right now, he worried about his mother.

Alex had heard the sob in his mother's voice—an almost unheard-of occurrence—and known it was time to pack and get moving. Young Michael was handling things pretty well, Maria had reported, but Alex would just have to deal with Elena's husband himself. His mother had reassured him that Kevin was a good man. He didn't think like a Cuchulain, naturally, but he was good for Elena. Or at least he had been, before all this . . .

The trip involved a stop in Spain first, to the Kufdani Industries distribution headquarters. The education effort operated out of Algeciras, and things would soon be getting more interesting for them too. After that, he meant to take care of the situation with Elena. He wanted to be on the ground in the US before things got even uglier.

ALGECIRAS, SPAIN

A DOUBLE CYCLONE FENCE SURROUNDED THE KUFDANI INDUSTRIES distribution complex in southern Spain. Armed, unpleasant guards manned the gates, and a complicated system of anti-intrusion cameras and devices determined who could and could not gain admittance. Alex, of course, was among the former. He told his driver to take his things to the apartment he kept within the complex, and walked up the stairs to the entrance of a flat-roofed, pastel yellow, two-story building.

Alex and Jerome had upped the company's security budget by a large amount a few years earlier, when Kufdani had gone into the medical marijuana business with the Berbers. Basically, Alex and Sino—the Moroccan defense minister—had convinced the king to sponsor the legal growing of medical marijuana in the Rif mountain region of Morocco, which was controlled by Berbers, ethnic indigenous Moroccans who had been selling *kif* on the black market. The case made to the king was that over time, legalizing marijuana cultivation could bring in an extra $20 billion of annual taxable revenue for the Kingdom. With good management, and with Kufdani Industries robustly distributing the product across Europe and the Middle East, that figure turned out to be $40 billion and growing. The company's educational successes with the Moroccan people had been a bonus, and the king was quite happy about both.

With the Algeciras warehouses filled with as much as ten tons of processed medicinal marijuana awaiting EU clearance, the proper-prior-planning assumption had been that someone, sometime, would try to break in and steal as much as they could. Jerome had initially complained to the locals about vandalism, then said he would handle security himself.

After a few days, a nice lunch or two with the local authorities, a convincing smile, and a bright blue Vespa delivered to one particular door, the authorities had given Kufdani Industries whatever permits were requested. Vague promises of ongoing political support and few questions about zoning sweetened the deal. Kufdani Industries had gone about expanding and lengthening the Algeciras airstrip to seven thousand feet, initiated a bonded cargo air service, and procured a small fleet of used C-130 airplanes from the United States.

The pastel yellow building was well tended and boring except for the flower beds surrounding it. Alex had long since told Achmed, his CEO at Kufdani, that he favored hiring women in the growth of the business and intended to foster that environment. So most of the building's occupants were women who took pride in the flowers. More than a few were women who liked to shoot.

Alex and Achmed had been childhood friends. When he was twelve, Achmed was ceremoniously "given" to the Kufdani grandfather, who had then "given" him to young Alex. It was an honor to be so named, for both Alex and Achmed—akin to the concept of the godchild in the Christian faith. Indeed, these two had an abiding faith in each other, and their friendship had flourished for several decades. Achmed was ambitious, but content with the traditional relationship. Alex, whose upbringing was more Western-facing, was less so.

"Why favor women?" Achmed had asked long ago.

"Because they cost no more than men and adapt to business at least as well" came the response. "If treated well, they may even have a better work ethic. There is also less competition to employ them, so we can spend time molding them to the Kufdani way of doing business." Alex then wanted to confirm this approach was acceptable to the CEO.

"Hey, you put me through the MBA program at IMD in Lausanne. I like Switzerland. You own me, literally."

Achmed had flourished at Kufdani Industries, and he now ran an organization of more than thirty thousand people across their trading market. Of the top thirty executives, thirteen were women. The most senior was Hala, who ran both the education effort and the European marijuana distribution business but always mentioned the education effort first, even though it was vastly smaller than the distribution business. To most people, Hala appeared to be the proverbial mystery wrapped in an enigma. Despite knowing her for years, sometimes intimately—with Caitlin's approval—Alex didn't *really* know her either.

Tall and dark, with a prominent nose and large brown eyes, she stood just inside the door, waiting to greet him. A graduate of a public honors college in western Pennsylvania and the IE Business School in Madrid, she spoke native Spanish, as well as several versions of Arabic and Pashtun, and was a single mother. A traditional hijab was wrapped around her head, as usual.

Alex stuck out his hand. "Good afternoon, Hala."

She took his hand firmly, nodded, and said, "Kufdani. Welcome."

They walked down the hall to a corner office, and Alex closed the door behind him. Hala sat back in her chair, waiting.

In all fairness, her focus on education among the Yahia Bedouin tribe and the Berbers in Morocco's hills had been a fabulously successful venture for Kufdani Industries. Literacy was at nearly 95 percent among children younger than twelve. Businesses were springing up, and post-sixth-grade education was soaring. Jobs were available with Boeing and other Western companies that needed educated workers. The Israelis were building factories in Morocco because good workers were available at a reasonable price, continuing the tradition of the Jewish community in Tangier, which had been part of the city's fabric for hundreds of years.

And all because of the Kphone, Alex thought, knowing Caitlin would insist on owing gratitude to Emilie instead. Speed was easy, but Emilie was cool.

Kufdani Industries had distributed several thousand Kphones in an effort to educate the Berbers and the Yahia Bedouin. As people learned, Emilie adapted her teaching style and speed to their needs, and soon the Kphone became a status symbol among students, and the learning accelerated. Emilie was valuable software, broadly applicable to education, business, and defense. She learned from her experience and her mistakes, as heuristic things do.

Kufdani Industries had built a new company out of Axial, partly on this effort, with Alex as CEO and lead investor, Brooks as advisor, lawyerly management skills from LuAnn, and the full-time commitment of Caitlin. Ten different divisions, with chief technical officers selected by Caitlin, were managed from afar by LuAnn, using Emilie's control of vast data.

Much of Axial's business with the NSA leveraged Emilie's inherent skills as the foundation for a particular project. As Emilie's libraries grew, with the base of available knowledge expanding beside better analytics, grown heuristically, costs continued to fall. Even though software was cheap to reproduce, Kufdani Industries' Axial sold value rather than effort, and prices continued to climb. Profits soared.

Now, according to Alex, it was time for an entirely new effort in using the AI chatbot once again as a force multiplier for education, not just war, and he was beyond excited. "We have a shot at educating all Bedouin children across the Levant and into Arabia—everything we've worked for," he explained.

"We are ready for that, Kufdani, and have been so for a year already," Hala said, her excitement visible on her face. "More than two thousand of our Muslim women are now members of the Piety movement, and we have trained them as active classroom monitors." The organization had found a ready market for helping children, in Bedouin grandmothers. "I have been following the 'P to the seventh power' approach that you emphasize, and I've taught it to the Elliot Scholars you had me hire. Thank you for the extra budget, by the way."

Alex nodded. "We need a flock more Kphones. I don't want to take back any of those we gave to students and administrators earlier."

"I agree," Hala said. "The Kphones are addictive. They provide everything you want to know, and they adapt to how you want to learn, and how much.

Absolutely essential." She smiled. "We should both do everything possible to thank Caitlin."

Though Hala did not realize it, she held far more than a cell phone that could teach in her hands. She was one hell of an operations executive, and the Kphone's speed enabled execution skills in abundance. *But you don't need to know about quantum computers,* Alex thought. The need-to-know standard was a given during his time in the CIA, and it still applied as far as he was concerned.

Kufdani agreed. "She just thinks of it as an Emilie accoutrement."

For a while, Caitlin had been very interested in how to adapt pedagogy to individual student needs and speeds. As she had found out, it was crucial to understand the students' psychic needs and then adapt to them for the lessons at hand. She had taught those methods to Emilie and then simply moved on.

"We should start to plan how to implement this next educational push," Alex continued, "and the details regarding rollout."

"I'm dying to know. Is it top secret?" Hala asked.

"Not to you," Alex replied. "It's just complicated. The Israelis are in the middle of some of it—West Bank stuff. I'll tell you at dinner ... if you're free."

Hala shook her head. "You know I won't do a two-person dinner. But I am happy to invite senior staff for a group event."

Alex gazed at her, making sure to focus only on her face. "Ah yes. Your ... personal obligations. I lost track of that. Sorry."

She had shown no interest in pursuing another intimate encounter with him. They had been together a few years earlier—several times—in Hala's attempt to have children immediately after losing her husband in an attack on the Kufdani Industries port facility in Yemen. The attempt was successful, as Alex's mother had recently become aware. In her role as one of the keepers of the complex's nursery, she had recognized the twins as her own grandchildren. She hadn't spoken to others of their parentage, but Alex knew that little escaped Maria's notice.

"Let's spend the rest of the day thinking through the particulars: who goes where and what support is needed," Alex continued. "I'm willing to share more with you than with your staff. And you may see some of Jerome's people checking security for the next several weeks."

Hala nodded. "I shall arrange housing and board if you don't want them at the airstrip."

"I'll let you know," he said, thumbing the personal memo icon on his Kphone's screen.

"For the first round of planning," Hala said, "I suspect we will need to work through tomorrow morning at a minimum."

"I'll give a short motivational talk to your entire staff just after lunch tomorrow, and then depart for Madrid the following day. And there's our schedule."

Hala nodded. "As you say, Kufdani."

MANY HOURS LATER, HIS MIND REELING from a thousand questions and conspicuously fewer answers, Kufdani headed from the education complex to his apartment, wondering what they had stocked for him in the refrigerator. After walking in, he dropped his jacket on a chair, swung open the refrigerator door, and—finding little of immediate interest—took out two bottles of water. Then he popped the cap on one, drained it, and picked up his Kphone.

"Hey, you," Caitlin answered. "Good day? All good with Hala?"

"It was a useful day," he replied. The upcoming meeting with Hala's staff had given him lots to do, given his belief that planning enables good execution. "I think she will do well. She understands planning, and she has a lot of experience teaching Muslims with Emilie's help."

"Well, I noticed that a long time ago, when you offered her the job of head dope dealer. Did you at least ask her to dinner?"

"Yeah," he said. "Same result."

Caitlin paused. "I haven't figured that one out. She was married once, but doesn't date now. You'd think she would welcome your advances, at least for a quick go. Or if she won't entertain traditional activities, at least take advantage of your . . . alternative services, which are world-class, indeed."

"As are yours, my love."

Caitlin chuckled. "Anything else on your mind? We are a long way apart for this kind of conversation."

"Yes," Alex replied. "I need a full dive on the Bollito crime family in the northeastern US. Names, faces, friends, lovers, in-depth organization structure, plus taps on the top fifty or so phones, with curation by Emilie."

"Not that she needs a reason, but—"

"They are in my way. Inconveniently."

"I'm on it," Caitlin said. "I was getting bored anyway. I have no one to play with."

NEWARK, NEW JERSEY

HAULING WEED STINKS, ALEX THOUGHT, WAKING UP JUST AS HIS IBERIA flight from Madrid touched down in Newark. He had caught a ride to Madrid from Algeciras that morning, a day later than planned, on one of the firm's C-130s and made a mental note to have the planes cleaned better in the future—or to bring an extra change of clothes next time. The subsequent flight to Newark Liberty International Airport had been smooth and uneventful, so he took the opportunity to steal a little dozing time as the Boeing 777 chased the sunset west across the time zones.

Feeling good and refreshed after his nap, he cleared immigration and customs quickly with his Moroccan diplomatic passport and strode through the busy Newark terminal, following the signs to baggage claim. There he spotted Elena, standing against the wall near the exit, poking at her cell phone.

Wearing faded jeans and an unbuttoned man's shirt over a cotton T-shirt, she was a little taller than most of the other women in the hall. Her dark hair was pulled into a bun, and she wore no makeup. With her square shoulders, big breasts, and long legs, no one would notice that she was perhaps twenty pounds overweight—except for a brother.

Alex grabbed his heavy bag from the luggage belt when it came out. Then he walked past the line of men in black, silently standing with signs naming their passengers-to-be, to the wall where Elena stood. "Hey, little brother," she said.

"Hey, Elena. What's the other guy look like?"

She threw an arm over his shoulder and turned her face from him, letting the side of her head fall against his cheek. Close up, he could see the fresh pink scar over her lip and another along her jaw, ending beneath her ear. "Thanks for coming," she said.

"You should have let me know," he said. "We're family."

"Yeah, like you would have called me if the shoe was on the other foot."

"Michael and Kevin okay?"

Elena glanced at him. "Michael is Mick's grandson in his soul," she said, "though I'd rather it had taken him a while to figure that out. He's only thirteen."

"Yeah," Alex said. "That's a bit young for this kind of crap. But Brooks says it builds character." He hadn't thought about his friend's similar bullying incident at fourteen for a long time. "I was in high school at least."

"Jesus, Alex! I haven't thought about that in forever. You were only sixteen, weren't you?"

"Yeah," Alex said, "but I remember it like yesterday."

The teenaged Alex hadn't trusted the pretty boy his sister was dating. So he'd followed the car she was in, and then jumped off his bike and hid in the weeds when it stopped, hoping she didn't catch him spying. He had forgotten the boy's name, but he would never forget how those assholes had pulled his sister out of the car and started on her.

"His name was Junior Harris," Elena said, as if reading her brother's mind. "His daddy was a big deal in town, as you may recall. You busted one knee and nearly popped out another guy's eye. The sheriff was upset."

"And *your* daddy took care of it for both of us, as I recall," Alex said. "That's what I plan to do for your family once I figure it all out."

Elena frowned. "Michael's not ready for military school or the Marine Corps," she said. "Maybe you can get Mr. Macmillan to shoot them for you. He sure fixed things in a hurry back then. You ever see him?"

"Occasionally, but I doubt he'll be shooting anyone," Alex replied. "Back then, I was out of jail and boom! A boot in the Marine Corps in no time. This could prove a little trickier."

The local roads across northern New Jersey were bumpy and pocked, with heavy traffic dodging the worst hazards and missing other bumpers by a few inches. Only tourists took the main highways. Along Elena's route, the landscape was a sea of low-rise shops, gas stations, and warehouses, punctuated by fleets of shingled houses with sagging front porches, many well past needing a paint job.

"And Kevin?" Alex asked, picking up the earlier thread.

"I'm still in love with him," Elena said. "He brought a fresh perspective, and I love him for that. We've had a good life so far, and I don't want anything to happen to him. But he can't do anything more in this situation, except get himself hurt." She glanced at her brother. "I don't know what you can do about this Cabrillo, but if you can help me find a way to kill him, I'll do it. You know about that stuff—don't try to deny it. I've heard the rumors. It runs in the family."

"I'm looking into it. Hell, Elena, if it were a matter of just killing Cabrillo, I'd do it myself. Or leave it to you." Alex grinned. "But it seems he's a mafia boss, so killing him might bring a whole raft of goons down on us."

"That Bollito gang—I know who runs things around here, I think, but the gang's roots go back to New York somewhere."

"I'll take it from here on the Bollitos," Alex said. "I know a guy." In New Jersey, you always knew a guy: He'll fix your window screen. He'll bring marijuana or get it for you wholesale. Alex would figure out the Bollitos. Emilie was a good "guy" to know.

"Don't we all," Elena said. "Just find one who knows what he is doing. And who we can afford."

She turned off the local highway and entered a suburban neighborhood of neat, two-story houses with attached garages and well-tended lawns. Most had flowers planted in rows beneath the railings of the front porch. She stopped in the driveway of a house ablaze with lights.

"You have the front guest room," she said, getting out of the car. "Mom said we aren't allowed to have you sleep on the floor."

NORTHERN NEW JERSEY

DINNER WAS SERVED FROM A TRADITIONAL MOROCCAN CLAY COOKING vessel—a bright green tagine that Alex recognized as a gift he'd given the family several years earlier. Chicken rubbed with tea leaves rested near the bottom of the conical pot, simmering in a spiced broth. The pointed tagine top trapped and vented the flavors, steaming the artichoke hearts to add a lovely spring flavor to the dish. Elena had paired the chicken with a lemony Grüner Veltliner from Austria.

It was a quiet meal. Nobody said much, and their bruises were more obvious for their silence. When Michael asked to be excused, Elena followed him upstairs, leaving Alex and Kevin to gaze at each other.

Kevin was tall—he had been a basketball player in college when he met Elena—and worked as an accountant at a local firm, where he had done well. He and Alex had found little in common the first time they met, at Elena's graduation, and not much had changed since then. The bruise from his broken nose spread across his upper face, and his lip curled up to the left, giving his face a slight sneer. The knuckles on his right hand were bruised and scabbed.

"Shall we attempt to talk, Kevin?" Alex ventured. He took a final sip of his wine and moved both glass and bottle aside.

"About?" Kevin asked.

"About the situation where we find my sister and my nephew. They are at risk, and I have much experience in dealing with personal risk."

Kevin eyed him warily. "You do have a reputation for that. And you think you can help . . . how?"

"I can fix it," Alex said, "but the solution will likely be complicated and a bit . . . messy."

"Even you, Alex—the legendary fucking brother, Cooch, the legendary fucking warrior, Kufdani, the legendary businessman and Islamic scholar—can't fix something like this," Kevin said. "Your three names won't help you. This is the fucking mafia we are dealing with. They own this part of Jersey."

"I can hardly make it worse than it is, Kevin," Alex replied. "Let me at least understand it. Give me some space to get these vermin out of your family's life."

"You can't kill Cabrillo, so there's nothing to understand," Kevin said, his voice rising. "He will beat the piss out of me while his son will beat the piss out of Michael, until we move out of here. Elena may get another slap or two as well if I'm not around to stop it, or at least try. Michael's school is a good one, mostly. I know there's family money from you, but we aren't going to use it because I don't like you or your money. Besides, this is our home."

"If it comes to it, I *will* kill Cabrillo," Alex said. "I just need a little time to think about the problem and the potential solutions. We'll only want to solve this once. I'll need two weeks, maybe."

Kevin sat back in his chair. "You know, I once considered taking a surprise swing at you, to put you in your place. Bloody *your* nose for once. What would you have done?"

"You would have missed. And missed again on the backswing." Alex paused. "Violence is what I do, Kevin. All I want from you is to stay out of the way—and keep your mouth shut about what happens."

"I never really liked you, Alex," Kevin said, "but I'll stay out of your way and try not to be judgmental. Get rid of this Cabrillo, and you're my new best friend. I'm worried Elena will try and do it first."

"Not gonna happen. Hide Elena's gun, somewhere she can't find it." Alex suspected his sister was fearless enough to go and do something stupid. "Hopefully, she'll hold off until she figures out what I have in mind."

He brought out three new devices, one for each of them—a cheap, plastic cell phone with a big screen, by the looks of it. Until this unpleasantness was in the past, he explained, they should keep it with them at all times. Despite its appearance, it was the latest model, with all the goodies—unfailingly secure and exponentially more useful than the average mobile phone.

"We call it a Kphone. Feel free to browse around the metaverse. You'll find lessons, maps, opinions, and many other things. And keep it handy. Trust me on this."

Kevin picked up the Kphones, stood from the table, and headed for the stairway. "Night," he said. "And . . . thanks."

Alex gave a curt nod. "I might have to leave for a bit, but I'll be back. Don't give my bedroom away."

NORTHERN NEW JERSEY

ALEX WOKE TO A WEAK MORNING SUN, ITS LIGHT FILTERING THROUGH either a smoggy layer or early mist. He thought about life in Tangier and Caitlin, decided the New Jersey fog was early mist, and rolled out of bed.

His sister had placed him in the small spare bedroom, as promised. The previous night, he had not even turned on the light—just peeled off his travel clothes in the darkness and hung them in the closet before wiping his shoes with a dirty sock until they shone again and then lining them up under the chair. Now, he crawled out from beneath the ironed sheets, pulled on a pair of sweatpants and a clean polo shirt, and walked barefoot to the kitchen.

Four places were set at the kitchen table. Elena stood at the stove, swirling eggs with the flat of a fork in a large omelet pan. Using the fork to pick up the edges, she tilted the pan, allowing the runny part of the eggs to flow under the congealing mass. Then she reached toward the countertop, picked up a small bowl of chopped peppers and grated cheese, sprinkled it with cumin salt, and dumped it into the center of the skillet. With practiced motion, she traded the fork for a small spatula, folded the egg in half, and, with a quick flip of her wrist, turned it over in the skillet.

In a moment, the toaster popped up four slices of toast with an audible *ping*.

"Breakfast is served," Elena said, sliding the omelet from the pan onto a large plate in the center of the table, then plucking the four slices of toast to another plate beside the butter dish. She sat down, sliced the eggs into four pieces, and took a piece of toast. "Dig in, guys."

Kevin, dressed for work in a white shirt and a repp tie, was quiet while he ate, reading the morning *New York Times*. Elena and Michael discussed math as Alex observed, feeling his blood pressure rise as he studied Michael's face—an interesting mess of yellows and greens. The teenager had a lump on his right cheekbone and a nasty, scabbed-over scrape at his hairline. His right eye was swollen nearly shut, and broken blood vessels made a bright red perimeter on the eye that peeked through the still swollen lid.

The previous evening, Kevin had asked Alex to speak with Michael. His expression had betrayed the reluctance of a concerned father, but Elena wanted it. "Do you mind?" Kevin had asked.

"I would very much like that," Alex had replied. "My own nephew, and I've never gotten to know him."

"I didn't *want* you to get to know him, Alex," Kevin had replied. "You're a killer, maybe even a monster. And a fucking Arab sheik, somehow."

Alex was two of those things, at least. But times change, and young Michael would have to be brought up to speed. "So, Michael," he said, picking a last bit of egg from his plate. "I'd like to spend some time getting to know you better. What works for you?"

Michael looked up at his uncle with one eye, taking in the large scar on Alex's forearm. "I'm not going to school today," he said, looking down again. "I'll miss a big math test, probably end up getting a shitty grade. So, I can sit and talk whenever you want, for as long as you want. Maybe on the front porch?"

"Sure," Alex said. "Bring your new Kphone, and we'll get you started on that. We can talk about whatever you want."

The swing on the porch creaked with Alex's weight, and the squeaking of the chains against the thick eyehooks above was pleasantly rhythmic. Michael sat on a cushioned wicker chair, facing him. The boy didn't speak or make eye contact. The tip of his new Kphone stuck out from his pocket.

"Do you mind if we speak Arabic?" Alex asked. "Lately, I think better in Arabic." He waited, recalling that his mother had praised Michael's language skills—the boy spoke Arabic well, which made Maria happy. She liked his Spanish, too.

Finally, Michael replied in academic Arabic, "Look, Uncle Alex, I don't even know you. My mom thinks you're wonderful, Grandma too. But my dad says it's best if I stay away from you."

"And what do *you* think?" Alex said.

"I don't know what to think," Michael answered. "Tell me how to figure that out."

Alex was silent for a few moments, listening to the sounds of the waking neighborhood. "I don't think you have enough data yet to decide. And any feelings you have for or against me don't matter right now. What matters is the situation at your school, and how we can fix it. It hasn't gone well so far, and that has nothing to do with you. You're just a convenient punching bag."

"No shit!" Michael exclaimed. "Look at my eye. Can you fix that?"

"You're a mess for sure. If it helps, you should know I've had a black eye more than a few times. In a couple of weeks, they fix themselves. I'm here to fix the situation that caused this damage," Alex said. "That's what I do best."

He could always take his shirt off and discuss all the healed scars, tell him about all the bullets and knives that had pierced his body, but he thought better of that. His sister didn't want that kind of life for her son.

These Cabrillos and Bollitos are pissing me off, he thought.

"What about school?" Michael said. "Cabrillo is going to pound on me every day for the rest of time. How can I get into college if I can't attend class? I'll never catch up."

"Not for the rest of time. I don't know how I'll fix it yet, but give me just a week or two. Now pass me your Kphone, and I'll show you how to be ahead when you get back to school, not behind."

"Fat chance," Michael spat. But he pulled the Kphone from his pocket and moved over to the swing.

Alex held the Kphone in front of his face. *Kid, if you give this a chance,*

Emilie will make you a star. "New student," he said aloud in English. "High school math. Go." He handed the phone to his nephew and stood up from the swing.

A middle-aged woman's soft, cultured voice said, "Well, hello. What is your name?"

Michael stared wide-eyed at the Kphone.

"It's just a phone, but it's one hell of a phone. Have fun," Alex advised. "And keep putting an ice bag on your eye. It helps, even after a week. Trust me."

LATER THAT MORNING, ALEX WAS ON HIS KPHONE, mostly dictating notes while sipping coffee on Elena's porch. He had received an early dump of data on the Bollito family and their support group, expertly curated by Emilie.

It turned out there were a whole bunch of Bollitos and their ilk spread across New York and New Jersey. From the newspaper articles and court summaries, this was a nasty bunch. Getting the phone intercepts working would be an important step. If Alex could hear what they were talking about, he'd figure out the rest. The organized crime folks probably knew the Bollitos well, and he had asked Brooks to gather pollen from a couple of the more useful agencies.

Alex took a sip of coffee and pushed his feet gently against the floorboards, giving the porch swing a little push. The chains still squealed under his weight. He watched Elena's neighbors pull late-model vehicles from their driveways and head off to work in the city, and wondered how many of those commuters had been beaten even once.

When his Kphone rang, it was Brooks Elliot. Alex had asked whether he knew anyone at the Drug Enforcement Agency to ask about the Bollito gang. Brooks thought he had a good contact.

"Found a guy I knew in the Navy," Brooks said. "Chaucer, pretty high up the DEA ladder. He knows the Bollitos well—intimately, maybe."

"And?" Alex said.

"And I shared the details of your family problem," Brooks said. "He says you should run away and run away fast. To hear it from him, the Bollitos are a scary, ruthless bunch. He says they do Hoffas on people."

"Hoffas?"

"Yeah, when they disappear you like Jimmy Hoffa, end up as one of the pillars in a fine sporting stadium built by union workers. I'll bet that scares the shit out of you."

"No worse than Thai druggies, cocaine gangs, ISIS assassins, Yemeni nutcases, and saw-scaled snakes?"

Brooks laughed. "We didn't get into your somewhat colorful history, but he knows you were once a serious badass with the CIA and unlikely to blow any smoke back on the DEA. No back smoke is important."

"My colorful history makes me feel more secure about my future and less so about the Bollitos'. Now, how do we get from here to there?"

"I told him you were just there to snap some photographs for now."

"Yeah, I'm a real Ansel Adams. So, did you find out anything useful?"

"I think so," Brooks replied. "Supposed to be a big meeting going down next week, Tuesday maybe. Outside Hackettstown in New Jersey, near the Pennsylvania state line. The meeting is on, but the details are not yet in. Although there's some talk about biker gangs, for crying out loud."

"Any idea exactly where?" Vivid images of men scurrying under gunfire, getting cut down like sheaves of ripe wheat, spilling fans of blood above their heads as they fell, came eagerly to Alex's mind. He smiled.

"He did get excited about the prospect of photographs, so I stroked him a little, but he still didn't want to give up the location," Brooks said. "He's worried about security for his own guys if he sends them in to take photos."

"And you told him how Jerome and I used to go unnoticed worldwide, taking snapshots for the president?"

Brooks chuckled. "Yeah, you two would vanish for weeks! I referred him to Mac, who told him about your CIA history. This guy was Naval Intelligence, so he already knew all about Mac."

"Did you get the location or not, Brooks?"

"I told him to keep his people out of the area, and you would snap some pics at the meeting." A sixteen-digit grid coordinate appeared on Alex's Kphone.

"I promise," Alex said. "Thanks, bro. Tell him to keep his people at least a quarter mile away. Jerome taught me to be twitchy."

AFTER HANGING UP WITH BROOKS, Alex went back to researching on his Kphone, leaving no stone unturned in his quest to determine the structure of the Bollito organization and any families in that hierarchy: the leadership, their addresses and life habits, and any connections, particularly in northern New Jersey. Upon notice of more information from the unemotional Emilie, he sat back to read through it all. After a moment, a piece popped up on cross reference, about someone named Edgeworth.

Edgeworth.

It was a familiar name.

Smiling, Alex read through the article and asked Emilie for more details.

Reading on, he discovered transcripts of phone conversations among the gang members that contained references to the upcoming meeting. A few purloined emails confirmed the date: Wednesday, not Tuesday. He sent a message to Brooks, along with a mild ribbing about the date change. Although Brooks got the day wrong, he would get a few points for alerting Washington to the meeting change—even if everything else went bad.

UPPER EAST SIDE, MANHATTAN

EARLY MONDAY EVENING, WHILE WALKING FROM HIS APARTMENT ON the Upper West Side, Alex dodged a few little old ladies who, without making eye contact, had dropped their shoulders for glancing impact. He didn't blame them: he was in the way of their progress.

As he neared Columbus Circle, he paused for a moment in the shadow of the skyscraper housing media conglomerate Edgeworth Studios. A tiny, fuzzy dog with a top hat affixed to its head by an elastic band defecated loosely on the sidewalk, only to be pulled along by yet another woman who also refused to make eye contact—or pick up after her dog.

Along the southern edge of Central Park, a tired horse stood on three legs at the curb while its driver napped on the buggy seat, waiting for the next group of vacationing tourists. Alex turned uptown at Fifth Avenue and made his way along the east side of the park to a brownstone on East 73rd Street, where he opened a steel gate and walked up three steps to a heavy wooden door.

Reginald Ketcher Edgeworth was a legend on Wall Street and in Hollywood who owned or controlled an abundance of media outlets: a TV network, several radio stations, and an international information empire of magazine and book publishing. Everything was interconnected, and it had made him fabulously wealthy and powerful. It was said that Edgeworth had two fingers and a thumb on the scale of the nation's thoughts and the world's attention.

But Alex's path crossed with Edgeworth's at a much closer degree of separation: he and Brooks Elliot had been prep-school roommates.

According to Brooks, Alex would be well advised to never sleep in the same room with Edgie. He was a legendary farter who tended to ruffle the covers immediately after a release, to let the hot air out. Alex thought such an arrangement unlikely, but took note all the same.

The door opened just as Alex reached for the doorbell. Alex was hardly surprised; quite a few security cameras were visible. A thick, fit-looking man in a gray suit said, "Mr. Cuchulain?" At Alex's nod, the man said, "Mr. Edgeworth is in his den awaiting you. I'll take you there."

The butler-slash-bodyguard had taken the time to look up the pronunciation of Cuchulain. It was *Coo-HULL-an*, but most people missed by a mile. The many histories written over the centuries disagreed about every possible detail surrounding the legendary Irish warrior, and perhaps the bodyguard had found an account that misspelled the name. Still, the butler had tried and come close. That was a good thing. And he'd said "awaiting" rather than "waiting for." To Alex, that counted for something too.

The heavy door closed with a solid *click*. The house was four stories with a small, enclosed yard—exceedingly rare in Manhattan—visible from the rear windows. It was all dark wood, mirrors, and leather, and it smelled of furniture polish and money.

Following the butler from the foyer into the large den, Alex took in the fireplace, the wet bar, several TV screens, and shelf after shelf of books, new and old. Seated in the center of the room was a man wearing pressed gray slacks, a maroon button-up cardigan sweater, an immaculate blue button-down shirt, and a repp tie pulled tight to the neck. Oxblood loafers, highly shined, filled out the preppie picture.

Edgeworth stood up from his upholstered chair and stuck out his hand. "Reginald Edgeworth. I understand you are good friends with Brooks Elliot. That makes you a friend of mine, until you prove otherwise.

"What would you like to drink, Mr. Cuchulain? And a cigar, perhaps?

I'm having a vintage port, but anything you favor is probably available, if not necessarily in the vintage you prefer." Edgeworth pointed to an upholstered chair across from his own.

Between the two men was a small table with a cigar ashtray, a cutter, and a gold Dunhill lighter in the center. An open crystal decanter partially filled with red wine sat on the wet bar alongside a closed, polished cigar box.

Alex sat, leaned back in his chair, and ran a hand through his hair. "A port would be delightful."

A nod from Edgeworth to the big man in the gray suit produced a Riedel port glass and a large pour. The butler returned the stopped decanter to the wet bar before walking out and closing the door behind him.

"I'm not quite sure why you are here, Mr. Cuchulain," Edgeworth said. "But Elliot asked that I meet with you, so here I am. Elliot was evasive about you and your relationship history, other than to say you are his dearest friend. That fact alone was enough for me to accept this meeting."

"Mr. Edgeworth—"

"You may call me Edgie. What can I do for you? I have as much time as you need. But first tell me: How did the two of you meet?"

"Call me Alex. We were both in the Navy when we first met, on a beach near a seaside resort in Lebanon," Alex explained. "Brooks was the SEAL escape shooter in a raid on an apartment complex where some bad dudes were hiding. And I was a guy who knew a bunch about how to blow things up, including apartment buildings."

"Aha!" cried Edgeworth, evidently amused.

"Later, we got to know each other well while at Oxford."

"So you were also a Rhodes Scholar? How unusual."

Alex smiled and took a sip of his port, rolling it in his mouth. "Good port. I'm a vintage port fan, but no Rhodes Scholar." He explained that he was at Oxford studying Islamic history and philosophy in the College of Oriental Studies. "I'm half Bedouin, half Irish American. I hold both Moroccan and American passports."

"Now that's interesting," Edgeworth responded. "I don't think I know anyone with that background."

"To cut to the chase, Mr. Edgeworth," Alex said, "I would like to hire you to do a job that requires your particular expertise."

"Wonderful," Edgeworth said. "I'll do anything I can. What have you in mind?"

Alex decided to start with the short version. "I plan to get the Israeli government to turn over the West Bank land and its settlements to their rightful Bedouin owners."

To his credit, Edgeworth just chuckled and shook his head. "You'd have to overturn the Israeli government to do that. To be blunt: no fucking way."

Alex smiled distantly, and his face darkened. He raised his port glass in salute and took another sip. "It's early days in terms of planning," he said, "and I suspect success may be a tad difficult to come by. That's why I need you—it's about public relations, and you are good at that."

"No one is *that* good," Edgeworth murmured.

"To start, I need to force the Israeli government's hand by convincing the majority liberal Jewish society that the Orthodox community, particularly the Haredim, is out of control—more trouble to the rest of them than is worth fighting over. Later, if we get lucky, we can convince them that Israeli national security would be better served by giving up the West Bank to their Bedouin citizens."

"How do you plan to do that?" Edgeworth said, his brow furrowing as a sardonic smile appeared on his face. "The Orthodox run roughshod over the Israeli prime minister. They vote in large numbers, and they breed like minks."

"Well, I'd like *you* to do it," Alex replied. "I'll provide information fodder for a PR campaign. You'll design the campaign, determine what should happen before something else happens, and plan what to do if things go wrong. It must be done right. I'm prepared to spend a billion dollars with you on the effort—success or failure."

Edgeworth shook his head.

"I'm aware that many pieces must be discussed before such an effort can succeed," Alex continued, "so I'd like to get started."

"Alex, it's just unreasonable. The odds of success are tiny, and the odds of pissing off the whole American and European Jewish community are astronomical. Do you even *have* a billion dollars?"

"I do, and more. Are we negotiating price?"

"God, no!" Edgeworth exclaimed. "What you're asking is not even possible."

"It may not be a sure thing," Alex said, "but I'd like you to try." He flashed his most sincere grin. *And I'm fairly confident that you will, given proper incentive.*

"I can't do it. The only sure thing is that I would destroy my reputation and lose a ton of money, both short- and long-term. It's too much to ask, even for Elliot. Hell, why not ask him to help you?"

"I already did. He came back with your name and a glowing recommendation. Brooks is in. His job will be trying to convince the president to stay out of the fray."

"I'm sorry, Mr. Cuchulain. It's too hard, and too dangerous politically. The answer is an emphatic *no*." Edgeworth held his hand out for a farewell shake. "Is there anything else?"

Of course there's something else, Alex thought, replaying in his head the details that Emilie had shared with him. *I came in with a handle to change your no to a yes, so I think I'll stay right here for a bit.*

"Well, I'm not quite finished with my port," he replied. "It's damned good. I'm thinking a 1977 Fonseca?"

Edgeworth leaned forward and raised one finger. "I—"

Alex held up an open hand and waved him silent. "Mr. Edgeworth, there's a reason I have survived as long as I have: it's a personal credo that drives my mind, whether in making violence or making dinner. I call it 'P to the seventh power': proper prior planning prevents piss-poor performance."

"I'm aware of the reference to the six P's of preparation, and your alliteration is cute," Edgeworth said, leaning back in his chair again. "But you've lost me."

"I care passionately about this issue," Alex insisted. "It transcends personal finances. I need it in my soul."

"Yes, but where do I fit in?"

You're going to provide the PR, somehow. Alex sipped his port. "In your case, I needed to find something you care for as passionately as I feel about recovering Bedouin land in the West Bank—something that brings your passion out, beyond tomorrow's win or the next infusion of cash into your well-stocked hoard. Some need that you would hate to take to your grave unfulfilled. I searched hard, Mr. Edgeworth. And I think I found it."

Edgeworth's face tightened. "There's nothing you or anybody can do about that. I've spent millions trying."

"Why don't you tell me about it?" Alex said. "It will give me a chance to finish this excellent port."

IT WAS A NASTY STORY, and Alex already knew most of it. By the end, Edgeworth's hands were shaking and tears were running freely down his cheeks. But once he started, he seemed eager to tell it, if only for the opportunity to feel the name of his son roll off his tongue again.

Edgeworth's son, Ketcher, had it all: smart, ambitious, caring, really thought about the people around him. He was president of his class at Williams and made Phi Beta Kappa. Not a great athlete, but enthusiastic about every sport he attempted. And he had a gift for business.

After graduation, he married a beautiful woman, Nellie, a Barnard girl. She was vivacious, fun, and interesting, and Edgeworth loved her too. She was the kind of girl who wanted to experience everything. And one night, while out with some friends, she ended up at a shady bar in Brooklyn, where she caught the eye of a young man in another group. She was a great dancer, and so was he. They spent several carefree minutes on the dance floor, showing off, all innocent fun—or so Nellie thought.

When the evening wrapped up, Nellie prepared to leave with her friends. The young man wanted her to stay, and when she refused, he grabbed her arm. She slapped him. He slapped her back, hard, and punched her in the stomach. Then he put her over his shoulder and started for the door. Nellie's friends tried to stop him, but his companions slapped them out of the way, giving one of the girls a black eye and warning them to keep their fucking mouths shut if they knew what was good for them.

The police were called, but the bar's management made it sound like a lovers' quarrel gone bad. They bought the cops a few drinks, and that was that.

The following morning, Nellie showed up at the emergency room: clothes torn, raped. More cops, rape kit, a big fuss. Then nothing. No witnesses at the bar, other than the women she was with, and they were terrified.

Ketcher, of course, refused to give up on getting the whole story and tracking down the guy who raped his wife. Naturally, his father was eager to help. They threw some money at the problem, as usual, and found out the guy's name. When they went back to the police, the guy was arrested and matched to a DNA sample from the rape kit. He made bail that afternoon.

That night, as Ketcher was coming out of his building in Queens, a couple of goons forced him into a car. The doorman called the cops with the license plate, but the car had been stolen. Ketcher was found the next morning down by the docks, beaten to death. His tongue was cut out, and he was castrated.

Edgeworth found out, too late, that the mob owned the bar and was running drugs out of it. So it came as no surprise when the rape kit was somehow lost, and no witnesses were willing to come forward. The charges were dropped. Nellie committed suicide a few weeks later. The guy never went to trial.

The grieving father made as much trouble as he could for them, complaining publicly about the illicit drug business. He asked his old pal Elliot to help, but Brooks could only encourage his DEA contacts to go after the mobsters generally, making trouble for their business. It barely slowed them down. They even tried to grab Elliot, but ended up with the feds all over them. Then they went after Edgeworth.

"And I've done nothing about it but hire more bodyguards and install more security," Edgeworth concluded, wiping his face with the back of his hand.

"So you know who's responsible for the crimes and all their aftermath," Alex said, "and your hands are tied. You can do nothing about it. And now you are also at personal risk."

Edgeworth nodded. "Look, Alex, I've known Elliot since prep school. We roomed together. I like him. He's tried to make life difficult for these monsters. But we haven't been able to touch them. They're expanding, not contracting. If I can't land a solid blow, with all the resources at my disposal, it seems unlikely that you'll be able to accomplish anything—except maybe get yourself killed."

"What would you consider a 'solid blow'?" Alex said. "Something you would go out of your way for."

Edgeworth walked to the bar, poured his port glass half full, and took a gulp. "Kill those motherfuckers. Kill them all. The rapist, his friends, the whole bunch of them. Put them out of business. Take their fucking power away."

"And what would you give for that?" Alex said.

"Anything I have. Everything I have." He waved the bottle at Alex. "I can make more money."

"You want them so bad, you can taste it." Alex had been aware all along that money would not motivate Edgeworth. He had already offered the man a great deal of cash for this particular job and been turned down. "I think we've found your passion, Mr. Edgeworth."

"Yeah? That doesn't change the fact that I'd be crazy to take on your little PR project."

"Why not? I have a problem . . . You have a problem . . ."

"Well, who will you shoot to change my mind?" Edgeworth asked in a choked voice. "Some of them? All of them? Who?"

Alex sipped his port. "I may not shoot anyone at all. But I will punish those who did this vile thing to you, to your family, and I will provide you with proof. And if I fix *your* problem, I want your commitment to fix mine. Or at least try."

Edgeworth eyed him. "What if I agree and then decide to screw you? What would you do then, shoot me?"

"That would mean that I misjudged you, as did Brooks. You would, therefore, be in my way." Alex grinned. "Anyway, screwing me wouldn't be that easy. Others have tried."

"Who the fuck are you?" Edgeworth shouted. "Your arrogance is astounding."

"But you're curious now, and you'll check me out further." Alex stood. "We've said everything that's worth saying, for the time being. But you should know: I'll try to figure out how to improve things for you." He nodded and moved toward the door. "Thanks for your time. And for the port."

The butler opened the door and waved him through.

"You should leave your coat unbuttoned and go with a waist holster, no cross draw," Alex said quietly to the butler as he strode out the door, deciding to call Jimmy and have him pay a visit to the Edgeworth residence.

The butler seems like a good guy, but he could use a little help discouraging intruders.

Brooks's resident thug and one-handed sailing master of his sailboat, *Old Fashioned*, Jimmy was a former SEAL, like Brooks, who was more dangerous with his prosthetic hook than most men were with both fists. Even before Brooks showed up, they were Cooch and Jimmy—drinking buds, or at least killing mates. Jimmy would know how to beef up Edgeworth's security system.

The big man just stared at him.

"The shoulder holster imprints the butt of the pistol on your suit. Plus, unbuttoning your jacket to get to it will take too long. I may send someone around soon to discuss this sort of thing with you," Alex explained, jerking his head toward the den. "I'll need him around for the foreseeable future."

WEST OF HACKETTSTOWN, NEW JERSEY

ALEX SAT IN A CLEARING AT THE END OF A DEER TRAIL, IN A LITTLE wooded valley near Hackettstown, chewing on a dried apricot and reading (yet again) *The Art of War*, by Niccolò Machiavelli. He appeared to be the perfect hiker: Attired in good, conservative leather boots over a Mossy Oak jumpsuit, he carried a large, heavy backpack with a map in the side pocket. Inside his pack were water and snacks, of course—but also a Heckler & Koch MP5 9mm submachine gun and a Sig Sauer 9mm pistol, both silenced, as well as several indistinct packages he kept stored in his apartment and others he picked up from Jerome's successor in the exotic firearms business.

When dealing with the ruling Medici family of fifteenth-century fame, Machiavelli was sycophantic to a fault, yet he also possessed a fine, under-appreciated military mind. Alex admired writers who could redefine the way wars were fought, and Machiavelli had done that despite having never served. He had changed the nature of force engagement by conceiving, arming, training, and mobilizing a citizen militia that could counter a mercenary force. Until then, the richest aggressors could rape and plunder any citizenry that failed to hire a corresponding mercenary force to get in their way. Ultimately, while mercenaries fought for money, the militia fought for a far more profound cause: home. He wanted the Palestinians to feel that emotion.

THE PREVIOUS MORNING, AT HIS APARTMENT on the Upper West Side, Alex had gotten reacquainted with Google Maps and its various cousins. He wanted to know more about the meeting site than its owners did. From sixty miles away, he'd learned that the site contained a large one-story building, a rambler style from the 1950s, on a cleared spot of about one-half acre. A broken-down shed and garage sat at the back, near a well-tended gravel road that led down about a quarter mile to the highway. Beyond the cleared space, the land was heavily wooded, with an upslope on the south side. A US Geological Survey map showed Alex the contours of the lot, including a gully to the east and a small stream running away from the house.

A few hours later, he'd gotten in his rental car, done a little shopping at some local gear shops—making sure to spread it around—and driven west to the spot near Hackettstown. As he'd surmised from the digital maps, the little valley sloped south to north, covering perhaps an acre. He slowly boxed in the site, walking edge to edge while narrowing his path to close the box with each iteration, scrutinizing the ground and dodging the ubiquitous poison ivy. Each round of inspection brought him closer to the house, until finally he ended up at the edge of the cleared area.

After shouldering his pack and entering the empty house, where he spent thirty minutes, Alex had come back out, sat beside a bush, and thought about the site, then again picked up his pack. Then he'd walked a hundred yards or so to a little depression in the dirt, turning to study it. He chose a flat spot with a view of the house and walked toward it, then did the same again—repeat, repeat, repeat. With a final nod, he began the jog back to his rented Subaru, down the deer trail and away from the entrance road, his pack much lighter.

At Elena's house, he had walked up to the porch and knocked. Elena had come to the door, looked him up and down, and said, "Love your outfit. Hiking date?"

"Hardly. I'm working," he'd replied. "Grab some coffee, and let's sit on the porch for a moment."

Elena had shrugged. "Kevin and Michael are out. Do we need them?"

"Later, maybe," Alex had said. "Your call."

Sitting across from Alex on the swing with her coffee cup in hand, Elena had raised an eyebrow. The scars on her face were healing nicely.

"They're going to have a big meeting, maybe seventy-five of them," he'd said. "Cabrillos, Bollitos, all of them. And I know where and when it's going down."

"How does that help you? Help us?" Elena had asked.

"I'm going to kill them all."

Elena had stared at him. "Yes! I should have guessed. What can I do?"

"You can make sure Kevin understands that to get one of them, we had to get *all* of them. Every last one."

His sister had nodded.

"Tomorrow afternoon and evening, be all together somewhere—someplace where people will see you. Have an ice cream soda in a crowded shop with visible security cameras, something like that. This isn't the movies. No cops. No crying. Life goes on."

"I can work with that," Elena had said. "What else?"

"Explain to Michael about being a Cuchulain. Remember when Dad said, 'If they're on the battlefield, you kill them all. There'll be no time to sort them out. If civilians get hurt, it's because they were on the battlefield.'"

"He's so young, Alex," Elena had said. "I'm not sure I can get him to think that way . . ."

"Remind him of the black eye, the loose teeth. What they did to his mother. Have him think about having to live like that for years. Or not to make it that far."

"I'll deal with Kevin," Elena had said. "If Michael can't handle it, I may send him to you."

Alex had laughed. "I'm going to be quite busy for the next several months. If you send him to me, I'll have Caitlin take care of him in Tangier until I'm available. If nothing else, you will get a well-trained graduate student in math and physics at age fifteen, a star student. He'll swim well. She'll be curious more about how he learns best than about being a caring provider. She won't be a touchy-feely kind of stepmom."

His sister looked skeptical. "That isn't going to work for me—or Michael. Let's just see how it plays out."

"Just stay strong, and it will sort itself out." Alex had stood up to go. "I love you, Elena."

"I love you, Alex. I trust you," Elena had said. "And if you need me to kill someone, I'm in. Bring a knife for me. I'm ready to slice Cabrillo's guts out."

Alex had laughed again. *If he wasn't wearing light body armor . . .* "The first thing you learn in this business is: don't bring a knife to a gunfight."

NOW, DRESSED IN HIS MOSSY OAK CAMO JUMPSUIT, he put down the book. Underneath a dark camo watch cap pulled over his head, his face was smeared with camouflage grease paint. Branches with leaves cut from the nearby bushes stuck up from the cap to break up his silhouette. He had been in place for many hours, dug into a depression in the ground and covered with a brown-and-green mottled ground sheet, reminding himself to bring a bigger piss bottle next time.

The Bollitos would never see him coming. They thought they owned this battle space by virtue of force and ruthlessness, but they hadn't thought it through. They merely had a minor, solvable advantage. The Israelis, Alex mused, thought the same thing: that superior technology would allow them to dictate to the under-armed, poorly led Arabs. But they, too, hadn't thought things through. Time and numbers were not on their side. Inevitably, both the Bollitos and the Israelis got greedy.

A little power, lots of greed. That was the way it worked—and sometimes it was the way to failure too. *How well had the Israelis trained their troops to operate without air cover and communications?* Alex wondered. *And how would they counter an attack from a trained citizen militia fighting for their home?*

He had hidden in a hole like this a hundred times, all around the world, waiting to kill someone or maybe just take their photograph—or both. Not for the first time, he thanked his lucky stars that he hadn't ended up a doctor or even a parachute rigger.

This is good fun.

In addition to the 9mm submachine gun and the Sig Sauer 9mm pistol loaded with Winchester hollow points, Alex was newly armed with a Swarovski-scoped, Smith & Wesson 6.5mm Creedmoor semiautomatic rifle with a foldable stock and five thirty-round magazines of 143 grain Hornady ELD-X ammunition. The Hornady rounds would fly at 3,200 feet per second, shooting flat; the enormous speed impact and expanding bullet were designed to drop a running deer.

He had dug in a Nikon 3500 DSLR camera padded with a low light, wide-angle lens that would allow a deep focus on blood and guts. A three-button garage door opener was at the front of his position, looped into a branch in the dirt. If he got caught somehow, they would lose many of their own before they ever got to him.

The first of the vehicles finally arrived in the afternoon: a Chevy Suburban loaded with supplies, followed by another. Alex spent several hours taking pictures of the arrivals, whether by truck, limousine, or Harley Davidson, and waiting for the meeting to begin. Hard, big-shouldered men, more and more of them as time ticked on, walked the perimeter of the clearing with automatic rifles and short-barreled shotguns. The US government would be vitally interested in who attended; the attendees, of course, didn't want them to know.

According to calls Emilie had intercepted, the East Coast mafia had made a deal with the country's largest of the Hell's Angels gangs; the Angels would then make deals with the smaller gangs and the various supremacy groups. The mafia would wholesale the drugs to these gangs, which would distribute them to trickle-down dealers across the country. All in all, it was an efficient mechanism for distributing a commodity desired by the drug-using populace and for reaping vast profits—and achieving a coup for the organizations that planned and executed it. Emilie had woven the phone talk and the emails effortlessly to illustrate the plan's details for Alex, including the names of the attendees.

Game on.

To his west, Alex spotted a big, bearded man in camo settling in to observe, no doubt anxious to strongly discourage any feds who might arrive with cameras. Alex watched through his Swarovski rifle scope as the man moved around like a tired dog choosing a spot for a nap. The camo man had a black rifle—a .308, likely—with a scope, that he bedded in for a good shot down the access road.

Twenty minutes after the last limousine had pulled up and the Harleys quit ticking, eight men in dark suits came out of the building and fanned out, some lighting cigarettes. A wait was in order. The meeting had begun.

Alex checked the sentries. Three of them were near the clearing's edge at the front of the property and could be a problem. Swinging his gaze back to the west, he saw the distant man in camo stand and hold binoculars to his eyes, still looking toward the entrance road—a one-trick dog.

Oh, well, Alex thought. *First things first.*

He pulled the rifle tight to his shoulder, settled the crosshairs of his scope on the chest of the man in camo, exhaled half a breath, and squeezed the trigger. The unsilenced rifle broke the stillness of the woods.

The recoil sent the muzzle of the rifle up and a few inches to the left before the crosshairs settled back to the original target. Alex dropped his aim and shot the man again as he fell.

Earlier, he had released the shutter delay on the Nikon, which would record until it ran out of storage or battery: one photo every three seconds, stored in a flash drive that would hold 7,500 18-megapixel photographs. He pushed one of the buttons on the garage door opener and leaned back into his 6.5mm Creedmoor scope.

Snugging the rifle butt into his right shoulder, he dropped the crosshairs to the chest of the first sentry, shooting the man even as he tried to locate the shooter. The scope rode up and back once more to lock onto the falling man. Alex shot him again.

The second sentry turned and prepared to run. Alex shot him in the head, twice.

Five seconds later, the walls of the house blew out raggedly, tops first, then fell slowly in a burst of smoke and a solid sheet of flame. The roof went straight up, propelled by flames and turning slowly as it rose, then began to drop. It made three turns before impact—a collision that set more fires.

This was a first for Alex. He had gotten two turns with an apartment building on the Lebanon coast with Brooks, and one and a half on a drug lord's wooden house in Thailand with Jerome. But three?

These new C7 plastic explosives are really cool, he thought.

One of the outer sentries was struggling and trying to get up. Another stood, dazed. Alex shot them both—first center chest and then in the head as they fell. Then he scanned the scene for more trouble.

A few painful screams came from the building, where a number of men were bolting through the doors and windows, aflame. Alex pressed a second button on the remote and heard six large explosions in succession, from concealed anti-personnel weapons known as Coochmores—the mines repeatedly improved by Alex and the CIA, based on the original Claymore of Vietnam fame. Each pointed a volley of 250 ball bearings toward the house along a precise, planned vector, much like a full-choke shotgun.

The six mines covered the entire perimeter of the house and anyone wandering out. The bearings were large and heavy, sometimes ripping holes in planks before speeding, deformed but still lethal, on their way. Mostly they hit running, burning people.

He watched the scene for a few seconds more before turning the Nikon off. Then he picked up the Sig Sauer pistol, spun off the silencer and put it in his pocket, and took a breath, ready to clean up anything that could be a problem. A gaggle of fat Harley motorcycles could provide refuge for an armed, frightened wayward soul, at least for a moment.

Four shots later, he returned to his hideout amid the brush to clean up. In less than seventy-five minutes, he would be back in his New York apartment, showered, his face wiped clean, and wearing shorts and a T-shirt, with his feet on an ottoman. He would sip a glass of 2003 Dancing Hares red wine—an unreleased vintage, received as a gift from its charming vintners, that he saved for special occasions—without a care in the world. The feds would figure the rest out.

Alex keyed his Kphone to make an appointment with Edgeworth, thinking, *I'll call him Edgie now that we're partners.* Then he folded the 6.5mm Creedmoor stock and slid the rifle into his pack along with everything else. He shrugged into the pack and began the jog back to his car. In the sudden silence, the crackle of the burning farmhouse seemed even louder.

He couldn't even hear sirens yet.

WASHINGTON, DC

BROOKS ELLIOT SAT IN THE EISENHOWER EXECUTIVE OFFICE BUILDING at the White House compound, chuckling and shaking his head at the photo collection Alex had sent. *He wanted pics, he got pics,* the email joked. *These should give him a little time to get the story right. Signed, a Kingdom of Morocco diplomat.*

A knock came at his office door. "Can you believe this shit from Cooch?" Mac said, grinning. "Fucking fantastic!"

"Yeah, eighty-three dead, none wounded," Brooks said, glancing up from his computer screen. He had watched the horrified anchors report it on the mainstream news that morning, but the batch of 250 live-action photographs that Alex had sent them told the whole story. "This will set the pinkos on fire. My DEA boy owes us a big one. It's like a post-op photo briefing of a well-rehearsed SEAL mission. Fabulous."

The phone on his desk lit up.

Brooks glanced at it and said, "I do believe that is the DEA's finest on the line right now."

"Put it on speaker," Mac said, sliding into a chair.

"Chaucer, my main man," Brooks answered. "How is the crime-fighting business? Eliminate any druggies lately?"

"Jesus Christ, Elliot, that was a fucking massacre!" the DEA man exclaimed. "What the fuck? Did you hang me out to dry or what? There must be fifty dead guys out there. Why would you do that?"

"The count is eighty-three dead, I think you'll find, and none wounded. As you may recall, in the SEAL business, that's a successful surgical strike. You got pics. You didn't lose any people. As a bonus, thanks to my talented friend, you even got a list of the newly departed. I'll let you match the names with the bodies. I'm sending the whole bit to you in living color—now." Brooks triggered a transfer of the photos.

"Oh, Christ! What am I supposed to do with them?" Chaucer asked after a pause to glance at the photo file. "Attach them to my resignation or my indictment?"

"Oh, please, Chaucer. Be creative! You sound like a fucking Yalie, seeking guilt for salvation."

Brooks told the DEA man to show the images of the camo guy with the black rifle to the agents Chaucer was going to send in. *How hard could it be?* he thought. That camo guy could have killed six feds at that range before they even raised their cameras. Then Chaucer could tell his director about what would've happened if the guy had started shooting federal snoopers with cameras at 146 yards.

"Consider this a career-enhancing opportunity," Brooks continued. "You almost single-handedly took down the biggest drug ring in the country and their plan to creatively expand distribution. You didn't lose any men. No civilians got hurt. And you got pictures for your favorite news whores to use."

"Well, yeah. Maybe, if I ever get that far. But—"

"Sure, the perpetrator is at large and you have no clues. But an investigation is underway." Brooks clucked into the phone. "You lack imagination, Chaucer."

"No way, Elliot. I'll have to arrest this guy that blew everything up. You've gotta know that! That was some serious shit, and he's gonna do some serious time."

"Chaucer, I have some bad news," Brooks replied. "Our mutual friend is traveling on a Moroccan diplomatic passport. We have no jurisdiction. I'm not even authorized to give you his name, although I suspect you'll figure it out over time, if you watch the news."

"You gotta be shitting me, Elliot. You didn't think to tell me this before?"

"Consider it a blessing, Chaucer," Brooks said. "Now, go ahead and package the story for your bosses: you're all heroes and successful defenders of the public good. Make it so."

There was a long silence followed by an extended sigh.

"Don't feel bad! Although you do owe me a big one. Maybe two." Brooks hung up the phone.

WASHINGTON, DC

<u>THURSDAY</u>

ALEX STEPPED FROM HIS RENTAL SUBARU OUTSIDE THE HAY-ADAMS, just across Lafayette Square from the White House. The hotel doorman retrieved his travel bag from the trunk and asked, "Will you be needing the car, sir?"

Alex grinned. "It survived the trip from New York City. Just turn it in to the rental agency, please, and I'll walk."

"Welcome back, Mr. Cuchulain," the reception clerk said. "Your room is ready. Just sign here. Your dinner reservations with Ambassador Elliot are for seven o'clock." He punched a hidden button, and a bellman appeared immediately, reaching for Alex's bag.

Alex followed the bellman to the elevator. In a few moments, they stood outside the door of a small suite overlooking the White House. Entering the room, the bellman hung his travel bag and checked the ice bucket. Then he nodded curtly and asked, "Will there be anything else right now, sir?"

"I think not," Alex replied, handing him a twenty-dollar bill. "Thank you." The bellman backed out of the room and closed the door.

Alex pulled a large bottle of water from the refrigerator cabinet and, collapsing into a chair by the desk, took a long pull on it to quench his thirst. He gazed at Lafayette Square and the White House in the background.

There were fewer tents and protestors down there than a few years before. It was as if the world had settled into two camps, and the tent protesters were not welcome in either.

In buildings fifty yards away, hundreds of diligent government workers did what they thought were their jobs. Meanwhile, higher-ups like Brooks and Mac tried to put their collective spin on things somewhere nearby. His Hackettstown venture had forced a few of them to look at what could happen when the rules of engagement changed.

Alex leaned back and tilted the chair on its rear legs. *Dealing with the Israeli military won't be all that big of a deal*, he thought. *It's a country the size of New Jersey, albeit with a vastly capable military.* But the Israel Defense Forces depended on the best combat communication system in the world. Communication, command, and control—based on solid intelligence—made it work well.

So far.

If he could force the Israelis to fight one-on-one with the Muslims, led by the Palestinians and assisted by the Bedouins—with no technological bullshit—they had a chance of achieving their goal. Because when it came down to it, there weren't nearly enough Israelis to overcome all the Muslims willing to fight for the idea of home. As he thought of it, the Hackettstown incident was part of the grand scheme to craft a story that would sell to its purpose: make the Israelis want to give up the West Bank.

The trick was figuring out how to make that happen.

Yet it would, inevitably, happen—Alex was certain of this. It was yet another repeat of the Thucydides Trap, this time being played out on steroids. The trap, as first described by the ancient Athenian general Thucydides, occurred when a dominant power (Sparta) was forced to attack a rising power (Athens) before the newcomer gained enough strength to displace it. In this case, Israel had taken fifty years of technical and intellectual dominance as a given, without paying much attention to how quickly that gap was narrowing and thus how inevitable an outbreak of war had become.

The Israeli military was, person for person, as good as any on the planet and fully interconnected. The IDF could act in unison against any direct threat from entities like Iran or Saudi Arabia. When challenged, Israel's numerical David grew to be a tactical Goliath as a result of its communications skills, but they had little experience or training to operate without solid intercommunications. But Israel in recent years had been leveraging that tactical power to move further away from its roots as a democracy and plunging toward becoming a theocracy.

Putting its boot on the throats of two billion Muslims could quickly prove to be cumbersome.

And dangerous.

A COUPLE OF HOURS LATER, Alex sat with a glass of red wine in a corner booth in the Hay-Adams dining room, freshly showered and wearing a blue blazer over a blue cotton shirt and a repp tie. When Brooks and Mac walked in ten minutes late, he was pleasantly surprised.

"I see you waited for us," Mac said, nodding at the wineglass.

"You're only ten minutes late," Alex said as he stood and shook hands. "An hour wouldn't have surprised me, given your boss's demands. A man could die of thirst waiting for the president's minions to show up for an appointment." Each man took a chair and shook out a napkin.

Alex reached into his jacket pocket and pulled out three devices, each the size of a smartwatch without the strap. He laid them on the table and pushed the center of one with his forefinger. A green light came on, blinked thrice, and disappeared. He pushed the other two devices toward Elliot and Mac.

"Caitlin's newest gadget," he said. "No one will be recording anything for the surrounding ten meters or so. Push the button and stick it in your pocket. Push it again, and it turns off. Inductive charging, so you can just forget about it until you need it."

Mac smiled and slipped the device into his pocket.

"And cell phones?" Brooks asked.

Alex shrugged. "Still a few bugs. Doesn't work so well on TV remotes either."

"So, how does it feel to have murdered eighty-three people with no trial and no chance to tell their story?" Brooks teased.

"Pretty good, especially for having so little time to put it together," Alex said, glad for the official confirmation that there were no survivors. Apparently, the last four he shot were the last of the living there. "A recording of the meeting before it ended so abruptly would have been nice. But the public relations effort, which is essential to reaching my goals, is up and running, And Edgie is on board. We'll begin working together soon, I hope."

"Yes," Brooks said, "he called to thank me for the introduction."

"Well done, lad," Mac said. "Clean, surgical."

"Thanks. It was a three-for-one deal," Alex joked. "I got to try out some fabulous new explosives. My sister and her family are safe. And we have Edgie for the West Bank effort."

He lifted a glass and raised a toast to Emilie. In curating the information he'd needed to protect Elena and her family, Caitlin's superpowered software had found a link between the Bollito gang and the drug stuff in Queens. Then Emilie had drawn the crucial line to the dead son of Reginald Edgeworth, the world's greatest PR guy. The idea had leapt right out at Alex, and the timing was perfect.

"Well, the president is up to speed on your latest caper in New Jersey, and I'm sure someday he'll get around to thanking you for killing off the Bollitos and their crime bosses," Brooks said. "In the meantime, Mac and I are somewhat impatient to be useful in your quest to regain the West Bank for your tribes. Our government has publicly and repeatedly objected to the rule-of-law situation there, but this is the first time anyone has really addressed it. The president has no official knowledge, but we need a sense of how this will unfold."

"Yeah, where's your head on the tactics if the Israelis come out shooting?" Mac said. "Still lots of moving pieces in your little homicidal puzzle."

"Of course, and I've been thinking about that," Alex said, sitting forward and placing his wineglass on the table. "First and foremost, we would have to disrupt the Israelis' ability to communicate among themselves. The IDF is good at combined arms operations because they are so well interconnected. Caitlin thinks we can interfere with that.

"Second, in order to obtain the goodwill of the liberal intelligentsia in Israel, we would need to avoid killing too many Israeli children and heroes.

"Third, if the shooting war started to get ugly, the leaders would have to see that the rules of engagement had changed to the point that both their soldiers and their society were at risk. That would be the hard part.

"I'm going to try to bring all of Islam into the fray as a matter of honor and faith," Alex continued. "I have a few ideas how to do it. But most of all, I have the need."

The early objective would be the return of the Bedouin land. The longer the Israelis let the problem go unsolved, however, the greedier Alex and his leadership would get in terms of a solution.

"Larger investments will create larger demands," he explained. "Jerusalem's sovereignty may come into play. Israel has to see the writing on the wall: they can't corner the market on the holy city forever. The danger comes when they figure out that their ironclad control of the city is slipping away. That's when the knives will come out."

"How are you going to handle that?" Brooks said. "I don't think the president will step up to any serious commitment of US resources. I'm pretty sure I would be unable to recommend it."

"It can't be allowed to get that far, and I doubt we'll need to," Alex said. "We'll be on our own. If it does come to that, I hope we'll have the Saudis and the oil bunch on our side."

The Bedouins were Sunni, after all—among the first worshippers in the early moments of Islam in Medina. There was a crowd of Bedouins in Saudi Arabia as in Israel and other Middle East countries. They were Muslim royalty, albeit without a country to call their own.

"If we do engage, I plan for Israel to suffer hundreds of wounded, yet very few killed, in the early moments of the conflict."

"Oh, boy," Mac interjected. "Global three-D micro-chess. This could be very entertaining."

"Moroccan diplomatic status, along with a note from the Moroccan king to the Israeli prime minister introducing me as the official representative of the Bedouin tribes across the Middle East, should keep folks from thinking this isn't serious diplomacy as things evolve. I doubt that I'm at serious personal risk."

"So you can be reasonably sure assassination is off the table," Brooks said. "But what do you expect to *gain* from this effort?" Brooks said. "In all honesty, how do you expect them to react?"

"I imagine I'll be treated courteously, given a pat on the head, and perhaps get a meeting with some of the power players on the Orthodox side."

"Then what?" Mac asked.

"We'll play it by ear." Alex grinned. "And that ear will be extra sensitive to whatever the liberal Jewish community is saying."

The game was afoot.

UPPER EAST SIDE, MANHATTAN

ALEX CAUGHT THE SHUTTLE BUS BACK TO NEW YORK THE NEXT morning. Manhattan was being itself. People were everywhere, each with a purpose and someone trying to get in their way. Alex threaded around them all, making a beeline back to the brownstone on East 73rd Street. When he rang the doorbell, the same big guy answered, but this time in a loose-fitting blazer.

"Much better," Alex said. "You look like the real thing now."

He followed the grinning man to the den once more, where two different televisions displayed Wednesday's chaos in Hackettstown. Fire trucks, state police, local police, and others milled about, taking notes and measurements, with TV trucks from all the networks jammed into the mix. The televisions' talking heads clashed: "... including four men found just beyond the explosion with close quarter .40-caliber bullet wounds to the forehead ... no one survived the blast ... dead sniper in the woods downrange ... two shots within two inches ..."

That one was nice, Alex thought.

Edgeworth turned toward him. "Elliot tells me this is *your* doing. Was it?"

"Do you really want to know?" Alex responded. "Do you care?"

"I want to know how they died. That they suffered."

"They didn't suffer," Alex confirmed. "That was not part of the deal." *Although that might have been entertaining to plan . . .*

Then again, he explained, burning to death was probably painful, not to mention having your eardrums blown out a split moment before the fire consumed you. And a few suffered from large ball bearings puncturing their bodies, so Edgie could console himself with that thought. Alex had shot a few outliers too, which didn't exactly tickle if it took them a few minutes to die.

"All in all, though, they just disappeared—eighty-three of them, including your target and his management," he continued. "It was the entire Bollito family, all the bosses and members of their organization. But if I missed a few, you should let me know quickly, and I'll deal with them. Loose ends can burn if left untended. I want to be sure I live up to my end of the bargain."

"God bless you, Alex," Edgeworth whispered. "Okay, I buy it. And a deal is a deal. Now, you better tell me how you think this Israeli thing will work, 'cause it's not going to be a day at the beach."

"But you are in? You are committed?"

"I am, God help me. I'm committed—zipper down, balls out. But I'd like to hear all the details."

Alex handed him a thumb drive. "A souvenir. Put that in your pocket for later viewing. Now, watch this." He held the Kphone in front of the two of them.

High-quality Nikon images started peacefully, with black limousines and motorcycles parked around a one-story 1950s-style building, and guards sitting patiently with rifles and shotguns. Then came the slow-motion destruction of eighty-three lives: The walls blasted open. Cars shook, and bikes fell over. Bodies were ripped apart. Then the flaming roof collapsed on the whole scene.

In two of the images, the end of the 6.5mm Creedmoor barrel jutted up from the corner, with a standing man downrange, his chest just above the barrel. The subsequent images showed each of the two men down and dozens of vehicles on fire in the background.

"Those are the details," Alex said.

Edgie put a hand on his shoulder. "I can see now that Elliot was not exaggerating. You are indeed the legendary Cooch."

"I am." Alex nodded. "Now, let's spend a few hours outlining my approach to our next collaboration—and your response. It will get hairier from here. And more fun, or at least that's how I look at it."

"It's not going to be easy."

Alex grinned. "Of course not. Changing the mindset of an entire country never is."

TANGIER

CAITLIN O'CONNOR WAS BORED, AS CAN BE EXPECTED WHEN YOU ARE the smartest person in the world. She had spent an hour working out with Tang, who had tutored Alex in martial arts for over two decades, and then some extra time in the gym on her own. But her swim time was always the best for thinking, which was why she needed to swim every day—she'd done two miles earlier that morning. Swimming took just enough effort that her brain could work and sort things out without interruption. Underwater, Caitlin could hear nothing, and the motion of her body gave just enough distraction that her mind was free to wander.

Besides swimming and sex, she knew of few ways to empty her mind so she could think properly or just relax. Taking in the view was one of those ways, and for that reason, the master bedroom in her apartment—the largest in the Kufdani Industries complex—had a large window facing the bay. Right now, though, she reclined in one of the two guest bedrooms tucked behind the master, where Lynn Shaler etchings were prominent, hanging large and small on much of the available wall space. Artwork could sometimes take her to that quiet place too. She went often to this spare room.

The Shalers were a visual representation of Caitlin's fondness for Paris (if only for a few days at a time). Released in small editions, the tinted etchings were dark in a calming, quiet, candlelit kind of way, strangely formal and full of unspoken pursuits. One piece depicted an old-fashioned library with a globe on the center table, and beyond it a small window that Caitlin told herself looked out over a river with cafés filled with smart, colorful, happy people. Shaler also drew great doorknobs.

Alex was on his way to Israel. He'd messaged Caitlin from his Kphone after stopping in Algeciras to handle some things around education planning. Not that Hala needed much help—she was smart, she was tough, and she had built a kick-ass executive team. Whatever it was, Hala could pull it off without much help. Things were really moving forward in that department, anyway.

Educate a million Muslims here, a million Muslims there, Caitlin thought, *and before long . . .*

Recovering the Bedouin lands would be easiest if the Orthodox Jews who were always pushing for the West Bank takeover were shorn of their political support. Alex thought that would be tricky. Caitlin agreed. He was better at figuring out that sort of thing, given the range of personalities involved and all the other determinants that didn't lend themselves immediately to math or science. But she still had a great deal of value to add—namely, in the endeavor to shut down communications in most of Israel and (she hoped) blow some electronics up if needed—and she was ready for something to happen.

Caitlin moved toward her office and sat idly in front of her screens, which were plugged into the Jerusalem city network and the Shin Bet technology, allowing her to observe various street scenes from the live cameras there and the occasional Israeli drone flyover. Transcripts of encrypted phone conversations floated across one screen, curated by Emilie according to the circumstances Caitlin had defined. Other screens showed drone views of Tel Aviv and the Ben Gurion Airport, south of Tel Aviv along Route 1. Dribs and drabs of written documents and newspaper articles also drifted by, all curated by Emilie.

Ever since Alex came back from the desert with his plan to restore the honor of the Bedouin nation and educate their people, Caitlin had focused Emilie's attention on Israel and the West Bank. At the moment, Emilie was hard at work figuring out the Israel Defense Forces: structure, operations, planning, personnel. She was snooping into Shin Bet—the state cops who answered to the prime minister—and the organization's director, Nabov Dayan. Unsurprisingly, there were quite a few moving parts, and Emilie was getting a little pushback from her probes: the IDF and that bunch were trying to block her and figure out her identity.

I may have to deal harshly with them, Caitlin thought, barely able to contain her glee. *Maybe blow up a few servers now . . . and some computers later.*

She didn't care so much about the Bedouins getting screwed out of their land, but Alex did care about the Bedouins, and she cared about Alex. A lot. She knew helping him would help with progress on their shared education goals—the glue that held their little group together. Besides, it was fun. But they both knew she would have helped him even without expanding education as part of the plan.

Caitlin didn't like the Israelis so much either. Too many of them were intellectually arrogant—an unjustified attitude as far as she could tell, although she had to admit that a few of them were exceptionally bright. She had even slept with a few of them over the years, and had learned a little something she didn't already know from each one—a tiny piece of thinking that contributed to her efforts to solve the evolving global puzzle.

Needle-dicks, she recalled now, *but they did take direction well.*

Having confirmed that Emilie was still at work and undetected, Caitlin found there wasn't much for her to do at the moment. *Maybe another swim?*

Jerome wasn't even around for a good run out into the desert. He was off in Germany at Rheinmetall, buying grenade launcher ammunition or some such. Alex had designed some new type of ammunition that was now being made by the thousands. She wasn't sure what this was, but she knew it would be brilliant.

He had also found a way to deliver her mobile EMP device. Using Alex's control software, Caitlin had managed to vary the blast radius and the lethality of the shootable EMP round. She had long since hardened their Kphones against EMP interference, and the satellites that the devices relied on were too far away to be affected by local blasts. It was a bit of very cool synergy, and she was confident Alex would find a way to exploit it.

The immediate goal was clear: get the Israelis to give up the West Bank and its development. The path to getting there was less so, but Cailtin knew one thing for sure: it would be quintessential Alex.

JERUSALEM

KUFDANI'S MIND WAS BOILING. TRYING TO SORT OUT THE RAGE, HE chose to walk—charge, actually—the mile back to his hotel despite the heat. He had just been spat upon by the Israeli government. Was the spittle targeted at the Bedouins, the Arabs, or Islam in general? He wasn't sure the specifics really mattered.

As he stormed down the street, passersby quickly turned elsewhere. A few women and fewer men glanced at his suit before turning away, thinking, *Good fit*. But most just avoided him, understanding instinctively that this huge-necked, slit-eyed monster was not to be confronted.

The prime minister's office had been a little fancier than most government offices. A bragging wall in the reception area displayed dozens of pictures, each featuring the office's current occupant with someone who was famous or controlled many votes. While waiting to be called in for the meeting, Kufdani sat on a sofa surrounded by three armchairs, browsing on his Kphone. Across from him, at a desk framed by an Israeli flag, a young, severe-looking woman typed at her computer and studiously ignored him.

He had been sitting there for more than an hour after identifying himself. Perhaps his outfit was the problem: Above his black, highly polished wing-tip shoes, he wore a gray, tropical wool suit with faint green pinstripes, a white shirt, and a green silk tie. Green was the Muslim color.

Finally, at a buzz coming from near the desk, the young woman looked up. She frowned and nodded to the closed door, saying, "The prime minister will see you now."

The familiar visage of the prime minister, sitting behind a very large desk with his shirtsleeves rolled up and his tie askew, was a bit disconcerting. Another man sat in an upholstered chair next to the desk, notepad in hand: Yakov Bernstein, the newly named defense minister. In addition to a disdainful sneer, he wore a white shirt, a black tie pulled tight to his neck, and a yarmulke from which long black ringlets of hair fell beside each ear.

Kufdani handed the formal introduction letter from the king of Morocco to the prime minister.

"Please, have a seat, Mr. Cuchulain. Or shall I call you Mr. Kufdani?" the prime minister said, glancing at the letter and setting it aside. "I understand that you were of great help to the IDF in the Iran venture. Thank you for that." He looked down, moved some papers on his desk, and looked up again, quizzically. "Is there . . . something else?"

"There is, Mr. Prime Minister," Kufdani said, absorbing the insult. "I would like you to sponsor a legislative effort to return the Bedouin lands in the West Bank to their rightful Bedouin owners."

"Owners? Hogwash," the prime minister scoffed. "Why would I do that? A great number of my voters live in that area. Perhaps you should discuss it with them."

"I'd be delighted," Kufdani said. "Will you arrange such a meeting and introduction?"

The prime minister stared at him briefly, shrugged, and reached for a piece of notepaper. He wrote on it, then pushed it across the desk, not making eye contact. "Contact this man. I will direct him to hold this meeting with you and listen to your arguments."

"Thank you, Mr. Prime Minister," Kufdani said, reaching across the desk to accept the paper.

Using one hand, the prime minister had waved him from the room without even looking up.

Arriving at his hotel now, Kufdani stepped into the air-conditioned lobby and nodded at the desk manager. Then he bypassed the elevators for the stairs and climbed to his room, three steps at a time. After ten flights, he stepped from the stairwell into the corridor, breathing heavily but smoothly, and dug in his pocket for the room key. After entering the room, he pulled off his tie, threw his jacket on the bed, and stripped off his sweat-soaked dress shirt.

He opened the little fridge and took out two bottles of water, drinking one and tossing the bottle in the trash. With a sigh, he picked up his suit jacket, placed it on a wooden hanger in the closet, and hung the tie over one shoulder. The shirt went into a basket for the laundry. He wiped his shoes with a dirty sock and arranged them, side by side, under a chair. Then he rolled into a handstand and, closing his eyes, took a long breath before letting it out slowly—then another, even slower. He settled his mind into his emotions and let them swirl until, slowly, his mind cleared.

The second water bottle was waiting when Kufdani spun right side up to his feet again and collapsed onto the bed, picking up his vibrating Kphone. "Brooks."

"Hey, Alex," Brooks said. "Back from your audience with the Prime Minister?"

"I am," Kufdani said. "It was more an exercise in contempt than an audience. What an asshole. His new Haredi defense minister was there. No one else."

Brooks chuckled. "So he failed to meet even your very low expectations? What are you going to do about that?"

"He gave me a name and number so I could pitch my case to a guy who would set up a meeting near the West Bank. I suppose I'll set it up and go."

"Why bother?" Brooks asked. "It seems a bit unlikely that it will do any good for your cause. They're the problem, not the solution."

"Yeah, I know," Kufdani said. "But our whole case will ultimately be about the optics. According to Edgie, I want to be able to say that I followed the path the prime minister provided, to no avail. If optics are the bulk of our effort, I may as well start now."

"I get it," Brooks said. "Seems like overkill to me, but you have a plan and you're executing it. So you're still high on Edgie as your PR guy?"

"So far, he makes sense. I like his intensity. He's marvelously smart and agile, and he's motivated. He wants us to move every stone to create a good positive image for the world to see."

"However one decides to define the target 'world,'" Brooks pointed out.

"Exactly. So next I'll head off to joust with my target world." Kufdani chuckled. "They may well see me as an unarmed jouster."

"Good luck with the meeting. I'm off for a few days on *Old Fashioned*. Gonna head up the coast from Connecticut to Maine, and then back to Annapolis."

Old Fashioned was a fifteen-year-old, ocean-going, 48-foot sailing vessel that Brooks had ordered from Taiwan, built to his specifications. It boasted many gadgets that real sailors found enviable, and Brooks kept it compulsively up-to-date with maintenance and modern electronics.

"I do so miss that boat. Tell Jimmy I said hello," Kufdani sighed. "May there be fair winds ahead of us both, my friend."

NORTH OF JERUSALEM

KUFDANI PUSHED THE LITTLE RENTED FIAT ALONG THE ROUTE NORTH from Jerusalem, following the GPS directions toward the old Jerusalem airport. From the tinny speakers of the car radio came the voice of Professor Alan Charles Kors from Penn, lecturing on Isaac Newton. He had heard this lecture once before—it was part of a Great Courses class—but he still liked it. Brooks was a historian of some note when it came to seventeenth-century Enlightenment thinkers, and Caitlin knew more about how Newton thought than maybe anyone alive. They verbally abused him when he fell behind.

Ha! He thought. *I'll be ready for them next time.*

Reaching the outskirts of the old city, he saw a road sign for the airport and continued heading north. Soon enough, he entered the parking lot for a small block of one-story buildings. He checked his notes and began to look for one with the proper marking. After a few minutes, he saw several cars and a panel truck outside a building with *2443* stenciled on the hangar door and pulled up to a halt.

As Kufdani exited his car, the marked door opened and a tall man, somewhat overweight, stepped out. The man wore a black fedora, a white shirt, and a black tie. His hair appeared in an arrogant show of enviable *payot* curling chaotically from beneath the hat. He was approaching quickly. Kufdani's hostility detector went through the roof.

"Mr. Kufdani? Please," the man said in Russian-accented English. He pointed inside the building.

Through the door, Kufdani saw a small room where five men dressed almost identically in Orthodox attire were seated around a table. One man stood and said in English, "Mr. Kufdani," indicating a seat beside another large man. He did not meet Kufdani's eye or offer to shake hands. "I am Yakov Bernstein. We met at the office of the Prime Minister."

Kufdani nodded, thinking, *No, we didn't "meet." You didn't even acknowledge my presence.*

"We understand you have new evidence in the matter of construction of settlements for our people on the West Bank of the Jordan River," Bernstein said. "Please, do fill us in."

Kufdani flattened his gaze, trying to maintain his cool. He hadn't driven here only to get spat on again. *Maybe I'll rip your face off and feed it to the swine someday.*

"There is only history," he said in an even tone. "The lands you confiscated belonged to Israeli citizens in 1948 and for two hundred years before that. Those lands are stolen and should be returned. The United States, the United Nations, and the International Court of Justice have officially and loudly condemned this travesty."

"So, no news," Bernstein spat. "You waste our time with the same flawed arguments your people have tried for years."

"You don't seem to be listening to me, Bernstein. Your government stands alone in the world with its regrettable public views on this issue." *And maybe when I rip your face off, I'll eat one of your ears. Just give me a reason.*

Bernstein snorted. "The Bedouins are Muslim. They have no rights in Israel, no matter when or where they were born. Israel is a Jewish state."

"Your arrogance is unfortunate," Kufdani growled. "We Bedouins will fight you for every inch of that land." He stood in order to stalk from the room.

A sudden burning sensation struck his left triceps. Someone was holding his arm with two hands. Kufdani spun and hit the man in the throat, then ducked as he felt a swinging motion behind him. The punch went over his head. Kufdani reached to pick up the man's legs from behind the knees, then stood quickly. As the man fell, Kufdani lunged for Bernstein, but the strength suddenly drained from his hands.

His legs wobbled beneath him. Everything went dark.

Someone grabbed the back of his shirt as he fell.

From a distance, he heard Bernstein say, in Hebrew, "Put him in the truck."

KTZI'OT PRISON, SOUTHERN ISRAEL

THE SOUND WAS INSISTENT: AN ANNOYING SCREECH WITHIN AN ERRATIC, abrasive scratching. Kufdani moved his head, and a lightning bolt passed between his eyes, then worked its way up the front of his skull. His brain pounded against his eardrums.

He opened his eyes.

A rat was digging at a crack in a concrete wall—the source of the insistent roar in Kufdani's head. The pain in his left ear seemed determined to split his skull in two.

A thin, brown wool blanket was rolled under his head like a pillow. He discovered that, under another thin blanket, he was naked.

When he swung his legs from the narrow steel bunk and sat up straight, a shooting pain drove across his hips and buttocks. The head pain settled down one level to marginally less than excruciating. Something had spilled across his hamstrings and buttocks, and his inner thighs were sticky with it. Bleeding scratches irritated his hips, and a foul, unfamiliar taste clotted his mouth. His teeth were scummy against his thick, pasty tongue.

Kufdani turned his head very slowly to see a small man, perhaps in his fifties, watching him. The man's remaining hair stuck out from the sides of his head like tiny white pom-poms, and his nose was crooked, newly healed but poorly set from a recent break. An orange canvas shirt, washed to near white, hung from his scrawny shoulders. Faded pant legs drooped over his rubber sandals.

"What are you staring at?" Kufdani asked in classic, unaccented Arabic, the dialect used almost exclusively in commerce and among the intellectual elite of Morocco and the Middle East. It hurt to talk.

"I'm supposed to keep an eye on you until Boxley gets back," the scrawny man replied with Bedouin-inflected Arabic. "He wants to talk to you. I think they're going to auction you off."

"Auction me off? What the hell—"

"Somebody doesn't like you very much. You're lucky you were out cold." The man paused. "The first time really hurts, and there were a lot of them."

Partial memories flooded back: bouncing along in a truck, bound, drugged. Tossed on a floor, clothes ripped off. Darkness—then the light, unfamiliar bodies, and new pain. Kufdani's face tightened as he decoded what the little man had said.

"Uh-huh. What do you do around here? Besides supervising sodomy, that is."

"You mean when I'm not on the wrong end of that act myself?" the man scoffed. "I run errands. I'm the house mother who cares for the cherries after they arrive at our hallowed correctional doors. They get broken in, just like you. One of the boys can always give Boxley a few shekels to organize a blowjob or back-door sex from me. I'm Boxley's property, so he won't allow use of me for free."

Kufdani pulled the flimsy blanket tighter around his shoulders. His mind flashed to a man behind him, holding onto both hips and digging in with ragged fingernails, having his rough way. *Oh, Bernstein. You got me.*

"Where are my clothes?" he asked, standing.

His cellmate shrugged. "House rules. You get clothes sometime after the second round, when no one else wants you. Right now, it's more convenient that you're naked."

Oh, Bernstein, Kufdani thought again. He had to admit: no one had ever gotten him this bad. *I'm going to find a way to hurt you.*

"And when, pray tell, does the second round commence?" he asked. "And how do I avoid it?"

"There's no avoiding it. They'll be coming soon, and you'd have to kill them all."

"Ah, necessity," Kufdani replied, moving toward the wall. The rat scurried away to parts unknown. "Your accent says you're a desert creature. Where?"

"Bedouin, from here in Israel. I ran off twenty years ago, fell in with the wrong crowd, and here I am."

"What's your name?"

The little man watched as Kufdani turned upside down against the wall in a handstand, stretching his legs by letting them drop to one side, then another. "Baadi. Thanks for asking."

"Okay, Baadi, you watch the door. Let me know when the first of them is coming. Then get out of the way. If you're useful to me, I'll let you live."

Baadi looked unconvinced, but still stepped up to the cell's opening and peered through the bars. After a few moments, he ducked back into the cell.

"They're here," he cried out. "Three of them—the guys who bought first, second, and third on your ass. One will hold your arms while the other two control your legs and take turns fucking your ass. The one holding your arms will go first on fucking your face."

Kufdani spun to his feet with a quick push and glided to a spot near the cell door. His hands were loose, and his thighs quivered slightly as he balanced in a slight crouch.

Now I guess we improvise.

The first man came through the door. Kufdani uncoiled to punch the spot on the human temple where bone is the thinnest. He felt the bone give way, under a single, extended right-index knuckle, to a mushy sensation. The man was dead before he hit the floor, convulsing.

The second man planted his feet to avoid the flopping mass below him. The follow-through from the temple blow had coiled Kufdani's muscular torso, sending the entire force of his well-trained, unwinding body behind the heel of his left hand. It hit the man just under his left cheekbone, driving his head into the steel and concrete of the cell door's edge. A gray mass tangled with red stripes exploded from his cranium and stretched in the air, splattering the third man's neck and face.

The third man moved to clear his face as the rebound from Kufdani's blow allowed him to slide his hand behind the man's neck, grabbing hair and ear while the right hand rose to grasp jawbone and whiskers. A quick counter-snap with both hands generated a sound like a broken twig.

Kufdani looked back at Baadi, who was hunched over with his rheumy eyes wide. "Three men," he muttered through bad teeth. "You killed three men in five seconds."

Backlit, Kufdani loomed like the naked Incredible Hulk, his lats pushing his scarred arms from his side and highlighting massive, veined deltoids. His face had transformed: The skin at the edge of his eyes swelled, hooding them atop the faint knife scar that furrowed through the wrinkled skin to his jaw. The tiny, curved scars on his forehead stood out against his darkened face. Breath whistled through his nose like an oncoming train.

"Probably more like four seconds," he murmured.

"The rest will show up soon," Baadi whispered.

Kufdani took one leg and pulled it up to his head until his toes pointed at the ceiling. He held it for a second. The stained thigh beside his face stank. He dropped it, his anger tugging at his control. Blending the two would be necessary.

"Don't get in my way once it starts, Baadi," he ordered. "And if you betray me, you'll know serious pain every day for the rest of your life."

Baadi scuttled to the corner of the cell and squatted with his hands against the opposing walls, his jaw quivering.

"Who's the big boss around here," Kufdani said, hovering over him, "and why?"

"There's somebody over Boxley, but I don't know who. You just deal with Boxley. He holds the power."

"And his chief enforcer?"

"Mustapha. Palestinian, I'd guess. Close to two meters tall, weighs a hundred kilos at least. Shaved head, thick scar tissue on his eyebrows. He's a brute, and he's big. Likes it rough. He rents me once a month or so." Baadi shrugged. "I'll be here for another eighty-four months, by my count, so I'll see a lot of rough. After a while, big doesn't matter."

Kufdani looked at him in wonder.

Then he heard his next set of friends approaching and peeked out through the open cell door. A ragged crowd, dressed uniformly in un-ironed orange prison garb, pushed, punched, and guffawed along a narrow concrete corridor, a steel railing on their right and the welded prison bars of repeated cells on their left.

Time for me to figure out how I survive this, he thought. *I'm supposed to be the planner here.*

His planning horizon had shrunk to today, not weeks or months from now, and he had about thirty seconds to figure things out. It occurred to him that a bunch of angry Muslims resided within those very prison walls. He wanted them to work for him, to be angry for him and along with him.

It's good to have the beginning of a plan.

"Shall we greet them?" he said calmly.

The lead man in the crowd appeared at the open door, large and thick with a ragged beard. At the sight of three inert bodies, he dug in his heels but could not stop. Slipping on the pool of red and gray matter, he crashed to the cement floor. The men just behind him stumbled over him. Two of them fell, and one caught himself against the corridor's steel railing. Behind him, another six or seven men managed to stop. They all gaped at the pile of live and dead men, and the naked man standing beyond it.

"Gentlemen," Kufdani said, seeming to fill the cell with his naked bulk. "Is there something I can do for you?"

"Yeah, cherry boy, I'm Abdul," said the man against the railing in a muddled Gazan accent. He was enormous—tall and wide, with loops of fat hanging from his chin—and breathing hard, partly from the short run and partly from violent lust. He stepped forward. "Nice dick, but I like your ass better. We came for a little more fucking. Maybe another blow job, too."

Kufdani shifted his balance forward and drove his right hand into Abdul's wide neck. Curling a thumb and three fingers around the man's larynx, he squeezed until the veins in his forearm stood out in thick cords.

The cracking sound was loud in the sudden silence.

Kufdani ducked slightly, then lifted with his legs, pushing the man hard. Once the man's back hit the railing, his obesity carried him slowly over the railing, his feet pointing up as they trailed the falling torso. There was no scream—only the slap of an inert mass hitting the concrete floor two levels below.

Take that, Bernstein. Your time is coming.

"He wasn't very polite," Kufdani said, "and I didn't like his agenda." He smiled at the man on the floor and then at the others just outside the cell door. His face was a caricature of malice. "If there are no more social comments, please come into my humble cell."

The prisoners pushed forward, forcing the first two men into the cell. "Baadi, what the hell is going on here?" one of them roared, staring at Kufdani. "That was my cousin. Who do you think you are? You'll pay for this."

"Maybe, but first take off that jumpsuit," Kufdani said. "It looks like it will fit me."

"Well, try and take it!" the man yelled, pulling his fist back.

Kufdani rolled his head to let the punch slide past his cheek, simultaneously grabbing the man by the face and slamming the back of his head against the steel bars of the cell, then again. Seizing the front of the orange jumpsuit, he pulled the man forward, then spun with the weight and threw him at the back wall. The man hit with a thud and slipped to the floor, perfectly still.

"I hate that kind of garbage. Baadi, take that jumpsuit off him. And try not to get any blood on it," Kufdani said. "It's mine now."

Baadi scrambled to his feet, stepped over the bodies on the cell floor, and began to strip the uniform from the inert man.

"So, gentlemen," Kufdani exclaimed, "I suppose you're my new best friends. Who's in charge around here?"

The remaining man in the cell stood with his jaw agape, but no sound came out. Kufdani moved to him and, taking the man's elbow in his left hand, dug two fingers into the socket where the nerves crossed. The man gasped and crumpled to his knees. Kufdani reduced the pressure and pulled him back up to standing.

Kufdani had practiced a certain look in front of the mirror a hundred times until it was exactly what he wanted. It was sometimes useful. Now was one of those times.

Allowing his head to sink to his chest, he then raised it with his face stretched into a grimace, his eyes slitted. The scars on his face stood out in white, and his muscled neck seemed larger than his head. He flicked his tongue in and out like a snake, turning slowly to gaze at the frozen crowd, sensing them.

The cell was eerily silent.

"Come on, people," Kufdani hissed, looking every bit the Gila monster. Brooks Elliot was always telling him to lose that look to avoid terrifying the civilians. "I'm not in a very good mood. Who's in charge?"

"That would be me," said a deep, calm voice from the back of the crowd.

The men outside the cell parted as a wheelchair emerged carrying a bearded man, in his fifties, with a pockmarked face. Pushing the chair was a very large man with a shaved head who glared at Kufdani from beneath bulging, tangled eyebrows. Beside the chair was a small, slim, nervous man who moved like a feral cat.

"You seem to have created quite a stir among my friends," the man in the chair said.

Kufdani scrutinized the man. "Boxley, I suppose?"

"I am Amad Boxley. This is my assistant, Mustapha. He is unhappy with you, it seems."

"Mustapha probably is worried I won't hire him down the road," Kufdani said. "And indeed I may not. He's too big to be useful."

"In that case," replied Boxley, "I think I'll just have him hurt you."

Mustapha shifted his weight to his front foot.

Time slowed down for Kufdani once again, into the freeze-frame slow motion that had evolved after countless hours of practice under the tutelage of the one and only Tang, one of the world's master artists of violence in motion. Kufdani's body turned, as his knees flexed. Then everything uncoiled in sequence: from his feet to an exploding drive of the legs, to a release and twist of the upper body, to a final snap of his arm, which drove a single, gnarled knuckle into that same point just below the center of the forehead.

The pain worked in reverse too, shooting from Kufdani's knuckle through his wrist and up his arm to his shoulder. Looking back over his right shoulder as his body continued to uncoil, he saw the eyes become wide, then glazed, then blank as Mustapha fell and his body completed its follow-through. Bone shards in Mustapha's frontal lobe had ended his life quickly, Kufdani knew. He endured his own pain and allowed himself a brief moment to admire one of his favorite moves. It was funny: even after all these years, his knuckle still hurt—maybe even a little worse than the first time.

Kufdani snapped his attention to Boxley and the small, wiry man beside him. The man in the wheelchair was stunned, immobile, and posed no immediate risk, but Kufdani sensed movement to his left.

The small man had a shank driven halfway to his shoulder. The ragged blade, attached with black tape to a small wooden block, was dark with some substance. Kufdani flowed back and reached for the man's forearm, pushing the motion of the blade over his shoulder, then spun the wrist and broke it. The shank fell to the cell floor as the man screamed in pain.

"I didn't kill you—yet—because that was a nice move," Kufdani said. "No warning, no bullshit. Just strike. I like that. I may have use for you."

He turned back to the wheelchair.

"So, Boxley, let's talk. I need to figure out who to kill next and who to keep alive to administer my orders. Plus, I'd like to get some clean clothes and—"

"Take him," Boxley snarled to no one, and he reached below his wheelchair.

Kufdani snapped a kick into the seated man's solar plexus, then grabbed his nose between two knuckles. The break was audible.

The room came into full focus again for Kufdani. The cell was still, except for the gases escaping from the dead. Faint groaning rose from the knife wielder holding his wrist. Boxley labored for breath as the blood flowed onto his orange shirt.

"I hate that kind of garbage," Kufdani said. Turning to Baadi, he stuck his index knuckle in his mouth and made a sour face. "I hope I didn't crack a knuckle again."

He felt relieved. He was fine, and it was time to get on with things. He couldn't kill them all, but he had gotten in front of things and taken control. Soon he would figure out where he was—and how to get out.

"The rest of you, move along," Kufdani ordered. "Take the dead with you. And Boxley will need a new pusher."

He told them to figure out what to tell the guards and let them know he was available anytime to meet with the head man.

"Oh, and one more thing: I am of the Yahia tribe and the appointed leader of all Bedouins. My name is Kufdani."

BAT YAM, TEL AVIV

ALWAYS RETALIATE FIRST, GUNS THOUGHT WHILE SITTING ON THE third-floor balcony at the apartment of Moishe Aman, overlooking the Mediterranean beach at Bat Yam. It wasn't something he'd made up on his own. It was a Cooch special—something the former CIA man had once told him, a key lesson for survival learned from his father, Mick Cuchulain: in a tough operation, it was better to attack before your opponent did.

Cooch is certainly in the middle of a tough operation now, Guns thought.

Out on the balcony, he and Moishe sat three floors up, allowing their dinner to settle, as a stream of bathers and diners moved up from the beach, beginning their trek back into the city. Dishes rattled in the background: in the kitchen, Guns's wife did the washing, and Moishe's wife dried and stacked the plates, glasses, and utensils.

For many years, Moishe—the revered, retired head of Mossad—had been Guns's sponsor within the agency, especially during the time Guns spent in New York. Moishe had protected Guns's back against the Tel Aviv Tarantulas, who prowled around Mossad headquarters looking for trouble and promotion. Thanks to Guns's many reports from New York, Moishe knew about Cuchulain, Masterson, Macmillan, and Elliot. He had read them all and often wanted to talk about them. It came in handy now.

Guns and Sheila Pelzer had already discussed Cooch's predicament. The current head of Mossad had no new advice, but she recommended that Guns go back and talk to Moishe. "Maybe he'll have a better handle on things," Pelzer had said. "He often does."

"My main man Cooch is in the Israeli jail," Guns said now.

Moishe looked startled. "Ktzi'ot?"

Guns nodded. "It's not quite clear how he landed there, but Shin Bet police seem to be involved. Someone calling in a favor, I suppose. It took me all day to find him." He explained the kidnapping—how Cooch had been taken soon after Pelzer had helped set up the meeting with the Israeli prime minister.

"Have you tried to get him out?"

Guns nodded again. "Mossad has no influence, no authority within Israel's borders. It's out of our purview—or so I'm told by a Shin Bet official."

"Did you tell him this particular inmate was carrying a diplomatic passport and operating on a diplomatic mission?" Moishe asked.

"I didn't have a chance," Guns replied. "He turned his back on me, wouldn't meet or take my calls. He reports directly to Dayan. I noted his name and position." *And we'll speak again.*

"How are you going to get Cooch out?" asked Moishe. "Ktzi'ot Prison is one of the roughest places on earth."

"I told Jerome Masterson where he is. Jerome didn't seem surprised, nor did he ask a lot of questions. We'll let the Americans get him out somehow. I want to see some outrage from the prime minister, not dilute the insult by begging for a favor."

"You think he's okay, our Cooch?"

"If he's not, no one would be. Cooch is one lethal human being."

"Well, I certainly hope he survives it," Moishe said. "I find myself quite cross at our prime minister for allowing a diplomat to be summarily kidnapped into prison. We simply can't have that kind of thing. Imagine if our populace heard of it!"

Guns chuckled. "Oh, I think they'll hear about it. Cooch will make sure of that."

Moishe shook his head. "You certainly have faith in this man. After all, he is a humble prisoner in one of Israel's most notorious prisons. That bunch knows violence."

"They just *think* they do," Guns quipped. "I've known Cooch for a long time. He's the quintessence of violence. He feeds on it."

Though he didn't say as much, Alex Cuchulain was also a friend. Guns knew Cooch couldn't have expected this attack, or he would have been prepared. He told Moishe about the Russian Orthodox Jews—including Yakov Bernstein, the new defense minister—who were present at the airport hangar when Cooch met with them at the prime minister's request.

"In that case, talk it over again with Pelzer," Moishe advised. "She'll have to be the one to deal with the prime minister."

"Not you?" Guns asked.

"I don't like him. I don't trust him, and he knows it," Moishe replied. "I could only do harm."

Looks like there's not much left to do but wait, Guns thought. The idea was unsettling. He was curious—and a bit nervous—about what might happen to daily life in Jerusalem while Cooch was in prison but the rest of his cabal was free to roam. But even before that, he would be interested in hearing how the prison officials were faring with Cooch in their custody.

KTZI'OT PRISON, SOUTHERN ISRAEL

WORD OF THE KILLINGS ECHOED RAPIDLY AROUND THE PRISON. THE guards were still trying to figure out where all the dead bodies came from—and who killed them. The usual snitches were surprisingly silent.

Whether or not the prime minister had prior knowledge, Bernstein had undoubtedly set Kufdani up, drugging and kidnapping him before dumping him into the notorious Ktzi'ot Prison in the Negev Desert—all in response to the valid political offer of great import to hundreds of thousands of Israeli citizens, an offer presented by a protected diplomat. And yet Kufdani had risen to the challenge so far by staying alive.

In fact, he had decided to take this opportunity to broaden his mission.

Kufdani had a late-afternoon visitor requesting entrance to his cell—a large man with broken teeth and burn scars along both forearms. "Yousef Salama would like to speak with you, Kufdani, at your convenience," the man said, bowing his head.

So, Kufdani thought, *my presence has become known among the next level of prisoner leadership.*

Surely they had heard of his status among the Bedouin. He quickly realized that the issue was poised to spread past the recovery of Bedouin land to become something far more complex: an insult to Islam itself. He had to figure out how to bring this broader denigration to the table.

I think it starts now.

Kufdani stood and pretended to brush detritus from his orange jumpsuit. "It is convenient right now," he replied. "I shall rearrange my schedule to accommodate Yousef Salama, whoever he is." He looked down at Baadi.

"I forgot about him," said his cellmate. "Palestinian political royalty, sort of the bosses' boss. He's a big deal. I've never met or even seen him."

"All the better," Kufdani said. "Save my messages, Baadi, and tell any visitors that I'll see them later. Shall we go, my good man?"

The broken-toothed man escorted Kufdani to a double cell: the first space contained the usual bed and steel toilet, while the adjoining cell had a small table in the center of four steel chairs with padded seat cushions. A man who looked to be in his sixties sat on one of them, studying Kufdani as he entered.

Flanked by a prisoner on each side, the older man wore the same faded orange prison suit as all the prisoners, but his was ironed. He pointed to a chair. Kufdani sat on the edge of it, feet under him, weight on the balls of the feet, alert.

"From the stories I heard about what remains of the prisoner leadership," the older man began, speaking classic Arabic with no regional accent, "you could kill me right here if you chose. Of course, then we would kill you."

Kufdani replied in scholarly Arabic. "But you requested our meeting knowing this. And in such a case, we would both be dead, along with perhaps a dozen others. Why would you attempt such a thing? Why would I? I have no reason to harm you. Rather, I wish to serve Allah, with your blessing."

"You may call me Salama," the man said. "You killed four men in the service of Allah?"

"It was actually five or six, I think, but yes. They were in my way." Kufdani paused. "The prophet Muhammad (peace be upon him) was a violent man in pursuit of his service to Allah. I suffer the same affliction."

"I should say," Salama agreed. "Do you enjoy it, or is it some form of duty to Allah?"

Kufdani smiled. "A little of both, I imagine. I was badly used when I was abruptly admitted to this lovely institution, which piqued my anger."

Salama eyed him for a long moment. "Yes, I do apologize for the unsatisfactory welcome you received," he said. "The guards circulated gossip about you being a Jew who had raped a Bedouin girl."

That perhaps explains the prisoners' lack of social skills. "Well, I thought I should disabuse the other residents of the notion that a second attempt would be easy or painless. I will admit that I enjoyed giving this lesson."

"And the service to Allah?"

"I would organize this prison and these prisoners in his name. There will be Muslim prayers five times a day, and many lessons."

Salama laughed out loud. "You know you are in Ktzi'ot? This is the most notorious prison in all of Israel, full of killers and thieves." The old man nodded to his right, and a teapot appeared. Cups of tin were brought out, and Salama himself poured from a battered copper teapot. "Please," he said, nodding to the tea.

"I mean no offense, sir," Kufdani said, "but may I kill the man on your left? Or if you prefer, would he put away that tiny revolver in his left pocket? I'm sure you are aware of the aphorism: Trust Allah, but tie your camel." He smiled. "My trust instincts are suffering."

Salama nodded at the man on his left and jerked his head.

The man glared at Kufdani and left the cell.

"Let's get to the point," Salama said. "More order in the prison and more thoughts of Allah could only be beneficial to us all. To that end, what do you want? And what do you expect of me?"

Kufdani relaxed, leaned back in his steel chair, and fixed the old man with his gaze. "Your people—these killers and thieves, as you describe them—suffer from the lack of organization and religious guidance. I would like to organize, teach, and preach. I'd like to know which of your Palestinian brothers have the potential for leadership and the ability and willingness to learn. And I want your blessing and support."

Salama's jaw dropped. "Who in blazes are you? Where did you come from? And why are you here, of all places?"

Gotcha, Kufdani thought. *Now let's see if I can sell this outrageous idea. When in doubt, tell the truth, I guess. Omissions are fine.*

"I am Kufdani, a Bedouin imam elected by all the tribes to represent the Bedouin nation. I am ready to do that. Yet I am here because I was drugged and abducted by Orthodox Jews, from a meeting sanctioned by my peers in service of Allah." Kufdani paused. "But it is clear to me now that Allah has willed this turn of events."

The old man sipped his tea and returned Kufdani's gaze.

"My ultimate mission is to recover the Bedouin lands on the West Bank that were stolen by the Israelis. I understand violence well, as you may have come to recognize, and will follow that path now that the diplomatic doors have been slammed in my face."

Salama nodded almost imperceptibly.

"On the way to accomplishing that end, I shall soon be forced to forgo further incarceration."

Salama spat out a mouthful of tea. "You want out? I've been here eleven years. If you can find a way out for us both, I will support you."

"And what do you want from me in return?" Kufdani asked. "What service may I provide in recognition of your devotion to Allah?"

"I am a Hamas elder. I want my leadership position in the Palestinian community recognized." The old man's eyes hardened, followed by his voice. "And I want you to give me hope of revenge on the Israelis for my hardships."

"I think I can give you more than hope, if your support is more than lip service."

"If you want lip service, talk to Baadi. You may keep him, by the way." The old man snorted. "I'll give you as much support as you can handle, though you might have to kill a few more to make it work."

"Inshallah," Kufdani said. "I won't let a few more dead get in the way of Allah's favor. The honor of Islam is at stake, not just for the Bedouins and Palestinians, but for all of Islam."

Well, there's the broadening of the mission.

Salama was still for a moment, then picked up his tea and sipped again. "I've been trying to get Islam behind our Palestinian effort for twenty years. Nowhere is where I got. Do you really think *you* have a chance?"

"I do," Kufdani confirmed. "I am a planner, and I have a plan." He described the events of the past weeks: how a million Bedouins across Arabia and the Levant had designated him as the one to fix the West Bank problem and restore their honor, and how he'd met with the Israeli prime minister and then with his designated West Bank operatives to discuss solutions. "Rather than begin to discuss remedies, the Israelis decided to toss me in here."

"Congratulations on the honor," Salama said. "But your Bedouin honor and your prison discomfort are hardly enough to strip the Israelis of their Jewish bigotry. Does your plan bring anything else to the table?"

"It does," Kufdani said, "but the details are rather confidential."

"I smell bullshit."

Time to impress, thought Kufdani. He would need Salama's support if this was going to work.

THE EXERCISE YARD WAS FULL the following afternoon during the designated free time at Ktzi'ot Prison. Groups of men awaited their turn on the exercise machines, watching Kufdani out of the corner of their eye. He stood in the classroom space not far from the yard as twenty-one prisoners shuffled in. None had asked for the meeting, but they were there as directed all the same.

At the front of the room, Kufdani held up his hand for silence. "At the request of Yousef Salama, I am taking the leadership place of Boxley, who was injured recently. Yousef Salama has given me his full support and authorized me to act for him in the enforcement of this support."

The previous day in Salama's double cell, Kufdani had mulled over how to disabuse Salama of his lack of trust, although he did not blame the Palestinian man. *I suppose I should tell him as much as possible now and worry about leaks later.* He would need Salama first and foremost to oversee the return of his Kphone, so he could contact Edgie and Jerome. *Caitlin is going to be pissed.*

Taking a sip of tea, he had sought to buy some time as he framed his answer: "I am rich. I own a big Moroccan trading company, and I'm already spending money on this effort to restore the Bedouin lands." He had revealed his military and diplomatic chops, bragged that his best friend spoke to the United States president nearly every day, and emphasized his Islamic education. "Most important of all," he had insisted, "I have a workable plan. I will get the Israelis to fight the Muslims one-on-one, unsupported by all their tech bullshit."

Salama was hooked. "We would slaughter them," he'd exclaimed, his eyes shining. "But before I champion your cause, how can I be certain that your claims are true?"

Kufdani shrugged. "If you could get my phone back to me, along with my Moroccan passport, I could prove my claims to you immediately. Then we could talk about my plan. I have constructed the salient pieces already."

The metal chair had creaked as Salama sat back, smiling and shaking his head. "The salient pieces of a workable plan to take Muslim land back from the Israelis? I'm closer to having an erection than I've been in years."

Now, at the head of the classroom, Kufdani was beginning to put those salient pieces in place. "We will pray five times a day," he instructed the prisoners. "Study in the practice of Islam will be held each afternoon. All will pray. The rest of the hours of each day will be spent in learning."

"Get out of my face," said one younger man, balding with a scruffy beard. "We don't want to spend our time learning about Islam from you."

"You have not done me the courtesy of even listening to my plans," Kufdani replied. "That offends me. Are there others among you with the same attitude? If so, please raise your hands."

Several prisoners looked around at the others, but no one raised their hand.

Kufdani walked to the man. "I don't deal well with the discourteous," he said, grabbing the hair at the back of the man's head with his left hand.

The man flailed his arms toward Kufdani's face, but his reaction was too slow. Kufdani took the beard with the other hand and snapped the man's neck.

"We must all be attentive to the lessons of the prophet," he said.

He almost felt bad about the dead man, but Salama knew the rules. Salama was accustomed to eliminating a problem without leaving fingerprints, and Kufdani had to set expectations of obedience.

"Baadi, I am preparing to teach," Kufdani said. "Please remove this man before he starts to smell. Now, where was I?"

Over tea yesterday, Salama had finally acknowledged that an inventory of leaders among the prisoners might reveal greater promise than one might expect in a dreadful place like Ktzi'ot. "Let me think about it," the old man had said. "I was considering, before our meeting, the cleanest way to kill you. But the religious aspect to your plan was . . . unexpected. It shows promise."

"The religious aspect is a means to an end—perhaps a violent end, as the prophet himself so often experienced." Kufdani had asked Salama to arrange a meeting with a group of twenty or so chosen leaders, without upsetting the prison staff—plus one man who had a big, gossipy mouth and whom Salama would be better off without.

"The prison staff is greedy, but more and more they are also fearful," Salama had said slyly. "A few have died under strange circumstances after interfering with our administration of the prison population. I don't think they will become a problem. Inshallah."

"Inshallah," Kufdani had replied. "Thank you for your time, Salama."

Now it was time to bring those twenty true leaders into the fold, and Kufdani would have to really work the crowd. From Muhammad's perspective, love of Allah paired naturally with the willingness to fight for Him. They would fight—if led.

"You are the core of the leadership effort selected by Yousef Salama. You will lead the others and teach them what you have been taught. Together, we will bring credit to Allah with our prayers and actions. So, there is a lot to do."

Kufdani pulled his Kphone from the left hip pocket of his orange jumpsuit, pressed at the touchscreen, and cast an image on the wall.

"But Allah's teachings are only the beginning. We'll also study small-unit tactics, and there will be instructions on management—how you will manage the men who must answer to you on the battlefield. And you will receive instruction on communications and the discipline that goes with it. Of course, we'll discuss a host of medical and logistics problems that must be sorted out."

Kufdani gestured toward the wall.

"The weapons I will provide, when the time is right for us to bring glory to Allah, will look something like this: the US-made Mk19, a belt-fed 40mm shoulder-fired weapon. So, our lessons will include tutorials on its ammunition and deployment."

Twenty men shifted in their chairs, murmured among themselves, and looked eagerly at Kufdani.

"We are leaving here before too long," he said, "and we wouldn't want to be unprepared to cut the Israeli army off at the knees."

HAARETZ ONLINE, TEL AVIV

<u>FRIDAY</u>

ELSA SACHS HAD A DAILY STORY TO GET OUT AND SEVERAL PODCASTS to organize. She still had some time before sunup, however, so she sat at her desk checking email before her workday started in earnest. She was hungry and still had sleepers in her eyes. Last night's blouse had a wine stain on the left breast, and she hadn't yet showered. And when the office lights blinked out and her PC flickered, switching to battery power, she was irritated but wasn't immediately concerned—until she looked out the window.

Tel Aviv was entirely dark.

Just minutes earlier and thirty minutes away, clustered in the shadows of a West Bank construction site just northeast of Jerusalem—on land that formerly belonged to the Bedouin—dozens of trucks, earthmovers, and bulldozers had stood ready to begin another day's efforts. New streetlights had illuminated the site, joining the interior security lights from five thousand recently completed apartments and another two hundred in final construction. One day soon, thousands of Orthodox Jewish Israelis would move in.

Anyone awake at that predawn hour might have seen a flash of very bright light near that West Bank construction site. It blazed for a split second only, and when the skies darkened again, the streetlight equipment and the newly finished apartments had gone as dark as the unfinished buildings. A faint stench of burning insulation wafted on the early morning air.

When the phone rang in Elsa Sachs's Tel Aviv office, the sound somehow louder in the early morning darkness, she felt around her desk, found it, and answered without thinking—just as the lights in her office blinked on again. Outside her window, the city was lit again too. All of Tel Aviv had been dark for just a moment. Thirty miles away, however, outer Jerusalem faced a more permanent blackout.

Over the past few years, Elsa had become the online voice of *Haaretz*, a role she had chosen without much sponsorship but, thankfully, little resistance from the family. Publishing was in her blood: a distant uncle owned the publishing company behind the *Haaretz* newspaper, the liberal beacon of the Tel Aviv intelligentsia. But Elsa had found her niche online and built an active following of nearly a million viewers. That was 10 percent of the overall Israeli population, and 15 percent of the country's Jews. She no longer worried much about the perception of nepotism.

"Hi," came an unfamiliar voice in English. "I turned the lights off in Tel Aviv for a few seconds so you would pay attention to me."

Elsa stared at the phone for a second. The number was as unfamiliar as the voice. "Who the hell is this?"

"My name is not important. I want to tell you a story that happens to be true. I want you to pay attention."

"I don't do stories with anonymous strangers," Elsa said, and hung up.

The lights of Tel Aviv blinked again, this time in a sequence of short and long flashes. Then all went dark for a brief second, and the lights were back on just as quickly.

Elsa's phone rang again.

This time, the voice said, "Do you listen to stories from an anonymous source who can play 'shave and a haircut, two bits' on the Tel Aviv power system?" The mystery woman sang the words a little off-key.

"Okay, you have my attention," Elsa admitted. "Tell your story, then go away. Who did you get to mess with the power system in Tel Aviv?" Now *that* was news her listeners would want to hear.

"I'll tell my story, but pay attention. You were recommended to me by a very reliable source, a big-time name that I will divulge to you in good time.

It's either you or Guzman at the *Jerusalem Post*. And I didn't need any help with the power system. This demonstration of credibility shit will quickly become tiresome."

Elsa sighed but tried to recover her composure. The voice sounded cultured and knowledgeable; perhaps there was something here after all. "Tell me the story," she urged, hoping she didn't seem too eager.

"So, there's this guy, Kufdani, who was recently named chief of all the Bedouin tribes. The tribal leaders want him to right the wrong in the West Bank—the Israeli confiscation of Bedouin land to build apartments for other Israelis—mostly ultra-Orthodox Jews. The Haredim, of course."

Elsa transcribed the caller's words with fluid shorthand. The story was getting better and better.

"Long story short: He's an influential guy, so he snags a meeting with your prime minister to make his case. Travels there on a Moroccan diplomatic passport, with an introduction letter from the king of Morocco. But the prime minister rejects him and instead arranges a meeting with key legislators in Jerusalem—Orthodox Jews and Haredi. When the Bedouin diplomat drives to the meeting just north of Jerusalem, of course those Haredi leaders turn him down too. And on the way out, the Bedouin is drugged and imprisoned in Ktzi'ot, complete with the false backstory that he's a Jewish rapist of Bedouin girls."

Elsa had heard enough. "This is clearly bullshit. Shit like this does not happen in Israel. I don't need to hear another word of—"

The lights blinked.

"Of course you do. Why else would I bother with this conversation?"

Elsa turned back to the computer screen. "And you can prove everything you're telling me?" Despite her journalistic skepticism, the faint whiff of a Pulitzer Prize kept her attention.

"Turn your printer on. I'll feed you things as we talk."

Elsa couldn't resist. "You can't turn my printer on? What's that about?"

There was a sigh. "Yeah, I know. I have trouble with devices that are turned off and not connected. It's hard, as much as I hate to admit that anything is. Turn it on."

Elsa touched the ON button, and the printer came to life. Thirty seconds later, two pages printed. The first was a smiley face with a flickering, pointy tongue printed out in eight colors. The second was a list of names.

"Those are the men who attended the meeting in Jerusalem set up by your prime minister."

"I don't recognize any of these names except Yakov Bernstein," Elsa said, throwing the smiley face in the trash.

"Four are Haredim. The others are Orthodox Jews of a less confrontational sect, but still, they took part and must face scrutiny if not prosecution. I am looking into their personal backgrounds as we speak."

Elsa said, "And the hard part? The matching up of these names with the story you're spinning?"

"I'll leave that to you. You are both an accomplished journalist and a committed Israeli. The facts are there. You just have to connect the dots, and you'll find that it's all true."

Elsa snorted. "If I'm going to go off on this wild goose chase, I'll need more than a list of names. It would be nice to have some confirmation. Are you planning to provide evidence or just hearsay? Blinking the lights is not enough to make me trust you."

"Yeah, good point. I'll email you a voice file of the meeting between the Bedouin and the government people. It lasted just over ninety seconds, but that should do it. But you'll have only two hours before it deletes itself."

Elsa was used to working to a deadline. "I have to ask: What is your stake in this?"

"My stake?"

"There has to be a motive for you. Why are you doing this? Are you Jewish?"

She heard a chuckle. "Another good question. If you must know, I'm in love with the Bedouin in question, and the way he has been treated pisses me off. But expect him to mount his own retaliation. I'm just helping out."

"I'll look into it," Elsa said.

"That's all I can ask. And oh, by the way, the largest West Bank construction site just went dark twenty minutes ago. Irreversible damage. Billions in losses, political bullshit—there's a storm brewing. Now, do I give good story, or what? Get on it, girl."

The lights blinked twice, and the call ended.

Holy shit, this might be real, Elsa thought. *What a fucking scoop.*

She dialed the number of a stringer she often used in Jerusalem. "Get your ass out of bed, and head out to the big apartment project at the West Bank. Take your camera. Get in their faces. If things break right, we're about to have one hell of a story."

She was right.

By full light, men in construction clothing would begin collecting in little groups at that West Bank construction site, watching as some of their colleagues tried to switch on each piece of heavy equipment, one by one.

"Nothing," one man said. "There's nothing. No power anywhere."

"It's spooky," another replied. "If it was just the power company, at least the equipment would start, right?"

None of the lights worked.

No equipment would start.

Puzzled, the men ambled down the slope, away from the finished apartments, shaking their heads.

MOSSAD HEADQUARTERS, TEL AVIV

GUNS EPSTEIN WALKED THROUGH THE DOORS TO HIS OFFICE AT 8:55 a.m., ready for the day. He flipped on the TV, then turned to his computer and his coffee. The TV screen showed a huge construction site surrounded by a cluster of emergency vehicles some with their lights engaged, still flashing. No construction activity was visible.

"No clue," a man in a hard hat was saying to the TV reporter. "My wife saw a flash in the sky, and everything went silent."

Transformer must've blown, Guns thought, sitting down at his desk. *And this is what passes for news these days?*

"No lights, no radio, no vehicles, nothing," the man continued, looking into the camera. "None of the vehicles will start or even turn over. Man, this stuff is fried, fried, fried."

Guns looked up at the television just in time to see a large banner rolling across the bottom of the screen: POWER FAILURE. POSSIBLE BILLIONS IN DAMAGES.

From a power failure? Guns thought, leaning back into his desk chair.

He turned his attention to his computer. Haaretz Online refreshed every morning at 9:00 sharp. Elsa Sachs's articles covered topics that other media outlets ignored, especially in the conservative environment created by the current government. Guns made sure to catch them whenever he could—HOL was big among New York's liberal Jewish crowd. The headline for today's top piece got his attention: ARE WE BEING LIED TO? BEDOUIN LEADER DRUGGED, KIDNAPPED AFTER GOVERNMENT-SPONSORED MEETING.

Reading on, Guns sat up suddenly, as if he'd been struck by lightning. "Oh, shit."

The article outlined the events the Mossad man had been aware of—Cooch's brief meeting with the prime minister, including a description of his diplomatic credentials, and the prime minister's rejection of Cooch's request to sponsor legislation that would return occupied West Bank lands to the Bedouins—but went on to reveal something shocking: Cooch had then met with Defense Minister Bernstein and members of the Orthodox leadership, after which he was drugged, kidnapped, and dumped into the notorious Ktzi'ot Prison in the Negev Desert.

Why? the article asked.

> *Mere arrogance on the part of our Orthodox brethren? Mr. Kufdani was traveling on a Moroccan diplomatic passport with an introductory letter from that nation's king to our prime minister. How is this possible? Is this the way a democratic world power should operate? How long are we going to tolerate this kind of behavior in the name of God?*

"No shit, Dick Tracy," Guns mumbled. "That camel is out of its corral." He scrolled to the next story:

SUSPICIOUS EXPLOSION LEADS TO BILLIONS IN LOSSES IN THE WEST BANK.

> *Reliable sources report that an explosion of some sort destroyed the electrical systems for more than five thousand completed apartments in the disputed West Bank and for all the heavy equipment that toiled at the site. The entire electrical system in the surrounding two*

hundred meters or so has been utterly, irreversibly destroyed—an
unprecedented, unexplained event that sources say were caused by
intentional tampering with the city's power grid.

What happened? Who is responsible? This makes the second
major incident in recent days threatening to disrupt West Bank
politics. When are they going to tell us the truth: that this was not
just an electrical glitch or a blown transformer?

The office phone rang. When Guns picked it up, his boss was already speaking. "Are you reading the Haaretz Online piece?" Pelzer asked.

"Yeah, I read it," he replied. "Time to check the West Bank for EMP damage. But quietly."

"Why quietly?" Pelzer demanded. "That journalist is bluffing. No one has yet managed to control an EMP burst that closely. Unless you know something different . . . ?"

"I don't," Guns said, "but I know someone who might."

Pelzer silently awaited his next words.

"Caitlin O'Connor," he said at last.

"The AI expert? Cuchulain's girlfriend?"

"According to Jerome Masterson, she's an EMP wizard. She helped design the stuff used in the Iran attack. And if we find that the West Bank explosion was some form of EMP, I rather doubt it will be the last."

"And on the Cooch matter? Did we really try to bury him alive in Ktzi'ot?"

"I think their next move will be to try and buy him dead," Guns admitted. "But he's been in there too long for that to work. I think it's about to get ugly, and fast. Let's just let it run its course."

"Agreed. If this is a domestic matter, let's stay out of it. Best-case scenario, we figure this out without rushing into the spotlight."

Guns hoped she was right. "After all, it's out of our purview," he said. "But we should be ready in case this goes onto the international stage. There may be a need for us after all."

"Be careful what you wish for," Pelzer said and hung up the phone.

TANGIER

<u>MONDAY</u>

IT FEELS GOOD TO BE BACK IN BUSINESS, JEROME THOUGHT. HE HAD always loved Cooch's tactics. He didn't relish the image of his old pal sitting on a cell bunk, locked up in a brutal Israeli prison. But Cooch had his Kphone. They were in touch every night after the prison dinner hour, and he was making shit happen. Jerome had complete faith in his friend's plan and his unique ability to bring it to life.

Jerome sat in his office with Caitlin sitting across from him on the couch, listening to the two ex-military men talk about Jerome's trip to Rheinmetall and the new 40mm ammunition being manufactured there. Cooch had instructed him to contract with the company for ten thousand razor rounds and a few thousand other specialties, like the anti-drone stuff that Jerome agreed was very cool.

Cooch had chuckled when Jerome told him about the West Bank attack and the online coverage of Israel's mistreatment of a Bedouin diplomat, singing his own praises about bringing Edgie on board. Now he was outlining the next steps of the plan as Jerome listened intently.

One of the Israeli Bedouins, an old man, would soon be pushing a wheelbarrow full of junk through the streets of the West Bank. Interspersed with the plastic and metal odds and ends were tennis ball–sized "rocks," and the man would possess a rough map instructing him where to throw the rocks. Although some were high-powered explosives, most of the rocks were in fact 3D-printed EMP devices that could be triggered via satellite—which Caitlin had hacked—and managed for range and lethality. The explosion at the West Bank housing development site had been caused by a blast from just such a device.

Jerome enjoyed the thought of the old man smiling as he followed his paper map and scattered forty-three rocks. A nondescript cleaning woman in Tel Aviv would be doing the same thing, although Caitlin didn't think they would need to take that extra step. Janitors and landscape caretakers at various military and commercial institutions carried a few rocks in their things too, prepared to distribute them among attractive industrial targets and naval bases skirting the Mediterranean Sea. Ben Gurion Airport would receive special attention.

Jerome had also ordered five thousand aging, US-built Mk19 weapons from his old company, all to be delivered within one month. Cooch knew he would get a good price and fast delivery because vast stores of the Mk19 weapons had already been made obsolete by a new, US-made, 40mm version with all the latest electronic technologies. And the Rheinmetall ammunition had been ordered to align with Kufdani's PR campaign: only the razor rounds, not the South African ammunition typically used by the Bedouins, would fit in the Mk19's slightly smaller chamber. This would ensure that razor rounds were the exclusive ammunition used during the first ring of violence.

Just slice up the first round of the attacking infantry, Jerome thought. *But if they won't surrender, then we can kill them.*

Emilie had cleaned up the old Mk19 training videos and translated them into Arabic, so they were good to go. Jerome was making another video for deployment in the first ring of upcoming combat, which would be tricky. But hundreds of Palestinians shooting well-aimed 40mm rounds should make the fog of war even foggier for the attacking Israelis. Controlling the process of wounding rather than killing, he knew, was critical. All these videos would become part of Cooch's teaching curriculum at Ktzi'ot.

Meanwhile, Jerome had received permission from Admiral Sino to use not only the South African 40mm weapons, but also three hundred or so of the eight hundred warriors who Jerome had trained—all Bedouin, mostly Moroccan of the Yahia tribe. Well, Brooks had been the one to obtain permission from Admiral Sino, who had been one of the friendly foreign officers selected to attend the US Naval War College, where the two became fast friends. The two continued to bond year after year while sailing the US Atlantic coast on *Old Fashioned*.

Jerome was just happy to be back in business, looked after all things weaponized and not being too concerned about Kufdani Industries' marijuana business or the education successes. There was enough money; that's all he needed to know.

"Tighten up the security around Kufdani Industries," Cooch was saying to Jerome on the Kphone. "Put some extra security around the ships and put an alert staff on the *Hog*." Cooch's special freighter, nicknamed the *Hog*, operated under contract with the US Department of Defense, testing new weapons before they were deployed to the US fleet. The captain, the executive officer, and the senior NCOs were all retired US Navy of Middle Eastern extraction. The crew was Bedouin. It was run as a tight ship—literally—and provided modern anti-aircraft coverage for a broad swath around Tangier.

Jerome agreed it was time to beef up the protection, but it was going to cost them. "We're getting into some serious pocket change here, and I don't want to run short. A billion here, a billion there . . . suddenly it's hard to scrounge up the cash quickly enough."

"Talk to Achmed about money," Cooch instructed. "And keep me posted about how they are treating the Bedouins around Jerusalem." Then he mentioned the Haaretz Online coverage again and how Elsa Sachs might continue to help get their story out, promising to talk to Edgie about her.

He might be onto something there, Jerome thought. Indeed, the Sachs woman might be useful in the near future.

OFFICE OF THE PRIME MINISTER, JERUSALEM

"WHO IS RESPONSIBLE?" SHOUTED THE PRIME MINISTER, HIS FACE reddening.

Yakov Bernstein glared at the other men in the room, who then looked at each other. The IDF man—a general, if Bernstein recalled correctly—stood up to give his report. "It has all of the earmarks of an EMP blast, but of some new sort that is yet unfamiliar to us."

"Unfamiliar?" the prime minister repeated.

"Yes, sir," the general stammered. "Our scientists are working through the evidence onsite. Only four or five people on the planet possess the knowledge required for a venture of this sort. We are checking on their whereabouts and will update you on our findings."

Bernstein sensed his moment. "This travesty has caused trillions of shekels of damage and will mean years lost in our efforts to build new homes for the faithful. We Orthodox will expect the government to make good the losses suffered." He paused as if considering a new idea. "To provide partial recompense, perhaps you feel this would be a good opportunity to move more of the worthless Bedouins and their smelly herds from our land. They no doubt were involved in this heinous crime. We will need to start anew, unfettered."

The prime minister seemed to be weighing his options, and Berstein knew he was inwardly counting the losses—and hoping he could save face among his most loyal constituents by dealing with the pesky Bedouins.

It's as good an excuse as any, Bernstein thought eagerly, striving to maintain his composure.

Turning to face the IDF general, the prime minister spoke at last. "Make a plan, then make it so. Do it fast. Move them someplace else." He dismissed them with a wave.

Bernstein smiled and nodded. Quite a few Israeli businessmen had large financial stakes in these West Bank housing development projects. Making them whole on their losses would be a very lucrative thing for all. *The US will pick up most of the tab anyhow.*

On his way out the door, Bernstein caught the general eyeing him. "We are fairly certain the blast in Jerusalem was the work of a Dr. Caitlin O'Connor, who resides in Tangier at the moment," the general said under his breath. "I will send the details."

Bernstein felt a wave of satisfaction. He would take care of that insolent Bedouin sheik causing chaos at Ktzi'ot, and then take care of the impudent woman behind the attack in the West Bank. Perhaps they could get this behind them quickly. They might even manage to blame it all—the blast, the prison fiasco, everything—on the Moroccans.

KTZI'OT PRISON, SOUTHERN ISRAEL

"GOOD MORNING, EDGIE," KUFDANI SAID. "HOW ARE THINGS GOING WITH our shared objective?"

"Morning? You're back in New York?" Edgie exclaimed. "I need to talk to you."

"Morning time for you, not me. I'm actually in an Israeli prison, in case you hadn't heard. And a fairly notorious one at that," Kufdani said. He and the other prisoners had just enjoyed what could presumably be called dinner.

"Having too much fun to leave?" Edgie joked.

"There's plenty to keep me busy until the time is right. But we can talk. Shoot."

"I don't trust this new phone."

Kufdani sighed. "Edgie, it's true that I sometimes forget things as I age, but I'm quite sure I've already explained that your Kphone is the most secure device on the planet," he scolded. "You can say, send, or receive anything you choose. Securely."

"Fine. I'm still working on influencing the Israeli news establishment. I see Elsa Sachs came through for us with the Haaretz Online coverage, as I thought she might."

"Yes, Edgie. Caitlin and I wanted to thank you for that."

"Caitlin O'Connor?" Edgie said. "Elliot's old girlfriend from Princeton? Blond hair, gorgeous, arrogant, big bazooms, 375 IQ?"

"Yeah, Edgie, that's the one," Kufdani said, rolling his eyes at the drab cell ceiling. "I had Caitlin contact the Sachs woman as you recommended so they could start working together. Those first two articles were a good start."

"Yes, I think Elsa Sachs is a good choice," Edgie agreed. "Now it's time to posture your story for the rest of the world. We have to take this thing bigger, influence upper-class Israel and the European and American diaspora—take your objective up a notch."

Kufdani grinned. "I'm about to do just that."

Baadi gestured frantically from his lookout post at the cell door.

"Gotta run. The guards are coming." Kufdani switched off the Kphone and put it under his mattress.

Two guards in uniform stood in the doorway to his cell. "On your feet, Kufdani," one said. "You're coming with us." The second guard took cuffs from his belt and held them out.

Kufdani stood and walked slowly to the cell door. With a sudden move, he pushed both of them hard at the same time, lifting from his legs and shoving from his extending arms. The two men shot backward, hitting the rail against their low backs, and slowly rolled over it to fall screaming to the concrete floor two stories below.

He went back to his bunk and retrieved his Kphone. "I'm going to visit with Salama," he told Baadi. "When the next guards come for me, tell them you haven't seen me."

LOOKING COMFORTABLE ENOUGH IN HIS CELL SUITE, Salama looked up from his reading and said, "Sheik Kufdani, my good man, what brings you to my humble quarters? Have a seat." One of his attendants brought a steel chair with red and green cushions.

"Two of our keepers just fell over the rail to their death outside my cell,"

Kufdani said. "Of course, I was here with you the whole time, discussing the Quran."

Salama smiled. "Indeed you were. What is it that brought you to their attention?"

"It seems that one of their big housing projects in the West Bank suffered a catastrophic, permanent loss of electrical power. The Israeli government has lost billions—a real pity." Kufdani grinned. "They seemed to think I knew something about the explosion."

Salama turned to an attendant. "Slow them down. Get in their way. Hurt a few more of them. It may be time for another prisoner revolt to protest our treatment here."

The man dashed out of the cell, beaming.

"Has it begun?" Salama asked solemnly.

"It has begun," Kufdani replied. "My cadre training is almost complete." He explained that Bedouin tribes and patriots had been dispatched to the borders of Israel in support of the upcoming action, and were now being trained and dispersed across Israel and Gaza. "Now we have only to await a series of stupid moves by the Israeli government. A week or so would be my estimate."

Salama smiled. "Please tell me you have figured out how to get us out of here."

Kufdani took the Kphone from his pocket and swiped at the touchscreen. The cell doors slammed shut, locked, then reopened. "This prison is an electronic marvel," he said, "and it is now *our* electronic marvel."

He advised Salama to sort through which belongings he wanted to take with him and to alert their fellow inmates that when the time came for their release, the prison administrators should be locked up but not harmed.

"That won't be popular," Salama warned. "Many of our keepers have been unnecessarily harsh and greedy."

Kufdani shook his head. "I'll leave it to you to enforce my directions, but you must do so. Maintaining our image as the oppressed, the unfairly treated, is paramount. We can kill a great many more down the road, if that becomes necessary to get our stolen homes returned."

"It shall be as you request." Salama bowed. "Yet naturally the prison guards may become a bit bruised in the transition."

"Inshallah." Kufdani bowed in return. "Nothing permanent, please."

TANGIER

"I'M TIRED OF WAITING," CAITLIN SAID. SITTING WITH JEROME AND LuAnn in the Kufdani Industries executive dining room, a regular spot for breakfast and catching up, she sipped hot mint tea from a green ceramic cup. "Alex is fat, dumb, and happy over there in jail, while we're just sitting here doing sweet fuck all."

Jerusalem was in a social tizzy over the West Bank attack, and the liberal press was stirring up the intelligentsia in Tel Aviv. There was outrage from the other direction too, and Emilie had picked up some progress in figuring out the source of the explosions. But still there was no offer from the Israelis to negotiate.

"So, what happens next?" LuAnn said. "A schedule of destruction designed to motivate?"

"I was up late last night, figuring out our next steps and looking over the landscape," Caitlin continued. "Our Bedouin rock tossers have given us a great set of options. We could destroy forty strategic sites with the touch of a button, if the need arises. Israel wouldn't deal well if, for instance, we shut down Ben Gurion Airport for six months or so."

Throw in a few closed ports, and the bigoted motherfuckers could starve, Caitlin thought.

"Cooch will be bailing out of there in a few days," Jerome added. "He gave us a list of things to do to help out at the right time. I'm hard at the stuff he needs for the breakout."

"Such as . . . ?" asked LuAnn.

Jerome shrugged. "Instructing the local Bedouin leaders on our plans going forward. They are continuing to train and take positions and will provide excellent support—*when the time comes*." He fixed Caitlin with a stare.

"I'm taking the steps one at a time, as instructed," Caitlin replied indignantly. "I did the West Bank stuff as a one-off, sort of a beta test of the attack concept. Alex said he'd let me know if we should delay things. I didn't get a call, so . . ."

"I know you're impatient to see Cooch again," Jerome said, "but let's not get ahead of things."

Caitlin laughed. "I wanted to see how it ran, see how the Israeli forces reacted, so I was up most of the night working with Emilie to lock things down. We dimmed a few lights in cloud data centers around the world, doing all the calculations to figure things out."

"Alex wants to avoid bloodshed where possible," LuAnn reminded her.

"I know," Caitlin said. "I'm just fucking with the Israelis. Everything is planned except the sequence."

If Israel responded against the local Bedouins in some hurtful way, she had nine different scenarios planned and available to use as retaliation, ranging from nasty to expensive to socially inconvenient. She would monitor things in case she needed to stop or modify a planned action, but otherwise Emilie was programmed to run through them all.

"Of course, I have my usual bag of electronic tricks," Caitlin continued, "but I'd be surprised if they manage to find me or mess with the plan."

Jerome stood and picked up his Kphone from the table. "Well, I have to work for a living, so I'm out of here."

LuAnn excused herself too. "My legal chops have been called upon. I'm looking at the mortgage structure on the West Bank and who owns what."

"Fertile ground," Caitlin acknowledged. "Fine. I'll head to the pool as usual."

LuAnn smiled at her. "I'll come back later. Don't want to interfere with the princess's swim."

IN THE LARGE OFFICE-SLASH-LABORATORY BEYOND Caitlin's bedrooms, deep within the mountain that housed Kufdani Industries, seven large display screens were mounted on the walls, operating from a massive server connected to 12,400 square feet of computer, 3D printing, and network equipment. The 3D printing operation was the most sophisticated outside of the United States, maybe anywhere.

An hour or two's swim every morning cleared Caitlin's head, but it wasn't kind to her hair. She waved the electric dryer over her short, towel-dried tresses as one of the machines, which she had personally modified with Alex's help, was printing through the lens of quantum mechanics, which was useful for EMP projects and Kphones alike. As usual, the NSA was paying for most of it without question.

At a soft knock on the apartment door, Caitlin laid the dryer on the sink and pulled on a polo shirt, followed by blue cotton shorts, thin cotton socks, and hiking shoes. LuAnn stepped into the room, glanced at Caitlin's hair, and said, "You don't miss a lot of swim days, do you?"

"I don't," Caitlin replied.

"I should be in shape like you," LuAnn said. "Are you ever going to need a bra?"

"As soon as I have a couple of kids, maybe, which is never." Caitlin turned to admire her profile in a mirror. Her busty protrusion was a defect, in one sense: it slowed her swimming, although it did attract men. For Caitlin, it was an acceptable trade-off.

Serious swimming was hard work, but having men around helped her forget all that. She needed to get off now and again, or her mind got clogged. Plus, she learned a lot in the process—as long as she chose the right men.

Alex hadn't been crazy about that requirement at first, but he had acquiesced and adapted.

"So, are we going downtown for lunch?" LuAnn asked.

"Yup, and then we'll stop and buy a goat bag or two from my favorite Bedouin grandmother." The vendor wasn't Caitlin's actual grandmother, she explained—just an old lady whose husband died a year or two ago, after which she'd started weaving satchels covered in goat hair. Now the woman was making more than she ever did before, which admittedly wasn't much. "Hey, a woman has to eat," Caitlin said.

"I like it," LuAnn said. "It's commerce responding to a demonstrated need, to the benefit of all." She was planning to gift-wrap one of the goat bags and give it to the First Lady. "That thing will drive Washington society crazy."

"Yeah, I guess," Caitlin said, seeing only the crushing poverty that had led the Bedouin woman to create such bags, and not the allure of scarcity and perceived compassion that would lead DC society women to purchase them.

She walked to the electronic teapot and poured a cup of mint tea, then raised her eyebrows at LuAnn.

LuAnn smiled. "No, thanks. I don't want any more tea. What I want is to understand what is going on in Israel." Brooks and LuAnn had signed on to Alex's project in order to help the Bedouins, but so far, all that had happened was a bunch of apartments blowing up. "You and Alex pushed the plan. I just want to be sure that plan is working."

"Alex pushed the plan on principle," Caitlin corrected her. "I just thought it would be interesting to engage the Israeli brain trust on such a fundamental issue."

"And now?" LuAnn said.

Caitlin leaned back in her chair and gazed at the ceiling, sighing. "I don't really have another project right now. The education push is my passion, and it's going well with the Berbers and now the Bedouin."

Emilie had told her to expect excellent scores in the pan-European standardized achievement tests. Even with a major success under their belt, however, getting politicians to worry about educating their nation's young felt nearly impossible.

Probably because kids don't vote, said Caitlin's inner cynic.

"So you're just trying to fend off the boredom?" LuAnn asked.

Caitlin nodded. "I've already smuggled into Israel everything I need to do whatever I choose. Alex and I defined and discussed the potential target list. Emilie is building files that I'm not sure we'll ever need."

"And I'm researching the West Bank financing stuff to see how we should play things down the road, if indeed those days come."

"But will they?" Caitlin said, her voice rising. "We're trying to make the Israelis change their behavior toward their Bedouin citizens. There should be chatter on the national security front there. There should be more political concern in the West Bank about what happened. If the Israeli government doesn't put a stop to it, they're facing vast damages and expenses. Israeli insurance companies have already seen several billion dollars go down the tube over what we've done. And yet Emilie isn't picking up anything!"

"Get a grip, Caitlin," LuAnn said.

"How can I? There's nothing of note on their networks, except some squabbling over Orthodox politics and how much of the West Bank replacement costs will be paid by the Israeli government with money from the US. There's still no discussion of politics involving how to actually fix the West Bank problem."

LuAnn shrugged. "Maybe you just haven't heard it yet. No one has time to listen to a whole country's chatter every day."

Caitlin sighed. Explaining how everything works was exhausting. *We broke them!* she wanted to shout. *We know everything they know. We know everything everybody knows! And we can change their records to say whatever we need them to say.*

"Yeah, you're right," Caitlin said. It was easier just to agree. "I have Emilie sort out the day's messaging for me. Mostly I trust her to look for things that interest me, and I can ask her to ramp up or down on granularity."

"What about encrypted messaging?"

Oh, LuAnn! So naïve.

"I broke Israel's encryption ten years ago. Since then, it's mostly a matter of how much information the NSA wants to share."

"How many people know you've broken Israel's encryption?" LuAnn asked. "That is enormously valuable news—a priceless secret."

"Not really. Hell, I broke *every* country's encryption ten years ago." *China was hard,* she thought. *Korea too. They've got some really smart people over there—devious, crafty little fuckers.* "We know everything there is to know about every computer system in the world that is hooked up to the internet. Want to know what the Chinese are telling the Russians about the Israelis? Emilie sorts it all out."

"You taught Emilie how to break any encryption anywhere?" LuAnn asked.

"Yeah, sort of," Caitlin said. She had taught the software to do quantum mechanics—really hard, but a total blast. After five years of that, she showed Emilie how to break the encryption. Emilie had already spent twelve years learning how to process vast gobs of data and sort through it for trends and shit like that. "Decryption is just a first step. We have too much data to return to normal—ever."

"And why am I one of the few with this knowledge of the futility of encryption?"

Caitlin just looked at her. "Because you're one of us. There are no secrets among the five of us, just things that aren't talked about."

"Well," LuAnn said, "let's talk about going into town for some lunch and some more mint tea—from a real tea house this time." She winked.

Caitlin grinned and put her teacup on the counter. "Tang will want to come along with us on security detail." She knew he would be standing or squatting by the front entrance of the complex, waiting for her. "Maybe he'll want to buy a goat bag too."

KTZI'OT PRISON, SOUTHERN ISRAEL

"WE NEED TO TALK ABOUT MOVING UP THE SCHEDULE," KUFDANI SAID into his Kphone. Several days had passed since their little demonstration in the West Bank. Since then, he'd been talking to Jerome and Edgie every evening after dinner, when the whole prison was locked down for the night.

"Fuck your schedule, Cooch!" Jerome replied. "My piece is easy: I drive trucks from the port to someplace well inside Egypt. I build airports. I order weapons and ammunition. Worry about your own part of the plan."

"Yes," Kufdani said, "but what about where our parts intersect? We need to figure out how to manage an unruly bunch of escaped Palestinian prisoners in the desert."

"Uh-huh. If, by chance, they wander off in the wrong direction and massacre three thousand Israeli civilians, that's a bit of a problem."

"Actually, I'm *sure* some are going to wander off." Kufdani chuckled. "These guys have anger issues."

"Cut to the chase, Cooch."

"We're going to need enough water and dried food for six thousand or so men, and someone to show them the way to Egypt—on foot. We're also going to need about fifteen hours to make it work."

"So we'll need to block the emergency vehicles, distract the reaction forces, and have Caitlin fuck up their communications," Jerome confirmed.

"Will it be a problem, do you think?"

Jerome scoffed. "I've got a hundred or so Egyptian Bedouins here with trucks and pack animals, for crying out loud! All looking to be useful to Sheik Kufdani. I'll make it work."

"Excellent. Keep the trucks in Egypt till we move. Rely on the pack animals. Plan for Saturday," Kufdani said.

"So soon? Goddammit, Cooch, you're ahead of the game. Don't you have anything else to do in there?"

"The nightlife is a bit limited—rather tiresome, actually," Kufdani said. "So I spend my time figuring out where I might have missed a chance."

"A chance to do what?"

"To shove a log up their collective ass."

THAT AFTERNOON, KUFDANI VISITED WITH Salama as he did most afternoons, talking through the early plans for engaging Israel. Hot tea was quickly poured. Each day, as he entered Salama's cell, an attendant brought the chair with red and green cushions, which seemed to have been selected just for him: red and green were Morocco's colors.

Nice touch, Kufdani thought. *He thinks I'm a big deal.*

Indeed, Salama had taken to calling him by a new name, if only in private: *Mahdi*. Translated from Arabic as "guided one," the Mahdi was understood to be a messiah-type figure offering deliverance, restoring justice and the true religion for a short utopian time before the end of the world. Kufdani knew of nothing that particularly identified him as the Mahdi, and in fact was convinced he was no such person—nor did he have any indication that any such man was destined to exist. But given what he was up against, the legend could do no harm.

Salama gazed at Kufdani and said, "We should figure out what to do about Hamas. They control Gaza. I was once a senior member of Hamas leadership, but after more than a decade in here things have changed. The man currently in charge of Gaza activities for Hamas was once a prisoner here, but was released on a prisoner exchange. Once in Gaza, I can pave the way but you will need to meet with him."

Kufdani nodded. "Good," he said. "I look forward to it." *I hope I don't have to kill him.* "I have been wondering about how to deal with them. One of the tasks of our prison leadership is to train Hamas fighters in the use of the Mk19. They won't be happy that it won't kill Israelis."

In their discussions over tea, one problem stood out for Salama: Israel controlled the electricity, water supply, and shoreline ports for all of the Gaza Strip and most of the West Bank. Kufdani wanted the Israeli population just outraged enough to attack the Palestinians and Bedouins in Gaza—but not so much that they would support the authorities moving to shut off access of essential supplies to Palestine. At least not yet.

In the meantime, one of Salama's chosen leaders was proctoring as Emilie taught four hours of classes daily through the Kphone, learning and helping and getting better at it each day. Emilie figured out the pace of learning for each student, and the prisoners were responding positively. Though he knew Emilie had no soul, Kufdani could not resist praising her for a job well done.

"And what is the news today?" Salama said, sipping his tea. "Things go well? Progress?"

"Progress," Kufdani replied. "We will be departing here soon. We have three days. Tell those you trust to get their things together. Deal with any leaks. Obedience to my command, given through you, is the key to our success."

"And our keepers?" Salama said.

"We'll lock them in cells, unharmed. We'll need the press on our side. The news will be late getting out, as the internet will be down during our escape. But eventually, the world will see how we handled this moment. We can't afford revenge. I want us to look like good guys, at least for now."

"What about transportation? We're a long way into the Negev."

"We'll walk," Kufdani said. "Plan for a trek of about sixty miles. Trucks won't work either after the blast, except for one we will provide to you, and maybe a few more for the weak and infirm among us. You should plan to go where you choose, but don't drive northeast. Food and water will await us along the path to the south, to Egypt." Jerome was going to have the time of his life setting this all up.

"And you?" Salama said.

"I'll stay here and wait for them to come for us." *I probably won't have time to rip Yakov Bernstein's head off and piss down the stump, but it's on my list.* "I think I'll spend a little time doing interviews in Tel Aviv."

Salama smiled. "And quite interesting interviews they should be. But be careful."

"As always," Kufdani laughed. Edgie was excited about the upcoming challenge. At his recommendation, Caitlin had secured an interview with Sachs for Saturday night.

Now Kufdani just had to figure out how to get himself there.

TANGIER

AS CAITLIN HAD PREDICTED, TANG WAS SITTING ON HIS HEELS BY THE front entrance, dressed in his trademark white robe, as she and LuAnn exited the complex. At their approach, he rose, almost floated, to his feet, with a small smile and a bow. Tang didn't make small talk.

"Good afternoon, Tang," the women said simultaneously. They started down the short cobblestone street that led to the casbah section of town, the ancient center of Tangier, full of shops and stalls where vendors sold food and other products to residents, tourists, and Kufdani employees alike. Tang followed several feet behind, alert as ever.

Near a butcher shop that Caitlin often frequented, several men emerged from the shadows and split into two groups, moving toward them. The women continued talking, oblivious to the danger. Tang moved on a path to silently intercept the threat.

Sensing movement behind him, he ducked and turned to see a man coming at him with a drawn knife held low and in front, its dirty blade targeting his stomach with a serrated edge seeking to disembowel him. A second man was pulling a soiled cotton hood from his belt.

Tang felt time slow.

He moved as he had moved a thousand times before, spinning from his core to bump the moving knife hand with his left hand, pushing it from its lethal path. As the blade whistled past his torso, Tang uncoiled his body and drove the heel of his right hand up and into the nose of the assailant. The click was audible when the nose bone broke, just before it slid into the man's brain.

Tang settled his balance and turned to the second man, who was stunned by his rapid response to the attack—but not as stunned as he was an instant later, when Tang's left foot drove into his throat, crushing the larynx and collapsing the windpipe.

Recovering from the kick, Tang sensed movement again and spun to face a third man. Sliding to the ground, he traversed the distance between them with a move he called the Crab. Just as he reached his target, he heard the *phut* of a silenced shot from a low-caliber weapon.

A hammer seemed to slam his chest.

"Tang!" he heard Caitlin yell.

Someone had grabbed Caitlin from behind and tried to slip a hood over her head. A twinge of pride washed past the pain for Tang as he saw her instincts kick in: She backed into the man, driving an elbow into his ribs, then again. Reaching back over her head with both arms, she grasped his face and drove two thumbnails where she thought his eyes would be. A scream and a curse told Tang that she was close. A year or two of training with him had been valuable.

Next to Caitlin, Tang saw that LuAnn, too, was encircled from behind in big arms that attempted to lift her. But she was married to a paranoid ex-SEAL, he knew. So it came as no surprise when LuAnn dropped her chin and snapped her head back, again and again, into the face of the man holding her. With a groan, the man lowered his captive to her feet but kept her confined in his constraining hug. The arms finally loosened when she stomped her boot heel into his right instep; she pushed free and fell to one knee, looking over her shoulder and preparing to come to her feet and run.

Struggling to get up, Tang saw a second man move suddenly to face Caitlin, burly and bearded, holding something in his fist as it swung toward her. She cried out, but the shock of the blow stunned her into silence before a deep punch to the stomach put her down. The big, Slavic-looking man reached for her and opened his mouth to speak, but a small red hole appeared on his forehead.

Reports of gunfire filled the air.

Ten feet away, another man was pointing a long, skinny rod at Tang—the silencer at the end of a pistol, with noiseless flame shooting from it. Tang struggled again to come to his feet, his eyes still fixed on the third man, his target, when he saw bright red blossoming in the middle of the man's chest. The man collapsed backward.

And then Tang, too, was collapsing to the stone pavement, a second rose of red spreading at the center of his white robe.

TANGIER

JEROME EASED INTO HIS DESK CHAIR AND LEANED BACK, SMILING AND placing his hands behind his head. Just back from the shower after his run, he was pleased to see that his monitors were all functioning, and everything was in the green.

Feeling pretty good, he ventured.

Then a red light flashed at Monitor Two, and a buzzer sounded.

Spoke too soon.

Jerome jerked his head toward the monitor, which looked out on the street below Kufdani Industries' main entrance. Caitlin and LuAnn were surrounded by men in dark clothing, whose hands and arms held them in various states of violence. Tang was crumpling to the stone pavement, his white robe stained red. Two men twitched at his feet, their feet and hands spasming as the three died together.

A man in a green hat, dressed like the others, seemed to be shouting orders.

Jerome reached up to the flashing red light, flipped up a hinged cover beside it, and drove his thumb into the big red button. The alert sounded through the klaxon and sent electronic alerts throughout the Kufdani facility for all security personnel to hurry to their combat stations.

The signal also alerted the computer center to stop all maintenance and be prepared to receive and provide combat data, including electronic updates of time, humidity, and temperature targeted to the rifle scopes of the guards on station. Medical facilities powered up imaging equipment and prepared for any wounded combatants and civilians to arrive.

Jerome had retained the organizational structure he'd learned in the US Marine Corps. His fire teams and its leadership had letter designations: Alpha through Kilo. Staff functions were numbered: S-1 for personnel, S-2 for intelligence, S-3 for operations.

He picked up his handset. "Alpha, put down the attackers—feet first if you don't have a decent shot. Delta, shoot green-hat runner: right elbow, left knee."

Jerome heard the pop from the two rounds being fired. Delta and Echo, former members of British Special Air Services, used the same rifle as the security duty shooters, who preferred a 55g bullet with an e-tip designed to expand on impact—for killing coyotes, deer, and other varmints, including humans. But Delta and Echo used a very low drag match 40g bullet that flew at 3,500 feet per second and was shaped for accuracy, not killing. The Varmageddon rifle from Nosler in Oregon shot a .22-caliber target round that would pass right through an elbow or knee without expanding much. The speed-driven force of the impact would largely destroy the targeted joint but keep the target alive.

"S-3, alert the hospital of incoming," Jerome continued, "and roll the medics to the front entrance. Women plus Asian man only. Priority one. Secondary support for wounded Zulu with the green hat. I want him alive and awake for questioning."

Jerome had long ago made a bet: that greatly reduced recoil from the 22 Nosler ammunition would vastly improve combat accuracy without meaningfully reducing lethality. When a shooter fired a round, the reaction to the bullet leaving the barrel was felt as recoil, pushing the rifle back into the shoulder of the shooter and lifting the gunsights up and to the side, away from the target. The trick was to bring it back on target quickly. He had trained his shooters to manage the 22 Nosler recoil such that an aimed shot could be fired within a four-inch group every three seconds. The range and wind didn't matter within three hundred yards or so: the bullet's path was so flat and so fast that any error was subsumed by the margin of error provided by a center body shot. Shooting practice was usually done with multiple targets within one hundred yards—a far larger area than his teams were working with right now.

"S-2, alert Emilie and direct her attention at the attack: who, why, conclusions. Get wound wagons and bring to company-run morgue—autopsies ASAP, collect fluids, particulars to follow."

Jerome glanced at the monitors as the fire teams carried out his orders. Within a minute, four men around Caitlin and LuAnn were down and still, with five other men down just beyond them. LuAnn was standing stock-still in the middle of the carnage.

"Nine now dead in the main group," Jerome reported to his intelligence officer. "Notify the Defense Ministry and our army units that the Kingdom may be under assault. Inform the local police and tell them to stay away for now. Tell our local NSA contact that Dr. O'Connor was hit, condition unknown—action underway, recording available.

"And send two men ASAP to recover Ms. Clemens. Bring her here if she's willing, or wherever she wants to go, but don't leave her alone. Watch for shock."

Within one hundred seconds, it was all over.

The green-hatted man was lying still on the cobbled street. Jerome hoped someone had not killed him yet.

"Fuck," Jerome muttered. Up until now, he had been having a good day.

NEGEV DESERT, SOUTH OF BEERSHEBA

NOT LONG AFTER MIDNIGHT, ON A DESERT RISE A MILE OR SO SOUTH of Beersheba—the largest city in the Negev, built on an ancient biblical site—four Bedouin men ripped the cover from a South African–made, belt-fed 40mm weapon launcher mounted to the bed of an old white Toyota pickup. Smuggled into Israel weeks earlier, it had been inspected and re-inspected for function. For days, the men and their followers had held continual practice sessions on aiming and firing the 40mm, referring to videos on a Kphone supplied to them by Sheik Kufdani.

Below the rise, a large truck was jackknifed across Route 40, the main north–south highway in the Negev. Traffic backed up behind it, yet when emergency vehicles converged on the site, preparing to clear the highway, there was no sign of either the driver or the keys.

At about the same time, the notorious, high-security Gilboa Prison in northern Israel malfunctioned, and the cell blocks holding the women and minors opened unexpectedly. As it was Shabbat, the Jewish sabbath that ran from Friday evening until Saturday evening, few of the Orthodox prison guards were on duty. On this day of rest and reflection, if simply riding in a car and using a telephone were forms of forbidden *melakhah*, caging and brutalizing rebellious Muslims surely would not pass muster. So when the alarms sounded at that early morning hour, the assigned police and IDF watch stations came to life, activating recall orders for the men and equipment that would be required to respond adequately to the interruption at Gilboa prison.

Phone trees were activated, with each initial contact alerting three other guards, each of whom then contacted three more, in order to recall as much manpower as possible. Radios were active with notification to higher authorities of yet another imminent prison break at Gilboa.

Then the wiring at a large, nearby power station melted, thanks to an EMP "rock" placed by a Bedouin mailman several days earlier.

Much of Israel, including the communications systems used for an armed response to prison breaks, blacked out. The sleeping population noticed little change yet, but the blackout made the recall of prison guards impossible.

Knowing none of this, but placing trust in their leader, the men on the old white Toyota sighted their South African–built weapons and shot their first 40mm razor rounds at the site: the initial test of the Kufdani design.

Round after round, tens of thousands of sharp, spinning shrapnel pieces woven from scored wire, coiled around the charge, drove down from the explosion point at ten feet over the calculated targets. The exploded pieces sliced the emergency workers and onlookers, causing heavy bleeding but seldom wounds that required immediate attention.

Cars began to flee the site, heading west. Despite the late hour, there were enough cars to block all service roads for Beersheba's main industrial park and tie up the secondary roads. As the news spread, lights began to wink on in the industrial park. Ambulances couldn't reach the wreckage but stopped to treat those who made it out of the impact zone. Nothing moved south.

After the fifteenth razor round, the Bedouins picked up three green-tipped EMP rounds from the bed of the Toyota and fired them carefully across the target zone—one, two, three—aiming at one building per round to ensure the blast covered as much area as possible, with a bias toward the industrial park. When they were done, every car and piece of equipment below was utterly ruined. Neither the machinery nor the wiring and lighting system for the industrial park would ever work again.

Then the four men wrapped the 40mm again in a tarp and departed. As they drove south, they unwrapped a box of a dozen mottled brown rocks, compliments of Caitlin O'Connor, and threw one beside the road every half mile. Pursuit could be discouraged.

Moments later, every last cell door at the large, troubled Ktzi'ot Prison in southern Israel unlocked and swung slightly ajar. The waiting inmates began making their way to understaffed guard chambers, where they achieved near-total surprise. Salama-appointed supervisors secured the guards in separate cells, most of them beaten badly but otherwise unharmed. Those doors were wired shut in the old-fashioned way. Keys were found, and the weapons locker was emptied. One guard managed to set off an alarm that sounded within the prison, but it was too late.

Twenty minutes later, the lights went out, and the siren ceased. Every electrical circuit from Ktzi'ot northward, beyond Beersheba, went kaput, with no hope of restoration.

The Israeli air traffic control system was inoperative. Local air support was unresponsive. Israeli forces in Beersheba mobilized and attempted to organize, but without communication capabilities, little was accomplished.

Meanwhile, Ktzi'ot inmates formed into teams as planned and—except for a few who took their weapons from the prison armory and headed east, seeking loot and revenge—began to move west toward Egypt. Small fires were lit. The path to Egypt was clear. Bedouin men and women, some of them armed, provided water, dry snacks, and first aid as they began the long walk.

Eighty miles away, Jerome continued to supervise the rapid installation of pierced steel planking in a flat field a few miles over the Egyptian border. He had planned for a five-thousand-foot runway to accept the C-130 aircraft soon to be en route with supplies, arms, and ammunition. If they stayed in Egyptian airspace, things were likely to be uninterrupted.

Jerome chuckled at the thought that nobody could really see him from Israel. They were busy dealing with a parade of escaped Palestinian prisoners, north and south—and Caitlin.

Caitlin was chuckling too, through the pain of a broken jaw, a bruised face, and several missing teeth. She sat in her Tangier office, playing with the controls in front of her and watching the Israeli electronics systems fail, one by one. The IDF had managed to get a few drones in the air. Emilie, with unmatched expertise, curated the images of pure chaos.

Overlaid by the panicked chatter from the drones' controllers, they only added to Caitlin's mirth.

KTZI'OT PRISON, SOUTHERN ISRAEL

"TO THINK I ALMOST HAD YOU KILLED," SALAMA SAID, BRIEFLY EMBRACING Kufdani as he supervised the old Palestinian's imminent departure from Ktzi'ot. A truck, acquired by local Bedouins and recently wrapped in EMP shielding, had been unwrapped and brought to the prison's main gate.

"You're about to become the greatest leader in Palestine, greater even than you believe," Kufdani promised.

"Like a son I love you." Salama waved as the truck pulled away. "May fortune smile on you. Let me know when you need me. I shall arrange a meeting for you with Hamas."

Kufdani had no doubt of it: Yousef Salama would be useful in the future, no matter if things went bad today. It was his time. Kufdani had plans other than personal fame or glory. Consolidation to a single leader in Palestine would be necessary going forward. *He will be good for Palestine,* Kufdani thought.

He walked to the warden's office, where the only useful light was from his Kphone, and sat back in the chair to send an email that bounced from a satellite: *Guns, come get me. I'm in Ktzi'ot.*

The call from Guns Epstein came quickly. "Okay, you've got everyone's attention," he said. "I'll bring a chopper, if that works—and if you promise not to kill its electronics. Or me."

"I'll be in the warden's office. Bring me some clothes. I've got a busy schedule, but I'll make time."

"I won't ask how you got your Kphone into Ktzi'ot."

"And I won't ask what the hell you were thinking, attacking Caitlin O'Connor," Kufdani said, and he slammed the Kphone down on the warden's desk.

He had managed to calm down somewhat since Jerome rang a few days earlier on his Kphone. "I'm sorry, Cooch. Caitlin has been attacked," Jerome had said quietly.

"What the fuck!" Kufdani had come off his bunk in a puff of smoke: sitting, then suddenly standing, his legs slightly spread and flexed. His face had begun to transform into that reptilian mask, and he breathed loudly through his nose. Baadi dove for the corner.

"In Tangier, outside HQ," Jerome had continued. "She was hurt, but it's not life-threatening. LuAnn got bruised up. And, Cooch . . . Tang was killed."

"Jesus Christ, Jerome," Kufdani snapped. "Who the hell is good enough to kill Tang? What the hell happened? They dared to attack Caitlin? Where were you?"

"I was a minute and forty seconds late to the game," Jerome had confessed. "Tang had already killed two. He was shot by a third. LuAnn needed stitches on the back of her head from headbutting her attacker. Your security people popped the main attackers even before the alert was sounded."

"How many Zulus dead? Were the survivors questioned? Any ID on perps?"

"Fifty-six total dead—eleven leaders, forty-five thugs. No known survivors. Collateral damage: one truck driver."

"And Caitlin?"

Jerome had paused. "She's gonna be okay, Cooch. I'm sorry. Her face was broken up pretty badly after she hurt the guy attacking her. He hit her in the face with something—a gun, maybe, or brass knuckles. Knocked out a bunch of her teeth and ripped up the skin. We've got the best medical people on their way from the US."

Oh, Bernstein. I can't just kill you anymore, Kufdani had thought then, seething in the darkness of his cell. *I'm going to have to humiliate you. We will keep you alive so we can watch you suffer.*

Now, picking up the Kphone from the warden's desk, he went back to rereading *The Art of War*—Sun Tzu's version this time. Two hours later, when the *flack-flack* of a helicopter came wafting through the warden's open office window, he smiled and marked his place in the book. Putting the Kphone back down, he started thinking about how he wanted this operation to end.

The cost of it ending now or in the future is a price someone will have to pay, he thought. *But the gap between the timing and cost of the two pieces could turn out to be vast.*

"Cooch, are you up there?" Guns yelled from outside the building as the helicopter shut down.

Kufdani was at the window in three strides. "You were expecting someone else?" Guns was alone, but he had brought protection for the chopper: men in body armor deployed around it, holding short-barreled Uzis.

Guns chugged up the stairs and, reaching the warden's office, stuck out his hand. His biceps stretched the short-sleeved canvas shirt he wore. "First things first: to my knowledge, Mossad had nothing to do with the attack on Caitlin."

"Tell me that you tried to get me out of here," Kufdani said, shaking Guns's outstretched hand and then pointing to a chair beyond the desk.

"I tried," Guns said. "I was told by Shin Bet that it was no business of Mossad. The prime minister chose not to intervene. I tried your Kphone— there was no answer. My hands were tied! So I called Jerome and told him about it."

"Water under the bridge," Kufdani said. "So, where are we? Has anything fundamentally changed?"

"Sure: you have Sheila's attention now. She would like to 'work something out.'"

"What's your guess?"

"I think meeting with you is her idea of a first step. Sheila wants to intervene with the prime minister on your behalf."

"I'm beginning to think your new prime minister is in my way. Perhaps he should be voted out—or booted out." Kufdani gave a soft laugh. "I'm not sure I need her 'intervention,' but I'll meet with Sheila."

"What's your plan then, Cooch? Give me some guidance," Guns urged him. "Tell me how *you* think I should play this, and why."

"My guidance for you is simple and clear," Kufdani said. "Do what will be best for Israel over the next ten years. Not five years—ten. Think through the extra time."

"And?"

Kufdani just looked at him. "Here is the tactical situation, the way I see it. It's complicated by the political situation, of course."

First, Israel had a land mass and population nearly identical to New Jersey's—nine million people—of whom 6.3 million were Jews. Meanwhile, there were 1.9 billion Muslims in the world, including more than 90 million in neighboring Egypt alone.

"That's a mismatch ripe for exploitation," Kufdani pointed out.

Second, Israel's power flowed from its collective intellect and accomplishment. Effective and coordinated communications, command, and control brought enormous force multiplication to the nation's very competent military, which was arguably the best in the Middle East. But Israel's arrogance in the face of these facts, Kufdani warned, was the crux of the problem.

"You have decided to create a theocracy that ignores the rights of its citizens," he said. "This theocracy is led by Orthodox Haredi, who arose as a group only in the nineteenth century, for crying out loud, and who add little or nothing to Israel's economic mix."

Further, most of the productive leadership in the Jewish diaspora and the Israeli intellectual elite had little conviction about the Orthodox situation and the seizing of West Bank properties. Kufdani planned to shake that conviction further, with some selective discomfort.

"So, you can expect me to change the rules of engagement and the battlefield in my favor," Kufdani admitted. "If a way can be found to engage Israel against Islam, man to man, it would be slaughter—and the end of Israel."

Guns remained silent.

"Now, let me change clothes, and we'll get out of this place. It holds bad memories for me." Kufdani felt satisfied with his explanation, thinking he'd been rather sporting about things. "Hopefully Sheila can offer a bit more in the way of hospitality."

MOSSAD HEADQUARTERS, TEL AVIV

SHEILA PELZER STUDIED THE LARGE MAN AS HE ENTERED HER OFFICE. Epstein had said he was important, smart, and connected. He was appearing more so by the hour. At the moment, however, his hair was still damp from the shower. He wore a loose, open-neck, white cotton shirt over black cotton trousers, belted at the waist. Cheap sandals were strapped to his feet.

Pelzer stood as he came close, almost recoiling at his closed face; it oozed hostility. A large, veined and corded neck stuck out above the rumpled collar. The eyes were flat, observing, catlike, hooded by thick flesh on either side. A lumpy scar wandered down from his left eye to his jawline.

He is big, she thought, *and he has the eyes of a feral cat.*

"Mr. Cuchulain." Pelzer extended her hand. "It's nice to finally meet you. I've heard so much about you over the years."

The large man smiled, an evil countenance coming to his face as he took her hand. "At the moment, madam, I prefer Kufdani, my Bedouin name," he said with icy graciousness. "And I have read about you, Madame Pelzer. It is unfortunate that we meet in such ugly circumstances."

"Indeed, Mr. Kufdani," Pelzer said, indicating a chair across from her desk. "Please, take a seat. You must accept my apology, and that of the state of Israel, for the way you were treated. It was dreadful, simply dreadful."

"I'm happy to accept your apology, madam," Kufdani said, sitting down to face her. "And if your prime minister apologizes personally for the involvement of the state of Israel in my difficulties, I'm happy to accept that as well. There are, of course, more urgent issues that must be considered."

Oh, dear, Pelzer thought.

"Our prime minister is hoping you would accept his apology by proxy, with me as his representative. The damage caused by the incident in the West Bank has made him very busy—and quite angry." She paused, seeking the courage to hold his iron gaze. "I must congratulate your people on a well-planned operation, but I have advised the prime minister that this kind of attack is unlikely to happen again—a one-off effort."

Kufdani glanced at Epstein, who was gazing at the blank wall, expressionless. "What I would accept," he said, "is the restoration of lands illegally seized from Israeli citizens, based on their religion, for the benefit of other Israeli citizens, based on *their* religion. So long as that happens, I'm pleased to accept your prime minister's apology as you offer it."

Pelzer looked at him over her glasses. "Let's stop beating around the bush, Mr. Kufdani."

Kufdani grimaced. "Give the land back, and we'll drop our nascent efforts to convince the world that Israel is a racist theocracy, unworthy of exceptional Middle Eastern support from the United States or anyone else."

"Do you think your 'nascent efforts' are sufficiently well funded to have a lasting impact?"

"I do," Kufdani said.

Pelzer took her chance. "Well then, would you be willing to tell me more?"

Kufdani shrugged. "Telling you won't interfere with anything. We plan to tell the world what we are doing in great detail. I'll just be giving you an early view."

"To what end?"

"To bring pressure to resolve this situation before it gets uglier. This is about Islam against a sovereign theocracy created by economic slugs and thugs. I am about to make that an international issue. The lands of the West

Bank will resolve their ownership in the midst of a larger engagement. I shall try to make that engagement an existential one for Israel. A standing Mossad in the rubble would be good, don't you think?"

Pelzer had to agree. She had long harbored the sense that Israel's best interests would be served by reining in its West Bank activities and begin returning the land to the Bedouins. Things were spinning out of control, and now—with this Kufdani in the picture—they faced the prospect of the Palestinians joining forces with the Bedouins.

At least the United States hadn't weighed in yet. But what if she was wrong about the one-off? What if there were more Jerusalem bombing incidents to come?

That will drive our leader crazy.

"And why would the prime minister do something as radical as simply giving the land back?" she asked. "Right or wrong, it's about politics. He answers to his voting base."

"Indeed, it is about politics," Kufdani agreed. "The objective of the Bedouin effort is to destroy the will of the prime minister, to break his resistance to fixing this illegal and unjust situation. If it is a matter of votes, then we will change the voting environment."

"Does your arrogance know no bounds, Mr. Kufdani?"

Kufdani looked at her with those flat, emotionless eyes. "The arrogance of the Israeli nation dwarfs any other," he spat. "You justify stealing our land simply because we are not Jewish, and yet your disdain prevents you from seeing the truth. Think about numbers—about history and common sense."

"How noble you are," Sheila said, "with your grand paths of destroying the will to resist! But the danger of pursuing this path is exceptional. The Israeli Bedouins have no arms and no organization to accomplish this noble objective of yours. You've had your little West Bank attack to demonstrate Bedouin unhappiness, and in response our government is forcibly moving the Bedouins again. What is your planned encore?"

"You can be sure we have planned further demonstrations of Bedouin unhappiness over our mistreatment. All Bedouin tribes across the Middle

East find their tribal honor violated and have selected me to resolve the issue with your government." He paused and cocked his head, unsettling Pelzer with his stare. "Of course, you can kill all one hundred thousand Israeli Bedouins. At that point, there will still be nine hundred thousand Bedouins screaming for retribution across the Middle East, but this is not just a matter of Bedouin Israeli citizens. A billion or two Muslims around the world will also be enraged—and coming for the six million of you."

Pelzer sighed. "We don't seem to be making progress in our discussion. It seems that I don't understand you, and I probably should."

Kufdani nodded at Epstein. "*He* understands me. He knows you shouldn't lose sight of me as this goes on. For eight years, I was on the sharp end of US power. I saw how it worked around the world. Since then, I've had more than a decade to study war and the people who wage it. Israel faces Thucydides Trap; your military edge will become moot within ten years because it is based on technology, and the world is quickly catching up. Israel's technological dominance fades more and more every day. Your edge is becoming dull."

He paused, giving Pelzer a look that was both thoughtful and penetrating. It made her rather uncomfortable.

Those eyes again.

"We have considered 'the danger of pursuing this path,' as you say," he continued, "and we find it acceptable. I have personally experienced the tactics of the Israeli Haredi opposition. It was unpleasant, but here I am. We will stand for no more."

"And we will identify and punish those responsible for your incarceration," Pelzer insisted.

"Please don't bother. It would just make it harder for me to find them and balance the ledger," Kufdani said. "Perhaps instead you could prosecute those Orthodox creatures near the West Bank who attack Bedouin children on their way to primary school. That would be a start to resolving things."

"Perhaps we should just make you go away and make the trouble you bring go away."

"Perhaps you should," Kufdani said. "But allow me a moment of transparency. You quarrel with a Bedouin tribe . . . mine. My flock is Islam, and we care about injustice to Muslims. I have tried to arrange things and direct my flock so that in case I disappear, the problem will escalate, not go away. The longer Israel fails to redress the West Bank situation, the more our efforts will engage the entire Muslim world in this ugliness and your demeaning treatment, with or without me."

"And if things get uglier and you are gone, with whom should we negotiate?" Pelzer asked.

"Caitlin O'Connor would be a good place to start. She's not Bedouin, but she takes a beating and comes back stronger than ever—as you well know," he growled.

"Mr. Kufdani, I don't—"

"And as you can see, you are well behind our technology curve." Kufdani chuckled as he stood and headed for the door. "Brace yourselves."

"TALK TO ME, EPSTEIN," PELZER SAID once the door had shut behind Kufdani. "How did this get so blown out of proportion?"

Guns sighed. "You are too busy doing politics to do your job, Sheila."

"He seemed more an intellectual than I anticipated."

He snorted. "Didn't you read any of the reports I've written up over the years? Cuchulain was once the most legendary special operator in the business, in demand from his perch at CIA special ops. Tactical instincts, a record of heroism, IQ off the charts, unfailing ruthlessness, savvy business skills . . . I tend to be thoughtful in my analysis, don't you think? And as I may or may not succeed you as director of Mossad—"

"He's still a thug," Pelzer said.

"And an enormously rich thug, not to mention a fixture in Moroccan society who carries a diplomatic passport, and who is now the designated chief and imam of a million Muslims threatening to shake down your very own neighborhood. Oh, and don't forget his girlfriend, who may be the smartest person in the world."

"Money? Can he be bought?"

"Probably not," Guns said. "Between him and O'Connor, I suppose there's billions of dollars in play. Maybe tens of billions."

"So he can cause us real pain," Pelzer said.

"He could, considering his resources," Guns said. "Their alliance is enormously dangerous to the state of Israel. And don't forget that Brooks Elliot, his best friend and essential advisor, is a well-connected centi-millionaire with an office in the White House. Pooling their money leaves them with the liquid financial resources of a small country. Kufdani's firm pays about 17 percent of the tax revenue of Morocco! Given his connections, the US president and the king of Morocco may just pitch in where needed."

"And yet someone in our government seems to have targeted the girlfriend?"

"Broke her face. And beat up Elliot's wife, too—a personal friend of the First Lady. Cuchulain thinks it was Yakov Bernstein, but I have yet to confirm that." Guns smiled wryly.

"I fail to see the humor," Pelzer said.

"O'Connor is somewhat famous for movie star looks . . . and her narcissism," Guns said. "Cuchulain seems to think she'll be unhappy with us and is enjoying the anticipation. The NSA is already threatening revenge."

"Over one woman who got beat up?"

Guns shrugged. "We're at the business end of her spear now. There's a reason they pay her so much, and we may be about to find out why."

"If so, we should plan another meeting with our glorious leader once we get debriefed by the IDF scientists about the West Bank attack and the EMP that Dr. O'Connor is thought to have designed," Pelzer advised. "And what about Mr. Kufdani's talk of loyalty among his budding flock?"

"Cooch thinks Israel should have a future, but not as a theocracy. To get his way, he's trying to become the voice of two billion Muslims. He says he doesn't want to keep fighting this battle over and over again, each time from another vector. He wants this to be an open battle between Israel and Islam, to be settled once and forever."

"And what do *you* think, Epstein?"

"I think we can deal with Kufdani later. He's busy and not an immediate threat. The NSA too. We're dealing with something even scarier," Guns replied. "An angry Caitlin O'Connor is a nightmare for Israel."

Sheila had to agree. Anything with moving electrons was at risk—and that was most definitely a nightmare scenario.

HAARETZ ONLINE, TEL AVIV

KUFDANI PAID HIS TAXI DRIVER AND GAVE HIM A NICE TIP AFTER THE ride toward the setting sun, from the prime minister's office to the offices of Haaretz Online in Tel Aviv, where Caitlin had arranged an exclusive television interview. Liberating his wallet from storage in Ktzi'ot had made him feel flush. He tried not to think about the items they had stolen from him: his dive watch and the knife and sheath that always hung at the back of his neck.

Two old friends probably sitting in a pawn shop in Jerusalem.

Stepping out of the elevator, he introduced himself to a receptionist who directed him through a set of large glass doors and down a long hallway to the outer room of a small recording studio. A young, attractive woman sat typing on her computer, wearing a simple blue suit with a single strand of good pearls—or great fakes. It was a good look for a reporter. Her hair and makeup seemed excessive, even for TV, but Kufdani thought she looked bright enough. Several other staff members scurried around her, preparing the studio, and she never broke concentration.

"Ms. Sachs, I presume."

The young woman's head snapped to attention, and he saw her face brighten with focus. "Holy shit, you're him. You came. This is the biggest fucking story ever."

"Indeed, I came, and it may well be a great story," Kufdani said. "It's been a busy day. There was a prison break around me, so I had to call a friend to get me safely out of Ktzi'ot and back up here for this interview." He reached out a hand and held hers briefly in greeting. "You'll want to continue planning your approach. I would try to keep the stories separate and then later blend them into the bigger story. It will evolve, so don't get ahead of it."

Her face flushed. "You're working me. Trying to get me to build your story the way you want it told."

"Of course I'm working you." Kufdani grinned. "That's why I'm here. I have a story to tell. You work me for the best of it. It should be great fun—or newsworthy, if nothing else."

Sachs shrugged and smiled faintly, as if to say, *At least he knows the game.* "Let's get you made up."

Sitting in a chair with a big towel wrapped around his neck and something thick being smeared on his face, Kufdani said, "I've just heard, from someone very high up, that the Israelis have moved the Bedouin tribes from the West Bank to another location. Herded them like sheep. No facilities, no public transportation, no nothing."

Sachs nodded. "Basically the same news as yesterday and the day before that, but yes, still outrageous. And nothing new."

The makeup woman was blotting concealer at the scar beside his eye, which was taking far longer than her work with all the little scars on his forehead.

"Well, *today's* news," Kufdani emphasized, "is that the appropriate response to displacing thousands of Israeli citizens to an area with no proper shelter or public sewage treatment is to equally simplify the lives of those who made such a reckless decision."

He glanced at his wrist as the towel was removed from his neck.

"I don't know what time it is, but my sources tell me this response is expected to initiate at five o'clock. Now, who would steal a watch from a humble prisoner?"

Sachs glanced at her own watch and turned to her assistant. "Call my guy in Jerusalem. Tell him what Mr. Kufdani just said. Big story coming in. Talk to me before he files it." She turned back to him, her dark eyes ablaze. "Now, Mr. Kufdani, come into my lair."

Inside the studio, they sat in the two identical, cushioned chairs facing one another. Two cameramen adjusted their machinery to the appropriate spots as their assistants measured distances between interviewer, interviewee, and the cameras. The bright, deliberate studio lights flicked on. One of the men nodded, and tiny red lights began to blink from each camera.

"A hundred different things are going on that are newsworthy. Which of them would you like to talk about?" Sachs began.

"They are all related, of course, but there is one immediate issue. Israel has stolen Bedouin land from Muslim citizens of Israel. It should be returned immediately."

"And if it's not?" she asked. "Which seems likely."

"If it is not returned, we will attempt to isolate the Orthodox Haredi community to the extent that the cost of carrying them along in privilege will be an unacceptable burden on the remainder of Israeli society."

"What exactly is your view of the Haredim?"

"They are economic fossils," Kufdani replied, spitting out the words. "Slugs—a drain on your society, hiding beneath the cloak of the Hebrew god."

"Fossils? Slugs? You should debate one of them," Sachs said. "They have some very smart men with nimble minds."

"A public debate?" Kufdani said. "They would never dare. I'd rip their Torah-loving beards off. They can't deal with logic or history. They are too busy grooming their pigtails and bragging about their erudition. And making babies they then use to control their women."

Sachs gave a soft laugh. "Tell us how you really feel."

"I will do more than that. What is about to happen in Jerusalem this evening is a metaphor for all of Israel: tit for tat. Of course, we'll have to throw in a bit of catch-up for all the wrongs of the past. But we won't tolerate a theocracy stealing from Islam."

"What do you mean by that?"

"The Haredim are driving national economic policy by threatening to withhold their votes for your prime minister—a man of questionable integrity, a record of venality, and an offensive personality. We're going to fix that. If there is bloodshed, it will be shed on both sides."

"How wonderful for you, until the IDF and Shin Bet get involved," Sachs prompted. "Then you go down in smoke."

"Or not." Kufdani shrugged. "There is my bet. If they support the Haredim by coming after the Bedouins or the Palestinians, the fight is on."

"Wait, I'm missing something here. The disorganized Bedouin tribes on one side, and Shin Bet and the IDF on the other? And you're calling this a fight?"

"This is Islam against Israel. I call *that* a fight. And, as you may know from your research, Muhammed (peace be upon him) was a warrior. In this fight, I hope to act in his stead."

Sachs looked up at a camera and brought her hand across her throat. The floodlights went off, and the intermittent red flashes ceased. "We are nearing five o'clock, Mr. Kufdani. A quick break?"

She stood and walked over to a long table against the wall. Lifting a teapot, she looked at Kufdani, who smiled and nodded. She poured hot water into one mug, then the other, and hung teabags over the edge of each.

"That was certainly an interesting opener," she said. "It should play well. How long have you been out of prison?"

"Almost all day, Ms. Sachs," Kufdani said. "Yousef Salama, the great Palestinian leader, was kind enough to include me in the group that departed Ktzi'ot prison early this morning. Now, shall we watch the Jerusalem festivities in real time?"

He pulled his Kphone from his pocket.

"Show drone views of operations in Jerusalem," Kufdani instructed Emilie. Three of the TVs in the studio switched to an aerial drone view of the city. "Show Jerusalem news on set four."

Over the next six minutes, the three screens displayed a new round of destruction in Jerusalem, this time targeting the city's strategic infrastructure—particularly in the areas where Orthodox communities were prevalent. Explosions and fires were followed by images of cracks, rubble, dust, and running sewage as blast after blast hit the city streets.

At the seventh minute, the TV monitor showing the news from Jerusalem abruptly switched to an anchor, over the headline ticker BOMBINGS IN JERUSALEM.

"What are we witnessing?" Sachs asked, her eyes wide.

Kufdani touched the Kphone screen, and all the TVs returned to their previous events. "That is a response to the way Haredi treat Bedouins. I can get you raw video to edit alongside our interview."

"Please." She nodded, and Kufdani spoke the instruction into the Kphone. "I can't believe this shit," she said, "but I am beginning to understand. So, you're also friends with the person who can make the Tel Aviv city lights blink?"

Kufdani nodded back at her. "Caitlin. My true love. If she wants the lights to blink, they blink."

"And you were talking to her on the phone, I assume?"

"No, that was our chatbot Emilie, mostly," Kufdani said. "But that's a story for another day."

Sachs shook her head. "I can't believe I'm having this conversation. It's like science fiction, the world of tomorrow."

"Tomorrow has arrived," Kufdani retorted. "You have the story lead. Let's see how you handle it."

Sachs sat down again. "Are you ready to finish the interview? We have plenty of time."

He shook his head. "I have time for just one more question. You ask, I'll answer. Then I'd better run. I imagine your folks will be looking for me soon, and they'll be unhappy. I'd rather not go back to jail."

She looked startled for a second, then nodded. "What is the question?"

"Ask, 'What do you want?'"

The floodlights switched back on, and one of the cameramen nodded.

"So, Sheikh Kufdani," Sachs began, "you're telling me that your people have caused untold destruction in Jerusalem this evening in response to the involuntary relocation of Bedouin Israelis from the West Bank. Earlier, most of Beersheba and its industrial production were destroyed in support of a prison break, which you also claim."

She paused, and he had to admire her clever phrasing: no question had been asked.

"Yes, I did tell you that." He nodded, playing along. "The days of us Bedouins living under the repressive thumb of a theocracy that specifically denies our rights under Allah are over. Beersheba attempted to interfere with Yousef Salama's return to glory among his people. But it is Jerusalem that is in the Bedouin crosshairs. If you make life uncomfortable for us, as you continue to do in the West Bank, we will make life uncomfortable for you, as we have just done in Jerusalem."

"Let's get to the point, Mr. Kufdani," Sachs said. "What do you want?"

"The answer is more than a single point. It has texture, Ms. Sachs," Kufdani replied. "We are Israeli citizens. We want our stolen lands back, and what is on them is ours to keep. Israel must walk away from this bigotry, this theocratic tragedy it has created, where the Hebrew god rules all of the world to his profit. Let's put this injustice to rest and get on with life."

"And if Israel does not reply to your satisfaction, Mr. Kufdani? Do you plan to destroy what remains of Jerusalem?"

"We will continue to respond, with more vigor and bloodshed—within reason. After all, what further we destroy of Jerusalem, we may have to rebuild ourselves. In any case, we have made our point and, so far, with little bloodshed. But if you shed our blood, we will no longer hesitate to shed yours."

"How can you hope to win?" Sachs said.

Kufdani shrugged. "Right now, our quarrel is with the Haredim and the petty, lying theocrat they have elected. We see no reason to target our retaliation at the thinking people of Israel, those who are able to examine facts and draw conclusions about their own interests in the face of this perfidy. Not yet."

"I sense a 'but' here."

"But if you deploy Shin Bet to fight us, we will respond in kind. If you send the Netzah Yehuda against us, we will respond ruthlessly. I can assure you that we will not be unarmed, and they may not survive. The world's Muslims outnumber Israeli Jews by more than three hundred to one. You would run out of bullets before you could stop us."

"And down the road?" Sachs ventured.

"We'll see. We will redefine Jerusalem, of course, perhaps as a Muslim city with rights for Jewish and Christian visitors and worshippers. We all are Semites, after all—part of the ancient, monotheistic Abrahamic religions. We share prophets and differ only on the nature of God and redemption. So, Jerusalem is easy."

Sachs squinted at him, a dubious look on her face.

"The rest is harder. But we will attempt to find support for our thoughts and actions, particularly among progressive, logical Jewish thinkers."

"Easy enough," she said drily. "Any final words?"

Kufdani looked directly into the camera. "Give up this brutal charade, good people of Israel. Keep the life you have, and send the Haredim back to the kibbutz. If you let it get ugly, it will get very ugly. None of us will like that."

Kufdani stood, and the cameras shut down.

"Put that story out in the world, and you'll be famous," he predicted. "Treachery, maniacal theocracy, and nasty, nasty people . . . you'll be a journalistic idol. I'll be responsible for earning you a Pulitzer. I know a guy that will get you on the US news."

"Yeah, right," Sachs muttered. "You figure that out, and I'll go down on you for a week."

"An hour or two would be fine." Kufdani grinned. "It's a deal."

The young journalist smirked back at him. "That's science fiction, too."

"We'll see," he replied, still grinning. "In the meantime, have fun with this. I'll get someone to give you a call about arranging our next interview. By remote webcast if necessary, but naturally I hope to see you in person." He turned and walked through the glass doors to the elevator.

Outside, a small white truck awaited his arrival. He climbed into the back seat and was handed a bundle of traditional Bedouin attire, slightly soiled. As the truck drove off, the Western clothes went out the window.

Kufdani was invisible.

OFFICE OF THE PRIME MINISTER, JERUSALEM

THE CONFERENCE ROOM WAS CROWDED. AT THE BACK WALL, SEATED around three sides of an oblong table, was a gaggle of staffers, officers, cabinet members, and agents. Among them, Nabov Dayan—the director of Shin Bet, the Israeli internal security agency and special forces—noticed Guns Epstein of Mossad and Yakov Bernstein, the newly appointed minister of defense, sitting side by side. Dayan couldn't think of two men who were more different. And yet all were there at the behest of the prime minister.

Also at the table sat the commanding general of the IDF; the director of Aman, Israel's military intelligence service; and Sheila Pelzer, the director of Mossad. As Shin Bet's director, Dayan was responsible for tracking down terrorists and ferreting out other sovereign threats within and beyond Israel's state borders. He had acceded to this post after recently commanding the Sayeret Matkal, which was modeled after the famed British SAS and sometimes compared to the Delta Force of the US military. Whereas the other branches of the security services were responsible to the Knesset, the national legislature, he reported directly to the prime minister.

At this moment, Dayan noticed, the prime minister sat at the head of the table, his face flushed and a vein in the center of his forehead bulging. And no wonder.

In Jerusalem the previous evening, beginning at 5:00 sharp, the small sewage treatment plant at Aomat, which mainly serviced the Haredim community, suffered a bombing that breached its walls. A second blast fried its electronic controls and all circuits within two hundred yards. Raw sewage began to run from cracks in the plant's infrastructure and into the streets. Ten minutes later, another explosive blast ripped a new hole in the sewage retaining wall, turning a trickle into a flood that filled the streets.

Another explosion disabled the bus terminal along with 525 buses within a three-hundred-yard radius, plus hundreds of cars, trucks, and service vehicles in the area. Rush hour traffic came to a complete halt. Two of Jerusalem's elevated train terminals were also disabled, causing a permanent interruption of that service. The telephone exchange most used by the Orthodox community was hit with another EMP blast; the city's main exchange was spared—some said graciously.

The prime minister did not agree. "These pipsqueak Bedouin terrorists have destroyed half of southern Israel, and no one can tell me how," he snarled, grinding the words out through his teeth. "More than six thousand Palestinians of the worst sort managed an escape from one of our most secure prisons, and we killed or captured only eleven of them. They have utterly destroyed our communication system. Nearly two days have passed, and only now have we figured out where the escapees went. They have heaped humiliation on us. And what have you done? Nothing. Nothing!" he screamed.

Dayan was paying close attention to his boss, yet he couldn't help but notice that Guns sat calmly on his back row chair. *Well, that sums it up nicely*, Dayan thought. *Why doesn't Epstein look at all rattled? He's supposed to be the Cuchulain expert.*

Dayan, too, was familiar with the legendary Cooch of CIA fame, of course, particularly his understanding of urban tactics and his profound intimacy with violence. Dayan knew enough to find Jerome Masterson and keep an eye on him. He and Cooch seemed to have outdone themselves on their opening gambit. And he anticipated that things were about to get far worse.

The prime minister was shaking a finger at him. "You find these no-good bastards and kill them! All of them!" He pointed around the table. "The rest of you, figure this out. These bastards are threatening our country, our people, our religion, our way of life! Provide everything that Shin Bet asks. Then do your jobs and get me some answers."

He turned back to Dayan.

"Now, you find that Bedouin bastard Kufdani and kill him. You figure out how these terrorists demolished much of Jerusalem and Beersheba. Find the people who did this, and kill them. Kill them all!"

He turned and stormed from the room, slamming the door behind him.

After a few seconds of stunned silence, Dayan stood and shuffled some papers. "I think I've been given my marching orders. I'll be in touch." He gathered his papers and walked out the door, the prime minister's words echoing in his head.

Kill them all!

TANGIER

CAITLIN O'CONNOR LEANED BACK IN HER DESK CHAIR, WATCHING THE prime minister's meeting. The two cameras covering the conference room in Jerusalem had been easy for Emilie to hack. Caitlin had taken the sound from Yakov Bernstein's cell phone—not the best quality of the seven phones recording there, but Emilie had cleaned it up a little to make it more tolerable. Alex had told her to start pointing the records of anything leaked at Bernstein, so he would be the obvious culprit when the Israelis sorted out the leak. Emilie had been instructed to modify other Israeli records accordingly, and Caitlin had left instructions for future opportunities of the same type.

Her face still hurt like hell. The cracked ribs hurt too. Under her bandages, the stitches along her jaw itched like mad. Worst of all, Tang was dead. Thinking about it, she felt the rising tide of a new emotion: rage. She hadn't yet figured out how to mitigate its impact.

Her Kphone lit up with a call from the United States: her NSA boss, sort of. Colonel Marilyn Ann Rieber of the US Air Force was the person who administered the NSA contracts with Axial and thus the relationship with Caitlin. LuAnn did the business part with Rieber.

Caitlin got along with Rieber, who was better than most. She had a master's degree in physics from MIT and a decent brain, as far as Caitlin was concerned. She was an Air Force Academy graduate who had been in and out of the NSA for fifteen years. She knew the rules and played by them broadly, which had made her safe to promote.

"This is Dr. O'Connor," Caitlin said. "What's up, Rieber?"

"Or what's down," Rieber said, laughing. "That was very nice work in the West Bank. EMP?"

"Cool, huh?" Caitlin said. "It was a bitch, but I figured out how to downsize it. Rocks, 40mm ammunition, whatever. I'm thinking a lot about new shit. This could be a hitter. I see good business in our future."

"EMP ammunition, huh?"

"Yeah. Fusible, blast adjustable. Cool shit. I'm thinking how to make smaller shit, like aircraft arms."

"We'll maybe talk about that," Rieber said. "We probably already own that technology in one contract or another that you've signed over the years. Now, we really have to talk about your security."

"My security? Get real, Rieber," Caitlin retorted. "I live in the most secure environment anyone could ask. Full-time armed guards, a monitored living and working space, sheer granite walls, all of it. All run by my true love, who is a gifted badass."

"The bottom line is, someone got to you and messed you up. You're still healing, for Christ's sake!"

"Do you think you could manage to kidnap me, bring me back to live in a less secure gated community near Fort Meade?"

"Probably not," Rieber said. "So I made that case to the director who was considering it, and I think I sold it."

"Yeah?"

"Yeah," Rieber said. "I left out the part about your Bedouin lover and his unique skills. What I couldn't and didn't sell was your travel security. You come back here once a quarter, then galivant all over the country while you're here. We can't secure every airport."

"What did you come up with, given that my schedule is *my* business?" Caitlin asked.

"Well, a US Air Force plane would be ideal, but that's too visible. A private arrangement with NetJets or one of that bunch is not all that secure, given that tail number tracking is also public, at least from the contractor side."

"You have a bunch of executive jets to ferry your generals around. Why not break one of those loose?"

"Not likely," Rieber replied. "They are spoken for and vigorously defended as a perquisite."

"Out with it, Rieber. What do you have?"

Rieber sighed. "I have a C-37B that was outfitted with all the new security goodies for the former First Lady, and then rejected as a budget buster by the new administration."

"A C-37B, huh?" Caitlin said. "If my capable memory serves, that is one of the Gulfstream models, the 550. It fits my image of myself."

"Yes to both," Rieber said. "It was purchased new, and we've been working on it for two years. The Air Force wants it off their books as quietly as possible. They're willing to write off the cost of the improvements."

"Imagine that," Caitlin said. "I have a secure transportation requirement, and you have a secure airplane that fits the bill. Let's make something happen."

Rieber said, "I'm going to figure out how to make the director happy and get this thing off my ass, but I'm not there yet. You have any ideas? After all, you're supposed to be the smartest person in the world."

"Fuck you, Rieber," Caitlin said. "I'll have to think about it."

"Oh, joy. How long will that take?"

"I'm pretty busy right now. Let me talk to LuAnn. She may be able to make this work."

She ended the call, then called LuAnn to explain.

"Well," LuAnn said, "it's an asset with long-term value, and we have a leasing company based in the US. A sale to us and leasing it back to them might work. How badly do they want this to work?"

"You propose a deal that makes public sense to the government, and I'll sell it," Caitlin insisted. "Keep in mind that the C-37B is used and junked up with enough superfluous security equipment that they can't sell it on the public market without ripping it out—or facing a public shitshow for the cost of bringing it up to standard for a used Gulfstream 550."

LuAnn chuckled. "You are preaching to the choir, but I'll keep it in mind," she said. "This could be a good deal for Kufdani."

"And me," Caitlin said.

"Of course, Caitlin," LuAnn said.

Caitlin hung up and thought on it for a few moments. This approach to travel—having Air Force security enhancements as playthings in a playpen she was beginning to covet—would make it harder for anyone to bust her face next time. It might even have a bed. She scratched absently at the stitches on her jaw. The itch was annoying, but it fed her rage in a way that was strangely satisfying.

She touched her Kphone and replayed the end of the prime minister's meeting. It seemed clear to Caitlin that the ball had been transferred to Shin Bet's court. They certainly had the assets. She had a decent handle on their communications facilities, but they were good—and aggressive about protecting their information. She was getting a fair amount of interference from Shin Bet, and decided to tell Emilie to clean things up so they didn't leave electronic footprints. Figuring out a whole new system would be a pain in the ass, so she and Emilie should hide from Shin Bet for now. A long history of major Shin Bet operations outside Israel's borders made plain that they did not play nice.

Was it Shin Bet who arranged the attack on me? she wondered, running her tongue over her new molar implants. Most of the plastic surgeon's work was still hidden under the bandages, and she didn't quite know how it would turn out. *I'm going to be careful around you guys, so I don't miss a chance to hurt you.*

Caitlin had an important phone call to make, but first she inputted the sequence for destroying the Shin Bet communications suite so that Emilie would make it look initially like a cascading series of electronic failures, something hard to fix. Alex would tell her when to execute the destruction.

He had a better sense of timing, but she wanted to be the one to execute, particularly if these were the motherfuckers who knocked out her molars.

With Emilie's help, she could make sure Shin Bet couldn't talk to each other (or anyone else) when they needed to—*and* make sure Alex heard everything they said.

At least she wasn't bored anymore.

HAARETZ ONLINE, TEL AVIV

WHEN THE LIGHTS DIMMED—NOT JUST IN HER HOL OFFICE BUT ALSO far into the city outside her window—Elsa Sachs was not at all surprised that her cell phone rang immediately afterward. The caller displayed as *Unidentified Sender*, but this time Sachs knew exactly who it was.

"Caitlin?" she said into the phone.

"Yeah, it's me," Caitlin said. "Alex spilled the beans, huh?"

"Alex?"

"Yeah. You know him as Kufdani."

An image flashed in Elsa's head: his huge neck, with thick veins wrapping up to his graying hair. He was sexy, she had realized in the past twenty-four hours, sort of the way a jaguar is sexy: awesome to observe from a distance. "He's not Bedouin?"

"It's a long story," Caitlin replied, "but he is as Bedouin as the pope is Catholic. I see that your printer is on. I'll send his background."

Elsa's printer started, and two pages printed out. "Read it later," Caitlin said. "We've got more important things to talk about first."

"Okay, tell me something I need to know. Give me a big story," Elsa said. "The last one was, well, acceptable."

"Is that right? Well, the prime minister had a big meeting today. He sicced Shin Bet on Kufdani and the Bedouins. He told IDF to help, but Shin Bet is in charge, and they're a bunch of ruthless bastards. He told them to kill them all."

"Bullshit, Caitlin," Elsa said. "I heard about the meeting, but it just wrapped up. Top secret. No way can you jump to such conclusions."

"Ha! Well, maybe I know a guy in government who recorded it. Check it out. I'll send you a summary." The printer started again.

Elsa scanned the page. "This stuff is a journalist's dream. If it's for real, it will make an incredible story."

"Elsa, Elsa. You know you can trust me."

"Do I? What exactly do I know about you?"

"Well, my name is Dr. Caitlin O'Conner, but you can just call me Caitlin. I leave the doctor stuff to my employer and my students—"

"Kufdani said you were his true love. Is he your employer too?"

"God, no! Kufdani is my lover and my soulmate. I live in Tangier with him. The NSA is my employer, or at least the source of much of my revenue."

I keep waiting for this story to get less weird, Elsa thought. "Tell me, Caitlin," she said, "what really rings your bell?" She heard a deep sigh.

"Education," Caitlin said. "If I can help fix elementary education around the world, I will have accomplished a vast public good beyond quantum mechanics or building a new bomb. That is what dominates my free time and thought. I want every child to have an even shot at a life of the mind—reading books, thinking about stars and galaxies, about history and economics, about quarks and photons. I would rather have the Nobel Peace Prize for teaching the world's children to read, write, reason, and calculate at the sixth-grade level than the prize for physics. Education is harder anyway. I like hard."

"And how is that going for you?" Elsa asked.

"I've been at it for ten years or so, and we're getting a foothold. We'll get another million or two with this Bedouin effort Alex is behind. But that's a story for another day," Caitlin insisted.

"Anything on your hot list for right now?"

"Yeah. I'm horny."

"Oh?" Elsa said. *That answer was . . . unexpected.*

"I just think better when I get off. And all the good vibrations that life or a wall circuit can offer—that doesn't do it for me. Alex is gone, and no one appropriate is available."

"So you're not into monogamy?"

"God, no," Caitlin said. "Different men as I can find them, or a woman but only if she's scary smart. And no one twice. There's a lot to be said for selective sport fucking."

"Sport fucking?" Elsa blurted out.

"Sure. Physicists, the occasional chemist—mostly a bunch of quantum mechanics guys who've just completed their PhD. I love spending a weekend picking a guy's fresh-minted brain, arguing logic, expanding my thinking base, and teaching him all the messy, juicy rest of it. Mossad sent me a pretty young man one time. Great fuck, but he didn't know anything. Mostly I just fucked with his head. He was—"

"Uh, Caitlin?" Elsa interrupted. "You might be oversharing. I'm guessing you don't want the word out, especially if Mr. Kufdani is your lover."

"It's true he's not crazy about the arrangement. He is the best of them, and I love him desperately. But that's who I am, and I'm worth it. He knew about it when he took the deal."

This is getting weirder by the minute. "And Kufdani?" Elsa couldn't resist asking. "Does he . . . play around too?"

"Of course," Caitlin replied. "But he doesn't have the same needs. He's not driven by sex like I am—just takes it where it presents itself. A friend of mine in New York hit on him recently at my request, and now she raves on about Kufdani, the pony-peckered Arab." She laughed heartily. "The guy is a great fuck, and he gives the best head on the planet. If you ever see him again, you should try him on."

The best head on the planet, Elsa thought.

"So is that enough about me for now?"

Elsa snapped out of her reverie. "Not exactly. I've got the meeting summary and the Kufdani bio. While you're at it, send me something on you."

"I'm the famous Caitlin O'Connor," came the response. "Would've thought you already knew everything there is to know about me." The phone went dead, but the printer started up right away.

Elsa read through the Kufdani piece: Alejandro Mohammad Cuchulain, former US Marine, master's in Islamic studies from Oxford, author of several papers and presentations on early Islam and the schism between Sunni and Shi'a. Elsa entered the URLs for the presentation videos and studied them for a few moments.

On one presentation, hanging out of Kufdani's thrice-rolled sleeves were massive, corded forearms attached to hands wrapped with veins and scars. A long, thick scar ran alongside the prominent veins on his right arm. Apparently someone had stitched him up pretty poorly. He might look like a thug, and he was big enough to fit the bill. But he certainly seemed to have a brain and be trained in its use.

Interesting, thought Elsa.

The bio on Caitlin O'Connor ran to eight pages. Elsa read the opening sentence: *Dr. O'Connor is perhaps the world's premier quantum physicist . . .*

PhD from Caltech, professorships everywhere, MacArthur award at age twenty-five, Fields Medal not long after. This woman had done everything before she was thirty.

"No wonder she can blink the lights," Sachs muttered to herself. "From the looks of it, she can do anything."

"WE ARE LOOKING FOR KUFDANI, BUT HE APPEARS TO HAVE DISAP-peared," one of the staffers reported. "Perhaps even left the country." Nabov Dayan sat at a rectangular table with six of his direct reports in a windowless room north of Yarkon Park, at Shin Bet HQ.

"No matter," Dayan replied, with more confidence than he felt. He knew of this "Cooch" from long ago, of his ruthlessness as an accomplished CIA operator. "We'll find him and deal with him when the time comes."

"We can always push the Bedouins around some more," suggested another agent. "We've received early intelligence that the tribes may have placed the weapons that caused the damage in Jerusalem. Maybe we could throw their leaders in prison?"

Not exactly the wisest option at the moment, Dayan thought. Plus, it was too soon to strike at the Bedouins again. "Let's just keep an eye on them for now. A drone or two should give us adequate warning if they look to become troublesome."

To get to the heart of the problem, he would have to see things through a wider lens.

"Shin Bet is under stress," he continued. "The full nature of the threat is unclear, but it is effective. Our nation is out of pocket billions of dollars for repairs and reconstruction. Incredibly, we don't know how this was accomplished or how far out the attackers have laid plans. But the prime minister has given us enormous power to avenge some of the recent travesties."

The faces around the table were grim.

"It seems to me," Dayan said, "those communications disruptions and electronic explosions are the source of many of our issues. Our efficacy relies on our ability to communicate, both among us and with our informant network. Step one is figuring that out. Any thoughts?"

Deputy Director Ehud Klinger spoke up. "These electronic bursts seem to be coming from miniature electromagnetic pulse devices—EMP, designed to destroy electrical equipment or circuits. We don't know how many of those devices they have or where they're located. Surveillance cameras show nothing unusual in the twenty-four hours before the blasts. But we do know the device was likely designed and produced by an American particle physicist, one of four people in the world with those skills."

Dayan looked expectantly at Klinger, who also served as leader of the IDF special forces and had a great deal of experience in the clandestine world.

"Dr. Caitlin O'Connor," his deputy said.

"Why her?"

"One, proximity, and two, opportunity. She is the Bedouin terrorist's lover, resides with him in Tangier. She is said to be the pointy end of the NSA's intellectual spear."

"Why not just grab O'Connor and kill her quietly?" Dayan asked. "Tangier is fairly open."

"A bunch of our Russian Haredi patriots tried that recently," Klinger explained. "Without our permission. We don't know precisely who was involved, but I'm betting on Yakov Bernstein. He's an impetuous prick."

"Fuck," Dayan said. "Save us from amateurs."

"Tangier may be open, but Kufdani's place is buttoned up tight according to Mossad," the deputy director continued. "We would need the IDF to breach it, and that would be enormously bloody. Thanks to Jerome Masterson, security there is both well-armed and well-trained—and over two thousand miles away. They have robust air defense."

Dayan shook his head. He knew of Masterson from long ago and had heard about his success in providing security training for the Moroccans. "What else?"

The man to his right pushed a few papers in front of him. "We could do an aggressive, armed push into Gaza. Take back some of the escaped prisoners from Ktzi'ot." Yitzak Galat, the head of Shin Bet's Arab department, was responsible for counterterrorism in Israel, including the West Bank and the Gaza Strip. "We know some have returned and are stirring up trouble among the populace. Could give us some extra time to figure out how to deal with this Kufdani."

Dayan liked the idea. After the recent losses in Jerusalem, the prison breakout had really rubbed their noses in things. "We'll recapture all that real estate in Gaza before long anyway. Might as well get the Palestinians used to that reality."

Galat nodded. "Give me a few days, and you'll have a plan. Shall we include some support from the IDF?"

Dayan thought for a second. "Why not? Let's give them a full show of power: body armor, armored personnel carriers, tanks, helicopters, the whole bit. IDF in support of Shin Bet. Search some houses, arrest some Palestinians. Maybe even shoot a few if they act up."

Galat's eyes widened in surprise.

"I don't think we need to be too careful about this operation and its optics for the press," Dayan confirmed. "Let us end this minor revolt. We need to display a ruthlessness that will get the Palestinians in Gaza out of our way."

Galat agreed. "They need to see us coming from a long way off and be scared."

"Tell me what you have in mind," Dayan said, adding, "If there is resistance at Mossad or the IDF, I'll ask the prime minister to deal with it."

Galat clicked his laptop and swung the monitor to face the Shin Bet director. "Before massing for the attack, we'll assemble in different areas in the Negev," Galat said, pointing to the map, "just south and east of Beersheba."

The roads north of there were still blocked, so the IDF forces would be less visible as they massed. Troops would have full-body armor with helmets and face masks and would be transported to the battlefield in armored carriers. Two companies of battle tanks would be available to the Israeli forces, to deal with any pockets of resistance away from the populace.

"But not too far away." Galat smirked. "It's time to teach them a lesson."

He suggested asking IDF to fly three jet bombers over Gaza as the battle was engaged, flying at very low altitudes and high speed. Then they would flood the area with drones—some armed with Hellfire missiles, the rest for surveillance—all by sector and controlled by commanders on the ground.

Dayan found the plan acceptable. "Shin Bet will observe and advise," he said. "This is an IDF show." The Israeli Navy would also send two armed corvettes to shell anyone or anything not visible to the drones, and to control any Palestinians or mercenaries who tried to flee by boat.

Galat traced his fingers along the map on his laptop screen. "We will enter the Gaza Strip just west of the Wadi al-Sarar, turn south in a line, and accelerate. They may launch stones with their slingshots and throw debris at our troops, but any armed resistance will be dealt with harshly. Tear gas is likely to be required, perhaps with a little nausea agent mixed in."

Dayan saw it all as clear as day: Gaza City would be isolated. When they had cleared the portion of the strip south of Gaza to the Egyptian border, they would reverse and move toward Gaza City, rolling back over those they had just crushed.

"Let's make it so," he said, standing up. "Put your plan together, and I'll run it by the prime minister." It would take a few days to get the logistics right, but in the end, these cretins would feel the force.

MOSSAD HEADQUARTERS, TEL AVIV

GUNS SAT IN FRONT OF HIS DESKTOP SCREEN WITH SHEILA PELZER AT his side, sipping tea and waiting for the 9:00 a.m. news release from Haaretz Online. It had been almost two weeks since the Sachs woman had written those pieces about the power outages and the kidnapping of Kufdani. The good news was that her articles were too small-time to garner the attention of the foreign press, particularly in the EU and the US. The bad news was that her readership was growing.

As both Guns and Pelzer well knew, Sachs had her pick of sensational stories: the second Jerusalem attack, the Ktzi'ot prison break, the plight of the Israeli Bedouins. Or she might go with all three. The first headline showed up, and the story was indeed shocking.

PRIME MINISTER ON PALESTINIANS AND BEDOUINS: KILL THEM ALL!

"Kill them all!" That was the closing directive from our prime minister in a senior staff meeting earlier this week. Kill who? Well, he's not quite sure. But there has to be someone to kill, doesn't there?

In what Bedouin leadership describes as a response to the

removal—by Shin Bet and the IDF—of thousands of Israeli Bedouins to appalling facilities, seemingly half of Jerusalem was destroyed last weekend, from a sewage treatment plant to the public transportation system to the vaunted construction project slated for the relocation of the "faithful" in the West Bank. And instead of working on a response to the massive, demonstrated incompetence from his administration that allowed this to happen, the prime minister issued a kill order on thousands of human beings.

Why?

Perhaps this order was an attempt to cover up involvement in the kidnapping of the Bedouin sheik who was drugged and tossed into Ktzi'ot Prison after a meeting with Haredi leadership. Or perhaps it was a cry of vengeance after the humiliating prison break on Saturday, led by the legendary Palestinian and Hamas leader Yousef Salama—the sudden release of more than six thousand prisoners who fled to Egypt, reportedly including Kufdani, the Bedouin in question.

Stealing Bedouin citizens' land is getting to be an expensive proposition, and the price is going up quickly, at least in Jerusalem. In Tel Aviv, how would we deal with that? And why should we? Is this approach to governing what we elected this political monster to do? Have we rolled over while the Haredim plan to steer our society backwards at his hand?

Do we want a personal theocracy led by an ineffective, backward-looking scoundrel?

Our exclusive video interview with Kufdani, which reveals his claims about human rights, who really controls Israel, and what he calls the "theocratic tragedy," may soon be aired on a top US network and is scheduled to air on Israeli TV unless our fearless leader generates a lie to stop it. He's good at lying to the Israeli people, but he has less influence on freedom of speech in the United States.

Theocracies, by nature, have limited international power, yet we allow ours to control us. "Kill them all" may refer to someone else this time. But can you be sure that next time it won't be an order to terminate anyone who doesn't agree with our scheming prime minister—perhaps even you?

Guns could see the distress on Pelzer's face as she finished reading the article. "The prime minister's actions undermine what we have fought so long for," she said at last. "The rule of law is fundamental to managing a democracy, and he is trampling it with land confiscations and assassination orders. If he continues on this path, he might soon actually have that power he's reaching for. It's really quite discouraging. Shin Bet is an unforgiving bunch, and a competent one. Now that Dayan is involved, the score will change quickly."

"Well, he was never our favorite guy," Guns agreed. He and Pelzer had known all along that the prime minister was not the least bit troubled by truth or ethics. "It's our job to minimize any long-term damage from his actions while protecting Israel from harm. And so far, the score looks like Bedouins 3, Israel 0."

"But you heard him direct Shin Bet to kill them all," she protested. "That simply is not consistent with the rule of law as we practice it."

"Neither was the seizing of the Bedouin land, but we did it," Guns pointed out. "We'll see how that works out. For now, we need to go about our own business and see how things play out on the ground."

"That makes sense. We need to continue our intelligence mission, not that the PM or Shin Bet has asked. Do we have any idea what your Kufdani will do next?"

Guns shook his head. "Not hearing any chatter on his whereabouts. I'm looking for Masterson too, and he doesn't appear to be in Morocco."

"That's bad news."

"Yes." According to Guns's sources, Caitlin O'Connor was eerily quiet too, and Kufdani Industries in Tangier had been tightened up for combat ever since the incident involving her unknown attackers. The Algeciras facility appeared largely deserted if highly guarded—both conventionally and, interestingly, by a large, well-trained, well-armed group of older women.

"What's your guess as to his tactics?" Pelzer asked. "Where will they attack next?"

"I believe they will await our next move and calculate their response accordingly. Cooch is trying to sell an appeasement program to liberal Jews here and in the diaspora. Tel Aviv should be safe for a while."

The head of Mossad dropped her head to her hands. "I was a college professor. I was happy. How does this happen?" she asked. "What are we to do with this mess?"

"We Mossad?" Guns shrugged. "We do what we can."

"No one in our government must decide to invade Morocco in an attempt to get to Caitlin. It's too far, and the United States would defend it aggressively."

"The logistics would be a nightmare, even without Cooch in the game—and he is in it, completely," Guns agreed. "IDF needs to know that loud and clear."

Pelzer nodded, looking more herself as she got warmed up. "We should figure out which US network became so interested, so quickly, that they would announce Mr. Kufdani's interview with such fanfare. Someone is waving a publicity baton that we don't know about, and our New York office is silent on the topic."

"We also need to make nice with the White House." Guns was only too aware that the Americans had been unhappy with the West Bank situation for some time. Only the New York diaspora had kept them from moving beyond bellyaching. "We should make sure the Jewish leaders in New York are with us. They have no love for the Haredim."

"That all sounds like a good start."

"I can arrange a call with Macmillan," Guns said, "if only to gauge the mood. As Cooch's ex-boss and mentor, he is quite familiar with the motivations of a stone-cold killer without a bunch of emotion to burden him."

"Yes, I've always admired that about him," Pelzer said. "And you'll talk to Brooks Elliot?"

Guns raised one eyebrow. "You mean the husband of the woman whose stitched-up head is proof that one of us almost took her out? And what would you have me say to the special ambassador to the president?"

Pelzer's eyes narrowed. "Fine, whatever. Let's get to work. But we'll both need to consider how we might deal with bad outcomes."

Things are going to be a little busy around here, Guns thought. "Pretty sure bad outcomes are on their way."

"But not on our watch." Pelzer smiled slightly. "Not yet."

WASHINGTON, DC

"WHITE HOUSE SWITCHBOARD," A VOICE SAID. "HOW MAY I DIRECT YOUR call?"

"Colonel Macmillan, in the National Security Advisor's Office, please," Pelzer said.

There was a pause, a buzz, and finally a gruff answer: "Macmillan."

"Mac, it's Sheila Pelzer."

"My dear Madam Pelzer. It's so nice to hear from you. Are we having lunch sometime soon?"

"Hello, Mac. It's not a social call. I need some advice. I don't know quite how Mossad is to handle the situation with Mr. Cuchulain or Dr. O'Connor. The attacks in Jerusalem and the West Bank are causing quite a stir."

Mac snorted. "Straight to business, eh? Well, by forcibly imprisoning a friendly agent, Cuchulain, your compatriots have done long-term harm to Israel's standing in even our dark world. That kind of thing resonates around the world and impacts trust. It certainly did with me. You'll be unable to escape the repercussions of that—not only from us but from others as well. As far as I'm concerned, Mossad should be pushed to the fringe: no informal information sharing."

That's harsh, Pelzer thought. "As I think you know, Mossad had no prior knowledge of that incident."

"Maybe not. Still, someone in your camp gave us the handle, so we're gonna push on it."

"And now? How are we to prevent further damage? What can you tell me about how to handle your Mr. Kufdani?"

Mac chuckled. "I have no advice about that other than to say I view Cuchulain as a son. Keep in mind that Brooks F. T. Elliot the third, chair of the US Senate Foreign Relations Committee, is quite grateful to Cuchulain for saving his son's life. And Brooks F. T. Elliot the fourth, the president's security advisor, views him as a brother. I could go on, you know. If he is ambushed again, a great many people are going to be very angry."

"What about Dr. O'Connor? That seems to be a more immediate and perhaps more serious issue. How do we deal with her?"

"My advice is to get the hell out of Dodge in case the NSA has its way and nukes Tel Aviv."

So much for "safe for a while," Pelzer thought. "Oh, dear. That bad?"

"Worse," Mac replied. "The NSA is outraged, irrational. They want to bring O'Connor back from Tangier to the US by force. She has threatened all-out war if they try. The president values her enormously and is very angry with Israel."

"And what do you advise?" she tried again.

"The last time we gave you planning advice, during our efforts in Iran—at some personal risk, I might add—you used it to slaughter radical Arab leaders with weapons we provided. Now you have taken the architect of that plan, drugged him, and threw him to the wolves in an Israeli jail. So, my advice is to get out of the way until the Bedouins get what they want. But failing that, bring your A team. It's going to be a fascinating spectacle."

"Perhaps Dr. O'Connor and I should sit down together and talk things through," Pelzer suggested.

"Sheila, that might be a tad premature," Mac said. "Right now, Dr. O'Connor is using just one collective word to describe the government of Israel."

"And that is?"

"Motherfuckers."

"Goodness," Pelzer said. "A bit irrational, wouldn't you say?"

"Perhaps. I've known O'Connor well for years, as has the president. This is the first time I've seen her homicidally outraged. It will take her a long time to work it off, at your expense. Don't expect Uncle Sam to kiss it and make it better; the NSA wouldn't allow it, and the president is pissed."

"We go back a long way, Mac," Pelzer said. "This is sounding less and less like a domestic disturbance, and more like an international incident. I need your help."

After a long silence, Mac sighed. "Get involved, Sheila," he said. "This situation is evolving quickly, and it could change the nature of US-Israeli relations for a long time to come. Your Russian Jews are out of control; that will be expensive to fix. It's safe to say you're about to face a one-two punch: asymmetric electronic warfare combined with one of the finest minds extant on the subject of urban guerilla warfare."

"Oh, dear," Pelzer said. "I'll have to sell our prime minister on the danger. He doesn't scare easily."

"He'll be hard to convince until it's too late, and then it's *your* problem to solve."

He's right, thought Pelzer. She had no response to give.

"I must run, Sheila, but one more bit of advice," Mac said. "Give up the Russians."

NEAR GAZA CITY

KUFDANI WALKED ALONG A NARROW PATH IN A VILLAGE JUST OUTSIDE Gaza City until he met Amad, a former physics professor and one of his better students from Ktzi'ot. They embraced formally, then continued along the path, passing several other Palestinians who stopped in their tracks and just stared at Kufdani.

Over a week had passed since the prison break, and the brutal life of a prisoner was becoming a distant memory, fading as fast as an unpleasant dream or a distant mirage. A new vision was taking its place, slowly building from the legend and dust of the desert, and from the yearning of the people who lived there.

"My countrymen have heard about you." Amad grinned, nodding at the gaping men and children. "You're becoming famous. They know who planned and carried out our freedom, who delivered them into the light of Allah through learning and prayer. They know the truth, no matter what Yousef Salama says."

"Amad, Amad, you're not thinking this through," Kufdani said. "Salama planned all of this. I just executed it. That is the story I want to tell."

Amad replied with a knowing look. "Yousef Salama asked me to set up a meeting for you tomorrow, with one of his Hamas colleagues. He will hear a different story, maybe."

"I hear the voice of Allah, and you hear stories. Amad, don't disappoint me."

Why does he believe he can choose where to place his loyalty? Kufdani wondered, knowing that Amad was asking him to lead them. But he had absolutely no interest in ruling Palestine or in politics generally.

As a scholar of Islam, he recognized this moment as an opportunity to get some of this Shi'a–Sunni split thing out of the way, through his plans for a literal and figurative offensive that would require all Muslims to speak with one mighty voice—and he did not wish to squander that opportunity. But if he could get the Israelis to roll over within a few weeks as planned, that would be the end of his foray into geopolitics.

"Listen to me," Kufdani insisted, "and learn algebra. I despise arithmetic and fail at it often. But I know this much: Salama must use the credit for these actions to gain political power. I am defending Allah's flock. It is the will of Allah I seek to carry out."

"Inshallah," Amad conceded.

Kufdani stopped at the entrance to a small hut. "Credit is interesting, Amad. Unlike in physics, it can be subdivided without losing mass. Take the case of our prison experience: Yousef gets credit for planning it and gets more power from that credit to become the Palestinian leader. I get credit among the masses as a follower who both thinks and kills, thus giving more power to the will of Allah. The sum of the two is *more* than their total, not less."

Amad nodded. "You have thought things through yet again, Kufdani."

Kufdani opened the door. "Make them ready to take orders, Amad. Make them want to kill for me. I demand that, as a messenger of Allah. You will tell the others. All must conform aggressively to the orders of Yousef Salama."

Amad met his eyes, nodded, and then turned to leave.

In the small room, Yousef Salama sat with a Kphone on the wooden table in front of him. Kufdani smiled when he saw the teapot and the vacant chair awaiting him: it had new green cushions.

Salama stood, and they embraced warmly.

"Yousef," Kufdani said. "I see you got the Kphone I sent."

"I did," Salama said, bowing his head briefly. "And I thank you for it. I envied its capabilities when we were together as guests of Israel. Now this Kphone knows my name as it does yours. Can it also teach the classes?"

"Your Kphone can do anything mine can do, as long as you're authorized for it," Kufdani replied.

He had ordered delivery of additional Kphones for Amad and the other leaders, who needed only to register with their name and credentials to gain access. All directions to control the upcoming battle would come from Kufdani through the Kphone, to be shared as though coming directly from the leaders themselves.

"Things are warming up," Kufdani continued. "If you want to lead Palestine, I'd like to help, but there are more immediate issues." He explained that Shin Bet was preparing to take another run at the Gaza Strip, with the IDF in full support, sometime in the next week or so. "You and the others do the on-the-ground planning and take the public credit, but promise obedience to the agreed plan. It's the method we will use to work together. Amad has arranged a meeting with your Hamas colleague for tomorrow."

Salama himself would control the largest group of warriors, in teams of three with each team handling the shoulder-fired Mk19 40mm that they had been studying in videos, along with a loaded six-round belt for each weapon. The videos, which would continue to be shown and reshown within each group until the Israelis attacked, described how to load and how to be accurate at one hundred yards against soldiers who dismounted their carriers and attacked with air support from drones and helicopters.

"No one is to engage until you give the order to Amad and the other leaders. We hope to take care of the helicopters and the drones separately, so no one should need to engage them. Your targets are men, and men only. Well, if we hit a few women, that's okay. We weren't the ones who drafted them."

Kufdani winked.

"Your people will have only razor rounds, as we discussed at Ktzi'ot," he continued. "We don't want them killed, just wounded and scared."

Salama bowed his head again. "You have made your message clear. And thank you for your kind words to the press about me," he said. "Is there anything more you need in return?"

Kufdani leaned forward and took a sip of his tea. "I'd like you to start the conversation about Palestine becoming a single political entity again. Fatah, Hezbollah, Hamas—all these warring factions are in the way of that. They must eventually become our allies in Allah, working together in pursuit of this monster that Israel is becoming. You must entice them, letting Allah lead the way."

"Only show me the way and, as an elder of Hamas, I will be delighted to do my part," Salama agreed. "The schism, as you call it, of Shiite and Sunni greatly reduces our economic and military impact. We must work together. I've come to respect your planning abilities. Bringing down the border crossing software at the Egypt-Gaza border was a stroke of genius. Our people just eased back into Gaza, carrying the arms and ammunition you provided, on the trucks that were modified as you specified. I'm told your man on the ground in Egypt was quite useful in figuring out how to move that much equipment into Gaza."

"Jerome is quite a useful man," Kufdani said. "I assume you have secured our packages until we need them?"

"As we agreed," Salama said. "The packages await an opportunity to be useful."

"Good. The tactics we discussed are important. The battlefield leaders will need to keep their troops under control and review the training on weapons use within the next week, using the Kphones I sent."

"We await our next move. Things are coming together. My leaders are enthusiastic."

"Great," Kufdani said. "And I'll do what I can to make you attractive as their leader, the one who can secure for them a better future. So don't get yourself killed."

Salama sat back and looked at him thoughtfully. *What an interesting man you are, Kufdani! So focused on the problem for our people, and not on your role in solving it. But do you not want to rule? Are you not destined to be the one who restores justice, the Mahdi?*

Kufdani denied this title once again, as he had at Ktzi'ot. But as he left the hut and returned to the narrow village path, local residents began to cluster around them, some shy, some clamoring for Kufdani's attention. The crowd grew, slowing his progress, and he shook the hands of some, patted the backs of a few others, even kissed a baby. He heard the whispers: *Mahdi. Mahdi.*

Flashing a mysterious smile, he instructed them to prepare for the coming battle, to have courage and follow the orders of their true leader, Yousef Salama. "Since death is our one sure destiny," he called out to the crowd, "why die a coward when you can be brave?"

The cries of *Mahdi* followed him all the way down the path.

HAARETZ ONLINE, TEL AVIV

REGINALD EDGEWORTH. THE REGINALD EDGEWORTH IS GOING TO BE calling. Elsa still couldn't believe it. She had decided to remain skeptical until she actually heard his voice, the one she'd heard on TV countless times. But so far, what Caitlin offered was pure gold, so Elsa was cautiously hopeful.

"I call him Edgie," Caitlin had said on the phone, "but you know him as Reginald Edgeworth. He'd like to meet with you."

"Reginald Edgeworth? Reggie fucking Edgeworth?" Elsa had shouted. The scent of a Pulitzer grew suddenly stronger. "I can make time for him at his convenience, of course. He just about owns the worldwide news and opinion business."

Caitlin had asked him to call at 3:00 Tel Aviv time, and Elsa had promised to wait by her phone. It was all moving so fast, and she had recruited a few staffers and stringers to help her work on the big stories facing Israel at this critical moment. This was career-making journalism.

The scheduled time was almost here. Elsa peered out her office window at the afternoon traffic beginning to build on the Tel Aviv streets below. Her stories on Jerusalem and Kufdani had been good and had attracted lots of attention. But the "Kill them all!" story had gone viral. She was getting calls from everywhere. Ad revenue was going up—*way* up.

Inevitably, she would be interrogated about her sources. How did she get inside the prime minister's secret meeting? She would have to defend herself without blowing up her only source: Caitlin O'Connor.

More important right now, however, was figuring out the next story and the one after that. It struck Elsa that the fastest way to do this was to get Edgeworth to commit to a plan, if he had one. And if he helped her learn more about this Kufdani person, all the better.

The best head on the planet, Elsa thought yet again. *Who the hell is this guy?* He was sort of handsome, she supposed, but sort of creepy too . . .

Her phone rang. She glanced at it and saw that the number was unlisted. "HOL, Elsa Sachs. How may I help you?"

"Ms. Sachs, this is Reginald Edgeworth. How nice to make your acquaintance, if only by phone. Is this a convenient time?"

"Now is convenient, Mr. Edgeworth. What can I do for you?" She hoped her voice wasn't shaking.

"I think we may be able to do things for each other in support of my client, Sheik Kufdani," he said.

"It's *Sheik* Kufdani now, Mr. Edgeworth?"

"You may call me Edgie, Ms. Sachs," he said, "and his name is whatever we want it to be, whenever we want it to be. The story we tell the world will present Kufdani in exactly the light we choose."

"And that story will end, you hope, with the return of the West Bank projects to the ownership and control of the Bedouin tribes."

"That is Sheik Kufdani's hope."

"And my part, Edgie?"

"We build the story. You sell it, with my help, to a world audience." He chuckled. "Journalism as it was meant to be."

"And if it doesn't work, and Sheik Kufdani gets his ass kicked in the next few weeks? What then?"

"Why, then what we have is a story with a very different ending to be crafted, but still a world-class story to be sure."

Elsa paused, choosing her words carefully. "Do we *care* whether he gets his ass kicked? It seems likely to me that he will."

"I care, but that is a mere aside to the story. If it's a good fight, Ms.

Sachs, it's a great story. But if *you* don't care to tell the story convincingly—a story that shares the message we've planned—then this conversation will be quite short."

She could almost taste that Pulitzer now, but there were still great pieces of this story that she didn't understand yet. "I think we are on the same page, Edgie, but walk me through what you see happening. Just how are we supposed to share this message?"

"I have spent far more time with Kufdani than you have," he replied. "Our conversations give me confidence that his plans are solid and workable. There will be glitches, of course, as in every great story. How they are handled will tell our viewers a lot."

"What kind of glitches?" Elsa asked.

"Well, for starters, he wasn't supposed to get drugged and thrown into an infamous Israeli prison."

"Yeah, that made for a good story. It didn't get picked up outside of Israel, but it did well in Tel Aviv. I liked it."

"I liked it too, Ms. Sachs," Edgie said, "and it will be a better story tomorrow for not having been picked up today. We're going to build an interesting mosaic around Kufdani." Each episode, he explained would fill in important blanks in the story they were selling. Slowly and powerfully, the full tale would come into focus.

"We can start with Mossad setting up the original meeting with prime minister—"

"Wait, wait," Elsa interrupted. This was a detail she hadn't heard yet. "Mossad? How did he get Mossad on his side?"

"Kufdani and the number two guy at Mossad, Norman Epstein, are old friends and collaborators. Epstein ran the US for Mossad for years. Kufdani was CIA special ops. They have an active history together."

Elsa listened carefully as Edgie divulged some of the other missing pieces of the puzzle, including how he supplied the Palestinians with the weapons necessary for their defense and smuggled them into Gaza while preparing for the inevitable IDF attack.

"And that's where we are right now, Ms. Sachs, the end of the story," Edgie said.

"The end?" Elsa asked. "Sounds more like the beginning."

"Of course, the story continues to unfold. We've got the raw material for the first chapter. Now we watch carefully and decide how to spin it from here."

"Are we sure that Kufdani has the stones for what comes next? Is he capable of killing the deadly people who will be coming for him?"

Edgie chuckled. "Quite sure. Capable to a fault, perhaps."

So he really is *the mean son of a bitch he looks like*, Elsa thought. *Guess that hard-looking body was well-earned.*

"So what do you say?" Edgie continued. "How about I fly you to New York and introduce you around; then we do a few specials and air them on my network? I'll arrange for the appropriate studios and production, first released as live shows and then rebroadcast as webcasts? The questions and answers will be carefully selected for our purposes, to maintain public interest and to reinforce our messages."

"Questions and answers?" Elsa repeated. "So I will be interviewing—"

Edgie laughed. "Of course! I will arrange for Kufdani to sit down with you again. Didn't he promise you another interview, Ms. Sachs?"

"Call me Elsa."

"Marvelous, Elsa. Now, you should consider what physical image you want to project to your new, larger audience. I'll be happy to consult on your new image when you come to New York, but it shouldn't be a problem." Edgie paused. "From what I've seen, you already have a face for television."

NEAR GAZA CITY

<u>TUESDAY</u>

KUFDANI CROSSED THE DIRT STREET AND WALKED TOWARD THE ADDRESS Amad had given for his meeting with Hamas. The café was perched on a dusty corner, and the unnamed Hamas officer for Gaza affairs sat alone at a tiny table inside. Kufdani was halted at the doorway, but smiled and voiced no objection, greeting the security people warmly. After releasing him, they took up inconspicuous stations outside the café, leaving the two men to their discussion. Tea was served, as always.

The Hamas officer wore the guerrilla's uniform: a thin, drab olive jacket, sleeves rolled up one turn, and a matching t-shirt. His hair was gray and his beard trimmed. His eyes were wary under steel-rimmed glasses. In his earlier days, he could have been a professor of history—and was, for all Kufdani knew.

"So, Yousef tells me that maybe you are the Mahdi," he said in a surprisingly deep voice. "What would the Mahdi have to discuss with Hamas?"

Kufdani continued smiling agreeably. "I'm not the Mahdi. Just a simple warrior and Islamic scholar. I come to you with a plan to engage Israel." He explained his strategy for confronting the Israelis when they came for him, speaking of nothing beyond the envisioned battle.

"Ah, Kufdani," the Hamas man replied. "You have a plan. We have a plan.

We plan to kill all the Jews in Israel. You plan to kill only a few, and send the rest home to fight again. It is not a difficult choice."

"We want our West Bank land returned," Kufdani insisted. "My plan is designed to make that happen."

"So you kill a few Israelis, and the Israelis kill a few of you? Not much of a plan." The man held Kufdani's gaze. "When we are ready, we will kill the rest of them—slaughter them in the tunnels of Gaza, our home. And then we will destroy *their* home."

The Hamas officer stood and looked out at the dusty street, where children kicked a bruised, weeping grapefruit around in a game of football.

"How many men and how much equipment will you need, and how may the forces of Hamas be of service?" he said over his shoulder. "My leaders are building stores for our own fight and may have little to provide to you."

"We ask only for your blessing—and for Hamas to stay out of this fight. We have been a long time planning it. We have what we need."

The man sat again and shrugged. "You are ready and we are not. Yousef Salama is gaining power within Hamas and supports you aggressively and without question. We will not interfere with your efforts."

Kufdani nodded his head and said, "Thank you. May Allah bless you for your understanding and patience."

The Hamas man nodded. "Inshallah."

Kufdani had gotten what he came for.

SHIN BET HEADQUARTERS, NORTHWEST TEL AVIV

OVER A WEEK HAD PASSED SINCE THE LAST TIME THE SHIN BET LEADership had gathered around the very same rectangular table. This time a seventh man joined them: Lieutenant Colonel Mati Shorch from the IDF, who was recently appointed commander of the 97th Netzah Yehuda of the Kfir Brigade. Formerly called the Netzah Haredi, the 97th was a well-trained volunteer battalion of nearly one thousand men, including two full companies and two in training. Although other Orthodox Jews had joined its ranks, causing the name change, the 97th was still vastly Haredim and favored by that community. The battalion was renowned for its bloody work in the West Bank.

Dayan stood and looked around the room, meeting each man's eyes. "The prime minister has decided the Netzah Yehuda should lead the attack in Gaza. The IDF has agreed. Lieutenant Colonel Shorch will fill you in."

Shorch stood from the table. "The Bedouins and the Palestinians have heaped shame on the 97th. They have destroyed the lives of thousands of Haredim and billions of dollars of equipment. Now it is time for retribution. We will plow through them, cutting a harsh swath with air and drone support, to remind them that in Israel, only Jews matter. The tanks and the rest of your units will mop up."

Still standing, Dayan said, "Anyone have a problem with that?"

"I can work it into our battle plans, of course," said Yitzak Galat, head of counterterrorism. "But have you worked into your planning the communications disruptions that attended the other recent attacks? The asymmetry in communication capabilities could signal trouble."

Shorch threw up his hands. "They're a bunch of Arabs. They don't have two brains to rub together! We're ready to go on a day's notice."

Galat shrugged. "I'll add your organization into the logistics manifest."

"The IDF won't be in the area long enough to need much logistics support," Shorch countered. "Now if I may be excused, gentlemen, I have work to do."

When the door closed behind him, Dayan looked at his team. "Any comments?"

"They'd better hope there's no serious opposition in the Strip," Galat said. "Getting back to our trains for food and water will be quite a haul. They need to be certain that they can contact us for a reserve."

Dayan shook his head. "They say they won't be there long enough. The prime minister was emphatic about executing Shorch's orders. He plans to carry out a lightning strike to the Egyptian border and then drive them back toward us."

Shorch had promised to deliver an operations plan by the following day. Although Dayan was no fortune teller, he had a feeling the prime minister would love it.

Dayan, on the other hand, had a bad feeling about it.

AL-BAYUK, GAZA STRIP

RECLINING ON AN OLD CANVAS AND ALUMINUM BEACH CHAIR WITH ONE of its back straps missing, Jerome Masterson eyed the local beer sweating in its amber bottle nearby, on the tree stump acting as his end table. His feet rested atop an old tree root.

He had supervised the outfitting of a personal command center in the town of Al-Bayuk, south of Rafah in the Gaza Strip, near the Egyptian border. After capturing the Israeli border agents at the Rafah border checkpoint and hobbling them in the back of their trucks, he had kept a few folks dressed as Israelis to man the checkpoint.

Yesterday, Jerome had watched as two S-300 batteries showed up—surface-to-air missiles, complete with crews. Cooch was pretty happy with Admiral Sino, who had approached his Egyptian counterpart about a chance to fuck with the Israelis. For the glory of Allah and a little revenge on the Israeli Air Force, the Egyptian defense minister was delighted. So was Cooch. Not only was the Russian-built S-300 one of the most feared air defense systems in the world, but Jerome and his troops would have the benefit of total surprise as well.

He had talked to some of the Egyptian guys, muddling through conversations even though their Arabic was different. Together they had sorted out the air defense tactics and then dug both the batteries in pretty good, so just the radar showed above the ground. The Egyptians had sent their A team, that was for certain—some seriously good people who had shown him around the S-300.

Those Russians build some heavy-duty shit, he thought, taking a long swig of his beer.

The Egyptian efforts would be billed as Islamic support for the Bedouins and the Palestinians—at least that was what the media would be reporting after the world saw the S-300s in use. At least Caitlin planned to have the video clip of the shoot-down. Edgie had written up something for Admiral Sino to pass along, together with what video Caitlin made available, to the Egyptian information minister: details to share with the press after the first attack.

Given the Gaza Strip's location up against the Mediterranean, Cooch seemed to think the Israelis would deploy their navy. So Jerome had positioned two trucks near the coast, each manned by a Bedouin team with a Javelin antitank weapon system and a supply of fragmentation and razor rounds. After shooting the first Javelin, the teams would need to shit and git, because those Israeli Navy guys would be pissed. Jerome had been able to get only six Javelins; there seemed to be a shortage even on the black market. The other four Javelins and a few Switchblade drones they got from the Iranians would be useful in destroying Israeli tanks if they became a problem.

As Cooch had told him earlier that day, things were getting hotter, faster. Jerome thought it was time to get back to checking things over—as soon as he finished his beer.

Jerome had moved his Bedouin teams closer to Sufa the previous day after they found firing spots within a thousand feet of the Israeli air base. Why the Israelis would put an air base right next to the Egyptian border was a mystery to him, but it was wide open to weapons that lobbed in destruction. He happened to have quite a few of those, in 40mm. Cooch had told him that Sufa's counter-batteries for artillery could detect no incoming smaller than 90mm. Plus, they would take seventeen minutes to come up to speed after being powered on in an electrical emergency.

Jerome smiled. *We'll be gone long before that.*

From Tangier, Caitlin had been inventorying equipment that Israel had positioned to use and messing with Sufa's electronics, so the Israelis were too busy to worry about a border station being out of touch. The fighter base had custom-made surveillance F-16s on its runways and housed a special forces unit, so he'd have to deal with that issue before he cut the border people loose—maybe pop an EMP round on every storage ramp, then rain down a bunch of fragmentation rounds on them. Maybe he'd frag them first, in hopes of blowing holes in any EMP hardening capabilities used by the fighter jets or other equipment, and then pop the EMP. Fun to think about. As usual, he'd make the decision at the last moment. But he was confident about fucking up, at a minimum, a billion dollars' worth of airplanes.

Jerome took another swig of beer and leaned back against the old beach chair. This was shaping up to be a major op. Time to review his end of the deal.

First there was the shopping list from this Edgeworth guy in New York. Jerome was flabbergasted by most of it. Five thousand flex-tie wrist cuffs? Those things were used to hobble prisoners with their hands behind their backs. Cooch was apparently planning to take more than a few prisoners. Empty ten-gallon water containers? They took up a lot of room on the trucks—he could have at least had them filled with good water from Egypt. The water here in Gaza really gave Jerome the shits.

The next few items on the list were particularly strange: thirty rechargeable electric hair clippers, ten gallons of red paint, and forty brushes. *Are we having some kind of party?* Jerome wondered. Go figure. But Cooch said to not get in Edgie's way.

The two hundred tubes of medical gel made more sense on a battle-field—probably to clean up the wounds from the razor rounds—although the Cooch Jerome knew would just let 'em bleed, so that was probably an Edgie thing, too. Cooch wasn't that touchy-feely. He'd just kill them on the battlefield, like his daddy taught him. Killing is cheaper, faster, and safer.

Cooch had specified all the things he needed a while ago, and Jerome was responsible for making sure they showed up. He sure would hate to get the stink-eye from Cooch for missing something important. Cooch did effective stink-eye: you knew you fucked up, you knew the impact of that, and you really felt like shit.

Jerome had supervised delivery of all that stuff to the command post that Cooch had set up near Bani Suheila, a small city just east of Khan Yunis in the southwestern part of the Gaza Strip. That pierced steel planking field across the border was pretty busy for an airstrip that didn't exist a week ago. C-130s were in and out of there three or four times a day, loaded with gear. Kufdani Industries was delivering the goods. Maybe it was just a busy runway rather than a true airport, but it sure was useful. When the trucks arrived at Bani Suheila carrying the goods, a bunch of Palestinians had offloaded it all.

Six teams of Moroccan Bedouins had stayed behind with them—eighteen of Jerome's finest, with South African 40mm weapons and a couple of pallets of 40mm special ammunition. Their ammunition would not fit the Mk19s procured for the Palestinians and a few local Bedouins to use. Cooch didn't want them killing people, so they got no ammunition to do that—typical Cooch.

Jerome was the shooter and worker, whereas Cooch was the thinker and planner. *Okay.* Jerome chuckled. *Cooch can also fight and shoot pretty good.* But that boy sure did have a bug up his ass about planning their little adventures, and this one was especially complicated. Why couldn't they just shoot them all? Dead people don't drink, eat, or try to escape.

Not killing them was clearly the plan, though, since Cooch had spent a ton of money on those razor rounds, which wouldn't kill shit. But they sure would fuck a guy up: bloody him and make him not want to fight. From a fused detonation altitude of thirty feet, they did a nice job shooting the spinning pieces of steel down in a ground radius of about fifty feet. If the target troops were bunched up, they'd be injured badly and quickly. If the troops were spread out, it would just take a while longer.

A few thousand Palestinians Cooch had managed to train somehow—not that Jerome was surprised—would be shooting a ton of razor rounds downrange at the Israelis. If they could get the Israeli troops out of their armored personnel carriers, those soldiers would be stepping right into deep shit. Their arms, their legs, and the backs of their necks would be exposed, and those razor cuts would really smart.

Cooch had designed that ammo well, shaping the charge for maximum impact. He'd also worked with Rheinmetall to design a spalling round for the tops of the APCs, intended to scare and cut until the troops decided to exit the vehicle. Then, after waiting for the baddies to organize, the Palestinian forces would cut them to pieces with razor rounds. Jerome had seen firsthand that the Rheinmetall guys were impressed and looked forward to selling a lot of that ammunition down the road.

The planning and preparation, the innovation and invention—in Jerome's eyes, it was all a thrill. Another thing he'd never seen before was a recording studio adjacent to a theater of war, but that was exactly what they had built a few days ago in Egypt, thirty miles from the border, at an old resort in the city of El-Arish. The outside just looked like a desert shanty, but inside—when it was lit up, and Emilie projected an image onto the white walls—the studio was every bit as modern as he'd expect to see in New York City. When it came to media equipment, that Edgie seemed to know his shit.

When Jerome first heard about it, he gave the studio building about thirty seconds before the Israeli Air Force decided they didn't want it there. Then he realized Cooch's plan was to deploy the first S-300 system in El-Arish and save the other one for the new PSP airstrip. Both would be well protected.

This was fun shit. Jerome loved being part of it all—being around when deals were made and billions were spent. But what he loved even more was all the violence and destruction that would follow.

WEST OF DEIR AL-BALAH, GAZA STRIP

THE STENCH OF DIESEL EXHAUST OVERPOWERED AN ACRID BODY ODOR. Strapped into their seats, nine Israeli soldiers of the 97th Netzah Yehuda battalion bounced and slid as the US-made M113 armored personnel carrier crossed into the Gaza Strip, sixteen miles north of the Egyptian border and a few miles east of Deir al-Balah—away from the city and its masses but still in the suburbs. A unit commander's helmeted, visored head stuck up from an armored cupola slot in the roof of the M113, like a cherry on a cupcake. The driver's head was another helmeted cherry, which allowed for easier driving: the view was better that way. Both could close their hatches quickly if artillery started exploding overhead.

The vehicle was just one in a long line of M113 armored personnel carriers snaking westward along the dusty residential route. The M113 was a holdover from Vietnam, improved from time to time over a half century but still vulnerable in the many ways that a fifty-year-old armored weapons carrier could be made vulnerable. Both driver and unit commander had radio wired into their helmets and were in contact with the battalion communications network. They had drilled often on this mission to the Gaza Strip to control the Palestinian populace, so today was a day on the job like any other—almost.

Dotted along the long, narrow Gaza Strip, the 97th Netzah Yehuda battalion leaders were encased in their respective M114 armored command vehicles, a smaller version of the M113 with space in each for a driver and a gunner, a commander plus one assistant, and lots of communications gear. Together, the heavy aluminum vehicles bounded over roads and fields, banners flying proudly from antennae, sometimes destroying crops but maintaining a rough line.

The battalion commander, Lieutenant Colonel Shorch, sat in his M114 on the rise at the eastern Gaza border, listening to the radio chatter. He watched the armored carriers turn in a line, with near perfect symmetry and timing, and begin driving south toward Egypt, with the Mediterranean Sea to the west.

Lieutenant Colonel Shorch's plan was for the 97th to travel in company-sized units. The battalion was deployed in three groups, each a two-hundred-man company, positioned about two miles apart but effectively covering the full six-mile width of the Gaza Strip from about halfway along its twenty-five-mile length. The fourth company lagged behind in reserve in the center sector, with wheeled support and logistics trucks farther behind yet.

Shorch checked with the two navy corvettes stationed two miles offshore, ready to move in to control the shoreline and support the assault if needed. He had five scout helicopters hovering above to survey the landscape for hidden Palestinians. IDF attack helicopters with their drones would follow, but Shorch didn't want them too close. He'd call them when he needed them. The prime minister had made clear that he wanted this nest of Palestinian vipers wiped out, and when things on the ground got hot, visual records were best avoided.

Shorch smiled. The hard part was over. No broken tracks. No stalled trucks. His unit was intact. When they encountered resistance, they would attack.

The 97th was ready.

KUFDANI COMMAND CENTER, GAZA STRIP

FIFTEEN MILES TO THE SOUTH OF GAZA CITY, KUFDANI SAT PERFECTLY still in the spacious basement of a squat yellow house on a small rise in the village of Bani Suheila. He saw, on three of the screens before him, the M113s turn south in unison, their banners advertising the intimidating presence of the 97th Netzah Yehuda. The images came from Israeli drones and were quite good. Thanks to Caitlin, who had hacked those very drones long ago, Emilie had been tracking the 97th since it assembled in Israel many hours earlier.

Extra power had been run to the yellow house so Kufdani could separate the signals from his Kphone into wall displays, allowing Emilie to manage both the display set and all interactions between Kufdani and his main players: Jerome was in the field, managing the most lethal of the 40mm weapons and the Bedouins who operated them, while also planning a raid on the Sufa air base and preparing for a potential navy attack. Caitlin was in Tangier, monitoring live video from Israeli surveillance cameras at various spots in Israel, and overseeing a list of communications points that would allow her to control tactical communications between Israeli units. And Edgie was across the border in Egypt, putting the finishing touches on the studio in El-Arish, ready to facilitate further contact with Elsa Sachs.

The plan was for Edgie to join Jerome soon in Al-Bayuk, so he could get a firsthand sense of the battle and be on top of all the great video when the balloon went up. So far, Kufdani's strategy had been to just get Edgie almost anything he asked for, especially if it kept him out of the way. Edgie was far from battle hardened: he could handle danger if he had a chance to think about it, but sudden explosions froze him.

The Sufa thing was interesting. Although it was founded as a kibbutz, where all income generated by the community and its members goes into a common pool, the site now contained an air base full of custom-built reconnaissance F-16s. Plus, from Mac, Kufdani had learned of a spook community in Sufa somewhere. He didn't want any well-trained special ops guys digging around in his backyard right now, so he figured a raid was an effective way to distract them.

Time to set the opening skirmish in motion, he thought, and smiled.

Kufdani raised his Kphone to his ear. "Go ahead with final planning for Sufa," he instructed Jerome. "The goal is maximum monetary damage to Israeli property. I'll have Caitlin send details on security. Do two strikes, use fire on the third, then run. I might need you." Then he messaged Caitlin, asking her to look into how Sufa secured its aircraft on the tarmac and whether the spooks were in town.

It was fun thinking about asymmetries: He could target a large area with three used trucks, each one manned by one of Jerome's three-man Bedouin crews, and the South African weapons mounted in the truck bed. A palette of Bedouin ammunition would comprise 90 percent fragmentation rounds plus the EMP devices and a few thermites to set things on fire. Kufdani estimated that in a quick strike, Jerome could damage thirty or so of Israel's prized fighter weapons, to the tune of billions of dollars.

A lot of 40mm ammunition had been distributed among his Palestinian forces—for the main event, they would use mostly Mk19 razor rounds. The trick would be stopping the drones and the helicopters with the more exotic 40mm rounds before cutting loose the razor rounds.

Kufdani saw, on the screens facing him, the scout helicopters catching up to the line of Netzah Yehuda APCs. His tired, scarred face lit up with a malevolent smile. In the shadows of the command center basement, which gave contrast and prominence to every feature, the scar on his face ran down his cheek like a serpent.

The Haredim had come for him.

Kufdani would not disappoint.

AL-BAYUK, GAZA STRIP

JEROME AND EDGEWORTH STARED AT THE WALL OF JEROME'S COMMAND center hut, where Emilie was projecting video of the emerging combat through Jerome's Kphone. "It's time, my little vermin," Jerome heard Cooch say through the open line on the Kphone. "Come into my trap."

The shooters were Jerome's own Bedouin troops from Kufdani Industries in Tangier, transported with three hundred of their colleagues from Morocco on a fast ship. Jerome had trained them all himself; they were good, but more than that, they were disciplined. Disciplined was what Cooch valued most right now.

"Blue two take the central corridor, stop first four helicopters," came Cooch's order. "Nets, I say again, nets. Confirm fire."

"Roger, wilco," came the reply.

"Blue one and three, engage helicopters when they come in range."

Jerome wondered what Cooch would think of the new anti-helicopter round. Several years ago, he had helped Rheinmetall with the design of the explosives but hadn't bothered sticking around to watch the test. Jerome had watched it, though, and subsequently bought a bunch for Morocco. He couldn't wait to see them deploy in the Gaza Strip.

The new 40mm round exploded, popping a fine wire net in the air above the helicopter like something out of a Spider-Man movie. According to design, the net was sucked into the downdraft from the whirling blades. Almost instantly, it stalled the rotor and thus the blades, causing the helicopter to lose lift.

"Red one, red two, red three, engage armored carriers in their backspace, then progress to lead," Cooch's voice said over the Kphone. "Disengage when they dismount. Confirm."

"Red one, roger."

"Red two, roger."

"Red three, roger."

Jerome chuckled as Edgie, his jaw hanging slack, watched the images on the wall: Two of five helicopters went spinning, fluttering to the baked soil of Gaza. A third limped away, losing altitude. The remaining two turned north for further guidance. The two men cheered when the transmission came through: "This is blue two. Two scout birds down, one wounded, two retreating."

Emilie continued to project assorted views of the battlefield. Explosions were showing up in red and yellow above the rear line of M113s—the ones carrying the reserve company of Netzah Yehuda. As the special 40mm grenades exploded over the layers of massed aluminum, the fragmentation not only directly impacted the aluminum roof, but also caused spalling on the underside of the aluminum armor as shards of aluminum on the inside surface broke loose. Drivers' spaces and drivers' faces were particularly vulnerable to these projectiles. Faces, hands, and arms were cut, blood was flowing, and the language inside the carriers was darkening rapidly. In the troop cabin, thighs were beginning to suffer as exposed legs were sliced.

Jerome sat at the edge of his seat, waiting for what he knew must come next.

Holding their rifles, the soldiers began exiting their vehicles with their rifles and moving to protected ground positions, seeking cover in ground creases and behind trees. They quickly sorted into their units and prepared to move south, continuing on their mission toward the Egyptian border.

Their chatter came through in audio curated and translated into English by Emilie.

The soldiers proceeded on foot through the suburbs, rifles ready, bayonets fixed. Thanks to Emilie's exhaustive research, Jerome knew that each soldier had a magazine of fifteen rubber bullets locked and loaded in the rifle and another in a magazine pouch. A third magazine was in the pouch, just in case, loaded with live, hollow-point ammunition.

Fat lot of good it will do them. Jerome smiled.

As he watched the screens, the 40mm anti-armor fire shifted to the main advancing lane, now far ahead of the reserve. "Fire discipline. Fire discipline," he muttered. "We own their sorry asses. Now execute."

One round every thirty seconds started to fall on the advancing M113s, then two, then three rounds. Jerome listened as the slow pitter-patter of the early explosions developed into a series of staccato bursts and then a regular pattern of attack: ten rounds or so every ten seconds. This was where they faced the greatest danger of failure.

The chatter between the armored vehicles' leaders remained constant and disciplined at first. Then Cooch's voice came through the Kphone. "Emilie, limit the communication contact within the target group. Eliminate contact of 97th with Shin Bet and IDF."

Emilie's translation from Hebrew started to run together.

"Red team, attack six M114 command vehicles," Cooch ordered. "Report when dismounted. Capture and separate leaders from others."

"This is red leader. Roger. Wilco," came the reply.

The chatter of radio talk diminished, interrupted by long bursts of static. All became chaos.

SHIN BET COMMAND POST, GAZA CITY

SITTING IN A COMMUNICATIONS TRAILER, THE SHIN BET LEADERSHIP was impatiently waiting for contact with the 97th battalion to be restored. Dayan had a bad feeling about it.

"Strange. The signals were good, and then there was just nothing there," Galat insisted. "They seem to be engaged but haven't asked for any help, so all must be well."

Dayan just looked at the counterterrorism expert, incredulous.

"I'm glad they haven't asked yet," Deputy Director Klinger said, "but I don't like any of this. Figure out where the communications went bad; then we'll see where we are." He instructed Galat to have Sufa send three of their pretty F-16s on a high-speed pass from north to south to take some pictures, one up each attack vector. "Then move the navy closer and shoot up the beach a bit. Shake them up a little, and maybe get better intelligence than we're getting here."

Dayan sat back, staring up at the ceiling. The trailer suddenly felt very small. "We have no enemy to attack," he muttered. "It could be a kill fest up there, for all we know. They could be killing them all!"

That phrase struck a chord, and in an instant, he knew.

It's that fucking Cooch, somehow.

AL-BAYUK, GAZA STRIP

THEY WERE ON THE VERGE OF THE END GAME—AT LEAST THAT WAS what Jerome said. Edgie had never seen a real battle before. He continued to be fascinated as this one unfolded right before his very eyes, thanks to Caitlin, Emilie, and the wonders of high-tech Israeli video surveillance.

The 97th troops had left their carriers not long after the red team's barrage began, just as Alex Cuchulain had anticipated. Nothing much happened for the next few minutes. Then the explosions began overhead. The soldiers on the ground began to dance violently, slapping at their arms and legs and the backs of their necks.

Hundreds of Palestinians became visible on Edgie's screen as Emilie curated the drone feeds, emerging in fire groups of three, their Mk19s firing six rounds per team from belts of razor round ammo. Most were aimed, controlled shots, but a few of the troops were just seizing their chance to do some damage to Israelis in retaliation for one offense or the other over the decades. As they watched, Edgie heard Jerome muttering, "Fire discipline," to himself, but for some of the shooters, any thought of discipline was forgotten. The shooting slowed, then finally stopped, when the Palestinians ran out of ammunition.

Edgie could hardly believe his eyes. Images of Israeli soldiers curled on the ground in fetal positions dominated the screens. Blood was everywhere.

Yet as he and Jerome continued to watch, the soldiers began to stumble to their feet—again, according to Cuchulain's plan.

"Alpha and bravo, deploy to site two," came over the radio from Cuchulain.

"Alpha leader, roger. Wilco."

"Bravo, leader, roger. Wilco."

A light-colored Toyota pickup truck came bounding over the uneven ground toward the fallen troops. It was flying a white flag. When the Toyota neared them, it spun in the dust. As the dust settled, a sign on the tailgate appeared that said, in Arabic and Hebrew, *Lay down your arms, take off your body armor, and follow me.*

A few startled-looking men got up without their rifles, blood running from their arms and necks, and walked toward the truck, then a few more. Edgie heard explosions to the north of the hut, then nothing, and imagined that the same thing was going on in the other two attack corridors nearby, where even Caitlin had apparently been unable to locate or hack any cameras. These soldiers clearly had not trained for this type of surprise operation.

Cuchulain is moving assets as planned, to engage the relief column expected from Shin Bet, Edgie remembered. That could end up being a far more lethal engagement.

The surrendering prisoners visible on the screen were intercepted by Palestinian men carrying handfuls of plastic flex ties. Groups of women pointed to the ground beside the Israelis, instructing them to stack their helmets and body armor beside the path. Their captors formed lines of prisoners and bound their hands behind them. Most complied without a fuss.

Then one Israeli soldier pulled a pistol from his vest and started to shoot.

Three Palestinian women fell to the ground, bleeding.

The pistol wielder spun backward suddenly, screaming and slumping. A bleeding hole had appeared in the middle of his shoulder.

Another soldier, with a pistol partway out of his vest, took a round through his right elbow, eliciting a rending wail of pain and loss.

Two Bedouin snipers were dug in, five hundred feet from the white truck, observing the surrender through the low-power scopes on their 22 Nosler rifles, ready to shoot when the first surrendering Israeli had pulled the pistol from his vest. Nosler 25-grain match bullets were accurate to a quarter inch at that distance, at least for the first careful shot. The bullets were not good at killing; they didn't expand at impact but instead went straight through. The impact of their flight speed destroyed whatever bone and gristle they passed through.

The snipers also had two thirty-round magazines, each with Nosler 125-grain hunting rounds that expanded on impact and would bring down a deer at five hundred feet. If necessary, these snipers could put a bullet within a virtual four-inch target box every four seconds until magazine change, which took eleven seconds. They heard on their radios that the two other sniper teams dealt with similarly bad behavior by the 97th soldiers.

After the three injured women crumpled to the ground fell, some of the remaining women fell screaming on the first wounded Israeli shooter, punching and hitting him. Others approached in large numbers, some wielding small knives and scissors pulled from their sewing kits and bags.

But that was not the image Edgie wanted the world to remember.

He backed up an image with his Kphone and froze it for examination: one of the falling Palestinian women with her hands shooting up in the air, her black hair spilling in a fan around her head and shoulders, the blood from her chest frozen in the air and contrasting with the white of her garment, her agonized face as she fell. He wondered if she was dead. He should check, and get a journalist to cover the grief too, if needed. Now *this* image was superb. It would sell.

A roar sounded overhead as high-speed jet aircraft made a pass above the command post. As the sound faded, Edgie heard the Kphone squawk. "Gyptair, weapons free," Cuchulain ordered from his command post—and then, directly to Jerome, "Five, attack Sufa."

"Five, roger, underway," Jerome came back, his instructions confirming the assignment of forces and granting permission to fire at will.

The first attack on the IDF's Sufa air base had begun.

SHIN BET COMMAND POST, GAZA CITY

THREE F-16S FROM SUFA ROARED OVERHEAD, HEADING SOUTH TOWARD Egypt. For the moment, Dayan and Galat diverted their attention from the complete lack of communication from their units in the evolving conflict a few miles to their west.

At least they were still in contact with their air cover, although not with the troops on the battlefield. The flight leaders transmitted in the bored voice of macho flyers everywhere. To Dayan, it was strangely reassuring to know that communications with the aircraft were intact.

"At the border, break right for a pass down the coast."

"Two."

"Three."

"Missiles! Break right, countermeasures. S-300." There was a squawk, then silence.

Dayan could barely contain his shock. An S-300 meant a new game where Shin Bet wasn't invited. *But we only do domestic shit . . .* , he thought aimlessly.

He started giving orders to his equally shocked staff. "Pull the navy back. Send the F-16s home, if any remain. Let's carefully retrieve our unit ground probe. Return fire, but don't initiate. We don't know what the hell is going on."

What was going on? The utter neutralization of the Israeli forces involved in the attack. And when those F-16s encountered the surface-to-air defense system at El-Arish—and then, under the Shin Bet director's orders—tried to return "home" to Sufa, no such home remained.

Across the width of runways, fragmentation rounds exploded at thirty feet above the targets, shrapnel slicing down through the Plexiglas of the unattended cockpits; the upper surface of the wings above the fuel tanks; and across the fuselage. As nearby trucks were hit, people tumbled out of them and ran for cover. Leaks of jet fuel dripped and sprayed on the tarmac, forming oily pools.

Alarms sounded. Trucks deployed to their assigned slots and prepared for pilots to arrive and man their planes. Armed troops deployed to the gates and other predetermined exposure points. Defense radars were manned.

Jerome Masterson had deployed a total of nine men—three teams of Bedouins—in three trucks, each carrying a half pallet of 40mm rounds of varying capability, plus a belt of ten rounds of high-explosive fragmentation rounds loaded into their South African 40mm launchers. Each team had as its target a ramp of parked, waiting F-16s, a thousand feet away, along with the support trucks and personnel working on the ramp and in the offices nearby. The Bedouin gunners worked through their calculations for thorough coverage of their target area, methodically walking the bursts through their arc of assigned coverage.

Upon finishing their ten-round belts of fragmentation rounds, each set of gunners loaded a belt of three EMP rounds. Their next fire plan: to disable the trucks, the service vehicles, and the entire electrical support system and infrastructure at the Sufa air base. The 40mm EMP rounds fell along three wide, blacktopped aircraft storage areas. Fuel trucks ground to a halt. Pilot delivery vehicles stalled in place. The lights in the support offices blinked and went out.

The gunners waited ninety seconds.

Then attack three began.

Taking two standard 40mm thermite rounds from each truck, the Bedouin gunnery crews fired them halfway across their assigned attack area. When the rounds exploded, the thermite reached temperatures of over five thousand degrees Fahrenheit, igniting the stray pools and trails of jet fuel. The fires spread quickly and began to consume fuel vehicles. Support staff on the ground ran for cover.

Their tasks at Sufa completed, the gunners quickly lashed the remainder of their 40mm ammunition onto dedicated pallets and sped away from Sufa in the direction of their next assignment. The current one had taken twenty-three minutes, start to finish.

Dayan did not know all this, of course—not just yet. But an incoming message from the IAF notified him that the Sufa air base was under attack, had suffered heavy damage, and was closed to incoming traffic. He picked up his papers and his radio, hoping he still had contact with his people.

"I told them not to put all that secret shit so near the border," he muttered to himself. "But no. They *had* to have the votes of the kibbutzim and the Haredim."

He continued barking orders into his radio, grateful that at least *it* worked.

"Pull the probe back slowly. Bring the vehicles with them. Confirm hand signals for movement direction. Take five tanks, and set a screen behind the retreating probe at five hundred yards. If they pursue, ambush them—gloves off. Let's start back to Tel Aviv with full flank security. Weapons free."

KUFDANI COMMAND CENTER, GAZA STRIP

KUFDANI WATCHED THE IMAGES PROJECTED ON HIS BASEMENT WALL as his men engaged the relief column with 40mm fragmentation fire. The lead vehicle in the relief column was falling back. Shin Bet was directing targeted artillery fire at the red teams, endangering civilians still in the area.

"Red teams, snipers, move to position three," he ordered. "Disengage."

Kufdani had picked a spot where Shin Bet relief forces, traveling along the center corridor, would be forced into smaller avenues of attack, bunching them closer. He had ordered the sites to be dug in and sheltered. From there, if Shin Bet kept coming, he would attack them with fragmentation rounds rather than razor.

It would be a bloody fight.

But when the lead units in the center corridor attack began withdrawing, Kufdani reassessed the situation. Five tanks were driving well behind the withdrawal, taking any shooters from his forces under fire. Shin Bet was still four miles from the spectacle of the surrendering soldiers of the 97th and out of radio contact with them. They had no idea what lay ahead.

"Do not engage the attacking tanks. Weapons are safe. They are withdrawing," Kufdani said into his Kphone. Emilie made sure his entire team received the message.

Their plan so far had resulted in unmitigated success.

THE COMPOUND AT BANI SUHEILA had been transformed into a prisoner processing facility, and the surrendering Israeli troops just kept coming. Each set of prisoners—a total of nearly eight hundred at first count—was force-marched four miles eastward to the flat, open field punctuated with a few low houses and huts. The surrendering soldiers stood in a line with their hands still bound behind them as Palestinian women used electric clippers to shave their heads, four at a time.

There was plenty of hair to cut. Palestinian children ran to pack it into rough bags as it fell. The hair of conquered Israeli soldiers could be woven and sold as souvenirs. Those who resisted were wrestled to the ground by waiting Palestinian men, who shaved their heads with manual clippers, with somewhat bloodier results.

The shaved heads continued behind a row of low buildings to the south, where a giant doorway was constructed of scrap lumber. As they passed through, each prisoner received a bright red splash of paint across the top of his bald head, again administered by laughing Palestinian women, some standing on low benches and wielding the brushes, others holding the buckets of paint into which they were dipped. Scuffles of resistance were fewer this time, yet many Palestinian men remained eager to help secure and decorate the prisoners.

Just past the painting station, more women waited to serve drinks of water from wooden buckets filled by hand from large containers dunked into local wells. Even at this point, while waiting to drink, the prisoners looked stunned. Most were submissive. This was so far beyond anything they had trained for that they were simply lost.

The prisoners then shuffled around another set of buildings and into a long, barren field, out of sight from the newer arrivals, where many more Palestinian men awaited them, pinking shears in hand. The prisoners were thrown to the ground and held while their shirts and trousers were cut off, then sent forward to a group of women with small squeeze tubes of a bright green medical gel. The women rubbed gel on the prisoners' many bleeding cuts. A few of the older women swatted at the prisoners' genitals with switches and old brushes loaded with new red paint.

By this point in the assembly line, most prisoners stood passively as their clothes were cut off and discarded. Palestinian men were able to cut the flex-ties that bound the prisoners' hands behind them and secure their hands in front of them with fresh flex-ties. There was little resistance.

When Lieutenant Colonel Shorch and his sixteen battalion officers were brought forward, their heads were shaved and their clothes cut off, and their bare genitals and buttocks were sprayed with the fluorescent green medical gel—similar to the others, albeit with extra paint and much more resistance. It might have been a fight too, if the prisoners' hands had not been bound.

Finally, four aviators from two shot-down F-16s and six crew members from downed helicopters were brought forward in their sweat-stained flight suits with their hands tied in front of them. They were provided chairs in the shade, where they nervously watched the armed Palestinian guards, but no one bothered them except to offer snacks and tea.

With little left to do, the shaved, painted Israeli soldiers stood nude in the afternoon sun. It had been barely five hours since they rode dramatically on a path to victory and dominance.

Stepping out from his basement command center, Kufdani surveyed this vivid, real-life portrait of chaos and order. Here and there he observed men with cameras, right up close with the prisoners: Edgie's people, the best in the businesses. Soon, all the world would see the heartrending images that Edgie was working toward: a visual portrayal of *too far, too fast, too much*.

The soldiers clearly hadn't trained for this. Nor had they been given any warning of what they would face. And now they were prisoners standing naked before their captors, stunned and overwhelmed.

NEAR RAFAH, GAZA STRIP

ON A SMALL RISE ON THE OUTSKIRTS OF RAFAH, NEAR SUFA, IN THE back of a white Toyota pickup with the mounting bracket for an Mk19 still bolted to the floor, Kufdani sat on a wooden storage box with Jerome and Salama at his sides. Marching beside the truck were ten Palestinian soldiers on guard. Strung out behind them was a ragged formation of nude men, followed by a growing mob of thousands of Palestinians, watching, jeering, cheering.

Kufdani put his Kphone back into his pocket and called for a halt. "Edgie needs another ten minutes to get his people in place."

The prisoners were starting to stumble anyway. They had been force-marched for six miles, moving relentlessly southeast, stopping every half hour to rest and drink. Some had bowel problems from the local water, and their legs were stained. Others had thrown up. Now they took a long break in the lessening heat of the late afternoon, a quarter mile from the air base, while Kufdani waited for Edgie to give the go-ahead.

Edgie had arranged for an event to be broadcast on his TV and online networks, available to be picked up worldwide by anyone with a signal. To support this effort, Caitlin had located and hacked a new Boeing satellite that provided sound and signal coverage for remote spots in a quality unsurpassed by anything local. Ads had been purchased or arranged the day before on media outlets Edgie found useful—mostly his.

Emilie had accessed video of the Sufa air base attack until the EMP rounds took out the base camera coverage, blinding outside eyes to the remainder of the blossoming debacle. Edgie had obtained recordings of the first few minutes, though, and Kufdani had confirmed that he planned to use them. Images of the destruction would soon be on screens across the globe. But first, Edgie would capture this moment of victory at Sufa, using his media savvy to both elevate Kufdani and portray him as a deeply religious, humble, unassuming leader of men.

Kufdani picked up a dark bulletproof vest from the storage box on the truck bed and offered it to Salama. "Put this on under your shirt. It will protect you in case anyone manages to smuggle in a small weapon."

"What comes next in your plan, Kufdani?" Salama asked.

"I will make a talk about our victory and Islam," he replied, "and then you will commit Palestine on behalf of Allah."

Salama reached for the vest. "This morning, I was waiting for an attack and wondering how many of us would die. This afternoon, I return eight hundred prisoners of war to the accursed Israelis." He shrugged. "It is all moving too fast, Kufdani."

"Do you trust me?" he asked.

"Yes, I trust you," said Salama. "Play on."

SUFA AIR BASE, ISRAEL

KUFDANI STOOD ALONE ON THE BED OF THE OLD, WHITE PICKUP, AGAINST a background of smoking hulks of F-16s, the skeletal remains of burned fuel trucks, and office buildings with missing windows. Four cameras were trained on him, each from a different angle, awaiting Edgie's activation. He wore a checkered scarf wrapped around his head, the ends dropping past his shoulders, reminiscent of Yasser Arafat, and a loose white shirt open at the neck. He was clean-shaven, and his scarred face appeared handsome, in a rugged, intimidating sort of way.

Edgie nodded.

Kufdani looked directly into the cameras and said, "Bedouins did this."

He swung his arm across the wrecked Sufa vista, and the cameras followed his gesture. Wild applause thundered from the crowd of Bedouins and Palestinians who stood before him. His voice echoed powerfully thanks to the microphone wired into Edgie's system and the speakers embedded in the ground, interspersed among the crowd.

"In the name of Allah and the sacred tenets of Muslims everywhere, we, the Bedouin nations and our Palestinian brothers in Islam, have graciously decided to return a group of prisoners of war to Israel. We are at the border crossing in Sufa, waiting for you to take them home."

At Edgie's instruction, the cameramen focused on the sea of red heads and green genitals belonging to the nude prisoners.

"The Israeli government attacked us this morning in the Gaza Strip, which is sovereign Palestinian territory and so designated by the United Nations," Kufdani continued. "They chose to send the 97th Netzah Yehuda, a full battalion of Orthodox armored infantry. All prisoners are Haredim, and it was made clear today that they simply are not capable. They don't have the fortitude of men, and we've adjusted their appearance temporarily to reflect this."

The crowd roared again.

"You are welcome to your Haredim," Kufdani spat. "They are worthless scum, and I now return them to you, relatively unharmed. The infantry surrendered nearly immediately once they came under fire, so there was no reason to kill them in battle. We have fed and watered them, and treated their wounds, because we understand—unlike Israel—that this is the humane thing to do. But this is Islam's final gesture of goodwill. We will not tolerate being robbed and humiliated by a theocracy—any theocracy, Jewish or otherwise."

The cameras swung over the cheering supporters once more. An undercurrent of sound rose from the crowd, indistinguishable at first but then as a growing whisper.

Mahdi! Mahdi! Mahdi!

"Our Muslim brothers in Egypt and Morocco have supported us in this encounter. If you force this conflict to go any further, all of Islam will support us."

The cameras' focus returned now to the speaker, standing tall and majestic on the old white Toyota bed.

"I am Kufdani," he said proudly, "a simple Yahia Bedouin scholar from Morocco. I preach on the apostasy of the schism between Sunni and Shi'a, and on the glory of the Islamic Golden Age. Together in Islam, we will return to that glory."

The cheers erupted again.

"I am the elected leader of a million Bedouins spread across the Middle

East, who are among the earliest followers of Islam. We have no government of our own, but since our first days, more than fifteen hundred years ago in Medina with Muhammad (peace be upon him), we have relied on Allah, not government, for guidance and succor. Allah has repaid us today."

In response to this, the applause and cheering grew even louder.

"Several years ago, the Israeli government confiscated Bedouin land on the basis that no non-Jew is permitted to own property in Israel—that Muslims have no rights in a Jewish society," Kufdani continued. "They stole Bedouin property to build housing for their Orthodox Jewish sect, the Haredi, with the profits also going to Orthodox Jews with Russian thugs among them, doing their dirty work.

"You have heard and read the recent stories by now, about a series of outrageous, incredible, disgraceful actions by the Israeli government in response to attempts to discuss—merely discuss!—the outrage of property confiscation on religion. I, Kufdani, led those attempts at finding a solution.

"I met with the Israeli prime minister as a diplomat, with a sealed introduction from the king of Morocco. I then met with the Haredi defense minister, Yakov Bernstein. And what did I receive in return for my diplomatic efforts? A sedative needle in my arm, and an unpleasant vacation to the Negev, to Ktzi'ot Prison. Did they expect no retaliation?"

Kufdani paused for a moment. *I'm coming for you, Bernstein*, he thought. *I am planning your demise.* Maybe he would rip the Haredi man's arm off and beat him to death with it. But no, that would be a mistake. Not enough pain.

He went on. "While I was in prison, an accident occurred at a West Bank construction site. Israel has produced no proof of who caused the damage, yet has used this excuse to evict all Israeli Bedouin, men, women, and children, from their homes. Again I ask, did the Israeli government, the IDF, the Shin Bet expect no retaliation?

"In response, the Bedouins chose to target Israeli infrastructure in Jerusalem and disrupt Israelis' basic civil rights, to show them what it means to be denied these things as they had been denied to us. We killed no one. We injured no one. And yet the prime minister issued a kill order for thousands of people, including me. He then authorized a vicious attack on my partner, my true love—and her friend, the wife of a US special ambassador. Did the Israeli government, the IDF, the Shin Bet expect no retaliation?"

Kufdani glared into the center camera. His eyes hooded into slits, shifting left and then right, and his face morphed from angry to evil. His long scar turned brighter. His enormous neck bulged from the loose, white neck of his shirt. His tongue flickering between his lips as if tasting the air.

"Mr. Prime Minister, if you take issue with me, please come and hurt me personally. I would welcome an opportunity to expose you for the cowardly, inept, worthless person you are. You were special ops in your youth, as was I. We know much about killing. How about killing me one-on-one instead of hiring people to dispense your filth? You may try, but I will hurt you."

But not as much as I'm going to hurt you, Bernstein.

Kufdani looked away from the camera, striving to recover himself. He looked over at Edgie, who glanced at his watch and raised a thumb. His message was coming through loud and clear.

Mahdi! the crowd continued to roar. *Mahdi! Mahdi!*

Kufdani made a conscious effort to relax, willing himself to lose the Gila monster look. "During my time as a prisoner at Ktzi'ot," he continued, "I became acquainted with a great man: Yousef Salama, the righteous Palestinian leader. He was kind enough to allow me to minister, to pray, and to teach Allah's lessons to the prisoners under his protection. Then, when our frustration and rage at the mistreatment of our loved ones spilled over, he allowed me to escape with him from Ktzi'ot. Together with thousands of other Muslims, we escaped to Egypt—again graciously sparing the lives of Israeli Jews, despite experiencing years of brutality under their prison guards.

"Today the Israelis came to punish us, the Muslims who live in Palestine and the Muslims who serve Allah without a country, we Bedouins. Yousef Salama named me as commander of our defense. I welcomed this opportunity. As you can see, I am a man competent in violence, as was Muhammad (peace be upon him).

"Under the orders of Yousef Salama, today I commanded our forces deployed to resist the invasion of Palestine by the Israel Defense Forces, Shin Bet, and the Israeli Navy. They came across our border with all of the might of Israel: armored infantry, navy, helicopters, and jet fighters. Here at the Sufa air base, you see the result of our resistance. We were not known to be armed with more than slingshots, so they did not fear us. But we had the blessing of Allah!"

Mahdi! Mahdi! Mahdi!

"The nations of Islam everywhere are uniting in support of the Bedouin people and the Palestinian nation," Kufdani continued. "My leader, Islam's champion, was victorious today, and we support him. We applaud our leader, Yousef Salama."

Salama stood and raised his arms. The crowd cheered wildly, and a few shots were fired into the air. The cameras panned over the Palestinians and Bedouins gathered there, before focusing once more on the prisoners of war.

"Rather than competent soldiers," Kufdani continued, "Israel sent these red-topped surrender monkeys whom we now return to their wives and mothers. They are cowards who gave up at the first shot. They abandoned their weapons and equipment, which we have now confiscated. The commanders of the unit are among them, no longer distinguished by anything but their lack of courage. We shall keep their armor and weapons in case of another attack, with real Israeli soldiers now that the 97th battalion is no more."

Mahdi! Mahdi! Mahdi!

Kufdani paused, glaring into the camera one final time.

"That fight will be very bloody."

MOSSAD HEADQUARTERS, TEL AVIV

GUNS TURNED TO THE TEAPOT, STARTING OFF THE PROCESS FOR A badly needed refill. He could hardly blame his boss. Sitting together in his office, he and Pelzer were reviewing, frame by frame, the Israeli drone videos of the day's fiasco—the tragedy unfolding in the Gaza Strip and at the Sufa air base. Thanks to the IDF link to the new Boeing 03b mPower satellites covering the Kufdani turnover of prisoners, the images were clear and distinct. Guns was forced to come face-to-face with the reality of the damage at Sufa, and with the image of Kufdani in all his glory.

"We suffered a major defeat today, no matter how the IDF and the prime minister want to play it," Pelzer was saying. "I want to understand how this happened, what we know about the planning and logistics, and what we do from here."

Another technology triumph for Caitlin and Cooch, Guns conceded. "I guess it's time to step it up a notch." The escalation had run its course: Israel had deployed fighter jets, tanks, infantry, and the navy against Kufdani—and had lost on every front. Guns hadn't anticipated this level of response. Perhaps he should have, even though the prime minister had instructed Mossad to butt out. "We've moved past the West Bank situation. Cooch has somehow gotten the Palestinians involved and under his control."

Without Cooch as their leader, the Palestinians would have killed all eight hundred of the 97th Netzah Yehuda. Guns knew this without a doubt. Sadly enough, it would have made things easier for him. Just think of all the sympathy for the dead, not to mention the grieving! The possibilities regarding an Israeli response would have been unlimited. But instead he was returning every last prisoner to Israel, live on global television.

"And now?" Pelzer asked.

Guns raised an eyebrow, and when Pelzer nodded, he poured for two. "We'll see soon, I imagine." The Cooch he once knew would have killed them all on the battlefield, gathered their weapons, and passed them out to be used for the ambush on the revenge attack. That was what his daddy had taught him: if they're on the battlefield, they are the enemy and should be killed.

Pelzer looked puzzled. "What do you think he wants?"

Guns handed Pelzer a steaming mug and sat down. "I don't know, but he's not operating from the goodness of his heart."

Pelzer took a tentative sip. "We must get on top of the public relations aspect. Our allies have a set of expectations. They believe in our military competence. For goodness' sake, this is the state of Israel against the great unwashed."

"Uh-huh. And we appear to be losing." Guns was feeling a little underwater. The Egyptians, the Moroccans, even the Iranians were making protest noises and vague threats about the need for a global Islamic response. The Egyptians were already in the fray, given that the S-300 had brought down two of Israel's F-16s in Egyptian airspace, according to the press releases, with promises of video to come. And IDF was telling them nothing thus far.

"Tell me what's going on, and I'll make sure you're the next head of Mossad," Pelzer said.

Guns laughed. "Thanks for the promotion, but it's a bit premature. The scope of this conflict has moved beyond the West Bank. Our nation is at risk."

"My word, that seems a bit extreme."

"Think about it," Guns retorted. "Kufdani has a plan that is now playing out."

The speech bragging about the capture of eight hundred IDF soldiers on Palestinian soil was just the first step, but it had been given the full propaganda treatment alongside fabulous photography. And Cooch had hired Reginald Edgeworth to manage his public relations. Guns suspected they would soon be hearing more from him.

Not only that, but Kufdani had suborned the most powerful online voice of liberal Zion, Haaretz Online. Elsa Sachs was increasingly being recognized as a bright and committed journalist—who was also very ambitious. Guns had heard she would soon be heading for New York and a major promotion. Given her recent journalistic disclosures, that couldn't be good for Mossad and its interests.

"Israel has suffered more than twenty billion dollars of damage and counting," Guns continued. "The president of the United States is furious with us. I'm thinking he's not exactly about to volunteer to fix what Cooch has broken."

"I get it," Pelzer said. "But what is Kufdani's end game?"

"I dunno," Guns replied, "but his midgame is coming into focus."

"To wit?"

"It's just as he told us: He wants our diaspora and the liberal Israeli community to give up on the West Bank. He wants our best public opinion on his side."

Pelzer took a sip of her tea and stared at a blank wall. "And from there?"

Guns looked at his shoes. "From there, it will get nasty. We need to begin planning for a new election." Of that, he felt sure.

"That isn't exactly the business of Mossad—"

"The survival of Israel is the business of Mossad," Guns said, "and the business of patriots. Let's let the midgame play out and continue taking the temperature of our colleagues."

Pelzer put her mug down and gazed at him. "How do *you* think I should be planning my time, Epstein?"

His answer came immediately. "Find a way to get next to Sachs. See where her head is. We're going to need a new prime minister, and she can help or hinder our candidate. Make her see our world the way *we* do."

Pelzer gave a wry chuckle. "I don't see Ms. Sachs and me sitting down to tea, unless she starts changing her message. And when is someone going to figure out who this next prime minister will be? That's a real hornet's nest."

"I've already figured it out," Guns said. He had yet to discuss things with Moishe, but he was sure his mentor would share his opinion. "You'll want to think it through, but no matter. You're good at that."

"Who is it?"

"Sheila, it's you."

EL-ARISH, EGYPT

FRESH FROM MAKEUP AFTER HER HELICOPTER TRIP FROM TEL AVIV (courtesy of Reginald Edgeworth), Elsa was sitting at the edge of her chair at the recording studio in El-Arish. She was both anxious and excited to record this next interview. The images from Sufa—the destruction, the cheering Palestinians and Bedouins, the nude prisoners with red heads and stained thighs—were compelling. Kufdani's speech from the battlefield was being projected around the world.

Edgie was delighted. "So far, our PR operation has exceeded my fondest hopes and wildest expectations," he'd told her a moment ago. He thought she and Kufdani had shown a certain chemistry during that first, brief interview in Tel Aviv. Now he wanted the world to see it again, in prime time. Another live interview would really put the level of global attention over the roof.

Perhaps Edgie's right, Elsa thought. *He's been right about everything else so far.*

Kufdani sat facing her, also newly made-up for the interview in a clean, white, flowing desert shirt that was loose at the neck. Elsa was distracted by the vertical scar zigzagging down from his left eye in bright white, but the rest of his face was relaxed. He was looking her dead in the eye and smiling faintly.

The display cameras scrolled through the camera views, so both interviewer and interviewee could get a sense of how they appeared to viewers at each angle. The art director called out orders to adjust the lighting in the studio, reaching for the right tone and the best use of shadows. Edgie and Elsa had discussed the politics of the Kufdani coverage at great length already, and now he was working with two technicians, directing Emilie to manage the image flow.

"So you have the images pretty much the way you want?" Elsa asked. There hadn't been much time, given that the battle had ended just hours earlier, but the editors in New York had done double duty. They had been working with the images and footage taken by Edgie's photographers—of the woman getting shot, the crowd's reaction, the Haredim surrendering and being treated—and were loving it.

Edgie nodded and smiled. "We're good to go. My client has precedence in the editing of all TV views. Any scripting from me is secondary. Get anything into the interview that you can, with that in mind."

Elsa nodded back. After seeing the footage from Kufdani's speech, she was determined to take a chance on getting to one viewpoint in particular: she was going to ask him about the Mahdi.

The supposed ways that Muslims would be able to identify the Mahdi were apocryphal, taken from one hadith or another. There was no disclosure from Allah in the Quran on this topic and little from the prophet himself. Nor was there any denying the cries for justice—and for the man who would restore it—among Kufdani's supporters.

Edgie waved for the cameras, waved again for action, and the lights winked on the cameras.

The first series of images ran on the screen, showing the blown-out windows, smoking F-16s, and abandoned service trucks of Sufa under the header BILLIONS IN DAMAGE TO ISRAELI AIR BASE.

"So," Elsa said, "once again, Sheik Kufdani, we meet about conflict."

The man across from her dipped his head slightly, his faint smile still in place. "We meet on my quest for the return of Bedouin lands and the protection of my people, who suffer under the Israeli theocracy. The conflict today was initiated by your country, thrown as a slap in the face of Allah. We merely reacted to Israel's attack—after giving you full warning, I might add."

"And now that violence has come once again to the Gaza Strip, how are you going to get out of that?" Sachs retorted. "All of Palestine will now become the bigger target."

"Palestine was attacked by Israel. The IDF sent armored infantry, navy corvettes, helicopters with drones, and fighter jets after us on our own land. Each infantryman, as we discovered in Al-Bayuk, was carrying one extra magazine of live ammunition in his vest, just in case." Kufdani lifted his head high now, still gazing directly at her. "Ms. Sachs," he said softly, "your 'just in case' just happened."

Elsa knew the camera was going to switch to her now. She sat without saying a word, allowing her silence to encourage him instead.

"You sent armor against us. It's gone," Kufdani continued. "You sent fighter jets. Two are gone, and your valuable air base is destroyed. You sent armored infantry with an abundance of live ammunition in their vests. We spanked them and sent them home, mostly unharmed, with their heads painted red to match their spanked bottoms."

He chuckled as the second series of images appeared on the screen. Elsa held her tongue.

"Israel had the temerity, the arrogance to send the Haredi battalion, the 97th Netzah Yehuda, against us," said Kufdani, the cameras back on him now. "These are the troops who have stolen our land and raped our children. They are cowards, rapists, and thieves. They come from a community of people who don't work, don't serve, don't educate their children. Instead, the Haredim study only their religious book, breed like rabbits, and vote for whom they are told. They are worthless scum feeding on a narrow interpretation of the word of Allah or the Hebrew god. And today, one of them murdered an unarmed, beautiful, young Palestinian mother of two."

With perfect timing, the screen displayed the image Edgie had singled out, of the Palestinian mother with her hands and black hair in the air, the blood spilling from her chest and the shock on her dying face.

The next image showed the moment the crowd of Palestinian women fell on the shooter in a rage. The header this time read, PALESTINIAN WOMEN ATTACK PRISONER OF WAR WHO KILLED UNARMED MOTHER OF TWO.

Elsa couldn't help but appreciate the juxtaposition of such raw emotion. *That Edgie really is a genius.*

"The murder of this young mother was but one among countless," Kufdani said, his voice hard. "We have neither the time nor the inclination to punish just one or two of these cowards, as today they have proven themselves to be. All must face retribution for their actions. Maybe the next time we'll geld them, as we do camels who are found wanting."

"And is that what this was, returning the prisoners of war to Israel in such a demeaned state?" Elsa asked. "Was that retribution?"

"You sent them against us, against me, against Islam. This was an insult to all of Islam. Next time they will come home far worse off."

"I understand the hyperbole, Sheik Kufdani," Elsa said, "but what conclusions do you think we can derive from this skirmish? How do we bring this unfortunate matter to an end peacefully?"

Kufdani looked away for a long moment.

"Moroccans rely on our king to grant us rights as citizens, so that we may live well and care for our property no matter our religion. Jews in Morocco have been successful owners of property and business for more than a thousand years. We value them. They are our brothers, with the Christians, in observance of Abrahamic religions.

"In Israel, hundreds of thousands of Bedouins have been citizens since the nation's founding in 1948. The Bedouins brought to their new Israeli citizenship property that they had owned for more than two hundred years, much of it on the western bank of the Jordan River—known as the West Bank."

On the screen now was an image of a West Bank construction site when it was still fully operational, followed by a series of past headlines announcing the international community's denunciation of Israel's moves to confiscate land there.

"We want our Bedouin lands back," Kufdani demanded. "We Bedouins and all of Islam want the world's leaders to condemn Israeli acts of confiscation. The world has already condemned this, yet Israel has ignored the world's opinion on the basis that Muslims have no rights in a Jewish society.

"Our actions in Jerusalem were designed to mirror your offenses against your Bedouin citizens, tit for tat. That's why your local communications were targeted, and your sewage treatment, public transportation, and apartments, all in Jerusalem. Yet Tel Aviv has been spared! No civilians were hurt! Even so, the destruction in Jerusalem failed to open the eyes of your leaders, who gave no credence to our claims and showed no understanding of what tit for tat means in the broader Israeli context. They fail to concern themselves with any understanding that this is the end of the beginning, that your nation is at the edge of a slippery slope."

As he spoke, the cameras cut to brief video clips showing the damage in Jerusalem, followed by clips from the day's battle.

"Now you attack us in our homes, sending a pack of armed cowards in the hopes of showing us just who is the boss. But where was the gain for Israel in this? Who benefits?"

"Who indeed," Elsa replied. "But one question is growing faster in the metaverse than any other: Are you the successor to Muhammad? Are you the Mahdi?"

Kufdani looked startled, then answered her question with his own. "And how will we know the Mahdi when he arrives? Of course, he will be a descendant of Muhammad (peace be upon him)—a *sayyid*—but there are many thousands of us. Would the Mahdi even realize that he was the one? He would be just doing his job in the service of Allah, as we all hope to do."

"In that case," she probed, "how do you know you are *not* the Mahdi?"

Edgie signaled his hand in rapid circles.

Just before the cameras cut to a commercial break, Kufdani grinned and said, "I don't."

BAT YAM, TEL AVIV

"THE RULES HAVE CHANGED," GUNS EPSTEIN INSISTED, TEARING HIS gaze from the television screen in Moishe's living room. The interview with Elsa Sachs was finishing up on replay—the tenth time he had watched it over the previous twenty-four hours. "I think I get it now."

"Pray tell," said Moishe. "I haven't a clue where this is going, but it can't be good."

"Well, we are under attack, but have no enemy to attack. Kufdani will make the world our enemy. He is attempting to enlist all of Islam to his cause, as he said he would. And although progress may be slow, I imagine he will succeed."

"Get to the point, Norman," Moishe ordered. "I am aging and retired."

"We are losing the support of the liberal Jewish community," Guns said. "He is undermining our position in the world."

Moishe stared out the window at the Mediterranean Sea three stories below his apartment. "Just as he said he would."

"No one in Israel has the stomach any longer for stealing Bedouin land or for housing the Haredim, no questions asked. It's becoming hard to support a bunch of 'red-topped surrender monkeys.'"

Moishe nodded. "Over the coming days, I imagine we'll see more polished, directed versions of the latest Sachs interview."

"Of course. That's why Kufdani hired Edgeworth," Guns said, also nodding now. "All those talented editors, creatives, and producers." How he had convinced Edgeworth to help him was beyond Guns, but Cooch could be very persuasive. The prime minister was furious with all the positive coverage of the Palestinian and Bedouin cause, splashed across all the newspapers and screens in the world. "This won't be the last time we see those shaved red heads and green genitals in living color, alongside a crafted narrative we don't like."

Moishe agreed.

Guns continued, "Our prime minister will like it even less."

Moishe shook his head. "He is not the ideal leader for us right now, if ever. He is headstrong and impetuous. Unethical. Even dishonest, perhaps."

"That's why I don't think Cooch will stop at asking for the Bedouin land to be returned. He's going to demand new leadership in Israel."

"That doesn't map well with the ego of our current leader."

"No, it doesn't," Guns said.

"And it's not good news for Sheila either."

Guns shrugged. "For a consolation prize, she gets to be prime minister. But she needs to get on board with the idea right now. It's time to get moving on this."

Moishe nodded. "I'll talk to her."

"I hoped you would," replied Guns. "I don't have the tact for that job."

OLD FASHIONED, CHESAPEAKE BAY

BROOKS ELLIOT AND MAC MACMILLAN SAT IN CANVAS-BACKED CHAIRS on the stern deck of *Old Fashioned,* sipping drinks and watching the sun begin to set. Six hundred yards from shore and below a protective point of land that jutted from the eastern shore into the bay, not far from Annapolis, the ship bobbed gently with the swells from passing powerboats and a light wind out of the west. *Old Fashioned*'s big, deep, heavy keel was designed to enhance ocean stability, so it was not ideal for the relatively shallow Chesapeake Bay. Finding deep anchorage like this was a challenge.

As sailing master for *Old Fashioned*, Jimmy was up to that challenge. He also managed Brooks's affairs in the difficult, sometimes clandestine situations that came up from time to time, such as folks trying to stop him from doing legal things they just didn't like. Jimmy's wife was the ship's equally competent cook and keeper. They even lived on *Old Fashioned* from time to time, transporting her to Tangier or wherever Brooks found convenient.

Two other former SEALS had joined them on board as crew for the recent trip up and down the Atlantic Coast: Snake, a sinewy, tattooed thirty-eight-year-old, recently retired, and Charles, a very large, slightly pudgy electronics expert who was keen on both sailboats and violence. The two men were busy stringing little cubes on a thin wire above the deck.

Josh Kim was coming tomorrow morning. Jimmy would be there with Snake to meet General Kim's security. And Alex was expected at any moment now.

"We find ourselves well buried in the shit this time," Brooks said, sipping at his glass of red wine.

Mac snorted. "Cooch has outdone himself. I'm starting to think he's serious about all this religion shit."

Brooks took his time and another sip. "Mmm."

He gazed at a channel pole with a reflective red triangle and an osprey nest on top. Lit up by the moving sun, the large, complicated nest had slowly transformed into varying shades of gray. It occurred to him that life, too, was an intricate puzzle with changing hues of right and wrong.

"I'm still getting my head around what we saw in the Gaza Strip," he said at last. "War has revolutionized itself one more time—and with it, the entire world."

Mac sighed. "I hate when that happens on my watch."

"Would things be better if it happened on someone else's watch?" Elliot replied. "Who do you trust to handle these things? I mean, who better than us?"

Mac swigged his beer. "Yeah. But I wasn't quite ready for this one."

Brooks looked back at the osprey nest, fading into the darkening sky. "Let's just see how it unfolds. Maybe we can add value."

The buzz of a small engine boat rumbled in the distance, moving closer. A bump on the hull announced the arrival of the tender, piloted by Jimmy. Alex sat beside him, grinning. As they pulled up, he swung over the rail, leaving Jimmy to tie up the tender.

"Hey, guys," Alex said. "What's happening?"

They embraced each other with much slapping of shoulders and backs. Alex settled in a deck chair with a cup of coffee as the pudgy Charles took his travel bag belowdecks.

Brooks didn't feel quite ready to tackle the big topics yet. "So, how's your sister doing these days? Is she happy with your solution?"

Alex laughed and told them about Elena's response to the 250 photos he'd sent her by Kphone, programmed to erase thirty seconds after they were opened. His text had read, *Someone appears to have solved most of our problems. Watch the news. Stay visible. Go to work and school.*

"And did they?"

"Of course! She's a Cuchulain," Alex said. "She's delighted they're all dead. Her husband has decided to tolerate me, and now her son has begun learning how we deal with problems according to family tradition. What could be better?"

The three men shared a knowing laugh and toasted, their three glasses coming together with an audible *clink*.

"Congrats on the Gaza thing," Mac started out. "Very well done. You outdid yourself with that fusible, miniaturized EMP trick—a real game changer."

"Thanks, but that was all Caitlin. What did you think of the razor rounds I designed?" Alex asked.

Mac shrugged and nodded. "Not bad. I didn't see it coming."

"I just handled the planning," Alex said. "Jerome took care of the hard parts. But it was still quite rewarding for me. I hate those Haredi fuckers."

"Yeah," Brooks said. "From the look of things, Edgie thinks you're the dream client."

"Edgie is having a ball," Alex agreed. "He adored being in the battle theater. And things are pretty well set up for our next PR win."

"And now that you have Israel by the balls," Brooks commented, "will their hearts and minds follow?" He wanted to understand whether the world could expect any true change in Israel's approach to its regional conflict. *What should I tell the president?* he thought. *Have the Israelis thought this through? Have they internalized the new state of affairs they are facing?*

"Guns understands, and probably a few others," Alex replied. "Israel can't continue acting as it has in the past, and they can't keep all the land and power they've acquired through nefarious means. The problem is getting from here to there."

"And defining what we should do about it," Mac said.

Alex shrugged. "That's the next step for me."

Time for a change, Brooks thought, stepping over to the large cooler and pulling out a bottle of 2013 Harlan Cabernet Sauvignon. "How much damage can you do on your own? What do you need from us?" he asked Alex.

"On our own, Caitlin and I can crumple Israel's entire electric system: no planes, no boats, no sewage, no phones, no so-called Iron Dome, no nothing driven by electricity. They'd be toast, and I'm tempted to seek revenge for her broken face, not to mention a jailhouse rape that I barely remember, thank goodness. For the Israelis, that's a bad outcome."

"What outcome do you prefer," Mac asked, thinking in 3D chess as always, "and what are the obstacles to getting there?"

"There's the rub," Alex replied. "I'm engaged with Islam. I represent millions of Muslims right now, and I've made promises. I'm not sure where to go with that."

You'll figure it out soon enough, Brooks thought, chuckling to himself. *You always do.*

"We're back to tire-spinning, folks," Mac said. "Let's look at the non-radioactive reality. What is actually realistic?"

Alex reached for his glass. "Let's drink now, gentlemen, and worry about reality tomorrow."

Once General Kim arrived, it would be time to get serious.

SHIN BET HEADQUARTERS, NORTHWEST TEL AVIV

KUFDANI IS BACK, READ THE LATEST HOL EXCLUSIVE ARTICLE. NABOV Dayan stifled a dour laugh. Three days after the invasion, this was old news to anyone with access to a screen device. But regardless of what he thought about her politics, Elsa Sachs had successfully captured everyone's attention once again. And regardless of what he thought about this Kufdani, he could hardly begrudge the man for his inspired battlefield tactics.

Dayan continued reading the HOL release on his computer. *Red-topped surrender monkeys . . . cowards, rapists, and thieves . . .* In the past few days, he had heard these phrases more times than he cared to think about. The IDF soldiers were of the 97th Netzah Yehuda, a unit composed almost entirely of Haredim, and had been accused of rape and stealing more than once in the occupied territories. This was the first time they'd been called cowards, and by broadcasting the story again and again, in full color, the Kufdani publicity machine was making it feel true.

Kufdani had led his people in the defeat and capture of a full battalion of IDF troops invading Gaza with both a motive—the destruction in Jerusalem and Beersheba—and the might of the Israeli army. What would he do next?

Despite access to the world's best known intelligence and security practices, Dayan had no idea. So far, his efforts had brought about only colossal failure.

He read on:

> *How could this happen? Israel has one of the best military organizations in the world. Yet we also lost two F-16 fighters and a full battalion's equipment, surrendered by the IDF. The air base at Sufa suffered billions of dollars in losses in aircraft and equipment. And eight hundred of our highly celebrated soldiers were returned home in humiliating circumstances: as nude, sunburned, shaved, and painted prisoners of war.*
>
> *Meanwhile, Sheik Kufdani is increasingly being called the Mahdi—the successor to Muhammad in the religious leadership of Islam—by his people . . .*

Dayan let out a long sigh. *Perhaps I should resign.*

Shin Bet and the Netzah Yehuda had gotten their asses handed to them in full view of the rest of the world. It seemed unlikely that the prime minister would take responsibility for his decision to send in the 97th to lead the doomed charge. And now the world was buying into the idea of Kufdani as a man who simply sought justice, honor, and dignity for his people. He was said to be the Mahdi.

Why did our foolish prime minister let IDF take up the baton? Dayan couldn't stop the rebuke from running through his thoughts. The IDF troops weren't invested in following Shin Bet's advice or leveraging its planning support. In the end, Shin Bet was just there, forced to watch all the nation's plans crumble and fail.

No, Dayan would not resign—not yet. He wouldn't give the prime minister the satisfaction of a scapegoat. He wanted to see what happened next, where this Kufdani would lead his people.

He turned off his computer and tried to push the phrase "red-topped surrender monkeys" out of his mind. He would just have to watch and wait—for now.

CHESAPEAKE BAY, MARYLAND

GENERAL JOSHUA KIM GLANCED DOWN AT THE GLISTENING LATE-MORNING light reflecting off the Chesapeake Bay as his three-car entourage continued east along US Route 50, over the Bay Bridge past Annapolis. Brooks Elliot had convinced him to break his schedule and spend a day or two in the bay, on a boat with the security of a floating fortress. The other important guest was a Bedouin who had just entirely fucked up battle planning for the US in the Middle East.

It was an offer he couldn't resist.

General Kim was a rarity among four-star officers: he had never seen combat. But his thinking on warfare—the result of a background in Middle Eastern studies and a gig under the North Dakota soil managing ICBMs, which produced some outstanding research and conclusions—was followed by those at the highest levels of government. He had served in various roles within the Defense Department, and the president had just promoted him to chairman of the Joint Chiefs of Staff. Despite knowing plenty about guns, planes, missiles, and the future of warfare, he had reached the pinnacle of his career through intellectual effort alone.

Kim had become friends with Brooks as they met more and more often during their years in Washington, with Kim advancing again and again through promotion and Elliot increasingly becoming a fixture at the White

House. Kim knew security would be tight anywhere Elliot went, and he'd heard plenty about the military mind of the one Bedouin who was currently at the top of everyone's news feed.

Still, he thought, *it can't hurt to be certain.*

When they finally reached the small dock where two men stood beside a small powerboat, introducing themselves as Jimmy and Snake, those introductions were followed by a show of IDs. You never could be too careful.

General Kim and one of his men joined Jimmy and Snake in the tender, heading toward Elliot's boat. *What was it called again?* Kim wondered. *The Old . . . something or other.*

The remainder of Kim's men stayed behind, retrieving bulky packs from the three Suburbans and spreading out in pairs along the rocky shoreline to spots picked from a map the previous night. They unpacked and checked their radios, set out ground radar, and then picked up their rifles and checked them. Despite the beautiful scenery, this was no vacation.

No one would get to General Kim easily from the shore.

Reaching *Old Fashioned*, Kim came aboard with the appropriate greetings and harassment. On deck near the command center, in the ship's stern, a huge, smiling, fortyish man stood and extended his right hand. "Mr. Chairman, I'm Alex Cuchulain," he said. "It's an honor to meet you."

So this is the Bedouin? Kim thought, grasping the man's hand and clasping his forearm. Cuchulain looked like a thug, huge and scarred, but his performance in Gaza—and in that recent event in Iran—was nothing short of astonishing, so he had Kim's attention. "The pleasure is indeed mine. Among other things, Elliot tells me you are a Navy brat, a former Marine, and his best friend."

Cuchulain nodded. "We go back a ways. He's insufferable, but who else do I know with a big fancy sailboat, willing to introduce me to the chairman of the Joint Chiefs of Staff?"

Kim smiled. "The king of Morocco, maybe?"

The men's laughter was cut short by the approach of Kim's bodyguard, a large man in a green t-shirt and camo shorts, stepping up the ladder from the galley. The man's hands were clasped behind his back, while beside him, Jimmy had rested his hook in a belt loop—not quite a mirror image.

"Is the security adequate?" Kim asked.

"More than adequate, sir," his bodyguard replied. "This is one awesome little battleship. It has monitors that would do a destroyer proud."

"Good. And our exposure?"

"From a silenced small boat or an attack launched quietly from the shoreline, sir. Small odds either way, given our preparation and coverage. An airplane attack could be a problem, but only if they hit us on the first pass."

"Fair enough," Kim said. "Now that we've confirmed all is well with security, I think we can agree to respect one another's confidence regarding this meeting. It's not exactly aboveboard, is it?"

The others nodded, and the four men took their seats in the canvas-covered teak chairs placed around a small, round slatted teak table.

Kim gestured toward Cuchulain. "Bedouins, with you in the lead, scored an incredible win over one of the best armies in the world, but I don't know how or to what ultimate end."

"I barely know myself, sir," replied Cuchulain.

"You can trust that I understand the ongoing shitstorm in the occupied territories," Kim continued, "and you seem to have won this round. Now you just need to mop up, as unpleasant as that may become. But what does the world's smartest woman say about this problem given her success in miniaturizing the force of EMP?"

Elliot laughed. "She dodges it. Says there are too many dependent variables that won't hold still."

"God's truth." Kim took a sip of his wine and leaned back. "I have spent my career reordering dependent variables to suit a purpose."

Elliot nodded. "Me too," he said. "And *I'm* not the smartest person in the world."

Kim turned to Alex. "Tell me what you think you have that would interfere with Israel's recovery of the West Bank lands."

"I don't need help with the West Bank fiasco. I can make that happen," Cuchulain said. "The problem is larger."

Kim nodded. "It seems to me that there is more at stake than the West Bank situation. What more do you want?"

"Now there's the question," Mac said.

Elliot said, "To cut to the chase, Alex and Caitlin have discovered a new approach to warfare. It's like having a cannon that will shoot accurately a mile farther than anyone else. As a result, you own the battlefield, writ large."

Kim shrugged and nodded. "Got it," he said. "Go on."

Cuchulain leaned back in his chair and took a sip of wine, looking at the western horizon. "The win in Gaza was an introduction, a demonstration. It worked, and now I'm not sure what to do with it. Careful planning is required."

Kim listened to his explanation of the two separate but related advancements they had implemented in their most recent venture: effective combat communications and weaponry. What he heard was astounding. Powered by a heuristic AI chatbot in development for more than a decade, Cuchulain and his crew were able to penetrate every connected entity in Israel, monitoring phone calls, listening in at meetings, and reading correspondence. The entire written and spoken record of every organization in Israel was at their disposal. The chatbot, known as Emilie, could disable every entity in Israel in any electronic and kinetic way possible, destroying individual pieces of electricity-dependent equipment as instructed, by overloading them.

"But what you describe takes enormous amounts of computing power," Kim protested.

Elliot picked up a strange-looking phone and held it in front of him. "Ten or so years ago, Caitlin O'Connor managed to put a quantum computer on a cell phone, and she has been learning to use that power ever since. We have hundreds of them. That's how she figured out the EMP downsizing. That's how she has been facilitating the education of Morocco's children. These phones can do everything at once and never break an idle."

Kim looked at Elliot. "As you promised, Elliot, this is a worthwhile meeting for me. I'm stunned. Governments everywhere are racing to field an operating quantum computer, and the NSA has had one for ten years! Why am I just hearing of this?"

"The NSA doesn't own a quantum computer," Cuchulain contradicted. "Caitlin O'Connor does. The NSA doesn't know how she can do the things they pay her to do. Emilie does quantum mechanics and acts as a launching base for solutions—a bit like a COBOL compiler or a smart server making life easier for the coder."

"So you've decided to bless me with this earthshaking knowledge of quantum success, even if it happened ten years ago. Why tell me? Why now?"

"You're in the death business. You're the chairman of our armed forces. You need to understand what's going on," Elliot replied. "And you can't understand it if you don't know about the Kphone."

"The global media and talking heads are jumping up and down, shouting about ChatGPT and OpenAI," Cuchulain said. "Yet even without considering the speed of the Kphone, these new technologies are infants in a huge market. We need to enlighten the Jewish intelligentsia about our new capabilities in AI and communications disruption, without scaring them into action. And we need you and the Department of Defense to sit back and watch for now, not get involved."

"Interesting," Kim said.

Alex smiled. "Yeah, it's not much of a fair fight."

"So you're telling me that your people can front-run any Israeli planning on how to conduct war?"

"And fuck it up in any way they choose," Elliot pointed out.

Mac sat forward in his seat. "This is gunpowder, Josh. It's the tank. This changes the game of war, for as long as that advantage exists. And it is a big, big advantage."

Kim stared into Cuchulain's intense eyes. "And the question is?"

"The question is, What, therefore, shall we do?" Cuchulain replied.

"What, indeed." Kim paused for a moment. "But what, other than taking a neutral stance for now, do you need from me?"

"I'd like to figure out how to mitigate the damage to Israel as we sort things out," Cuchulain said. "They need new leadership. Once they get it, I'd like to leave them with a society to lead, because regardless of what some Muslim leaders might believe, it is a valuable society. But Israel's current leadership appears to be digging in for the big fight. The latest word from Emilie is that they plan to send special ops troops to American soil to do their bidding."

"Probably Sayeret Matkal," said Elliot, "and as you know, they are very good."

"We need to figure out how much damage Israel can tolerate, and, by implication, how much we should tolerate." Mac pointed to Cuchulain. "Sheik Kufdani here represents Islam in the negotiations, and they seem to be in the catbird seat."

Kim turned his sharp gaze on Cuchulain once more. "You're an American," he said quietly. "You'll do as your country asks."

Cuchulain's lips turned up into a wicked smile. "Of course, I'm an American," he said. "That's why we're sitting here discussing things. But I have no intention of taking orders from you or from the US. That ship has sailed. I'm also a Muslim Arab by birth. I have a Moroccan diplomatic passport. I am the appointed leader of the Bedouin nation, which represents a million people. I represent the people of Allah. If you need to negotiate with Islam right now, I'm it."

Elliot waved a hand as if to cut through the tension. "It may be useful to remember that Alex is not only trying to restore humanity to his people, but also trying to develop a plan that works for all."

"I'm all ears," Kim said.

Cuchulain shrugged. "Given our original commitment to react to Israeli violence in a tit-for-tat fashion—they do something bad, we do something bad in return—we Muslims are behind in the game. That is the state of things today. They attacked us in Gaza, and we handed them their marching papers."

"But the Palestinians and Bedouins have no infantry, no armor, no fighters, no helicopters, no navy, so true tit for tat is not possible," said Mac.

"That's right," Cuchulain continued. "We humiliated them, however, and continue to do so in the daily news, so they will no doubt try again to punish the Muslims. They control essential services for the Palestinians, such as fresh water and electricity. I can imagine them shutting off those services and letting Palestinians sit in the dark, thirsty, can't you?"

Elliot nodded, sipping from his wineglass. "And it seems likely that they will rush into absorbing the West Bank into Israel without compensation to its rightful owners."

"Yes," Cuchulain said. "We have seen zero movement from the Israeli government on our demands, despite the damage and humiliation we have shown ourselves capable of causing. So, as promised, we will up our game and engage the rest of Israel."

"You have already made such a plan?" Kim asked.

Cuchulain's face darkened. "At some point soon, we will destroy Israel's infrastructure in a way that makes life more difficult for their people. Of course, we could destroy their airports, their mass transportation and delivery system, their gas terminals, and their fuel supplies. Then we would disable the Iron Dome system, and the rockets from the Syrians and Iranians would be free to start falling on the population centers."

"That's not a plan," Kim said, his voice rising slightly. "That is Armageddon for the Israeli people. Unacceptable."

"Yes, quite," Cuchulain replied in an even tone. "I'd like Israel to survive, but not as a theocracy. Staging that effort is the hard part. We may need your help."

"We'd like you to sit down and think through the rough pieces with us, then join us in keeping the president on the rails," Elliot suggested.

"It's worth a try," Kim agreed. "But no promises."

The four men continued to chat for several hours over crab enchiladas and plenty of drinks, about important things, as well as all the little things they had in common. As the sun dipped below the horizon, Cuchulain stood and stretched.

"I'm going to let you guys figure out how to solve the rest of the world's problems," he said. "I'm having dinner tomorrow with the Saudi deputy ambassador and the director of the Arab League, so I'll need my beauty sleep."

Cuchulain turned and shook Kim's hand.

"It was fun getting to know you a bit, sir. We'll no doubt run into each other again—if Sayeret Matkal doesn't get me first."

The four men chuckled, but Kim recalled that comment instantly when, just after 2:00 a.m., a quiet, insistent knock came at his door. Kim snapped awake and opened his stateroom door.

"Threat scope's flashing," Cuchulain said, scowling.

Despite all of Kim's security precautions, something was approaching *Old Fashioned.*

OLD FASHIONED, CHESAPEAKE BAY

IN HIS SMALL STATEROOM NEAR THE STERN OF *OLD FASHIONED,* KUFDANI had awoken a little before 2:00 a.m. Having gone to bed so early, he knew there was no getting back to sleep, so he dozed and watched the crew and the scope through his cracked stateroom door.

When the scope started to flash, he popped alert.

He was up and moving within seconds, heading for the command center, where Jimmy, Charles, Snake, and General Kim's bodyguard had been alternating duty: two men watching the equipment, two men snoring on bunks.

Twelve-gauge pump shotguns were racked beside silenced rifles with night scopes and fifteen-round magazines sticking out from them like blackened teeth. Jimmy had taken special care in organizing the goodies stowed against the wall, labeled in green, yellow, and black: an array of spears, two late-model Stingers, swimmer's ears to blow the eardrums out of anyone submerged within two hundred yards, a variety of explosives—even a Coochmore at the bottom of the stack. Four compact Kimber .45-caliber pistols hung on web belts with matte black seven-round magazines secured on the webbing, just beyond the bulkhead.

Jimmy took a shotgun. Kufdani grabbed one Kimber and then another for good measure. Each of the others took a scoped rifle.

Kufdani stole a moment to be grateful that he'd spoken to Jerome before going to bed. Caitlin and LuAnn would be well protected in Tangier—suddenly more secure there than if they'd decided to return overseas to the colonies.

It was a move they'd considered, especially now that Caitlin had acquired new, secure transportation from the NSA. As Brooks had explained to Kim the previous night, LuAnn had handled the sale-leaseback deal for Kufdani. "It's one of yours," he'd said, "a C37B that was modified for our former president's wife. Sixty percent of it belongs to Kufdani, the lessor."

"That's not going to work," Kim had replied. "I know that plane. I tried to get rid of it. Too many secret tech goodies to let it run around unsupervised."

"According to LuAnn," Brooks had said, "it comes with a crew of eight, all active Air Force, for which you will be reimbursed by the NSA. I suggest you vet that crew, as Caitlin is in weapons mode—all excited about the new C37 electronics. They could learn a lot."

"The NSA thinks what they do is what drives the nation, so they just sell our airplanes to meet their needs," General Kim had said. "We paid over $50 million for that thing! But I suppose this Gulfstream 550 is off the Air Force books and no longer a C37B, which is another thing off my list."

So at least Kufdani, keeping his head low while duck-walking along *Old Fashioned*'s deck to the bow, wasn't distracted by concern for his true love in Tangier. He heard someone moving on the deck above him and bumped his knuckles against Brooks's door.

"Heads up," Kufdani said quietly.

Brooks stepped into the passageway behind Kufdani. "Fuck," he said. "That didn't take long at all."

Next Kufdani knocked lightly on Kim's door and heard the rack of a pistol slide before the door even opened.

He'll do, Kufdani thought, smiling into the dark.

"We're under assault," he murmured as Kim joined them in the passageway, holding a 9mm Sig Sauer pistol. "I suggest staying down here for the moment. Let Jimmy and the others go see what these bastards are planning for us."

Kufdani repeated the action at Mac's door, and the bulk of Macmillan slid in beside them, a trench knife in his hand. "You didn't hear about the folly of bringing a knife to a gunfight?" Kufdani whispered, pushing a Kimber at his mentor.

"Fuck you, Cooch," Mac grumbled, pulling the slide back to check for a round in the chamber. He stuck the knife in his belt. "Life was good until you showed up."

The four men reached the ladder to the main deck, and hid in the lower deck shadows just as the ship bobbed slightly.

Six unknown figures slid noiselessly over the stern rail, each wearing night vision gear and webbing, and carrying rifles with long tubes extending from their muzzles. One had small boxes in his free hand—enough explosive, Kufdani later discovered, to potentially reduce *Old Fashioned* to toothpicks. Another raised his hand and counted, then nodded and waved his colleagues forward.

Standing near the bow, almost unrecognizable in his night vision goggles, Jimmy triggered the remote in front of him and yelled, "Now!" The men of *Old Fashioned* dropped their head and closed their eyes.

A quarter-second later, the ninety-three flash cubes that earlier had been strung around the deck detonated at once, blinding the intruders. Each of the *Old Fashioned* men stepped out from the shadows and methodically fired into the six invaders, center body. A strange cacophony of pops and thwacks filled the salty air as the Heckler and Koch silenced rifles cycled through their magazines of 6.5mm Creedmoor rifle bullets.

After multiple rounds of ammunition were fired, Charles ran for the outboard rail, pulling something from his clothes. An outboard motor came suddenly to life, slicing the silence. But when Charles threw a grenade pack at the rigid inflatable boat accelerating away, it hit the boat's large, silenced outboard motor and exploded. The pilot was thrown into the waters of the bay. Charles shot him once, then four more times, just to be sure.

Snake walked across the deck, inspecting the six bleeding bodies. He stomped on one man's throat, then raised a hand to high-five Charles before the two men started rummaging through the dead intruders' pockets. Jimmy stood behind them and grinned—P to the seventh power and all that, but mostly because his shotgun was unfired. It tended to do bad things to *Old Fashioned*'s rigging, things that took days to repair.

Several shots sounded from the shore: General Kim's shore-bound security was cleaning up the escape route. Kim grinned and looked at Elliot. "I heard them fire the first shots, didn't you?"

"I did, and I have witnesses," Elliot said. "These poor blokes on the deck refused to surrender, and now look what they're doing to my boat."

"There really is no justice," Kufdani said. "I guess I'll have to help with the cleanup, but let's get some good facial pictures first, before they get too pale. I'll send the photos off to Caitlin. Maybe she and Emilie can identify them."

"Send them to me, too," Mac said, wiping blood from his hands. "The president will be fascinated. So will the CIA."

Two hours later, the men sat together on deck, finishing coffee and freshly baked rolls. The deck had been swabbed of bloodstains. The bodies had been moved to shore and loaded into two of the Suburbans for a trip to the morgue and perhaps some answers. Kufdani had called to inform Jerome of the morning's events, sent Caitlin the photos, and shared his suspicions about who was behind the assassination attempt.

Elliot rang his wife with the news that Jerome would escort her and Caitlin to inner offices with no windows facing Tangier harbor, if only for a few days. Edgie hadn't answered his Kphone, but Emilie had alerted his security team to button him up too. They were now targets—all of them.

Kufdani thought it would be best for his sister to take a much-needed family vacation. "Go for a nice visit somewhere, and don't leave any message or trails behind you," he told Elena. Kufdani Industries would pay for everything. "Do it now," he advised.

It was time for Kufdani to get on the road. After the early morning's excitement, he would need a rest before meeting the Saudis. "The Israelis will have to regroup. I doubt they planned for this one to fail, but I still want to get about my business before they hear the bad news."

After backslaps and handshakes, winks and nods of approval, and more than one round of high-fives, Jimmy was at the rail, ready to take Kufdani on the short boat trip to shore. He turned for a last wave goodbye, hoping that when the news broke about the attack, some of the details would remain under wraps.

Kufdani drove his rental car through Prince George's County and into the District of Columbia, down New York Avenue toward the Hay-Adams. After he got to his hotel room, he drank two bottles of water, hung up his garment bag, cleaned his boots, and took a nap.

WASHINGTON, DC

EARLY THAT EVENING, KUFDANI STROLLED THROUGH THE STREETS OF Washington, DC, until he came to a brick wall with greenery growing uniformly along it and stepped through a small wrought iron gate into the courtyard of Tagine, a restaurant near Georgetown University. Well known for its Moroccan cuisine among the substantial Arab crowd laboring in and around the US government, the restaurant comprised small indoor and outdoor eating spaces. At the center of each table was a colorful tagine resting on a wrought iron stand, with a gas burner installed below.

Inside the gate, Kufdani saw the Bedouin owner, Freddie, sitting on a high stool in his usual spot near an open fireplace. Freddie leaped to his feet and lifted a hand in greeting. "Kufdani! Welcome!" He led his honored guest to a chair by the fireplace and began to gossip in Moroccan Arabic, that fluid, staccato lingua franca, spattered with French derivatives, that is a source of pride for Tangerines, although largely unintelligible to most other Arabic speakers.

"Tea!" Freddie boomed. "Bring more tea."

Kufdani surveyed the seating arrangement. Dr. Abdul Al-Fraih, director of the Arab League and a personal friend from his years at Oxford, had called with regrets that he would be a few moments late. On the bright side, the deputy ambassador from Saudi Arabia would be joining them, at Kufdani's request. This would be the first of several meetings, Kufdani hoped, that would bind the Bedouin efforts with the larger Muslim world—and bring them closer to the money and influence required to finish his efforts.

A few minutes later, just as Freddie's repertoire of recent events within and about the local Arab community was winding down, a booming voice echoed from the restaurant's entrance. Two men—one heavy-set and another smaller, both wearing the headscarves of the Saudi Arabian ruling tribe—were walking through the courtyard, their faces lit up with smiles.

"It is so good to see you, Kufdani!" the heavy-set man bellowed. "You have been making trouble for the Jews, I hear. Good for you! A bunch of bigots who shit on Muslims. Come meet my friend Abbas."

"Good for you, Sheik Kufdani," replied Haasim Abbas, the deputy ambassador. "I didn't think the Palestinians had it in them. Red-headed surrender moneys, indeed!"

"It pays to use sunblock," Kufdani said, grinning. "You never know when you will have to stand nude for five hours in the hot sun. Being a coward is tough duty sometimes."

Introductions were made, and they headed for a table that Kufdani had chosen—partially inside the building but facing the end of the courtyard. Three ornate chairs with bright cushions were arranged around a small steel table covered with a white Egyptian cotton tablecloth, set for a full meal. Kufdani sat between the two, facing the courtyard.

Freddie came to the table with a bottle of 1989 Chateau Mouton Rothschild. "I trust this wine is acceptable to you?" Al-Fraih smiled warmly. "I keep a small cellar here at Freddie's."

They made small talk about the original artworks commissioned for the vintner's label, the grape varietals used, and the Muslim approach to drinking alcohol.

"It's a Pauillac," Al-Fraih said. "That makes it a winner for Arabs like me who don't drink—much."

"You haven't bought a bottle of wine in ten years," Abbas said with a laugh. "Every time a Muslim diplomat gets transferred, you end up with the good wine he was saving for a special time."

"Bah! They are all sinners," Al-Fraih replied. "It makes them feel better to give it away, especially to a pure spirit such as me. So I do what I can for them—thus, my cellar." At his approval, Freddie poured the wine, and the three diners went through the ritual of sniffing and snuffling and sipping, as one must do with a noted and expensive French red Bordeaux.

"Al-Fraih said you wanted to speak to me personally," Abbas began at last. "How may I assist you?"

Kufdani looked around the courtyard and lowered his voice. "I'd like you to arrange a private meeting for me with the Crown Prince."

Abbas's eyes widened. He bought himself a moment by drinking another tiny sip of wine. "Just you?"

"Just me," Kufdani confirmed. "It is time to address the larger issues of Islam in the world."

Abbas sighed. "I'm afraid you do not understand how such things work, Sheik Kufdani. I am the twelfth son of the fifteenth most senior prince in Saudi Arabia. I have no power to attract the attention of ABS, the Crown Prince. Nor do I have the ear of any intimates of ABS intimates."

Kufdani chuckled. "Yes, I know how family politics work. ABS was once in the same boat as you are: he had a distant father with limited power."

Abbas bowed his head slightly, his eyes never leaving Kufdani's.

"I understand the feeling of powerlessness," Kufdani continued. "My own father was a noted US Marine, but that gave him no power to bring peace either. Yet now I am the appointed leader of one million Bedouins, tribes without their own country or government. I commanded the humiliation of the Israelis with minimal defensive losses, disrupted their efforts at diplomacy, and damaged their status in the United States, a very important source of funds and political support. Are you certain the Crown Prince will view me with such disinterest?"

"That may be enough to get his attention," Abbas admitted, "but it will take far more than that to get his ear."

"Is that not your job, Abbas? Make this a showcase effort. Find out who I really am. Build a dossier to share with the Crown Prince. Do your research. Am I rich or poor? An expert in violence or just lucky? You get the idea. In other words, do my mind, my background, my accomplishments, my ambitions make me compatible with ABS? I have done my research, and I believe they will."

"And I should do this . . . why? I take no orders from you," Abbas said, his voice rising.

"Abbas, listen to me. When an Arab does a bad thing, he gets stomped and humiliated in public. When an Israeli does an equally bad thing, he merely gets scolded. For many years this has been true. We are going to change that, and ABS will want to be a part of it."

Abbas regarded him thoughtfully.

"I'm giving no one orders. I do that only in battle. But now you must think carefully about my offer." Kufdani's voice hardened, and he locked eyes with Abbas. "Bringing to the Crown Prince the best idea he has ever seen, wrapped in a chance to be revered as a leader in Islam and in the world, will raise you mightily in his eyes. I believe that is what he really wants. He was educated in his own country by a talented British Algerian. He understands how the Western world views him, and he wants very badly to matter." He paused. "It is a point of honor."

Abbas leaned back in his chair. "Al-Fraih, what do you think?"

Al-Fraih shrugged. "It seems to me that the worst that can happen is that ABS says no to the meeting, and you have wasted your time."

Kufdani's back was straight. His hands rested loosely on the edge of the table. The big vein in his neck pumped the blood at an insanely low rate, maybe fifty beats a minute. He waited.

Abbas sat for a long time before speaking. "A dossier," he repeated, "a solid and thoughtfully researched dossier, on a person whom ABS will most certainly wish to meet, one-on-one." As he looked up and fixed his eyes on Kufdani, a smile crept onto his face. "A dossier that also makes the Saudi deputy ambassador seem underappreciated, perhaps even underpaid."

"Yes," Kufdani encouraged him. "All of Islam is depending on you, Abbas."

Abbas frowned suddenly. "What about the Wahabi? Are you ready for those who practice a radical form of Islam, who follow Allah's will in the strictest sense?"

Kufdani relaxed, thinking, *Done deal.*

His plan was falling into place.

"Oh, yes, of course," he said. "I am a messenger of Allah, an imam, a Bedouin who commands all Bedouins. We can arrange a meeting as you see fit, either before or after I meet ABS—perhaps with the Grand Mufti, with his entourage if that is best."

"They'll tear you apart. In public."

"Perhaps. Others have tried."

ON THE DRIVE TO NEW YORK late that evening, Kufdani checked in with Brooks and Mac. The US president had been outraged when he heard about the attack on *Old Fashioned*. Although they had no proof yet, being able to pin it on the Israelis would help send him over the edge—and prepare him to put up the boatload of money required to bring the Middle East together at last.

Next Kufdani rang Caitlin. It was very early in the morning in Tangier, but he was hoping to hear that her injuries were healing and all was well with her molar implants. They chatted a bit while he drove north on Interstate 95, about not just her face, but also those faces Emilie had been working to identify, looking through years of photos from every enforcement agency on earth. He asked Caitlin to take a hard look at the electronic devices belonging to the Israeli embassy in Northwest DC, as well as the country's US consulates. Those intruders were coming from somewhere, and someone on American soil had to know about it.

Kufdani excused himself from the conversation with Caitlin when he saw that Jimmy was calling. "Hey, pal. All good?"

"Not so good, Cooch," Jimmy responded. "I'm so sorry. They got to Edgeworth. Pros. Sniper, two rounds to the head."

EDGEWORTH STUDIOS, MIDTOWN MANHATTAN

THE STUDIOS WERE ON FULL ALERT. THE WORLD-FAMOUS, SUPER-RICH, highly protected Reginald Ketcher Edgeworth had been assassinated the previous day as he got out of his limo, in front of his Upper East Side apartment. The whole city—the whole world—was in shock. And tonight was the third in Elsa Sachs's series of interviews with Sheik Kufdani, this time right here in New York.

Arriving at his apartment on Manhattan's West Side the previous evening, Kufdani had felt the sorrow that always washed over him when comrades fell. He would look at all those people in his mind at some point later on. It was never pleasant.

"We got one of the guys, but dead men don't speak," Jimmy had said. "No ID, no clothes labels, great rifle. Really professional job. We had our best guys on him, Cooch. We're all so pissed. We liked him."

"I liked him too," Kufdani had replied. "Tell your guys they are now employed directly by me. Details to follow. Use them to button up Elsa Sachs now that she's here in New York. Do it now, and make it tight. The rest of them go on the general security team. These are Sayeret Matkal." He had thought that being an Israeli Jew would protect the Sachs woman, but now he wasn't so sure. "Let Brooks and Mac know. Hunker down. Arm up."

"Roger that," Jimmy had said. "Wilco."

Setting all the alarms and leaning a twelve-gauge pump shotgun by his side, loaded with no. 4 shot—one in the chamber, thumb safety on—had made Kufdani feel a little better. So had the extra two security guys Jimmy stationed across the hall in the vacant apartment that Kufdani Industries kept there.

It was late when he'd returned from DC, but still he had called Elsa Sachs himself and told her to expect more security. Then he told her about Edgeworth.

"Oh my god!" she'd said. "How awful! How did this happen?" She paused. "Should I cancel tomorrow's interview?"

Kufdani had to admire her priorities. "I'm fairly sure it was Sayeret Matkal, the special forces arm of Shin Bet. And no, we shouldn't cancel our interview. We should play it up."

"Hm, yes. Dedicate the show to Edgie. Dress it up for him."

"And get you that Pulitzer," he'd said, trying to lighten the mood.

"Hm. See you at seven, then. We're live at seven-thirty, full network coverage."

"I'll be there," he'd said. "You're going to be famous. Oh, and Ms. Sachs?"

"Elsa."

"Okay. Elsa?"

"Yes?"

"Welcome to New York."

TWO CHAIRS WERE SET UP in the recording studio, with a small table between them. The art director had chosen the skyline of Tel Aviv as a background. On one side screen was a huge photo of the Haredi troops, standing nude and defeated with their sunburns and bald, red heads. On another huge screen was the now-famous image of the Palestinian mother falling in a fan of blood. Multiple cameras were manned and ready for lights, cameras, action.

The studio audience was live this time: two hundred strong, highly vetted, and under the watchful eye of two men in long, dark coats standing alert behind the last row of seats, and two more stationed outside the doors. The crowd murmured excitedly as Kufdani and Elsa walked from opposite ends of the stage to the center, shook hands, and sat down. They were dressed in contrast—Kufdani wore a loose, white flowing shirt and dark slacks, and Elsa wore a dark outfit with her single strand of pearls—yet they seemed to complement one another somehow.

"So, Sheik Kufdani," Elsa asked. "How was your yesterday?"

There was more murmuring from the audience and a little nervous laughter.

"Well, as you know, my friend Reginald Ketcher Edgeworth—an American leader, and your boss—was killed by cowardly sniper fire." Kufdani spoke softly, with intensity. "He was a friend of Israel, but no friend of the Haredim."

"Yes, we were all stunned by the news of Mr. Edgeworth. I knew him only a short time, but he was loved by many." Elsa's sudden tears were endangering her mascara.

Kufdani nodded. "It is a terrible loss. Yesterday was a difficult day."

They both bowed their heads in a brief moment of silence.

"In fact, my difficulties started even before this tragic news," he continued. "In the middle of the night, six men came over the railing of a sailboat where I was sleeping. They had silenced weapons and enough explosives to sink the boat."

Kufdani knew that the attack on *Old Fashioned* had been disclosed to the press already, with some of the details strategically excluded—including the presence of General Kim. But he also knew that people slobbered over exciting news, especially when there was intrigue and danger involved.

Elsa nodded. "I heard about that. You were on the sailboat of Special Ambassador Brooks Elliot and . . . someone from the National Security Agency?"

Kufdani nodded.

"The attackers were killed," Elsa continued, shaking her head, "and you walked away without a scratch."

"It's true. We believe I was the target, but the other two were unhurt as well." He gave a small smile. "The boat seems fine."

"What did you do after the attack?" she asked.

"I got the hell off the boat and headed for DC. I had an important dinner and didn't want to fight any new wars."

"And how was the important dinner?"

"Delicious. I had a marvelous experience at a very nice restaurant named Tagine in Northwest DC."

"I'm happy to hear it," Elsa said, acknowledging the crowd's light laughter. "And who were your assailants?"

"We're working on facial recognition from photos."

"Sheik Kufdani, do you know who is responsible for the attack?"

"Of course," Kufdani said. "The Israeli government."

Gasps could be heard from the crowd.

"Go on," Elsa said.

"They are angry over their losses, their poor planning, the exposure of their cowardice."

Elsa paused, squinting at him. "I'm sorry, Mr. Kufdani. That seems unlikely. Who would authorize such an incursion into US territory?"

"Why your nutcase, slimebag prime minister, I assume."

Again there were gasps, and this time some tittering from the studio audience.

"I am not a fan of our prime minister, as many know," Sachs said. "But it's hard to believe that he would order such a thing. Why do you believe it was him?"

"Who else?" Kufdani replied. "He commands Shin Bet, and Shin Bet commands the Sayeret Matkal—the Israeli version of the US Delta Force. Six assassins have been killed—maybe seven. Very professional. They have been photographed. We will identify them."

Kufdani looked intently into the nearest camera.

"Until then, we have as evidence the humiliation he has faced at my hand, and the devastation of parts of Jerusalem and Beersheba that is attributed to me. But most of all, they hear what the people say: that I am the Mahdi, come to restore Muslim glory. For this, he and his cronies want me dead. They don't want an effective Arab warrior on their doorstep. So they have tried twice to kill me, while endangering and harming those around me."

"Will these attacks on you slow your efforts to reverse the course of Israeli occupation in Gaza and the West Bank," Elsa asked, "or accelerate them?"

Kufdani paused to give the impression of deep thought. "Well, the Israeli government seems to respond only to a tit-for-tat approach in the occupied territories. So I have decided to oblige them. Our next 'tat' will happen tomorrow morning."

Cries of surprise rang out from the audience.

"Wait, wait," Elsa exclaimed. "Did I just hear you say that you're going to attack Israel . . . tomorrow?"

"Yes, yes, tomorrow morning at rush hour or thereabouts. I'm afraid the Israeli prime minister has left us no choice."

"That is quite a bold claim, Mr. Kufdani. I don't—"

"Attacking me on US soil, however, requires me to act here as well. So I have decided to disable communications in the Israeli embassy tonight."

"The . . . embassy? Did I—?"

"Yes, you did hear me say that," Kufdani said. "Israel's embassy in Washington, DC, and its other consulates in the United States are dark even now, unless they have generator backup. Either way, they certainly don't have internet."

"And Israel's consulates around the United States? Is that truly necessary?"

"Yes," he confirmed, "the consulates too, or at least the ones in the eastern US. I do apologize to the American government and people, but technically this operation—which is happening right about now—is occurring on property that is considered Israeli foreign soil. And from my perspective, the operation is indeed necessary, because it will make me harder for Israel to shoot down. I'm sure you understand, Ms. Sachs."

She stared at him. "How would you net things out thus far, Mr. Kufdani, in your fight to reclaim the West Bank?"

"That is no longer the scope of our fight." Kufdani leaned back in his seat and smiled. "We consider the West Bank perfidy by Israel to be rejected already by truly thoughtful Jews and by the rest of the world. The issue now is a much larger one: Israel in a fight against Islam."

Elsa's jaw dropped.

"Tomorrow's damage will be relatively minor. More will come to Israel, however, if we don't see its government paying attention to our demands."

"And those demands are?"

"As a Muslim imam speaking for all of Islam, I will share those terms when Israel comes to the negotiating table," Kufdani said. "I still lead the Bedouins, but that fight for the West Bank is over. Israel has lost."

Elsa Sachs fell back against her seat. At the producer's signal, the show stopped for a one-minute commercial break. The camera lights stopped blinking.

Elsa picked up her notepad and scribbled furiously. "I assume the embassy blackout is practically old news by now. And we'll see about Israel in the morning. What else?"

"Ask whether I'll negotiate with the current prime minister," Kufdani advised.

A thirty-second warning sounded: the show was about to resume. Elsa checked her makeup, and Kufdani took a drink of water.

"Action!" the director cried out, and the cameras winked on.

"Your relations with the Israeli prime minister have not been smooth, Sheik Kufdani," Elsa said. "How do you think he will deal with an offer of negotiations?"

"Let me be blunt, Ms. Sachs. I will never negotiate with a coward like him. He lies to the world, to his own people, to his country. He is not to be trusted."

"Harsh words from a man *without* a country."

"I speak for *Islam*," Kufdani insisted, "and we will not tolerate a theocracy that hoists up its religious faithful by standing on the backs of Muslims."

"With whom *would* you be willing to negotiate?"

He paused, allowing a wide grin to spread across his face. "That's up to the Israeli people, isn't it?"

Elsa looked stunned. "It sounds as though you're encouraging the call for a vote to elect a new prime minister. Does that mean you're ready to give up on violence as a negotiating tool?"

Kufdani looked at her intently. "I am a violent man, Elsa, as was Muhammad (peace be upon him). I do not abhor violence. I have survived every one of Israel's attacks. Now it is time to test Israel's appetite for violence and ability to survive privation."

"That sounds . . . frightening. And you're saying that it starts tomorrow morning?"

"Yes. We will engage Israel until its people realize that a Jewish theocracy that cheats its Muslim citizens cannot stand. Israel has lost its technological edge. The world is catching up," Kufdani concluded. "Your emperor has no clothes."

UPPER WEST SIDE, MANHATTAN

<u>FRIDAY</u>

WHEN THE INTERVIEW ENDED, ALEX DUCKED OUT A SIDE ENTRANCE OF the studio and into a black Cadillac Escalade, which then drove quickly up the west side of Central Park with a matching Escalade trailing behind. At a side entrance of his apartment building, two armed men opened the door. They escorted him in and led him to his apartment.

After locking the door and resetting the alarms, Alex fixed a drink for himself. Then he collapsed into a chair and called Caitlin in Tangier.

"Hey," she answered, yawning. "Calling about the embassy?"

"No, just wanted to check on my beloved," Alex replied. "But yes, I suppose you should tell me all about it."

"I managed to find a connection and blew out their central server," Caitlin said. "I just caused it to spin on itself until it overheated and blew up."

"Very cool."

"Yeah, it will take weeks to fix properly. I took out the phone lines and disabled a few small servers too."

"Consulates were easier?"

"I only blew up a few—the ones on the East Coast that are most likely to be hosting the bad guys. I left the others alone, so Emilie can start tracking their response."

"Good for you," Alex confirmed. "You ready for tomorrow?"

"Yeah, tomorrow should be interesting. The Israelis' internal calls are full of talk about your TV interview. They're trying to figure out what you're going to do and how they can stop you." She sniffed and then yawned again. "They're not even close."

"Take a nap until it's time to get started?"

"I will, but I'm really looking forward to messing with Shin Bet and Bernstein," she said. "I hate those motherfuckers. And I miss the view from my windows."

Alex laughed. "Good night, my love." He hung up the phone and checked the time, deciding a nap was a good idea. When he dozed off, he was still smiling.

HE AWOKE AT 1:00 A.M., and sure enough—at 8:00 a.m. local time—Israel's largest solar facility, near Ramat Hovav on the Mediterranean coast, just north of the Gaza Strip, suffered an extensive EMP attack. From her windowless new perch in Tangier, Caitlin had triggered six 3D-printed "rocks" that had been placed there weeks earlier by an elderly Bedouin employee of the Israeli government. The EMP had a particular affinity for silicon and copper, and solar panels comprise an abundance of both. The facility was irredeemably fried.

Caitlin moved on.

At 8:10, Ben Gurion Airport ceased to operate. A series of EMP explosions destroyed the airport's electronics and control structure. With no air traffic control system, the controllers sat in their dark tower, trying to communicate and beginning to panic over the thought of thousands of incoming passengers with nowhere to land.

Behind a small hill on the other side of Route 1, a small white truck was parked, idling, as three Bedouins in the truck bed fired 40mm fragmentation rounds at the apron of the airport, where fifty-nine airlines had anticipated their regularly scheduled service. Terrified employees and passengers ran for cover. A repeat of the earlier attack on the kibbutz airfield left planes and trucks leaking fuel from small, ragged fragmentation holes. The fire trucks wouldn't start, and the pumps didn't work anyway. Then fifteen thermite rounds plummeted to the ground, and Ben Gurion Airport lit up in flames. The Bedouin men covered their truck bed and drove off to bury their 40mm weapon beside a pallet of 40mm ammunition, stored and ready for another day.

At 8:30, Haifa—the center of rail commerce in Israel—was congested with commuters and shoppers. An explosion at Bat Galim railway station, next to the central bus terminal, was followed by relative silence until, a moment later, screams of fear and anger could be heard. Two trains operating on electric power were destroyed, and the overhead line that powered them was fried for miles. Dozens of buses and hundreds of cars were disabled. Traffic lights went blank. Everything stopped in place—a chaotic stillness.

At 9:00, Caitlin turned her attention to the Ashdod Oil Refinery overlooking the Mediterranean Sea—the terminus of the pipeline from Israel's key Tamar natural gas field, one of only two major fields inside its claimed borders. An EMP explosion there shut down operations and turned off all the lights. Eleven billion cubic meters of natural gas typically flowed through the pipeline annually to power the electrical infrastructure of industrial Israel. It would flow no more, at least no time soon.

At the same time, thanks to a single EMP explosion that Caitlin implemented almost as an afterthought, the floating liquid natural gas facility just up the coast at Hadera lost its pumping capabilities. Without electricity the facility could not pump LNG from the freighters to the shore.

But Caitlin had saved the best for last.

Shin Bet headquarters in northern Tel Aviv was ravaged when the surrounding area was pulsed, as fifteen custom fragmentation rocks detonated around its perimeter, breaking windows and collapsing walls. The explosion killed fifteen men and women working there, and the vaunted Shin Bet computer facility was destroyed.

And thanks to Emilie, Alex's Kphone offered a curated selection of video clips showing the step-by-step annihilation of Israel's infrastructure. Alex stayed awake for several hours, until it was almost dawn in New York, so he could think about next steps while watching it all.

MOSSAD HEADQUARTERS, TEL AVIV

GUNS WAS EXASPERATED AND INCREDULOUS. KILLING REGINALD EDGE-worth was a stupid, vengeful act. But attacking the American Joint Chiefs chairman? And almost taking out one of the president's good friends? Either the prime minister was losing his marbles, or this Yakov Bernstein was even more of a hothead than Guns had anticipated.

All that, just to get the man they call Kufdani? he wondered.

It was no wonder Cooch was hitting back so hard, even though Guns was practically certain his unruly acquaintance had planned his response in Israel long before snipers took out Edgeworth or intruders climbed over the rail of that sailboat.

As if Cooch's interview and the latest word through the intelligence grapevine weren't bad enough, the news on another round of EMP attacks had just come in—this one far more extended than in Jerusalem and Beersheba. Without electricity, there would soon be no way to get food, fuel, and other goods (much less people) into or around the country.

"I do believe that we are about to see a demonstration of how to starve a nation," Guns said. His coffee cup had just been refreshed: he and Pelzer had been up all night seeking information that might mitigate the next attack by the Bedouin leader.

Behind her desk, Pelzer watched her computer screen as the updates kept rolling in. "Dreadful," she muttered. "Simply dreadful."

Her coffee was fresh too. Ever since the TV interview had set off alarm bells throughout the Israeli government, they had been trying to forecast specific targets.

"The least we could have done is bring Moishe in," Pelzer continued. "I don't remember him losing sleep like this when he was director."

"Let Moishe sleep," Guns advised. "We may need him fresh. Has the prime minister realized yet how badly he messed up?"

"Who knows?" Pelzer replied. "His intel was good. He told Dayan to go ahead, but just not get caught. He wasn't exactly rational about this operation, I'm afraid. He seems to have a thing about killing Kufdani."

"Well, he failed," Guns pointed out. "Shin Bet and the Sayeret Matkal are very good, the best we've got, and they failed." He had to admit, even knowing Cooch's capabilities, that he was surprised.

"They wanted to get him as soon as he landed in the US, before he made it to New York and his next PR move there. His security was always going to be too tight in New York, so they tried things another way. Thought they had a chance."

"Dayan must be very unhappy."

Pelzer nodded. "Yes, but the prime minister is downright livid."

"And here we sit, with rush hour upon us, completely outmaneuvered," Guns admitted. "What do you think Cooch will do next?"

"I'm afraid to think about it," Pelzer said. "What do *you* think?"

"I think whatever he does, he's been planning to do for a long time. Getting the public on his side was just the opening act." And it had worked—that was the worst of it all. The whole PR stunt had been vintage Reginald Edgeworth. But what was the point of killing him now? The damage was already done.

"And the negative publicity for us has just begun," Pelzer said, her voice gloomy. "Especially with our prime minister and his security forces going off-script."

"And with Cooch, on the other hand, toeing the line on a path to negotiate for what he wants," Guns said. "He didn't destroy anything military, didn't bother Tel Aviv much, and has certainly made his point to the world. Now we just wait and see who's listening."

"Perhaps we should attempt to take the lead on—"

"Not yet," Guns urged. "The diaspora will comment soon. That should influence the prime minister, if anything can."

"Good advice," Pelzer said. "We'll see who's the last man standing."

Something in her comment recalled a phrase Kufdani had used with Guns two weeks earlier, about what would be left in the rubble. Perhaps Mossad had a critical role to play here after all.

"Cooch is probably looking for a way in, someone to lead negotiations from our side," Guns said. "He doesn't want to have to do this all over again. Remember his comment? 'A standing Mossad in the rubble'?"

"It's not rubble yet, but I think we get the message."

"And today the Knesset may be a bit concerned about the state of our economy."

Pelzer smiled and nodded. "And perhaps less concerned with the votes of the Haredi."

OFFICE OF THE PRIME MINISTER, JERUSALEM

YAKOV BERNSTEIN SAT IN THE PRIME MINISTER'S OFFICE WITH A NOTE-pad open before him, but so far he had written nothing on it. What was there to write? He was too busy fielding insults to even think straight.

The prime minister was on the phone with the leader of the largest supportive Jewish community in New York, getting a high-volume scolding of his own. "You fucking tried to kill our chairman of the Joint Chiefs?" came the angry voice over the phone. "Are you a fucking moron?"

"It's more complicated than that," the prime minister tried to explain. "General Kim just happened to be with the target, a person who is an immediate threat to our republic."

"The Bedouin? Horseshit!" the angry voice shouted. "Save that 'threat to our republic' bullshit for the press. And kill the Bedouin when he is by himself, you fucking idiot, not holding hands with a representative of the United States government!"

"I'm sorry, sir," the prime minister replied, gritting his teeth. "It won't happen again." He shot an irritated look at Bernstein, who started pretending to scribble on his notepad.

"It won't happen on *my* fucking watch again—I'll tell you that. I'm taking truckloads of shit here, from American Jews and Israeli nationals alike. You'd better find some new fucking leadership over there, Mr. Prime Minister, because you ain't it. *Capiche*?"

"Let me get back to you, sir," the prime minister said, his eyes closed. "I'll speak with our defense minister and figure this whole thing out."

"Bernstein? Yakov Bernstein is a bigger fucking idiot than you are. I've tried speaking with him already. He doesn't even return my calls. Fuck Bernstein! And fuck the horse he rode in on!"

The phone disconnected.

The prime minister was fuming. He shot another look at Bernstein. "You didn't return his calls? What the fuck?"

Bernstein fumbled with his phone. "I . . . I haven't gotten any calls," he stammered. "My phone doesn't . . . doesn't seem to be functioning properly—"

"Get out of my sight!" the prime minister yelled. "Go away! Go home!"

"Well, Mr. Prime Minister, I . . . I will need a ride," Bernstein said. "My car is not working. My wife's either."

"Then call a cab. Or a friend, if you have any." The prime minister sunk his head in his hands. "Just get out of my sight."

Yakov Bernstein stumbled to the door, still fiddling with his seemingly dead phone, shaking his head in confusion.

TWO THOUSAND MILES AWAY, IN TANGIER, Caitlin was smiling so hard her new molars started to throb. The conversation had amused her to no end. This Bernstein was the guy who had gotten her face broken, the guy who threw Alex in jail. Bernstein may be unable to hear the conversation, but she could hear it from his phone just fine.

But that would not be the end of it. She planned to make Bernstein's life unpleasant for a very long time to come.

THE WHITE HOUSE, WASHINGTON, DC

BROOKS ELLIOT SAT ACROSS FROM THE PRESIDENT IN THE OVAL OFFICE, waiting for his next comment. He glanced at Macmillan, who sat to his right, equally patient. Sitting back in his high-backed chair, the commander-in-chief sighed. The devastation in Israel was all over the national news. The president was hoping it sounded worse than it was.

"So far, the screams from the US Jewish community are less strident than I would have guessed," the president said. "Perhaps the damage is not as widespread as we fear."

Brooks shook his head. "I don't think the press has sorted out that Israel has been blockaded, Mr. President. No rail, no buses, no air support. Their food supply can't get to them. Heating their homes will soon be a problem too. Their supply of natural gas has been reduced by half, for at least six months, so maintaining electricity is not going to be easy."

"The Israeli military is unscathed, and we believe that is by design," Macmillan added. "So, they can still defend themselves against invasion. They are less prepared for domestic problems, however."

"Why is that?" asked the president.

"Shin Bet headquarters got beat up pretty good, according to the satellite images from a few hours ago," Mac replied. "They'll have to find a new home."

The president sighed again. "Well, gentlemen, what is your recommendation?"

"It's Israel's move," Brooks argued. "Of course, we must respond with rage and diplomatic threats over Israeli attacks on our politicians—and on our soil. But we didn't lose anyone, so after a little while, we should let that blow over."

"Perhaps you could call for a pause to all aid and financial support from us, in response to Israel's breach of diplomacy," Mac suggested. "At the same time, we don't want to abandon the Israeli people. So maybe we agree to fly in food and necessities for a while."

"What does the State Department say?" Brooks said.

"They're still in shock over the attacks on Israel's infrastructure," the president said with a little grin. "They want us to be prepared to support Israel should any ground attacks come from their Arab neighbors."

"Good advice," Mac replied. "And then we wait it out."

The president nodded in agreement.

"We can't sort this out for them, Mr. President," Brooks added, "but I'd guess that Israel is destined for new leadership."

UPPER WEST SIDE, MANHATTAN

AFTER STAYING UP HALF THE NIGHT TO WATCH THINGS FALL APART IN Israel, Alex was quite busy trying to figure out Israel's next move. But when his Kphone rang and the caller ID showed it was Elsa Sachs, something prompted him to answer. "Hello, Ms. Sachs."

"Elsa."

"Yes, of course. Elsa."

"Have you watched the news?" she asked, sounding a little cross. "My friends and family are a little on edge—well, scared shitless is more like it. Your last move is really hitting home. They're worried about getting food. There's a run on the grocery stores."

"Good," Alex said. "Then things are going as I expected. Don't worry, I won't let your family starve. What about you?"

"What about me?"

"Are you feeling a little on edge? How's my security team treating you?"

"Your security team is a pain in the ass," she retorted. "They almost undressed the housekeeper, searching her for weapons when she came to clean the room. They surround me wherever I go. They tasted my breakfast before I was allowed to eat it. They're driving me mad."

Alex couldn't resist laughing. "What can I do to make you happy, short of removing them from their sworn duty?"

"Well, I'd like to go home to Tel Aviv, but I can't. You blew up the airport."

And the train station and the bus station, Alex thought.

"You're stuck. Why don't you come over here?" he suggested. "I'll make you dinner, which should guarantee your food is safe. And *I* can be your security guy for a while. Your regular guys can hang out with my guys in the extra apartment and . . . clean their guns or something."

"I don't know . . ."

"I promise," he said, "no swine."

Now it was Elsa's turn to laugh. "It's a deal."

They all work for Jimmy anyway and I pay Jimmy, or at least Kufdani Industries does. He made a mental note to send a bottle of 2003 Dancing Hares to Brooks for loaning him Jimmy and his crew.

Alex busied himself going through his refrigerator and pantry: chicken, a selection of vegetables, bone broth, plenty of spices—that would do nicely. He pulled the tagine out of his pantry and checked the wine fridge, which was overflowing as usual.

When his security team admitted Elsa, they took extra precautions. After all, they had just lost a high-profile client to a sniper.

"Put the extra people in the lobby," Alex told the team leader. "If they come, it will be up close and personal."

The windows were reinforced to stop the kind of shot a sniper would have to make. Anyway, Jimmy and Jerome had deduced the best spot for a sniper shot at Alex's windows and had rented that apartment and installed a security system to alert them in case anyone entered.

Dinner was predictably scrumptious, and the conversation was easier than he'd expected. They avoided politics at first, which was just as well, and connected on the topic of music instead. Elsa had recognized most of the tunes coming from the high-quality speakers mounted in the ceiling.

"Klemmer," she said, putting down her fork and identifying the alto sax player as John Klemmer. "From the album *Tapestry*, right?"

Alex nodded, putting his fork down too.

"I haven't heard this piece in years," Elsa continued. "These days I'm all about Bill Evans, but this is nice too."

Alex picked up his Kphone and instructed Emilie to play Evans's *Inner Spirit* after the Klemmer piece finished. After a moment of comfortable silence, a piano opened with applause in the background. The subwoofer showcased Marc Johnson on ever-so-subtle bass and Joe LaBarbera in spectacular form on drums.

"You probably know this piece," Alex said, "and the story Evans tells with the music, about struggling against his addictions and losing."

"Yes, beautiful. I've listened to it often," Elsa said, studying him. "You continue to surprise me, Alex—excellent chef, great taste in music . . . What can't you do?"

Moving into the living room, Alex fixed them each a cocktail before settling on a big easy chair. Elsa sat on the couch, observing the living space of this strange and accomplished man. He saw her gaze fall on the small table beside his chair, with an old Quran on it, marked by a green ribbon halfway through its pages.

When the conversation turned to the elephant in the room, it came as no surprise. Given the mangled, failing state of things near Elsa's home in Tel Aviv and all around Israel—and Alex's role in creating it—the discussion was hard to avoid.

"But physically, Tel Aviv seems largely untouched," Elsa said. "Was that intentional?"

"Pretty much," Alex confessed. "As I told my friend in Mossad, the objective is to frighten the liberal voices in Israel but essentially leave their reality unharmed."

"Why? To what end?" she said, her eyes narrowing. "You are on your way to destroying my country. The rest seems easy for you, at least until the nukes start flying. What do you need us for?"

Alex chuckled. "Have you no faith in me yet? You've agreed to enable me and my message by putting me in the news and on television. Everyone in the free world, and most everyone else too, hears when I speak. How could I manage that without you?"

"And the rest of us?"

Alex bowed his head slightly. "Indeed, I'm well on my way to destroying your theocracy. And I need your bunch—liberal, progressive Jewish voices—to help me pick up the pieces and fit it back together."

"With the theocracy piece missing from the puzzle," Elsa said.

"That's right. I need you to tell that story to the world," Alex replied. "Elsa, you're becoming famous, and that makes you powerful. People listen to you, just as Edgie planned. He thought that they would come to you, and I agree."

He paused, looking carefully at her. He had not really noticed her beauty until now—only her youth. But now he realized there was more to it.

"Use that power for good, Elsa," he urged. "Use it to make the world a better place."

Elsa was quiet for a bit, thinking about Alex's plea and listening to Bill Evans make magic on his piano. She patted the cushion of the couch and said, "Bill Evans sounds better from here. Come sit by me."

Across the room, a large oil painting of fishermen pulling in their bulging nets caught her eye. Rays of early morning sunshine glittered from the scales of fish and the sweaty male bodies straining at the nets. The hazy face of Gibraltar was in the background, counterpoint to their glistening shoulders. As Alex moved from his chair to the couch, Elsa thought about what this painting might mean to him. The mystery was more exciting than any true answer could be.

A fleeting thought came to her: *Why don't I feel threatened by him?* After all, they were saying he was the Mahdi, that he would restore the Muslim world to its rightful place of honor—perhaps at the expense of her own people. This thought was followed by a more practical question from her inner journalist: *What's his Mossad connection?*

But when Alex sat beside her, all else disappeared. Elsa leaned forward so his arm would fall to the back of the couch behind her. Then she leaned back and listened some more. Eventually, her hand slid to his thigh.

"I'm famous, Alex," she pointed out. "Does that make me a journalistic idol?"

Alex's expression was puzzled. "I suppose you could say that."

"*You* said it," she retorted. "And I said if that happened, I'd go down on you for a week."

He frowned. "I thought the deal was that you would get a Pulitzer Prize."

"Close enough," Elsa said. "So, is this a good time to start?"

"Don't be crude," Alex replied. "Listen to the music."

Elsa let her hand drift slowly up his thigh. "A deal is a deal. I want to find out about the pony-peckered Arab." She moved her hand even closer and felt him stir.

A single, soft beep came from his Kphone as he switched it off. "You've been talking to Caitlin."

LaBarbera's drums were becoming a little more active, and so was Elsa's hand. When her eyes turned to meet Alex's, he smiled softly. Evidence of his arousal was more pronounced and starting to tunnel down a trouser leg, making itself known. She slid from the couch to her knees on the carpeted floor and turned to him, reaching.

A deal is a deal, she thought.

She puzzled for a moment about how to get the pony out of his pants. Tugging at his belt buckle, she managed to release the creature in question. She had uncovered the only fat on this man's body, and it resided abundantly along the stalk of this mushroom.

Grinning up at him, she said, "I'll do my best Jewish girl on this. Brace yourself, Arab."

She offered the first faint tickle of a tongue and then repeatedly engulfed him, alternating active thumb contact at first and then finally contributing both hands to the effort.

Just as she was losing herself, he stopped her.

"This is lovely, but there are more comfortable ways to do this. After all, you are my guest. Let's try the bedroom." He stood and led her by the hand, turning back the covers and ironed sheets on the king-sized bed and pushing several large pillows aside. "Join me, and we will continue our previous conversation."

Elsa watched him undress: a big, dark middle-aged man in such terrific shape that the scars on his chest only heightened the attraction. As he reclined against the last remaining pillow, the infamous pony pecker, veins and all, protruded far enough to reach the lower ridges of his stomach.

I'm not sure I'm ready for that, Elsa thought, *but at least I'm no virgin. Let's just see what happens.*

"Jump in and say hello," he suggested, and she did.

The kissing started immediately but without urgency. As their tongues tangled, and his hands began to move over her body, she reciprocated and explored. Evans was still on the bedroom speakers, playing softly.

Elsa began to slide across his chest, but Alex stopped her and slid beneath her arm and down the bed. He explored her inner thighs, kissing and nuzzling, then moved farther upward—a pleasant start. Before long, her mind began to drift pleasantly, wandering briefly to her conversation with Caitlin O'Connor: about her lover's mastery of the delicate art of synchronizing his sensual ministrations to the beat of any complex music with a good bassist. *His Brubeck is spectacular*, Caitlin had claimed.

Elsa had thought that was quite a weird thing to say, but now she understood. *Anyway, tonight is a Bill Evans night,* she thought happily, more relaxed than she'd been in forever. As the tingle became more insistent, her jaw began to clench. Evans was hitting his stride, as was Alex.

If he doesn't give the best head on the planet, she thought a few minutes later, when words had returned to her, *I want to meet the other guy.*

After a while, she slid down on the bed and said, "My turn again. You should watch." She gave her best Jewish princess impression and, for a long time, investigated every one of his bumps, ridges, and veins. She added one or both hands as was called for, stroking to the rhythm, and finally picking up the pace as she sensed the finale.

"Well, Alex, that was quite an experience," Elsa said then. "We're even?"

"Not yet," Alex vowed.

UPPER WEST SIDE, MANHATTAN

ELSA LEFT EARLY THE NEXT MORNING AFTER BAGELS AND COFFEE, politely thanking Kufdani for a wonderful evening and trying not to limp as she walked down the hall between her two security guards.

Kufdani dropped his robe and stretched in front of his full-length looking glass, which showed a slab of a man with a respectable waist and the ripped abdominals of a young gymnast. Blood vessels stood out on his deltoids: his biceps were like cantaloupes atop vein trees. Nothing could match the ragged zippers and assholes all over his body, but his face was getting uglier too, with age building wrinkles in and among the scars. But the price and cost of his years in the CIA special ops unit had prepared him for the role he had now, and for that he was glad. He had become Mac's employee and then his friend. He had become Tang's student and later his friend too.

He missed the crabby voice of Tang, telling him that he was fat and sloppy, that he stank of alcohol. In the early days at the CIA's Farm in Virginia, a more patient Tang showed him how to sense, move, and strike, with recovery as part of the next violent move—he missed that too. Twenty years of studying with Tang, and now Bernstein had killed him.

Bernstein, you turd. You'll get what's coming to you.

Tang had left no one else behind to mourn him, nothing except for an untouched, growing pile of cash from the wages Kufdani had paid him all these years. But he'd also left Kufdani with a priceless personal gift for sensing motion and practicing the violent arts, not to mention anticipating changes in his life and responding to them in real time. It was a useful legacy, and not one that Kufdani took lightly.

He rolled into a handstand against the wall, letting his legs drop together to one side and then the other. Then he did ten slow pushups with his feet quivering above him, then dropped straight down, pushed up, and spun to his feet, refreshed. Sometimes he thought better upside down.

He put his robe on and sat in the reclining chair, picking up Larry Freedman's *The Future of War*. As a man of a certain age, he sometimes liked to turn pages and feel their thickness—without the benefit of Emilie's unending clarity. He was halfway through the book already, but had been distracted by its failure to deal with the reality of the Middle East. At least he was still trying it: Steven Pinker's *The Better Angels of Our Nature* was back on the bookshelf, destined to be a re-gift. Kufdani didn't see the world as inherently benign the way Pinker did.

It was late morning, just after he came out of the shower, when his Kphone rang: his old friend Dr. Al-Fraih.

"You can trust the Kphone security," Kufdani reassured him. "What's up?"

"Abbas did his homework on you and sent the dossier to someone on the Crown Prince's staff," Al-Fraih reported. "He followed up this morning and spoke with this person at some length."

"And?"

"I've just learned that you have a personal appointment with ABS in Riyadh, five days from now. You have just one hour officially, but I happen to know that ABS freed an extra hour for you, just in case. Apparently, he was impressed with your leadership in Israel. And he has heard the rumors."

"Rumors?" Kufdani asked.

"That you are the Mahdi."

It's all coming together, Kufdani thought, surprised to feel relief.

"You are a gentleman and a scholar, Al-Fraih," he said. "I'll make arrangements."

"You can work with Abbas on the details. You owe me one."

Kufdani chuckled. "I'll figure it out. Petrus, maybe?"

"Quite," Al-Fraih replied, "if it is a decent year. Merlot smooths nicely after ten years in the bottle."

Kufdani called Brooks to share the good news and discuss security for the trip, first to Tangier for a few days and then on to Riyadh. Brooks was hardly surprised, though. Both he and Mac had heard from Abbas in a roundabout way, and had made Kufdani sound like if not the Mahdi, then the second coming of Muhammad. They hung up, and agreed to talk again after Brooks talked to the president and Kufdani got back to Tangier.

Twenty minutes later, however, the Kphone rang again. It was Brooks. The president had insisted he take an Air Force executive jet to Tangier because LuAnn hadn't seen her husband for two weeks, and the First Lady was getting cranky about it. Taking Kufdani along, Brooks explained, had been an easy call.

Kufdani set about packing the few things he had brought from Tangier, then set the electronics to secure the apartment. At the door, two quick knocks alerted the guards, who came in and closed the door.

"We are going to Kennedy Airport, destination Tangier, so bring your passports. We will meet an Air Force C37B, a Gulfstream 550, at the FBO. Ambassador Elliot will be on the plane. You two will accompany me as bodyguards. Check your sidearms with the crew if they ask. Note where they secure them. We leave in sixty minutes."

Three Escalades wheeled out of the parking lot of Kufdani's apartment building. At the first intersection, the lead vehicle turned on its behind-grill lights and gave a *blurp* on its siren. A traffic cop in a bright orange vest pushed a remote that turned the oncoming traffic light to red. He stepped out, holding up his white, gloved hand, and waved the small caravan through the turn to the tunnel.

The feds are on point, Kufdani thought.

After moving smoothly through Queens, they drove past the iconic terminal associated with John F. Kennedy International Airport—now a stylish, modern hotel—and down a side road to the gate of the fixed-base operator. A few hundred feet past the gate, a sleek, two-engine executive jet in dull gray, with round windows and US Air Force markings, stood idling. Its passenger ramp was descending.

Two uniformed officers in camo and vests with M4 rifles stood back from the vehicles while six more walked to the Escalades. When they stopped, all the doors opened, and the passengers got out. IDs were checked, the cargo area was inspected, and then two golf carts came out of a nearby hangar and picked up Kufdani, the two bodyguards, and the small amount of luggage they'd brought for the trip. The carts headed for the jet. The other men and the three Escalades turned back through the gate to drive back to Manhattan.

Kufdani had to admit he was impressed: the White House's approach to security continued to err on the side of caution.

EN ROUTE TO TANGIER

<u>MONDAY</u>

THE PLANE—A GULFSTREAM 550—WAS FAST AND, AFTER QUICKLY reaching its 45,000-foot cruising altitude and leveling out, quieter than most. The flight attendant, in his briefing, had pointed out the features of the aircraft before asking Brooks about drink choices and nodding when both men ordered water and coffee.

Alex had spent most of his Air Force flight time in the back of a C-130 or, on good days, freefalling out of a C-141, wearing an oxygen mask that reeked of the nine guys who had used it before him. Now, buckled into an aft-facing seat behind the flight deck, with Brooks sitting in a forward seat across the aisle, he confessed, "I could get used to this."

Brooks laughed.

"How's the president's head?" Alex asked.

"Well, he is really pissed at Israel," Brooks replied. "Everybody's screaming about things—and mostly screaming them at him. He doesn't like that." This airplane trip, he explained, was the president's way of giving people the finger.

"What do you hear about what's going on in Israel?"

"The populace is starting to figure it out," Brooks said. "It ain't pretty, because it ain't fixable anytime soon. Without enough food, electricity, and transportation, and with no way to get much of anything else they need, they'll find it hard to make ends meet for the foreseeable future. Harsh things are being said about the prime minister."

"What does the power leadership of the diaspora say?" Alex asked. "They swing a lot of weight and a lot of money."

"They're saying harsh things about the prime minister too. Then they're shouting about sending aid to the Israeli people."

"When are they going to dump him?" Alex said.

Brooks shrugged. "Publicly? Maybe in the next few days—that's what State thinks. According to the US ambassador in Israel, support for the Haredi is nearing zero. The prime minister is many votes shy of a mandate."

"Good," Alex said. "I want to see him squirm, the arrogant prick."

"Get over it." Brooks took a sip of his coffee and a big gulp from his water bottle. "So, what's the next step? How do we make this work? How shall I advise the president?"

"You gather advice and then do as you choose, same as always," Alex replied. "That's how you maintain your personal values in that sleazy bunch."

"Mmm," Brooks said, staring out the oval window at the Atlantic Ocean eight or nine miles below.

"Have the president gather favors by bringing up poor past advice he has been given and acted upon. He should be hurt and confused, which makes him quite angry and lets him make crazy proposals in order to observe reactions."

"I suppose the trick will be finding a way for him to both support the solution *you* prefer and believe *he* was the one who thought it up." Brooks laughed. "They call that 'managing the morphosis.'"

Alex looked skeptical. "They do?"

"Yup, they do. It's from the Greek for 'the process of forming.' You, all about steering things in the way you want to see them develop."

As the flight attendant served their meal, Alex shifted in his seat to look at Brooks. "So, about my one-on-one with ABS—"

"Ain't that the shits?" Brooks laughed. "One day you're a CIA bomber carrying a bleeding SEAL off a beach in Lebanon, and the next you're having tea with the ruler of Saudi Arabia."

Alex grinned at the Navy SEAL in question. "I'm going to take Caitlin's plane to Riyadh. It's a lot simpler and may even impress him a little." If she let him, that was. If he wanted her to blow up anything else in Israel, he'd better pay some attention to her when he got to Tangier. "What are your plans?"

"I'm having dinner with Sino tomorrow—"

"Sounds like fun—"

"Could be, although being an ambassador really complicates my travels. I hope they don't decide on a welcoming band and speeches when I arrive."

"Poor you," Alex quipped.

"I know," Brooks said. "So, got a plan for Riyadh?"

"Not yet," Alex said. "It's tricky. At some point I'll have to figure out how to deal with the Wahabi Muslims. I need them on my side long-term. But first I have to get around the ABS ego and learn how to manipulate his thought processes to match mine as they morph, all in the space of an hour. I've never even met the man."

"But you've read a lot about him, I assume?" Brooks asked. "You know a lot about him, thanks to Emilie?"

Alex waved a hand. "I thought I did, but it's mostly pablum. I did manage to learn some from Al-Fraih and Abbas. But I'll need to learn more if I want him to view me as an important ally in his most cherished quest."

"And what's that?"

Alex pointed at his friend. "Exactly. I have to figure out how to get inside his head—manage the morphosis, I suppose."

"Good luck with that, my friend," Brooks said. "Not sure if this might help, but the president did mention the petro-yuan deal that ABS and the Chinese are talking about. No one in our universe is crazy about it."

Alex nodded. "I imagine plenty of US folks worry it might mean the demise of the petrodollar deal from the 1970s."

"Using the dollar as the world's reserve currency allows us to spend much more than we make." Brooks shrugged. "Of course they would hate to lose that gift."

"If I get a chance to fix that," Alex said, "the president owes you big-time." He sat thinking for a few moments. "Manage the morphosis, eh?"

"Mmm-hmm." Brooks dropped his head back on the seat and closed his eyes.

"So whatever I'm trying to sell to ABS, he will buy only if it's in his self-interest, however he defines that. So we need to agree on what that is."

"Mmm-hmm."

Alex glanced out the window just as a pair of Moroccan Air Force F-15s appeared off the C-37B's wingtip. Through the cockpit window, the lead pilot was grinning at them and giving a thumbs-up.

"Looks like Sino sent a welcome without the band," he joked.

EN ROUTE TO RIYADH

IF YOU WANT FOLKS TO SUSPECT YOU ARE THE MAHDI, YOU DRESS LIKE *the Mahdi.*

Kufdani heard the engines change pitch and felt the plane's nose tilt down, so he stood to adjust his new outfit, shifting everything into place. He checked the mirror mounted on the back of the closet. Yes, this would do. All white was a good look, one of purity.

Aboard Caitlin's NSA travel perquisite, an almost-new C-37B still in its US Air Force livery—painted a dull gray, with a darker shade not quite covering the *United States of America* lettering above the round windows on its fuselage—Kufdani heard the sound of wheels coming down and the flaps extending from beneath the wings, breaking the silence of flight. After more than three thousand miles, barely six hours from takeoff in Tangier, and a quick roll down the runway, he had arrived for the first time in Saudi Arabia.

The past several days had been both busy and invigorating, with Kufdani and his cabal reviewing the damage they had caused in Israel and considering how to move forward. After he boarded the flight at 6:00 that morning, the smell of brewing coffee had caught everyone's attention, from Kufdani in a forward seat to his two bodyguards comfortable aft. Even the flight attendant buckled into his seat next to the galley, still wearing US Air Force flight attire—the politics and protocol of a leased airplane and flight crew dress codes were yet to be resolved—had seemed eager for a second cup.

Kufdani hadn't slept much the previous night. Upon his return to Tangier after what seemed a lifetime, Caitlin had been hornier than a three-balled billy goat. She had heard from Elsa Sachs about their dinner date, which had seemed only to arouse her all the more. She also seemed rather frisky now that she was back in her sleeping quarters at the front of the mountain, where there was plenty of sunlight. Both she and LuAnn were happy to return to their view of Tangier harbor. Living quarters and offices got old quickly with four rock walls and spaces smaller than a Motel 6 room.

Kufdani had relented on this point after Israel's prime minister lost a confidence vote by a margin of three to one, putting him under great pressure to step down. It now seemed unlikely the prime minister could convince anyone at IDF missile control to put a projectile through a window at Kufdani Industries. It had never been all that likely anyway, but planning prudence had made him unwilling to take that chance with their lives.

At dinner on the previous evening, LuAnn had mentioned that Kufdani Industries now owned the mortgages on the apartments and land on the West Bank in Israel. "They were suddenly selling for ten cents on the dollar with a decent interest rate," she pointed out. The fire sale was based on the fear that Israel would disavow the debt or be unwilling to pay the rent, given Kufdani's recent show of power. Israel's government had declared guarantees, but many French and American lenders—mostly Jewish—still had little faith. "I negotiated for payment in gold at our choice at the current rate in dollars, since the collateral was at great risk," LuAnn continued. "The Israeli government bought it."

"Good for you, LuAnn," Kufdani had said. "Wars are expensive."

Stepping onto the tarmac at King Khalid International Airport in Riyadh, Kufdani was met by a black limousine assigned to transport him to the Royal Palace. As he watched the sparse traffic, and the orderly pedestrians walking along the streets—with women fully covered and always accompanied by a man—he thought about his goals and how to present them, and about the Crown Prince's place in the city, the country, and the future. ABS and his Wahabi advisors promised to be a formidable combination to confront, each with their own agenda.

Kufdani hoped wearing traditional garb was the right choice. A *thoab*—a light, white cotton shirt that hung to his knees and was open at the neck—was matched with white cotton trousers called *serwal*. A white *shemagh*, or keffiyeh, the traditional Arab headdress, was wrapped around his head with the ends hanging in front of him, secured by a white *agal*. Pure white was typically recommended for those embarking on the mandatory Muslim trip to Mecca, the *Haj*. Kufdani wanted to present an image of an immaculate Bedouin imam on a mission. If anyone mistook him for the Mahdi—well, all the better.

Upon arriving at the Royal Palace, Kufdani was welcomed by a guard in ceremonial dress, who took his two packages in hand and directed him to walk through a metal detector. He was then escorted down a red-carpeted hallway to a massive metal door, with two guards on either side, that opened at his approach.

A uniformed guard walked Kufdani into a spacious and opulent room, decorated with gold wherever a place could be found, where ABS sat on a large chair near a long table. Standing up and extending his arms, ABS exclaimed, "Kufdani, welcome! I have heard much about you."

Kufdani dipped his head slightly in acknowledgment. "I am pleased to make your acquaintance, Your Majesty, and I have also heard about you. Much is written."

"Bah! What do they know?" He waved Kufdani to an open chair. "Congratulations on your magnificent victory over the Israelis. Red-topped surrender monkeys, indeed! What a wonderful image you have shared with the world."

Kufdani grinned. "It seems to help the news get around, Your Majesty. But there is work yet to do, which I hope to discuss with you." *Right now, I have an hour, so I should push a little.*

ABS gestured to the two packages, which had been carefully rewrapped and laid on the table. "What gifts have you brought to impress one of the richest men in the world?"

Kufdani picked up the larger box and began to unwrap it. "I brought what I, as the leader of the Bedouin tribes, would be happy to receive."

ABS nodded.

"The all-white tagine is a rarity in Morocco," Kufdani said, extracting the item in question. "Bedouins covet them and view them as priceless. Only the most talented of Moroccan pottery artists make them."

ABS picked up the tagine, looked it over with apparent interest, and set it back on the table. "Thank you."

Kufdani then opened the smaller package and took out a simple wooden box. Opening the box, he removed a weathered item: an ivory cylinder with images carved on its sides and Arabic lettering encircling the top. "This was a gift to me from my grandfather Kufdani many years ago," he explained. "With it came a note that said, 'For your friends who are not.'"

"Yes, beautiful. Thank you." ABS reached for the cylinder and inspected it carefully. "But this note from your grandfather intrigues me."

Kufdani looked into the eyes of the Crown Prince. "Friends who betray friends were anathema to my grandfather. And he refused to reject violence in his lifestyle. As do I."

"This is good to know," ABS replied with a smile.

"Use your palm to push in the base of the cylinder, Your Majesty, and turn it in a circle."

As ABS twisted the base of the ivory cylinder, a long, thin blade sprang up from its top. Startled, he looked up suddenly to see a grinning Kufdani.

"Twist it the other way, Your Majesty, and the blade will disappear."

ABS twisted the base again to see the blade disappear, and then looked for the opening, which was obscured among the intricate carvings. "That is a most wonderful gift, Kufdani. I thank you," he said, twisting in both directions once more before slipping the cylinder into his pocket.

"To own such an ancient device is an honor among Bedouin men, Your

Majesty," Kufdani said. "It is indicative of great status and influence. I wanted you to have it. You are unlikely to see another."

Taking their seats at the table, they made ceremonial tea and ate tiny snacks for several minutes, sniffing, sipping, and belching as polite men do. Kufdani reminded himself to relay every detail to his mother the next time he visited Algeciras. She would be pleased to know her father's gift had been so honored by the Crown Prince of Saudi Arabia. Many years ago, she had once shown him how to work the blade, never dreaming it might smooth the way toward a more harmonious future.

When ABS wiped his mouth with an embroidered napkin and tossed it on the table, Kufdani knew the niceties were over.

"So, Kufdani," ABS said, his eyes blazing, "you have been presented to me as a master strategist and a ruthless, thoughtful killer. But why are you here on this trip? What is it you want?"

Kufdani held the Crown Prince's gaze. "I have a new vision for the Middle East and a plan to get there," he revealed. "I need your help to do it."

ROYAL PALACE, RIYADH

"A VISION AND A PLAN, YOU SAY?" THE CROWN PRINCE RESPONDED, glancing at an impossibly thin gold watch on his wrist. "And you need my help?"

"Yes, Your Majesty," Kufdani confirmed.

ABS sighed. "Most people do. How much do you need, and when?"

"I don't know how much. Perhaps some backing to sort out the remaining pieces of the Israeli–Palestinian mess. But a billion or two in US dollars, I could fund myself."

Is that so? ABS thought, wondering whether even he would remark in such an offhanded manner about a billion dollars—or two.

"It's your status I may need instead, Your Majesty."

And now we reach the most important part. "Why do you need it?"

"I wish to remake the Middle East with a grand gesture involving you, Israel, and the United States. And I wish to start with Jerusalem and the West Bank."

ABS sat quietly for a moment or two. "Yet you are not a politician, nor the ruler of a country with the influence and might of Saudi Arabia or America, but a noted killer. What plans does a noted killer have for me?"

"I think of myself not as a common killer, Your Majesty," Kufdani replied, "but as a warrior for Allah, just as Muhammad (peace be upon him) was a warrior for Allah. He killed often and many. Recently, while unarmed, I killed three men in five seconds—all in the service of Allah. But I shall tell you what I plan, and you may tell me whether you would choose to be involved."

ABS bowed his head slightly. "Go on."

"I wish first to remind you of Alexander the Great, who is remembered not for his great battles and victories, but rather for spreading Greek culture from Gibraltar to Punjab—for his role as a statesman," Kufdani began. "And that is what I see for you: leading the spread of an enlightened form of Islam across a vast swath of the world, starting in the Middle East. My plan is the first step in that quest. I am the warrior. And you are the statesman, bringing enlightenment to the world."

"And here we are—the pitch to save the Middle East, or at least make it much better." ABS smiled and leaned forward. "I await your next words with great impatience, Kufdani. The whole bit. But without a price tag, I presume?"

"I plan for Jerusalem to become an international city, open to Muslims, Christians, Jews, and pagans alike. I plan for Israel to survive this turmoil as a vibrant intellectual society with a constitution that proscribes a Jewish theocracy. I plan for twelve-year-old Middle Eastern children as a group to score, each year, in the top quartile of students in the world tested for mathematics and communications skills. I plan to have medical schools, business schools, and liberal arts schools across the Middle East, and more. You have begun that process with your new university here in Saudi Arabia."

ABS grinned. "That seems a modest enough set of goals. Anything else?"

"I plan to return the Arabic-speaking world to the glory it held in the ninth century, before internecine warfare set us to killing other Muslims in line with some obscure logic," Kufdani continued. "The schism between Sunni and Shi'a is apostasy in the eyes of Allah; good Muslims being killed by other good Muslims is an abomination in His eyes. You can help me do this."

"Allah be praised, that is a lot to do," ABS said, amused, as he leaned back into his cushions. "I would certainly be interested in being involved, if things happen as you say. How long do you think this transformation will take?"

"Decades, at least," Kufdani said. "Probably not in our lifetimes."

He is honest, at least, thought ABS. "You are both a realist and a dreamer. Do you really think these things go together?"

"The prophet thought they did," Kufdani replied, "but he had Allah and the Angel Gabriel to help him. I could use some help."

"I assume you are the leader of this vast effort that you fantasize about?" ABS demanded.

"I am no politician," Kufdani said vaguely. "I am a warrior."

"Fine, let's break it down," ABS said. "What do you need first, and when?"

"Probably a few billion for Jerusalem," Kufdani said, chuckling. "I've blown a lot of it up."

"And when do I get the bill?"

"I have spent a lot of time thinking about the whole picture. I do not expect to sell this vision to the Israelis without difficulty. First, I must instill in them a greater fear of oblivion."

"You are already planning for this?"

Kufdani nodded. "And then we will make our grand gesture: an offer to split the costs of rebuilding Jerusalem and setting up an international city there, with Israel, the US, and Saudi Arabia footing the bill together."

"Has the United States government agreed to this improbable scheme of yours?" ABS asked.

"I have not yet tried to sell it to the US president yet, because without you, it doesn't work. But the transition solves many problems for the Americans. The president has to make a whole group of powerful Jews happy, so he will agree to the first step at least, about rebuilding Jerusalem."

"And then?"

Kufdani paused. "You will need to reassure the president by reaffirming petrodollar status and relegating any sort of petro-yuan arrangement to the background."

ABS thought for a second. "The petrodollar won't be a problem. We will simply need to discuss the mechanics of publicly disclosing support in a way that best serves our interests."

"Indeed," Kufdani agreed.

"And Israel?"

"Israel doesn't know anything of this plan, and I don't plan to tell them anytime soon. Their current government is not to be trusted. As I say, I have a plan in the works that will do more to convince them."

"And who *will* know the whole plan?" ABS asked. "Is this a secret between us?"

"Not quite," Kufdani replied. "Our plan will remain a secret among a small group of us, including top officials in the US and my trusted team."

ABS placed his hands together and thought for a moment. "I see the wisdom in this. Yet how am I to convince my religious leaders, our Wahabi, of this wisdom as the plan gains bulk?"

"That will be *my* job," Kufdani declared, "and I look forward to it. It is a matter of Allah's will. Words of the Quran provide clear, unequivocal guidance. Allah will not be denied."

As if in answer to his words, the midafternoon call to prayer rang out through the city.

"As it is time for prayers," Kufdani said, "I believe my time with you is up. I thank you for it. I believe Allah thanks you for it."

ABS smiled widely. "Perhaps we could continue this discussion after prayers and over dinner, my friend? Unless you have other plans."

Kufdani dipped his head. "My entire evening happens to be free, Your Majesty."

EPSTEIN RESIDENCE, TEL AVIV

MIRIAM EPSTEIN SET A BOWL OF DRIED RICE CEREAL IN FRONT OF Guns. "There is water or thawed bone broth. No milk. Your choice."

"Bone broth, I suppose," Guns replied, as he had for several days in a row. As a government official, he was entitled to better treatment, but his wife had agreed they should refuse. Shouldn't he live as others in Tel Aviv were living? The population was digging in for a long period of shortages and was loudly unhappy about it. Store shelves were empty. Shop fronts were boarded. The streets of Tel Aviv were nearly deserted.

Sheila Pelzer had been elected prime minister of Israel the previous morning, by a large margin. Her first action was to appoint Norman Epstein as her replacement at Mossad. She had promised to give a report to the Knesset and the Israeli people within a week. With no real progress on rebuilding Israel after the recent damage, violence, and now privation, things were likely to get progressively uglier in the short term.

Pelzer wanted to give her people something of a wake-up call: things were not going to get better anytime soon and could get worse. But that would not be a big hit.

Sitting down next to her husband at the kitchen table, Miriam poured the remaining bone broth into her cereal bowl. "Norman," she said, "is your friend Alex receptive to any sort of accommodation? I remember some of our conversations in New York. He seemed polite, normal—not an irrational killer at all."

Guns had to laugh. "He is all of those things, Miriam. Also, we had plenty to eat in New York. Things change in a hurry, don't they? We don't know what he wants."

Guns had been trying to reach Cooch since yesterday's election, but the stubborn Bedouin was not answering his calls. Playing hard to get, most likely now that he had the upper hand. *He knows why I'm looking for a conversation.*

Pelzer wanted to meet with Kufdani again, this time in her new role as prime minister. "If he agrees, things should be interesting," she'd confided to Guns just after the election. "It's not like we come from a position of strength." She was hoping to get a grasp on a new outlook for Israel.

Guns didn't think they were going to like it.

"We had our chance, and we let our collective ego rule us," Pelzer had said wistfully. "Now we shall see the price."

When the phone rang in his kitchen later that morning, Guns was not at all surprised to hear the familiar voice. "Top of the morning to you, Epstein," said Cooch.

"Yeah, fuck you too, Cooch," Guns countered. "What's next, a cherry bomb in my toilet?"

"And mess up the last remaining set of balls in Israel?" Cooch laughed. "Nah. I'm gonna just let you starve."

"Ha, ha. We need to talk. You, me, and Sheila."

"Seems like a good idea," Cooch replied. "How about the airfield in Egypt, at El-Arish? The day after tomorrow, high noon.

"I'll bring Elliot as an observer, to save time. Security only. No IDF, no Shin Bet. And for sure no Sayeret Matkal."

Guns snorted. "We'll be there. Bring fresh food and milk. No grains."

"It's a date," Cooch agreed. "I'll be sure to have lunch waiting."

EDGEWORTH AIRFIELD, EGYPT

THE GULFSTREAM LANDED ON A HASTILY REFURBISHED AIRSTRIP IN El-Arish—already they were starting to call it Edgeworth Airfield. Twelve US Navy F-16s made a pass, in formation, at one hundred feet overhead, with four others visible far above, watching over the proceedings. The Gaza Strip just fifteen miles north was, after all, very recently a battlefield.

Kufdani was grateful that the takeoff and flight from Tangier had been smooth. He had already logged more than twelve thousand miles in just over a week, with three thousand more expected for tomorrow's return trip. Caitlin's airplane was luxurious at least—not to mention secure—and *someone* had to consume the 60 percent that the NSA didn't own.

The crew was still (somewhat inexplicably, Kufdani thought) attired in US Air Force flight suits. And there was some mild consternation during preflight duties, when a flight attendant found a strange, magnificent blonde in the electronics room in the aft section. Somehow she had found user's manuals at a secure online site and was fiddling with the high-end techie stuff, and had to be escorted off the plane before takeoff.

Their flying escort had been a bit of a surprise too. When the buzzer for Kufdani's phone in his armrest sounded, the pilot had said, "Sir, we have company. Open your shade."

Kufdani had flipped the switch so the window view became clear: four F-16s flying in box formation above their port wing. His phone monitored the radio traffic: "Charlie 37 Bravo, this is your Navy escort to Edgeworth in Egypt. Flight of sixteen in place." Kufdani had grinned and asked their pilot to pass along a message.

"Navy, this is the former Air Force 271," the pilot had said. "The message from the passenger is, 'Semper Fi to a bunch of squids.'"

There was a chuckle as the formation of four broke left and climbed to join the others. "Roger that. Spoken like a jarhead. Safe travels."

Kufdani had known since Saturday, when the call from Guns Epstein lit up his Kphone, that the crew would likely be preparing the plane for use again soon. Inspired by Admiral Sino's display as they arrived in Morocco last week, Brooks had talked the president into an expensive display of pageantry and support. On the ground below, Guns surely got the message.

Brooks drove them near the recently refurbished hut in a golf cart, where they met Guns and Pelzer disembarking with a small, armed security detail from a helicopter marked *Israeli Air Force*. Standing beneath a wide canvas canopy outside the hut, the four shook hands.

"Cooch, Brooks, good afternoon," Guns greeted them. "Mr. Ambassador, may I present our newly elected prime minister, Madam Sheila Pelzer."

Brooks stepped forward. "It is an honor to make your acquaintance, Madam Prime Minister. Just to be clear, I am here as an observer only. You may ask me to serve as an intermediary, of course. But I have no role in our discussions, on the part of Islam or the United States or any other group."

"And, Cooch," Guns continued, "I believe you and the new prime minister are . . . old friends?"

Kufdani nodded and shook hands. "At least we're not old enemies, Madam Pelzer."

Inside the hut, which smelled of fresh-cut wood, an air conditioner roared in the background. On a small table surrounded with four cushioned chairs, alongside an array of notepads and pens, sat a tray of mixed nuts and four large bottles of water. A huge tray of sandwiches and a jug of milk sat on another table nearby, with plenty of water bottles also for the prime minister's security guards. Kufdani wanted to remind them: he had access to food.

"There is no one here to impress, and I assume any recordings are confidential and will be destroyed in due time," Pelzer said as the four took the seats. "So, I think we should start by me making a statement on behalf of Israel."

Kufdani nodded. "Please."

"Israel has made some severe miscalculations recently and is responsible for some unacceptable and violent actions," Pelzer stated. "This airfield is being renamed to memorialize one of the lives destroyed by those actions then. We accept responsibility and want to quickly negotiate for the guarantee of Bedouin sovereignty over the West Bank. If there are to be reparations to the injured parties, it will be handled. We understand the need for a new approach."

Kufdani nodded again. "Thank you, Madam Pelzer. As part of that new approach, I now speak for Islam and no longer exclusively as the leader of the Bedouin nation. Let's be blunt: your government has allowed itself to become a theocracy that spits in the face of Islam. It steals from Muslims because they don't happen to be Jewish. That is unacceptable to Islam.

"To support your position, agents of the Israeli government have attacked me and those who are close to me again and again, including the ambassador's wife, both in our homes and on foreign soil. You have hunted us down, persecuted us, and attempted to assassinate us—not to mention murdering Reginald Edgeworth. We all know your government has authorized, at one level or another, the missions of these individuals from the IDF and Shin Bet. But in case evidence is required, you should know that we have positively identified the assassins from the ambassador's sailboat as known members of Sayeret Matkal. As they say, the remainder of the exercise is left to the student."

Kufdani smiled darkly and thought of the arrogant, brutal Israeli defense minister. The last time he'd checked, Yakov Bernstein had been in northern Israel, somewhere south of Nazareth. Now he was just another missing piece, but if pressed, he would reveal other atrocities committed in the name of Israel.

If I find you, when I find you, you will sing like a bird, he thought, *and cry like a baby.*

"The media outlets have all the raw meat they can handle right now. They are doing so well with the speculation that we've served up, we don't want to overburden them. And people are starting to feel sorry for the Israeli people, who face privation if not starvation—as you know. But if our negotiations end poorly, we are prepared to disclose these truths."

"We understand your game, Sheik Kufdani," Pelzer said. "When are you going to get to the point?"

"Ah, the point," Kufdani said. He described the nonnegotiable points as far as he was concerned: The West Bank settlements would be deeded to the Bedouins in a contractual context that he would provide. Mortgage holders with Israeli government backing on payments would be made whole, or the monthly payments would be made under the terms of the contract; others should not be punished for Israeli sovereign perfidy. Much of the West Bank debt was held outside of Israel, and those debt holders were not at fault.

Brooks exchanged a brief smile with Kufdani. Both men knew the unspoken gold concession was genius on LuAnn's part. Business was business, and the future looked pretty good for Kufdani Industries.

Kufdani took a drink from his water bottle. "That was the easy part."

"We have not agreed to any of these outrageous demands," Pelzer said, her voice rising.

"Of course, you haven't, but you will," Kufdani said. "And there is much more."

"Why don't you skip over the middle, then, and get to the hard part," Guns suggested.

In other words, 'Quit fucking around and tell me the deal,' Kufdani thought, laughing inwardly, *'and we'll figure out if we can sell it.'* He felt a deep appreciation for his old acquaintance, the new director of Mossad.

"The hard part, from your perspective, is that Jerusalem is destined again to become an international city," Kufdani continued, "with the areas of religious significance—any Muslim, Jewish, and Christian holy sites—protected and open to all. The city will be administered by Israel under strict UN supervision, with no cute games on your part. Jerusalem is no longer Jewish nor owned by Israel. You just administer it."

Pelzer paled but managed to recover without allowing emotion to cross her face. "That won't happen, now or ever," she said in a hard, slow whisper. "I can't sell that to our people, and I won't try."

"She's right," Guns said. "The Knesset won't buy it. The situation defies their concept of being Jewish. It denies their entire concept of reality."

"And yet without taking this first step," Kufdani said quietly, "your future will continue to be messy and dangerous."

Guns leaned back in his chair and put his hands behind his head. "I am trying to envision Israel in ten years, as I was once advised. How do you plan to move forward from here, and how is the US government involved? Israel is a key ally of the United States. Our people face starvation. What will the world say to that?"

"When you find a solution, the US will be on your side," Elliot said. "We have a vocal and intensely interested Jewish community. They vote. They provide money to politicians. They count. They are loud and worried. And they want to see a way forward here."

"We have not disabled your military capability nor yet shut down your Iron Dome defenses against missile attack," Kufdani added. "Your technology companies are intact, if temporarily out of commission. Your Leviathan oil field is still in operation, supplying much of your critical needs, if not your people's comfort. If you cannot see this as your opportunity for a ten-year vision, all of that would go first—with a single digital command."

"This is outrageous," Pelzer announced. "I won't be party to this discussion."

"Madam Pelzer, you are already party to this discussion," Kufdani reminded the prime minister. "The issue at hand is whether you choose to go a step further and suffer an invasion of thousands of Muslims set loose on the streets of their longtime oppressors in Tel Aviv and Haifa—looting, raping, shooting, what have you. Our plan to move forward seems likely to take that path, as you are demonstrating little willingness to cooperate with our efforts to find a just solution."

"We would slaughter them," Pelzer declared. "We have the best army in the world."

"Perhaps," Kufdani replied. "But these Muslims will be armed, and I will likely lead them. You will be fighting us one-on-one, with your vehicles at a standstill and your communications disabled. To paraphrase Chairman Mao during the Korean War: What am I going to lose, ten million Muslims?" Kufdani said. "There are only six million of you, while there are two billion of us."

"Not a pretty picture," Guns admitted. "Oceans of blood will flow. We have no place to go, so we will fight to the death. And we know how to fight."

"Do you really think you can arrange that sort of confrontation, Sheik Kufdani?" Pelzer asked. "Or are you merely posturing for a better deal, now that they are calling you the Mahdi?"

Kufdani turned to Guns. "What do you think, Director Epstein?"

"I don't like any of the alternatives, and your strategy thus far has been effective," Guns replied. "So, Cooch, what is next on your playlist? You have oceans of blood to spare, as you point out, and blood is now on the table. I know you have an endgame. Enlighten us. How is your solution good for Israel? How do we get from this mess you created to something we can all live with?"

"*You* created this mess." Kufdani took a gulp of water from his bottle and looked at each of them in turn. "The ten-year view is a transformation of the Middle East with Israel in a leadership role, albeit with diminished power."

"If you don't mind, Sheik Kufdani," Pelzer retorted, "I have a country to run and people who are demanding to know what I propose to do about this crisis. You're the strategy maven, so sort this out for me. What is your plan for this fantasy transformation of the Middle East?"

Three hours had passed by the time it was all hashed out. The negotiators did not shake hands, but everyone knew the conversation was over when Guns said, "Okay, we got it. It's insane, but let's see how it evolves."

Stepping outside the hut, he waved his index finger in a circle. The others followed him into the fresh air, and the rotor on the Israeli helicopter began to whine and turn.

"I just hope that you're the consummate planner you claim to be, Sheik Kufdani," Primer Minister Pelzer spat out. "And, Mr. Ambassador, 'oceans of Jewish blood' is not a winner for your president either."

"Oceans of blood, indeed," Brooks muttered as the helicopter left the ground.

Who knew politics could be so bloody? thought Kufdani, knowing all too well that a blood debt was sometimes necessary. It wasn't creating the puzzle that got things done, but seeing it through when the pieces started to mesh.

TANGIER

THE FOLLOWING AFTERNOON IN TANGIER, KUFDANI AND CAITLIN CROWDED into Caitlin's office with Brooks, LuAnn, and Jerome to watch the debate thirty-five hundred miles away in Jerusalem. Pelzer had wasted no time in bringing the proposal to an emergency session of the Knesset, and Caitlin had hacked the recording of the session by the Israeli government, so they had good seats.

Explaining that she had met with Kufdani, who now claimed to be the representative of all Islam, she brought forward the best proposal she could negotiate to end the systematic destruction of Israeli society. She glossed over the West Bank situation, simply saying it was largely resolved and would involve no further bloodshed. Her explanation was met with cautious murmurs but no direct outrage, as though most politicians were already resigned to a new approach there. But when she spoke directly of Jerusalem and the holy sites, the room erupted in cries of denial, shock, and anger.

The encrypted text messages that flew around the Knesset chamber were unintentionally displayed on their screens in Caitlin's Tangier office, curated by Emilie. Howls of protest burst forth from the ultra-Orthodox representatives, while many others grumbled about the message this would send to the world.

Several hours passed before a vote was called. The result: a resounding rejection of the concept of a Jerusalem that was not Jewish. There would be no further discussion and no further votes. A roar of approval came from the legislature.

In Tangier, five people in a room overlooking the harbor exchanged heavy looks, and one person prepared to set the next stage of Kufdani's plan in motion with a single digital command.

Kufdani's message was loud and clear: *Hey, folks! You're not paying attention. Let me mess with national security a little and see what you say then. That will cost you another twenty billion dollars or so . . .*

Just twenty seconds later, a few miles south of Tel Aviv near the cities of Rishon LeZion and Yavne on the Mediterranean coast, sixteen Coochmore mines armed with two hundred fragmentation ball bearings and fifty EMP ball bearings detonated within the active area of Israel's most important air base: Palachim. It was a severe blow.

The base was an open secret, so it benefited from little more security than any other Israeli air base. Its cleaners, handymen, and landscape and maintenance crews, hired through a contractor, were mostly Bedouin. The mines had been in place for weeks, blending in with the rocky, dusty ground.

The on-base members of the Israeli Air Force, their families, and the base staff heard the ragged booms of the Coochmores but saw only wisps of smoke—at first. But five minutes later, the lone Coochmore loaded with thermite ammunition and programmed with a broad shot pattern discharged in a whoosh of flames. Some on the base worried about loved ones; others worried about their lives.

Ten minutes passed before the next EMP device struck, this time at the massive new Tel Aviv central bus station, one of the largest in the world. Hundreds of buses were disabled, the shops lost power, and a mass of people streamed from the building. Some 230,000 square meters of offices, shops, and transport hubs went dark. Without electricity, nothing moved.

When Kufdani's phone rang in Tangier, it was ABS calling from the

Kphone that Kufdani had left for him. "Congratulations on your tactical riposte," he said. "Where exactly are you?"

"I'm sitting in a chair in a crowded office with all my good friends—all but you, Your Majesty. We were watching the Knesset debate on the hacked legislative network."

"As am I," ABS said. "Expensive hack."

"And no longer relevant," Kufdani pointed out. "Ten minutes ago, I destroyed nineteen percent of the Israeli Air Force. Unfortunately, a few hundred innocent people had to die. I did not destroy their central communications system . . . yet."

There was a long silence from ABS. "You seem to have done what you claimed you would do. I was skeptical, even though I like you. You can understand why, I'm sure."

"Naturally," Kufdani responded. "Are you a believer now?"

"Yes, I am—for now," ABS said. "Let's see how they react. Typically, when threatened, they are ruthless."

"We too are ruthless," Kufdani insisted. "They must face this truth before we destroy their society and—"

"And have to rebuild it for them? What a mess that would be!" ABS said, laughing. "Are you sure this phone is secure, Sheik Kufdani? There are probably fifteen Israelis listening to this conversation."

"It is secure," Kufdani confirmed.

"Then we should plan to talk once a week or so, to allow me to keep up."

"Friday morning?"

"Yes, that is good," ABS said, ending the call.

The monitors in Caitlin's office continued to pick up images of the retaliation organized by Kufdani. Traffic lights were no longer operative. Cars, buses, and trucks were stalled on the open road. There was no public information about the attack on the Palachim air base—or about anything at all.

Throughout much of Israel, all was silent.

OFFICE OF THE PRIME MINISTER, JERUSALEM

GUNS KNEW THE GAME, AND HE KNEW COOCH WAS A MASTER AT IT. Now that his plan was in motion, he could step back and leave the mud fight to the clowns. But Guns didn't think Cooch was interested in chaos for chaos's sake.

"What do you think the impact of Sheik Kufdani's actions will be?" Pelzer asked.

"You mean besides the physical damage, the lack of basic necessities, and the complete lack of information and communication?" Guns replied. "Well, the foreign media will certainly make sure attention is paid to our predicament. And Elsa Sachs is in New York now. She'll let the diaspora know what's going on, and loudly."

"I suppose you're right," Pelzer said. "And at some point, our Knesset leaders are going to have to deal with reality. How much time do we have for them to mobilize before your pal Cooch provides even more incentive?"

"Let's find out," Guns said, picking up the phone—and grateful to find that it still worked even though most of his neighbors' didn't.

"Guns, my main man," Kufdani answered. "Knesset got you down?"

"Fuck you, Cooch," Guns said, jumping to his feet. "What are we going to do if they don't fold? You're running out of targets. The prime minister is here, and she wants—"

"Wants me to stop pissing off the diaspora? Wants me to hesitate short of crippling Israel's ability to defend itself?"

"You are too close to the problem, Sheik Kufdani," Pelzer said. "Fine, go after the diaspora. Seduce them. Convince them. Let *them* convince the Knesset, because I suspect *you* cannot. Neither can I."

"Yes, I managed to watch the Knesset declaration," Kufdani said. "It was . . . impressive."

Pelzer put her head in her hands. "They are not ready. And quite frankly, another killing blow may undermine our very existence. Please, Sheik Kufdani, give us a little more time to change into the society we must become."

"Well, you can start by locating a new defense minister who can implement the plan while keeping your Haredim and other hardliners, well, in line."

"Any thoughts about who you might be able to tolerate?"

"Make it Nabov Dayan," Kufdani confirmed. "Shin Bet has no home. And Dayan has nowhere to work, so he's available. He has credentials and brains. He wants to make a difference."

"But he's the one who sent Sayeret Matkal after you!" Guns protested. "And unsuccessfully."

"That's just business," Cooch explained. "If they had crossed the boat's bow on two sides, they would have been harder for us to kill. But time was short, and they wanted us badly. They let emotion get in the way of planning." His chuckle came through the phone as a low rumble. "Dayan won't do that again."

"Dayan it is," Pelzer agreed. "He knows our security structure. We can make this work." She sighed. "I still hate this deal, Sheik Kufdani, but you're right: if the future you seek is going to be sold to the Israeli people, the diaspora is going to have to do it."

"That sounds like good advice to me, Cooch," Guns said. "Better do a good job of it."

"Madame Pelzer, you certainly have a better feel for your people than I do," Kufdani said. "But yes, it seems to me that the pressure has to come from outside Israel, from the diaspora."

Guns agreed. "They're removed from the situation, so they can see the big picture better than any of us here have been able to do."

Pelzer sighed. "The diaspora is well identified, and Kufdani will have to be engaged face-to-face with television, with interviews, with close and frank discussion if he is to influence them. But this is the show you created, isn't it? So break a leg, Mr. Kufdani."

"Well, then," Cooch sighed, "let's make it so."

EDGEWORTH STUDIOS, MIDTOWN MANHATTAN

"WELCOME, SHEIK KUFDANI. OR SHOULD I CALL YOU . . . MAHDI?"

The cameras were blinking as Elsa began her fourth interview with the man she sometimes called Alex. "Well, since the last time we spoke, you have destroyed most of my country. You seem destined to get your West Bank property back for the Bedouins. And now you want Jerusalem. What else?"

"Let's be clear, Ms. Sachs," Kufdani retorted. "I want Jerusalem not for myself or for any one individual or group. I want the holy city to be an international city open to all religions, as it once was, not so long ago. And I want Israel to lead a revival in early childhood education while remaining the technical leader it is today. And that's just the beginning."

"To do that, you destroyed a sovereign nation?" Sachs said.

Kufdani feigned shock. "For the record, Ms. Sachs, we have damaged Israel's social institutions, not destroyed your sovereignty."

Elsa's expression was equally sarcastic. "You see a difference between the two?"

"Of course. Islam has been careful not to destroy Israel's ability to defend itself. It has half the natural gas available to it before all of this started, with the second half in the ground, waiting to be delivered. Israel survives, and it can still thrive."

"Your past has you targeting the Haredi," Elsa said next. "What do you propose now?"

"This is not my problem, but I happen to know that Prime Minister Pelzer is developing new rules that will forbid using public finances to support a decadent lifestyle. No work, no public money."

Elsa scoffed. "Sheik Kufdani, there is no work at the moment! There is no money! People are hungry. Cities have been destroyed. You say you want to see Israel survive. Where does the money come from to do that, to rebuild?"

"Allah will provide," Kufdani said confidently. "Ask instead what your Knesset is doing to seek a better way forward, other than thumping its chest and making declarations as your people starve." He paused. "How old are you, Elsa?"

She was taken aback by his question, or rather by his timing. "Why do you ask?"

"The prime minister and Mossad director get it. The members of the Knesset don't. They don't seem interested in a practical plan for the future, and little of real value can be accomplished until they are. I just hope you don't die of old age before the Knesset gets off its ass."

"Sheik Kufdani, you say you're a representative of Islam. What do you pray will happen?"

"I pray first for the reemergence of a single, enlightened Muslim faith under Allah—a modern faith without extremism or divisive sects, a faith of people who follow Allah's word without destroying lives."

"And regarding the survival of Israel?" she asked. "My parents are hungry. My staff in Israel has no power in their homes. Life is very difficult there now. Things are not pretty."

"We Muslims have lived among Jews since the beginning, and vice versa. In the earliest centuries of Islam, Jews were an important segment of our society. Like Bedouins today, they had no government to care for them, yet they prospered. And today the Jewish people in Israel are at a precipice. But I would not think Allah wants them to disappear."

"No?" Elsa asked. "But as representative of Islam, *you* have brought war to Israel."

Kufdani studied her carefully. "Have I, Ms. Sachs? Perhaps you would take a moment to remember that my plans for the future—for education, justice, and religious freedom that we can all live with—are what stands between your nation and mobs of screaming Muslims who would like nothing more than to cross Israel's borders seeking revenge."

"And why do you stand between us and them, Sheik Kufdani?"

"That type of war wouldn't be an ideal solution, for Islam or Judaism or any other religion."

"But it is war *you* have created, is it not?"

A concerned look crossed Kufdani's face. "The war is ongoing, Ms. Sachs. The modern Islam that I speak of will do what it must to maintain the rights of its people and to destroy theocracy—of any kind." Then, looking directly at one camera, he asked, "Who of you is going to lead in this effort?"

The cameras winked off.

"What now?" Elsa asked.

"Now we wait," Kufdani said. "Things in Israel will be worse tomorrow than today. But maybe the day after, if my plan is on target, we'll find that Israel has remained in one piece."

"And if a sniper gets you, or a nutcase?"

He laughed. "Then the Iron Dome goes down, more air bases are disabled, and the second half of your natural gas supply goes offline for six or eight months."

"That sounds close to the end of Israel," Elsa said.

"Sounds that way to me, too," Kufdani replied.

THE WHITE HOUSE, WASHINGTON, DC

THERE WERE FOUR OF THEM IN THE OVAL OFFICE: BROOKS, MACMILLAN, and Kufdani on one side of the president's desk, with the president on the other. The three were trying to carry out the informal plan they had discussed for the president on the question of funding for Kufdani's new vision of Israel.

The president sighed. "How do you recommend we play this?"

Brooks leaned forward. "Very gently, Mr. President. We sit on the sidelines mostly, until Israel has agreed to the plan. Meanwhile, we gain favor by offering an airlift of food, medicine—stuff they're panicked over. With Ben Gurion Airport nonfunctional, the airport in Jerusalem has extended its runway, so we can get in there eventually. This will be an epic time to build international favor for the United States."

"But they will resist us," the president insisted. "They want the money, but not the deal attached to it."

"We should probably work it through you eventually, as the voice of the government," Brooks suggested. "But initially the First Lady could choose a less intense effort—one that would make us look sympathetic to Israel without providing a commitment to any solution, which could leave us in a sticky spot."

"Maybe something like, 'We can't allow children to starve or face a lack of essential medicine while we have the means to help'?" Mac suggested. "Put her on national TV. Have her give an address at UNESCO or one of those UN agencies."

"Some of the biggest Jewish American names have been hounding me," the president complained. "With all the technology issues over there, they can't send boatloads of aid to Israel like they usually would."

"The Israeli government can't hold out forever," Mac added. "Folks over there are getting really scared. There will be big opportunities to get things moving soon. Before we arrange the airlift, we offer to pay a third of the cost of rebuilding Jerusalem—but only if the Knesset votes to allow the city to become international."

The president looked at Kufdani. "Can you commit Saudi Arabia to paying their third of the Jerusalem bill when it comes due?"

Kufdani shook his head. "I cannot, Mr. President," he said. "That decision belongs to ABS alone."

"Will he do the right thing?" the president asked.

"I believe so. After all, we Muslims destroyed it, and now we're getting what we want. If Israel pays its part of the bill, then the Muslim world will contribute another third."

"Elliot?" the president said in his usual way. "Comment?"

Brooks nodded. "That's the idea: You step up and look like a statesman for the free world. ABS steps up for Islam. And Israel rebuilds with their troops intact and their money, up to a third of the total."

"I get the benefits for me, for our country," the president said. "But what's in it for ABS? How does helping Israel help Islam?"

"He gains a legacy of greatness," Kufdani explained. "The Crown Prince of Saudi Arabia leading on the path toward uniting the Muslim world. Not in his lifetime, of course. But he will die as a growing legend in the minds of modern Muslims everywhere."

The president looked skeptical. "And that's what he wants? Both down the road and right now?"

Brooks shrugged. "It will take years."

"Years, my ass! We're talking decades here," the president retorted. "Macmillan, don't any of these young folks have a sense of time?"

"Mr. President, I've been around for a long time too," Mac said. "This may be the best shot at world peace I have seen."

"If Kufdani's plan works," Brooks added, "then you, your successors, and ABS will rule the world for thirty years. It will change defense budgets, votes, and politicians, with you and ABS charting the course—mostly you, Mr. President. It's coming from you, as your invention, so be sure to take credit."

"Not only that," Mac continued, "but we'll deal with the Chinese from a position of great power. We control oil and technology. China is aging. They can't fight a war without oil, and population is hard to create quickly. Abolishment of the petro-yuan should be part of this deal."

Kufdani laughed. "Mac does have a way with tactics, Mr. President. He's a trained killer. Maybe you should fire him as a gesture to the pinkos."

"Fuck the pinkos," the president said. "It makes sense to me. I'm in."

"Excellent. I'll inform the Crown Prince," Kufdani said. "He'll have to decide what to say."

"And you will help him with that speech," the president said.

"I will, quietly," Kufdani said, watching another puzzle piece fall into place. He had been at this for ten years. It was working. "Mr. President, Islam needs this to work."

EDGEWORTH STUDIOS, MIDTOWN MANHATTAN

ELSA SACHS WAS OVERWHELMED IN HER NEW YORK OFFICE. THE MORE time passed, the more the pressure built. She had developed a public relationship with the infamous Kufdani, and now, for most people, she was the only known communications avenue to the man who held the future of the Middle East in the palm of his hand.

Her phones were ringing off the hook in synchrony with an orchestra of alerts on her social media accounts. Everyone wanted to meet with Kufdani, but most would eagerly settle for Sachs. The Pulitzer looked like a lock. Now that it was no longer an unlikely fantasy in her life, however, the accolade had somehow faded in importance.

The fact that her entire nation was suffering didn't help.

Finally, she gave in to the urge and picked up her phone. When he answered, she said, "Kufdani."

"Hey there, Sachs," he replied. "How are you enjoying life here in New York?"

"The press is driving me crazy."

He chuckled. "You *are* the press."

"But they all want *you* for an interview," she pointed out. "And for most, I am your only conduit."

"Well, that's the role Edgie envisioned for you," he reminded her. "We need the full, screaming support of the Jewish community in the US and Europe, now more than ever. You can help deliver that. Then they won't bother you as much—but you might miss it now that you're known world-wide as a crackerjack journalist."

"Why 'now more than ever'?" she asked. "And if I help you get their support, what's in it for Israel, for me?"

"The president has agreed to fund a reconstruction effort in Israel, mostly Jerusalem," Kufdani said, explaining that he had committed ABS to funding an equal amount and attempting to bring in the other Middle Eastern money players.

The ultimate goal was to build a relatively peaceful society in the Middle East, where Israel pays a third of the cost and leads from a technology perspective while the oil-rich countries fund the new infrastructure needed: schools to teach the children to read and write, universities to develop the region's brightest personally for the good of all—all the trappings of a modern society.

"As for what's in it for you," he continued, "it's not about you. It's not even about me. If everything works as envisioned, we could finally see the unimaginable: the Middle East as a safe, good place to live and grow for all men, women, and children."

"Liberty and equal rights for all? In the Middle East? That sounds like Enlightenment bullshit," Elsa said. "You'll never be able to achieve that."

"Oh, ye of little faith," Kufdani chuckled. "I didn't say it would be done by next week or even the year's end. It's a process that will take decades. Your piece is to build a following among the diaspora, where they lean in to get the job done and influence others to join in—and to reach into their pockets." He paused. "And who knows? Maybe you can leverage that Pulitzer we talked about into a Nobel."

Elsa had to smile at that.

"Any Jew who thinks this is a bad idea is stupid," Kufdani continued. "You must make the world believe that and denigrate that kind of thinking. Your job is to convince the liberal Jewish world that this is the best hope for peace they will see in their lifetime. Plan it out. Build a national image, and use it. Then get married and have babies who can expect a bright future."

"Maybe," she replied vaguely, "but first I'd like to go back home."

TANGIER

IN TANGIER, CAITLIN WAS DOING WHAT CAITLIN DID BEST: EMPLOYING her wealth of skills and technological dominance to monitor the convergence of Kufdani's plan at a near-planetary level.

Amid growing cacophony among liberal Jews demanding action in Israel, the US president delivered his message on national television. The support for his ideas among the Jewish diaspora in America, particularly New York, was loud and growing.

The Crown Prince of Saudi Arabia added to this crescendo when he announced his support for the effort in the name of Allah, promising twenty billion dollars to help rebuild Jerusalem as an international place of worship. "It is time for modern Muslims to rebuild our rightful place in world society," he insisted. "We must educate our young and reinvigorate our squandered legacy. This is an important first step."

In Israel, the Knesset had finally stopped squandering time, and convened again for a new vote, approving the internationalization of Jerusalem with almost universal support. The Haredi had objected but were shouted down. With the United States brokering the arrangement and Saudi Arabia on board, Israel had agreed to fund a third of the rebuilding effort from its own resources. Financial support from the other Muslim autocracies would follow. Kufdani's plan was truly coming together.

Caitlin was eavesdropping on the prime minister's office just after the appointment of Nabov Dayan as the new Israeli minister of defense. Pelzer instructed him that Kufdani was now off-limits: there would be no offensive operations targeting him. Kufdani had won the battle and won just about everyone over to his side—Israelis, Palestinians, Saudis, Americans—and now they would all need him. Plus, Kufdani would be able to keep a close eye on Iran given their desire for nuclear capability.

A conversation between Madam Pelzer and Guns Epstein also revealed that Yakov Bernstein was still missing in northern Israel—the latest news hinted at something about a car wreck, but despite attempts to investigate, the local hospitals up there had no official record of treating him.

Out of our hair at least, Caitlin thought. She knew Alex was still yearning for revenge, and knew Yousef Salama was working diligently to help out with his contacts in northern Israel.

"We must redirect the IDF," Pelzer was saying to Dayan, "from an externally faced organization to one that is focused on a controlled rebuild of Jerusalem, and a safe environment that would encourage education for children of all religions. We must continue to lead our world in research and technology, not oppression and war."

Caitlin listened carefully, grinning as the prime minister outlined her goals for managing this sea change in the IDF's mission: from killing and destroying to building and educating. This inside information would give her the edge she needed: the technology for education must come from an external, proven source. And who better than Kufdani Industries to administer the building of education facilities and curriculum? Just as she was about to sign off, Caitlin overheard an interesting comment made by Guns: the new director of Mossad was preparing to schedule a prime-time interview with Kufdani, to be televised on the new *Elsa Sachs Show*.

Caitlin knew who she wanted to hear from next: Elsa Sachs herself.

Her first few calls to Elsa's studio office went ignored. Elsa now had three assistants to handle the callers clamoring for her attention, and Caitlin couldn't seem to break through the wall of silence. So she tried Elsa's private phone next, with a more favorable outcome.

"Hello, Caitlin," Elsa said. "Are we just about done yet?"

"Hey, Sachs," Caitlin said. "Yeah, just about. This one played out better than I thought it would. The NSA isn't happy with me, but Alex is. Should've known he never bites off more than he can chew."

"How is he?"

"He's okay," Caitlin said. "A little tired of all the Mahdi bullshit, but I guess it was necessary. And on the personal side, pretty much the same as usual. I can't see that you taught him much of anything. What was the music?"

There was a long pause. "Bob Evans," Elsa replied.

"*Inner Spirit*?" Caitlin whistled. "Marc Johnson is a find, isn't he? Gives me shivers just thinking about Alex keeping time with that bass . . ."

Elsa chuckled. "You taught him well, Caitlin."

"Well, in all honesty, he was already quite talented when I met him long ago."

Caitlin recalled what Alex had said to her one time: *It's dark, it's damp, and the view never changes. The target is predictable and not hard to handle. The goal is mutual, and I seldom miss.*

"How romantic," Elsa drawled.

"That's where the jazz comes in. Look for a connection with the music, and you can't go wrong. If there's a next time, try Bob James and Earl Klugh, *One on One*."

"Thanks for the advice. Anything else, Caitlin?"

"Yes, as a matter of fact," Caitlin said, "I may be back in the colonies for a visit soon—mend some fences at the NSA, get a little plastic surgery. Alex has been hogging my new airplane, and I want to show it off. Will you be around? Maybe we'll take you on a ride someplace."

"Caitlin, I don't—"

But Caitlin had already disconnected the call. She smiled to herself—turning to look out the window at her second-favorite view, Tangier harbor—and decided to keep Alejandro Muhammad Cuchulain to herself a little while longer.

TANGIER

KUFDANI HAD KNOWN THE INTERVIEW WITH GUNS EPSTEIN ON THE *Elsa Sachs Show* would be critical to achieving the final stage of his plan, but he never expected it would receive such unprecedented ratings. Excitement across the political and cultural spectrum had led to overwhelming Israeli public approval of the plan as they described it, which had been agreed upon by the Crown Prince, Madam Pelzer, and the president.

Power had been restored to Israel. Jerusalem's airport was booming, and Ben Gurion was well along in its repairs. Primary schools were being planned for construction as soon as possible, under Prime Minister Pelzer's leadership but with Kufdani Industries the most likely (and most capable) option for handling the educational programming.

Kufdani sat in his Tangier office going over the new education statistics. Things had been quiet in his little hole in the mountain: LuAnn was safe and happy at home in DC with Brooks. Jerome was hard to pin down, now they were out of the shooting business for a while—or shooting at Israel, at least. He had freshly blooded warriors to pin medals on and reposition, lessons to be analyzed, weapons to inventory, tactics to update, and Admiral Sino to keep happy. For Jerome, it was basically a vacation.

Elsa Sachs had been nominated for her Pulitzer Prize, as promised, and was being considered for even greater honors. Without Edgie, however,

New York and Edgeworth Studios just didn't feel right. She had decided to return permanently to her offices in Tel Aviv, so she could host the *Elsa Sachs Show* from Israel, now a center of exciting opportunity.

Yakov Bernstein had finally been found, after no word of his whereabouts for about a month. He'd been mistakenly swept up in the return of escaped criminals and placed in the general population at Gilboa Prison, which was slowly coming back online. Bernstein had suffered an incredibly long list of injuries, from two broken elbows to shattered knees to a tangled web of internal injuries.

His long hair had been ripped out over some period of time, and iodine had been applied to the bleeding scalp, staining it a startlingly appropriate red. The older wounds were healing well, and an investigation was underway. Well, two investigations: Bernstein had been indicted in his absence for treason—something about recording secret meetings on his phone and distributing them.

Talk of Kufdani being the Mahdi still raged across the lands like wildfire. And it was Friday morning, the time he and ABS caught up on things. *Time to bring the plan to completion.*

Kufdani picked up his Kphone. "ABS, my friend," he said heartily. "All is good at your end of the world?"

"Yes, my friend," the Crown Prince replied. "You actually pulled it off! This pleases me greatly."

"But it was just step one, Your Majesty," Kufdani reminded him.

"Yes, step one! The great cooperation between our three countries—our investment in the future," ABS continued. "I am received with open arms wherever I go. I am invited to speak at prestigious events. My people cheer as I drive by!"

"Good," Kufdani said. "Now for the hard part."

ABS sighed. "Yes, the hard part—restoring Islam to greatness. This part of your plan is already well underway. But there has been increasing resistance from the Wahabi here in Riyadh. They don't like the new freedoms I have pronounced."

"Is it anything you cannot handle, Your Majesty?" Kufdani said. "It is their power that is reduced, not yours."

ABS sighed again. "The Wahabi have started to preach about the Mahdi."

Here we go, Kufdani thought.

"They say you are an apostate, Sheik Kufdani. They say you have influenced me with your claims to be the Mahdi. They say you should be put to death."

"I never claimed to be the Mahdi," Kufdani pointed out. "Nothing in the Quran provides guidance for identifying the Mahdi, nor any indication that such a personage even exists."

"How do you think I should deal with the Wahabi?" ABS said. "Did you foresee this difficulty?"

"I have thought about this problem a great deal," Kufdani replied, "and considered how we would know if the Mahdi had appeared. To know for certain, we must see evidence that the glory of Islam is restored to where it was in the ninth century. This requires building new relationships between Muslim nations, both Sunni and Shi'a—and a new world status to reflect this."

"Indeed, Sheik Kufdani, you are correct."

"But all of this will not happen without some measure of strife and turmoil, including dealing with your Wahabi. Bumps in the road are inevitable."

"That makes sense," ABS said. "And how do you plan to deal with them?"

"I am a warrior and a businessman, Your Majesty. I can deal with the Wahabi at your request. They are in the way of the will of Allah. We will deal with other bumps as they occur."

"Hm." The Crown Prince paused as if in thought. "I must admit, there are many skills you will need to develop."

"I have no plans to develop those skills, Your Majesty."

"Whyever not, Sheik Kufdani?"

"Those are the skills of a statesman. I am not a stateman and have no plans to become one. It will be up to another of Allah's children to undertake those tasks."

ABS was silent for a moment. "Nobody comes to mind, Kufdani. Have you identified an alternative?"

"I have long considered an idea that is compelling to me," Kufdani replied, "and I now feel certain that I can persuade the world to accept it."

"And what have you concluded? If not you, then who?"

"It is you, Your Majesty," Kufdani said. "You must act as the new Mahdi. You have the skills, the power, and the status to make things happen. You are already seen as the statesman transforming the Middle East."

"But I am not the Mahdi. I am not worthy."

"Just as I know that I am not the Mahdi."

"I would know if it was to be me."

"How *would* we know?" Kufdani asked. "Will Allah send the Angel Gabriel to anoint you or me in Mecca? We have no reason to believe that to be true."

"Sheik Kufdani, *I* am not the Mahdi."

"Your Majesty, perhaps it doesn't matter. If you do the work and bring Islam to glory, the Muslims of our world will praise you and remember you in their prayers. The Christians and Jews and others will adapt as they always have." Kufdani paused to let it all sink in.

ABS answered at last. "I had not thought of this. As the Mahdi, I can speak for Islam. The Wahabi will listen."

"And if it turns out you can't handle them, I'll give it a try," Kufdani declared. "You are the Mahdi, but I am forever your warrior. And I don't mind killing a few more to ensure your work succeeds. Now you must step forward and be seen as a world leader, not just the Crown Prince of Saudi Arabia."

"I am willing to make the effort you describe," ABS said, "but only for the glory of Allah."

Kufdani explained that this would be the essence of his leadership in the coming years. "Let them call you the Mahdi, but always deny it," he advised. "You are just a servant of Allah, doing what you can for your Muslim brothers and sisters. And perhaps you will never know whether you are indeed the Mahdi. Perhaps Gabriel will come to you on your deathbed and praise you. Perhaps not."

"May Allah bless you, Kufdani. I shall try my best. And if I need a warrior, I know where to find you."

"Inshallah," Kufdani said.

ABOUT THE AUTHOR

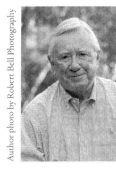

EAGLE SCOUT, SHOOTER, SOLDIER, ENTREPRENEUR, philanthropist, venture capitalist, vintner, and author, Robert Cook is a United States Army Vietnam veteran who attained the rank of Major. He holds the Parachutist Badge, the Bronze Star Medal, and the Army Commendation Medal.

Cook was named a KPMG Entrepreneur of the Year for the metropolitan Washington, DC, region in 1988, and is now an active philanthropist. He endowed the Robert E. Cook Honors College of Indiana University of Pennsylvania, which was covered in Donald Asher's book *Cool Colleges for the Hyper Intelligent, Late Blooming and Just Plain Different*. See www.iup.edu/honors for more information.

Originally from Altoona, Pennsylvania, Cook holds a BS in mathematics from Indiana University of Pennsylvania and an MBA from the George Washington University. This is his fourth book in the Cooch series.

Made in the USA
Middletown, DE
14 April 2024